USA TODAY bestselling author **Kristine Rolofson** has written more than forty books for Mills & Boon. She and her husband of many years call Rhode Island, Idaho and Texas home depending upon the time of year. When not writing, Kristine quilts, bakes peach pies, plays the fiddle and sings in a country blues band. She collects vintage cowboy boots and will not tell you how many are in her closet.

Christine Flynn is a regular voice in Mills & Boon True Love and has written nearly forty books for the line.

April Arrington grew up in a small southern town and developed a love for films and books at an early age. Emotionally moving stories have always held a special place in her heart. During the day, she enjoys sharing classic literature and popular fiction with students. At night, she spends her time writing stories of her own. April enjoys collecting pottery and soaking up the Georgia sun on her front porch. You can follow her on Twitter at https://twitter.com/april_arrington

Her Mistletoe Magic

KRISTINE ROLOFSON
CHRISTINE FLYNN
APRIL ARRINGTON

MILLS & BOON

First Published in Great Britain 2019
by Mills & Boon, an imprint of HarperCollins*Publishers*
1 London Bridge Street, London, SE1 9GF

HER MISTLETOE MAGIC © 2019 Harlequin Books S. A.

The Wish © 2015 Kristine Rolofson
Her Holiday Prince Charming © 2013 Christine Flynn
The Rancher's Wife © 2016 April Standard

ISBN: 978-0-263-27937-5

1019

Printed and bound in Spain
by CPI, Barcelona

THE WISH

KRISTINE ROLOFSON

With thanks and love to my husband,
who makes every Christmas fun.

CHAPTER ONE

"Is it true? The Barrett wedding is canceled?"

Grace Clarke looked up from her phone. "Yes."

"Wow." Patsy McLean, Mirror Lake Lodge's longtime business manager, entered Grace's office and plopped down in one of the overstuffed burgundy chairs that fronted her glass desk. "This is not good."

"No. It's not." She tossed her phone aside and eyed her friend. "I'm trying not to hyperventilate."

"You never hyperventilate. Not even during the clown reunion. Remember that?"

Grace shuddered. "I still have nightmares."

"The big curly-haired clown had a crush on you," Patsy reminded her. "He wanted you to wear polka dots and learn to play the harmonica."

"And the one with all the tattoos thought you should join the circus and live happily ever after with a man who turns balloons into animals."

Patsy sighed. "There are times when I think I should have gone with him." Her daughter was in the middle of a nasty divorce and had returned home six months ago, her twin toddlers in tow, while she and her cheating ex worked out the details. Patsy and her recently retired husband were still reeling from the chaos.

"It's too late," Grace declared. "No circus clowns for us."

"Speak for yourself, sweetie. You're still ridiculously young and so pretty. You could have all the clowns you want."

"I guess that's a compliment?"

"It is. I wish I had your figure, your skin, your age." Patsy sighed. "Please tell me you're going out with that real-estate agent who found the condo for you. What is his name?"

"Brad."

"Did he ask you out?"

"Not exactly. I believe his exact words were, 'If you ever get, like, really lonely, give me a call and maybe we can hook up.'"

"I'm sorry I asked." Patsy eyed the various cardboard boxes lining the walls of Grace's small office. "So, what happened with the wedding? Did the groom get cold feet? Did the bride run away with the best man?"

"I'm not sure. Right now it's a mystery." She leaned forward and took a sip of very cold coffee from a mug that said Fail To Plan, Plan To Fail.

"Who told you?"

"Both of them, actually. It was pretty grim. Julie

did the talking. And the poor groom just looked stunned. Like he didn't know what hit him."

"So she's the one who has the cold feet? Or another lover? Or her parents hate the groom. Or she found out he was cheating on her. Or all of the above."

"I don't know what happened. They've been an easy couple to work with. But I guess you can never tell what's going on under the surface." She looked at the shipping boxes that represented months of planning. Red glass Christmas ornaments embellished with the bride's and groom's names and the date of the wedding, pinecones for place-card holders, fat ivory candles, canning jars to be filled with battery-operated fairy lights—all destined for a seven o'clock wedding on Christmas Eve.

"True. But it does seem pretty dramatic, calling off a wedding so close to the ceremony."

"I'm going to have to look up an easy way to remove glitter-glued names from a hundred ornaments. Julie said she didn't want any of the decorations and I hate to throw them away." The wedding would have been absolutely gorgeous. Grace had planned on taking lots of photos to use as inspiration for other brides considering the Mirror Lake Lodge for their wedding.

"There's always eBay, I guess. Maybe another Mason and Julie will be getting married next

Christmas." Patsy peered at the boxes—one of the open ones was stuffed with pinecones. "What about the pinecones? I thought they were cute."

"I'll save them. I can use them for something else. But the little canning jars are my favorite." She had planned on taping the battery packs to the underside of the jar lids. "Festive Country Elegance" was her theme for this particular wedding.

"If you still want to assemble them, we can put some on the mantels. Or maybe the restaurant will want to use them for the Christmas buffet."

"Okay."

"Speaking of the restaurant," Patsy drawled. "Who's going to tell Nico?"

Grace shot her a pointed look.

"Oh no," Patsy said, her silver-and-red curls bouncing around her face. She threw up her hands. "That is so not part of my job description."

Grace wished it wasn't part of hers, but as the events coordinator for the lodge she had no choice but to discuss the cancellation with the lodge's most famous employee. The smoldering Italian chef would not be pleased. He'd worked on the menu for over a month, combining classic and elegant dishes to the delight of the bride, the groom and the bride's quiet mother. They had all been thrilled with his creative ideas, particularly when he incorporated his now-famous cheese bar.

Nico loved parties.

He was not going to love this news.

"He's going to throw a fit." Or worse, ask her to join him for a glass of wine while he flirted shamelessly.

"No, he isn't." Patsy frowned. "Well, maybe a little fit. Did you see the episode when he got really angry with that actor, the one who was the villain in that time-travel movie, I think."

"The tall guy," Grace said. "He thought it was funny to keep adding extra salt and pepper to the food whenever Nico turned his back."

"I thought Nico was going to punch him."

"He came close," Grace recalled. The YouTube video of those fifteen minutes of television time had gone viral.

"And the time the chicken wasn't cooked properly in that restaurant he was trying to help. He told the cook to leave and never come back. In Italian, I think."

"'Raw chicken *kills*'," he said. Remember? And then he threw those pans out the back door and two of the waitresses were crying—and then they went to a commercial."

"I wonder what happened to that restaurant. I should look it up."

"He's never thrown anything here, has he?" Grace had heard he was a perfectionist and an exacting employer, but nothing about violence.

Still, he had a reputation in the tabloids for his passionate nature.

"Well, just some utensils. But not at anyone directly," Patsy replied. "I think he just cooks with gusto."

"Gusto," Grace repeated, thinking of Nico's enormous energy. She wondered if he ever slept—he always seemed to be in the lodge's kitchen.

"He loves weddings," Patsy reminded her. "The bigger the better, he says."

"Well, everything has been paid for. The bride understood it was too late for refunds. Flowers, food, music, cake, everything. I hate to think of it going to waste."

"There's always the food bank. We've done that before with leftovers."

"I'll make some phone calls in the morning," Grace said, wondering if anyone would want ruby-red wedding decorations with pinecone placeholders and fairy lights.

"Ask Brian or one of the interns to take these boxes to the back room. Don't do it yourself." Patsy looked at her watch. "I'd better get back to the desk. I said I'd help Noelle with the tour group's arrival at one o'clock."

"But they're only here overnight, is that right?"

"Yes. A quick in and out—a celebratory dinner, a sleigh ride to the cabin, and then they're on to Boston in the morning after a leisurely brunch.

Nico has planned some kind of decadent French toast for them." She mock shuddered. "The man's food is so good just the thought of it gives me chills."

Grace eyed the half of a protein bar she was saving for a late-afternoon snack. It sat on her desk next to her now empty coffee cup, mocking her and her perpetual diet, daring her to throw it in the trash. "Eating his food would make me gain ten pounds in one day."

"It wouldn't show," Patsy responded loyally, but Grace knew better. At five feet two inches tall, she had to watch every calorie in order to fit into her clothes, like the size eight petite red sheath dress she'd worn to match the lodge's decorations today. Tomorrow she thought an ivory sweater and matching pencil skirt with dark gold suede boots would be appropriate, especially for the staff's Secret Santa breakfast. She planned to wear her new dark burgundy lace dress for Christmas Eve. Grace believed that blending in, looking as if she belonged to the lodge, was a necessary part of her job.

"Keep me posted on the wedding," Patsy said, heading toward the door. "If there's anything I can do—"

"I'll let you know," Grace promised. But she didn't intend to keep her friend away from her busy family and excited grandchildren during the holidays, no matter how many events were canceled. Patsy had already volunteered to work the desk on Christmas Eve so Noelle, who had a young son, could take the day off.

It wouldn't last forever.

Five more days until Christmas craziness was behind her.

Grace Clarke eyed the oversize calendar on her glass-topped desk and took a deep breath. She stayed organized using cell phone reminders and sticky notes, but she relied on her old-fashioned paper calendar to help her keep track of the Big Picture.

And the Big Picture had just shrunk.

Today was Monday, December 21. Yesterday Grace had overseen an intimate wedding between two eighty-year-olds and their immediate families, a Christmas party for the local chamber of commerce and a special family dinner for the resident bride and groom and their families.

The dinner was to have kicked off the wedding festivities, which would culminate in a Christmas Eve ceremony for a couple who appeared to be made for each other. The bride had been cooperative throughout the entire year they'd spent making arrangements and, despite some strange behavior during a dress fitting yesterday, she'd been a joy to work with. The groom, a physician, had been agreeable and patient.

In other words, he'd behaved the way a perfect groom should.

Until he'd been dumped.

Grace empathized.

She consulted her agenda on the iPad. She needed to make sure that the twenty-six people from the tour bus would be seated in the dining room for dinner at five thirty. Their sleigh rides had been confirmed for eight o'clock, with a return between eleven and twelve. There were the shuttle buses to Santa's Village to oversee—the guests' children loved that particular tradition. She'd had some luck helping the manager of the Village fill a Santa vacancy for tomorrow—one of the wedding guests turned out to be familiar with the role. The much-anticipated and very casual staff party would be held tomorrow morning, but she had nothing left to do for that event.

As far as she knew, the lodge was full, though Grace was pretty sure the groom and his family would be leaving the hotel and heading home. She made a note to check with Patsy on that. The maid of honor had arrived today, so either she hadn't known about the cancellation of the wedding or she was here to support the bride. Or maybe she loved to ski. After all, the bride and her mother had decided to stay for a few days and turn the visit into a vacation.

A vacation without lace, flowers, rings or promises of enduring love.

Grace couldn't understand it, but what Julie Barrett did or did not do was her own business. It was up to Grace to pick up the pieces.

She stalled for another two hours, making phone calls and going over the week's events. Finally she emerged from her office, which was conveniently tucked along a hallway next to the front desk in the main building. The double-door entrance facing the lake was decorated with the customary greenery and white lights. Each wreath was adorned with a red velvet bow and a set of tiny dangling sleigh bells. Patsy had Perry Como crooning through the stereo system.

"I will get even," she murmured as she passed the front desk where Patsy and Noelle huddled over the computer monitor. "I just downloaded 'Boogie Woogie Santa Claus' from Amazon."

"Bring it on," Patsy said. "You can't possibly compete. I have forty-seven easy-listening Christmas albums on my iPod, including Elvis."

"Kill me now."

Noelle looked up and smiled. "I heard that Nico loves Andrea Bocelli."

"Gosh, really?" Grace feigned surprise, which made both women grin, and she headed up the polished wooden stairs to the restaurant. She loved the lodge, with its elegant white exterior and porches, stone fireplaces and pine walls. She loved the views of the lake, piles of snow framing ice perfect for skating, and the Oriental rugs on the polished wooden floors.

She did not love Christmas, not this year. This year it was merely a holiday to be endured. Her father was on a cruise with his latest fiancée and Grace's only other relative, Aunt Ellen, was in Arizona with her daughter's family and a new grandchild. It wasn't the holiday she'd envisioned eighteen months ago when she'd been planning her own Christmas wedding, but she would make the best of it. On January 4, when the lodge's many Christmas trees were stripped of their sparkly decorations and Patsy's CDs were returned to the drawer labeled Boring Holiday Music, Grace would breathe a sigh of relief and look forward to a lovely, hectic ski season.

Grace stepped into the restaurant and waved to one of the waiters.

"He's in the back," the young man called out.

"Thanks, Tom." She made her way past the elegant linen-covered tables and white chairs, the empty tables set with the lodge's trademark white linen napkins and December's emerald tablecloths. She approved of the holiday flower arrangements, shades of cream and white dotted with silvery jingle bells, all very elegant and tasteful, as sophisticated as the chef himself.

The restaurant was a spacious room, much longer than it was wide, with windows along the wall that faced the lake. The far end could be enclosed for private events, something Grace had done many times in the past four years. Tonight's tour group had opted to sit in the main area of the dining room, and she saw that a table for twenty-six stretched along the windows across from the stone fireplace. Eight or so tables held the last of the lunch crowd and, as usual, the long room was immaculate.

Mirror Lake Lodge was known for its many stone fireplaces. Not every venue in the Lake Placid area could boast so many beautiful public rooms, which made her job booking events easier. All she had to do was show potential brides the Wildwood Room, a private dining room and wedding venue separated from the main restaurant with a view of the lake and, of course, its own massive fireplace. Then there was the Mirror Lakeview Ballroom, just a few steps up from the Wildwood Room through a set of French doors. Floor-to-ceiling windows highlighted a huge room designed in the Victorian summer-home style, with wooden walls painted white and dark wood floors. It boasted two rustic stone fireplaces, one on each end of the rectangular room. Since its construction ten years ago, the Mirror Lakeview Ballroom had been the setting for many weddings, reunions, fashion shows, civic functions and "celebrations of life."

Julie Barrett's wedding ceremony was to have taken place in front of the fireplace in the Wildwood Room, with her reception for eighty-five people up half a flight of stairs in the ballroom. She'd wanted room for dancing, and had been thrilled that the two large Christmas trees would be decorated and lit. She'd even requested Grace's specialty, the hot-chocolate bar, to add to the cozy winter atmosphere. So, what had happened?

It was none of her business, she reminded herself as she weaved through the tables toward the kitchen. But still, what made love start and stop? She found it all a little sad.

A young waiter carrying two silver platters of homemade cookies burst out of the kitchen and headed her way.

"Teatime," Brian announced, stopping to lower one of the gaily decorated platters in front of Grace. "Want one?"

"No thanks." Tea and cookies were provided in the lobby each afternoon, much to Patsy's delight. Their guests loved the tradition, of course, which added to the lodge's popularity. "Is he in?"

"Of course." The boy grinned. "He's training two more interns."

"Uh-oh." She inhaled. "Those smell so good."

"Hey, you know baking cookies is the highlight of Maria's day," he called, hurrying out of the room.

Maria had been the lodge's pastry chef for thirty-one years. Her cookie recipes were highly guarded secrets, though Patsy swore she'd replicated the almond cookies once. Maria was a sweet, quiet woman in her fifties who rarely spoke, but she had a gift for baking, if not for conversation. She made a different kind of cookie for each day of the week and Mondays were oatmeal raisin.

"Grace! You are looking for me?" Dominic "Nico" Vitelli stepped out of the kitchen and smiled. "Finally!"

His smile lit up his eyes. That genuine smile of his had attracted viewers of all ages to his television show last year. The tall rangy body clad in a white chef's jacket and jeans, along with dark curling hair and surprising blue eyes, looked good on camera. Grace, who had little interest in cooking, had watched the show several times, but only when she was channel surfing on a rare Saturday afternoon off. And during those times she had been mesmerized by the man's sex appeal. He made cooking look seductive and sensual. She often wondered why his show had been cancelled, why he'd returned home after that failure—and it must have been devastating—instead of continuing his exciting Hollywood lifestyle. But here he was. Smiling at her.

"Finally?" She couldn't imagine why he'd be looking forward to seeing her. She kept their meetings brief and to the point. All business, all the time. She didn't want to be flirted with, had no desire to play games with the former television star. She longed to meet a quiet accountant who dreamed of living a quiet, ordinary life devoted to his wife and family.

Unfortunately, the accountants she met at the lodge were all married, snapped up by women who knew a good thing when they saw it. Unlike Grace, who fell for charming men with commitment issues.

"Of course." He waved her closer. "Come into the kitchen. I want you to try the special tonight, ravioli with pesto cream. And I have a bottle of Chianti breathing on the counter."

"I have something important—"

"Good. We'll discuss it. Come," he said, holding the door open for her.

She had no choice but to step into the kitchen, Nico following behind her. Grace scurried around the corner and into the gleaming kitchen. Nico's World, someone had nicknamed it shortly after the chef had been hired to return the restaurant to its former glory. The kitchen was usually noisy and loud, filled with bustling servers, cooks and dishwashers, but this afternoon only a handful of prep cooks lined the stainless-steel work counters.

In another hour the restaurant would be chaotic again. Right now the smell of freshly baked cookies competed with the aroma of garlic and bread just out of the oven.

Grace greeted the staff and trotted across the stone floor in her ruby-red heels. Suddenly her right foot slipped from underneath her. Her ankle twisted and she was falling backward into the arms of the handsome chef.

"Whoa," he said from somewhere above her head. "What the hell—"

"Sorry," she managed to say, until he attempted to set her back on her feet and her ankle buckled again.

"Hold on." He gripped her waist so she was lifted off her feet. "Chair!"

Three white-coated interns rushed to find a chair and within seconds an intern set one down in front of Nico and Grace. Nico placed her carefully on its brown leather seat.

"Thank you," Grace said, surprised at how much her ankle had started to hurt. "I don't know what happened."

"I do. I think you slipped on these." He bent over to pick up a tiny cluster of metal jingle bells and held them in the air to show his staff. "Ideas, anyone?"

"The cookie platters, Chef," one of the young

women said. "They must have fallen off the cookie platters."

"Ah." He frowned at the bells and shoved them in his jacket pocket before turning back to Grace. He knelt down to peer at her foot. "Those are ridiculous shoes."

"I'm glad the heel didn't break. I love them."

"I loved them, too," he muttered, lifting her foot to his thigh. "Until a few minutes ago."

"Just give me a minute to catch my breath and then I'll limp out of here." It was so embarrassing. One minute she'd been ready to discuss business and then she'd landed against a surprisingly wide chest and into a pair of extremely muscular arms.

Must be all that chopping and whipping and stirring, she decided. Cooking was not for wimps.

"You're not going anywhere."

"Chef?" An intern pushed an empty chair closer. Nico positioned it in front of Grace and sat down, then carefully removed her shoe. Grace held her breath until he was finished. "Joan, check to make sure there are no more hazards on the floor. Check the dining room, too. Where's Brian?"

"Here, Chef." The young man looked at Grace and gulped. "I'm really sorry, Ms. Clarke. They must have fallen when—"

But his boss interrupted. "Yes, yes, it was an accident, Brian. Now, get some ice. And a towel."

"Yes, Chef."

"It's all right, really." She smiled when Brian returned. "I've tripped over all sorts of things in this job. Fallen, too. Don't worry. This is nothing."

"It doesn't look like nothing," Nico said, forming an ice pack with the towel. He placed it near the top of her foot. "It's swelling. You may need X-rays."

"Ow." She made a move to pull her foot back, but Nico held her calf to keep her still. She smoothed her dress and made sure no one could see her matching red panties. She was sure Nico was the type to appreciate such things. And she wasn't going to give him any more reasons to flirt with her.

"Definitely X-rays," he said.

"It's just a little sprain," Grace countered. "I'll take the ice and go back to my office—"

"Don't we have doctors staying here for Thursday's wedding?"

"Yes, but—"

"I'll see if Noelle or Patsy can track one down, give us an opinion. Brian? Go ask at the desk. Otherwise, we'll head to town."

"Patsy can take me. You're busy with ravioli and sauce and dinner and the twenty-six sightseers."

"Patsy can't carry you. And my staff is perfectly capable of making ravioli." He arched a brow in their direction and a chorus of "Yes, Chef!" followed.

Grace didn't want to like him. She didn't want her toes to tingle every time his fingers shifted the ice pack. She didn't want to believe he was actually pleased to be taking care of her.

There were rumors he'd dated three actresses at the same time. His picture had been on the cover of *In Touch* magazine, along with his glamorous raven-haired producer and the caption hinting at a surprise pregnancy. He'd cooked for George Clooney and been featured in Oprah's magazine along with his recipe for eggplant Parmesan.

"You must salt the eggplant and let it rest," he'd been quoted as saying, as if that information unlocked the secrets of the universe, eternal life and the cure for cancer.

"Why do you let eggplant rest?" she said suddenly.

He beckoned one of the interns over. "More ice, please."

"Yes, Chef." The college student hurried to do Nico's bidding.

"Okay," he said, looking at her with those dark blue eyes of his. "Why do you let eggplant rest?"

It took her a moment to realize he thought she was making a joke. "No," she said. "You told Oprah to let the eggplant rest."

There was that sexy smile again. She couldn't stop herself from blushing, but she hoped he would assume the heat of the kitchen was to blame. The pain in her foot blossomed, burning toward her ankle and up her leg.

"It must be salted to sweat—to release liquid—so it won't be soggy."

"That's interesting." She was babbling about eggplant. Could this be any more embarrassing?

"Would you like some? Dinner service doesn't start until five, but I will put aside—"

"Thank you, that's very nice of you, but—"

"You don't like Italian food."

"I love Italian food. Who doesn't?" She shivered as he ran his index finger along her ankle. His touch was so gentle she didn't feel any pain. Or maybe her skin was frozen from the ice. She was just being silly. Grace gulped. Time to get back to business. "I came to tell you that the Barrett wedding has been canceled."

He frowned. "I heard. Why have you waited hours to tell me about it?"

"You knew?"

Nico smiled. "There are no secrets around here. One of the house cleaners heard the mother talking about it. Would you like a cup of tea, Grace? A glass of water?"

"No, thank you. About the wedding, Julie and Mason have apologized for the inconvenience. And they know the refund policy."

"I'll let some of the staff know they will have that night off, after all, but they were looking forward to making the extra money. And I will have beef Wellington specials on the menu for the next ten days."

"I know. We've all worked so hard getting ready." She wondered why he was taking the news in stride. Maybe in Hollywood, canceled weddings happened all the time. "Well, I'd better get back to work. If you would help me stand up—"

"Is there someone I can call to help you?"

"No, I'll manage."

"Give it another minute," Nico advised. "Has anyone ever told you that you should always wear red?"

Oh, for heaven's sake. She wanted to roll her eyes, but caught herself. "You are such a flirt."

"Grace!" He pretended to look insulted. "It was merely an observation. You've made it clear you aren't interested in going out with me, so I won't ask you again. Think of me as an impartial observer. And a paramedic."

"Right." She hid a smile.

He was heart-stoppingly attractive, disarmingly kind. And charming, too, with that eyebrow lift that sent his staff scurrying to do his bidding. But she was going to resist, just as she had since he'd joined the staff. It was a matter of self-preservation. There were lots of reasons to avoid this man. It was a "father thing," Patsy had informed her after Tom bailed. Patsy had just read a biography of Jacqueline Kennedy and was up to date on "father things." Daughters with playboy fathers tended to repeat the past in an effort to change it, Patsy had declared.

Grace hadn't argued. She'd read plenty of articles on topics like How to Tell a Keeper From a Loser, and she'd come to the conclusion that a little more self-awareness couldn't hurt.

CHAPTER TWO

"EVERYTHING GOOD HAPPENS in the kitchen," his grandmother used to say. She was a large woman, almost as wide as she was tall. Nico had adored her. And now, with the beautiful Grace Clarke immobilized in his very own kitchen, Adalina di Prioli's words had never been more true.

"Someday I will have to tell you about my grandmother." Nico replaced the ice pack with a colder one. The original was sufficient to help with the swelling, but he liked to keep the interns busy and, besides, he wanted to pamper this lovely woman in red.

He'd noticed that no one else seemed to. After a few discreet inquiries, he'd discovered she had no family in town. She had been in a relationship with some guy who moved away, but apparently that had been over for a long time. She seemed to spend most of her time at the lodge; she didn't party in town or spend her days off on the ski slopes. She drank red wine if she drank anything other than Diet Coke and she emceed the animal shelter's annual dog fashion show.

"Was she a cook, too?" Grace asked.

"She certainly was."

"And she taught you everything she knew?"

"Yes." Nico had perfected Mama Lina's meat-ball recipe by the time he was eight, her lasagna at nine, and he began inventing different kinds of ravioli fillings by the time he was ten. "Her lasagna and her meatballs are on the menu. Have you tried them?"

"The lasagna. It was delicious." He watched her try to wiggle her toes and wince. "We were here for Patsy's birthday in October. You made tiramisu, and we had a cake."

"There was a lot of wine poured that night." He remembered Grace's short black dress. She'd worn pumpkin earrings that dangled to her shoulders and threatened to tangle in her blond curls. He'd asked her to go out with him—dinner and a movie—and she'd very politely refused. "Was that the first time I asked you out?"

"I don't remember."

"No." He pretended to think about it. "I believe I invited you for a drink the day I was hired. I should apologize for that."

"You don't need to apologize."

"But I embarrassed you, I think. And gave you the wrong impression. I was ecstatic that day," he admitted. "It took two months to talk the owners into hiring me." At her incredulous expression, he added, "They didn't want to risk hiring someone who wasn't going to make a real commitment."

"I can certainly understand that," she huffed. "But I would have expected them to jump at the chance to have you."

"Not exactly," Nico drawled.

"We heard you cost a fortune." She smiled. "We thought you'd bring your movie-star girlfriends and illegitimate children with you."

Well, *that* was irritating. "Do you always believe everything you read at the grocery store? There was no pregnancy. I never even had a date with Scarlet, and the woman who was on the cover of that stupid magazine? She's a friend of mine who happens to be gay."

"Lake Placid must seem very tame compared to LA."

"If you knew my family, and there are a lot of them, you wouldn't say that." He thought of his mother's dismay over that particular magazine headline. Theresa Vitelli had not been pleased. And his sisters had been horrified. There had been so many texts and voice mails the day the magazine hit newsstands that Nico had ended up tossing his phone to the floor and stomping on it.

Not one of his finer moments. Nico took a deep breath.

"I shouldn't have bothered you that evening," he continued. "But you were walking by the bar just as I finished signing the contracts and you looked friendly. You had a clipboard, which seemed charmingly old-fashioned, and I saw you comforting a young girl, a Girl Scout, I think." He didn't tell her the weepy Girl Scout had been his niece. "You seemed nice. And I just wanted to celebrate." He didn't mention that she'd looked like a curvy golden goddess, and he was so nervous about talking to her that his tongue had dried up in his mouth.

"I don't have drinks with men I don't know," she said. "I'm sorry if I was rude. The Girl Scouts had organized a dinner for their parents in Wildwood and I was really busy."

"You were perfectly polite, but you broke my heart." No lie. He hadn't been that disappointed since Sharon Winn turned down his invitation to the junior prom.

"I'm sure it healed itself after a few minutes."

Nico chuckled. "You're right. The bartender bought me a scotch and welcomed me back to Mirror Lake. We played basketball together in high school."

He lifted the makeshift ice pack and studied her swollen foot. It didn't look good, but he didn't want to worry her. "I think it's time you got that ankle checked out."

"I don't—"

"Let's get you back to your office and see if

there's a doctor in the house." He grinned. "I've always wanted to say that."

"You're sure you can leave your ravioli? And your wine?"

"They'll keep," he said. "We can always have supper later on, if you're up to it."

"There's an eightieth birthday party at seven and I have to make sure that the entertainment arrives. It's a surprise."

"In the ballroom, yes. It's a seven-course dinner for fifty-one people. What's the entertainment?" Nico handed the ice to an intern, preparing to carry Grace from the kitchen. He knew she would protest unless he kept her talking. She was trying to wiggle her toes again, but pain flickered across her face as she stretched out her leg.

"A polka band. The guest of honor loves to polka, so his children organized a little dance. We're having the party in the ballroom because, according to the kids, the polka takes up a lot of room and their father can be quite exuberant when he dances."

"Anything else?"

"A fund-raiser in the bar, but I don't have to do anything for that. The tour group is all set, I think. You're offering hot buttered rum and dessert after the sleigh ride?"

"Absolutely. They'll be available in the lobby when the guests come staggering in, frozen from the cold and thrilled with the moonlight." He bent over and lifted her into his arms. She let out a little squeak of protest, but her arms curved naturally around his neck as he headed toward the door.

"Michael!" His second in command looked up from the pasta machine.

"Yes, Chef?"

"You're in charge."

Michael winked at him and gave him a thumbs-up. "Absolutely, Chef. You take all the time you need."

Nico stifled a smile. He had no qualms about leaving the kitchen to the staff. He'd trained them well these past four months, had hired and fired until he was satisfied that he had the best team possible. He handed her the ice pack to take with her. She was going to need it in the next few hours because that foot sure as hell wasn't going to get better anytime soon.

"I've never done the polka," he said. "Have you?"

"No." She sighed. "I was looking forward to it, too, if I got the chance. This is so embarrassing."

The handful of diners looked up curiously as Nico made his way through the dining room with Grace in his arms.

"You're enjoying this," she said, her hair tickling his chin.

"I am not," he said, chuckling. "I hate having a beautiful woman in my arms. I would rather be rolling out pasta dough and scolding the interns.

I would rather be scrubbing saucepans and cleaning ovens."

"You're too important to wash pans yourself, and you certainly don't clean the ovens. Hi, Mr. Stanford. Did you ski today?"

"Sure did, Gracie," the gray-haired gentleman replied. He had the remnants of a chocolate cake and half a cup of coffee in front of him. "What happened to you?"

"I twisted my ankle a little."

"I hope you're being well taken care of," he said, giving Nico a warning look.

"I'm going to get her to a doctor," Nico assured him. "Right now."

"Good." He smiled at Grace. "I'll check with Noelle later and find out how you're doing."

Nico managed to get out of the restaurant, down the stairs and to the front desk with only about nine more people asking Grace what happened. Three young women in ski gear had giggled, obviously thrilled to see such a romantic sight, two men had eyed him suspiciously and several children asked Grace if she was being kidnapped.

Patsy met him at the bottom of the stairs.

"I just heard," she said, peering at Grace's foot. "It doesn't look good, sweetie, but I love the red nail polish."

"I had it done yesterday," she said. "You can put me down, Nico. Really. You can."

"All right." He headed toward the sofa that fronted the fireplace. "Is this okay?"

"My office—"

"Doesn't have a couch," Nico said.

"It's not as bad as it looks, but it's starting to hurt a little bit more," she told the hovering Patsy. "Nico has kept ice on it and that really helped."

"What happened? Brian said you slipped and needed a doctor. I've called the two that I know are here, but they're either still on the mountain or in town. I'll take you over to the clinic. I called and they don't close until seven."

"I'll take her," Nico said, reluctantly settling his dream woman on the couch. She'd felt good in his arms, all curves and soft skin, her yellow curls tickling his face. She smelled of vanilla. Hand lotion, maybe? Or perhaps she used the homemade soap from the fancy bath shop in town.

"I think I just need to rest it a bit," Grace said. "There's no reason to make a big deal out of this."

Patsy exchanged a look with Nico.

"One word, Grace," he said. *"X-ray."* He turned back to Patsy. "If you'd get her coat and purse and whatever else she'll need, I'll take her over to the clinic." He hated the fact that she had hurt herself, hated that she was in pain. And since she'd hurt herself in his kitchen, he felt responsible. Getting to spend time with her was the silver lining on his guilt-filled cloud.

Grace protested again. "I just need some Tylenol and the ice pack. I'll go home and take care of it myself."

But Patsy wasn't buying it. "And just how are you going to get up the stairs?"

Nico ignored the crowd that had gathered around the sofa. Children held cookies, parents held coats and the most recent guests checking in stood next to their luggage and stared. He tucked another velvet pillow behind Grace's back. "Stairs?"

"She lives in a second-floor condo," Patsy informed him. "Outside stairs. No elevator."

"Grace can come home with me," Nico declared. "I have four bedrooms. And a ramp."

Patsy looked impressed. "Why do you have a ramp?"

He shrugged. "Grace will find it easy to get around. I live right down the street."

"Stop talking about me as if I'm not here," Grace grumbled. "Are there any rooms available?"

"I'll check." Patsy tried to hide her smile, but Nico saw a twinkle in her eyes when she turned back to him. "But I think Noelle already filled the rest of the rooms."

"That was fast," Grace said. "I thought we'd have cancellations after the guests heard about the wedding."

"I have some news about that," Patsy said. "But I'll call you later and fill you in."

"Hey, Pats! Grace! What's going on?"

Nico turned to see three burly young men approaching. They were stuffed into identical navy down jackets and looked as if they'd been outside for hours.

"I slipped and fell," Grace said, looking mortified. "Do not make a big deal about it, okay?"

One of the guys edged Nico aside and lifted the ice pack. "Uh-oh. Looks like a bad sprain or even a fracture. Come on, babe, let's do it."

Babe? Do it? Nico couldn't let that go. "I'm taking her," he said.

"It's no problem," the kid said. "We've got the vehicles here and Doc will have her fixed up in no time."

"But what about the fund-raiser?" Patsy asked. "Aren't you in charge of that?"

"Yeah, but there are enough other guys coming early. They won't miss us." He grinned, showing acres of white teeth. "We can take care of Gracie, easy enough."

"Fund-raiser?" Nico wanted to deck him, if for no other reason than the sight of his hand on Grace's bare leg.

"For Search and Rescue," Grace explained. "You're catering the appetizers, remember?"

"Oh yeah." Twenty pizzas, and cheese and crackers. Done and done. Not exactly a culinary challenge, but that's what the group ordered.

"I'll get your things, Grace," Patsy said. "You'll be back here in no time and I'll see what I can do about a room for you."

Shoved to the sidelines, Nico watched as Grace was bundled into her black cashmere coat. In a matter of minutes she was out the door, being carried by one of the local EMTs and surrounded by two others. The men joked and laughed as if they were going to a party.

"Don't look so sad," Patsy said, touching his arm to get his attention. "You'll have your chance."

"I just did. And there it went."

"Maybe, maybe not."

That got his attention. "Please tell me there's no room at the inn."

She grinned. "There is one room available, but I won't tell if you won't."

"Deal."

"Don't you dare break her heart."

"I won't. But she might break mine."

"I know." Patsy tapped his chest with her finger. "I've watched you mooning over her since you started working here."

"It's that obvious?"

"Oh yeah. For a big TV star, you're kind of pathetic."

"Not anymore," he declared. "Not anymore."

CHAPTER THREE

"I FEEL A lot better now." Grace tried to sound emphatic, but her voice quavered a bit as she wobbled against Nico's side. He'd been in the clinic's waiting room, seated in the midst of texting teenagers and a mother with a screaming baby, when Grace had limped out, crutches under her arms and a medical boot on her right foot. On her left she wore one of Patsy's running shoes, which her friend kept in her office in case she decided to use the treadmill in the workout room. A nurse had put an athletic sock over her injured foot before showing her how to put the boot on. "I can go back to work."

"Sorry," he said, not sounding sorry at all. "But that's already been decided. Patsy said to tell you that she'd take over for you at the fund-raiser and she'd see you in the morning. If you're okay to come to work in the morning, that is. What's the verdict?"

"A nasty sprain, but nothing is broken. I need to stay off of it as much as I can, treat it with ice and keep it elevated."

"Okay. Let's go get it elevated and iced."

"I have to pick up a prescription. Would you mind taking me to Kinney's?" Her foot ached, but the twelve-year-old doctor had called in a prescription for painkillers at the pharmacy. "If you could help me get home, I would appreciate it."

Nico was silent as he opened the door and helped her down the freshly shoveled ramp to the parking lot. His familiar Toyota 4Runner sat in a handicapped spot.

"Isn't that illegal?"

"At seven thirty at night? With a woman on crutches?" He beeped the doors open and settled her into the passenger seat. "There. How bad is the pain?"

"I'm trying not to cry," she admitted. He looked so concerned. She wanted to tell him not to worry about her, that she would be fine, but he backed away and shut the door.

"First stop, drugs," he announced once he was behind the wheel. The car was warm, despite the cold temperature and the light snow flurries that danced in the air.

"Thank you." She adjusted her seat belt and turned toward him. "I would have called Patsy for a ride home. I didn't expect anyone to be waiting for me." She'd felt a surprising mixture of relief and pleasure when she'd seen him sitting in one of those uncomfortable plastic chairs and reading an old issue of *Sports Illustrated*.

"Is there anyone I can call for you? Family?"

"My father lives in Boston, but he's out of town for the holidays." Not that he would have been at all helpful. "And my aunt, who lives in Saranac, has gone to help my cousin, who just had another baby. In Arizona." She had friends, good friends, but it was four days before Christmas and no one needed an injured friend in their spare bedroom, or worse, on their living room couch. Even Karen, the one person she would have called after Patsy, had a houseful of in-laws and a set of eight-month-old twins.

"So you're stuck with me." Nico shot her a grin.

"I didn't say that."

"No, but you're thinking it."

"Just a little." She couldn't help laughing. It was either that or burst into tears. She wanted to curl up in her bed and pretend it was July.

He left the car running while he picked up the prescription, which gave Grace time to wonder how Nico was going to carry her up a flight of stairs to her little condo. He'd had no trouble carrying her down the stairs at the inn a few hours ago, but going up was a different deal. She could sit down and scoot on her rear, step by step. It would be cold, slow and undignified, but not impossible.

This was starting to get complicated. Maybe Patsy had found her a room at the lodge. If she could just get into a bed and lie down for a few hours, she was sure she'd feel better.

Nico returned with a bottle of water, her pills and a plastic bag filled with junk food, which he plopped in her lap.

"My sisters always wanted M&M's when they were hurt. Marie and Cathy said that pain burns calories, and self-pity can be treated with Pepperidge Farm Milano cookies. Beth, on the other hand, believes in chicken soup. It's all in the bag, so take your pick."

"Really?" She peered inside. Sure enough, there were enough treats inside to compete with an especially good Halloween haul. And the soup was the boxed kind.

She loved the boxed kind with the little flat noodles.

"Thank you."

"You're welcome." He started the car and put it in Reverse. "You haven't met my sisters? There are three of them, all older than me. They've been to the restaurant several times."

"I don't think I have." She would have remembered. His parents had been to dinner, though. She'd seen them in the lobby but hadn't met them yet. "You grew up here. Why did you come back?"

"My family owns Vitelli's."

"I know." Vitelli's was a large brick restaurant in the center of town. Famous for its pasta dishes and pizza, it was hugely popular with locals and tourists alike.

"I have a very *large* family," he said.

"You're lucky." She thought about Aunt Ellen, so far away in Arizona this holiday. She'd texted photos of the new baby, a little girl with yellow fuzz on the top of her perfect little head.

"Yes," Nico agreed. "I am."

She fumbled in her purse for her cell phone and called Patsy. If she couldn't haul herself up the outside steps to her condo, then a cozy room at the lodge was the next best thing.

"Sorry, honey," her friend told her after Grace gave her the medical report. "Every single room is booked. You know how it is over the holidays."

"That's okay. Nico will help me get up the stairs at home."

"No," her driver said. "Nico won't."

"You're not going home," Patsy said, using her best motherly voice. "I went to your place and packed up some things for you and I gave them to Nico. He lives right down the street from the lodge, so it's convenient."

"It's not convenient," she protested.

"It is," Nico said. "I have a very large, very empty house."

"It is," Patsy agreed. "Everything you need for

overnight is in a suitcase or on hangers. By the way, you have an impressively organized closet. I've never known anyone who organized her outfits for the week and hung them on hangers labeled Monday, Tuesday, et cetera. It was quite amazing. Did you see that on Pinterest or invent it yourself?"

"Pinterest," Grace admitted. "Every Sunday I organize my clothes. It saves time in the morning."

"Someday you will have children and all of this will be a thing of the past."

"What about putting a rollaway in my office? There would be room if we moved some of the boxes."

Patsy sighed, "And have you limping back and forth to the ladies' room? Wearing your flannel nightgown?"

"Well…"

"Did you get crutches?"

"Yes. And a boot I can take on and off."

"Okay, then, sweetie. Are you on speakerphone?"

"No."

"Go home with the handsome, sexy TV star. Let him cook you dinner and carry you around that big, glorious house he just bought. He's a good guy, you know. Everyone likes him. He feels badly that you fell in his kitchen, so let him make it up to you." With that, she clicked off, leaving Grace holding a silent phone.

"All set?" Nico drove past the lodge without slowing down.

"I can't go home with you." She actually heard herself whimper, for heaven's sake.

"Why not?"

"It's too…personal. I don't even know you. Not really."

"No time like the present," he declared. "It's not like we're sharing a bed. You'll have your own room. On the first floor. And you'll have a private nurse." He grinned.

"You."

"Yep. Me. I'm going to bring you ice packs and hot tea and, if you're lucky, I might even read you to sleep."

She leaned back against the cushioned seat back and closed her eyes. "I do not believe this is happening. This morning I thought I had everything under control."

"You have another option."

"I do?" She kept her eyes closed. She didn't believe it for a minute, especially since his voice held that thread of humor she had begun to recognize.

"I can, somehow, with enormous brute strength, haul you up your stairs and get you inside your home."

"Sounds good to me. What's the catch?"

"Then I stay with you. I can fetch and carry and dispense medication and sleep on the couch. You have a couch, don't you?"

"Nope," Grace lied, finding the idea of this almost-stranger poking around her home embarrassing. "I only have an antique rocking chair. Oak. Hard as a rock."

"No big brown recliner with cup holders?"

"Not even a lumpy futon."

"Well, that settles it, then."

She reluctantly opened her eyes. They were well on their way out of town, heading away from her place and toward Mirror Lake Road. Her foot throbbed. She was hungry and thirsty and sleepy. She reached into the plastic bag and pulled out the M&M's. It only took a few seconds to open the candy and self-medicate.

"YOU REALLY DO have a ramp."

"Yeah. You thought I would lie about a ramp?" Nico carried Grace from the neatly plowed driveway toward his house. "The previous owners were a hundred and ten years old."

"You didn't have to carry me," she said, protesting once again. The woman was extremely hard to spoil, he thought. Here he was doing the knight-in-shining-armor routine and she'd rather be limping downhill in the cold, dark night. He wished he could have pulled the car into the garage, but it was filled with a boat, six kayaks and two Jet Skis, all of which belonged to his sisters and their assorted husbands and children.

"It's fifteen degrees out, in case you haven't noticed. This is faster." Plus, he got to hold her in his arms. He shook his head at the sappy thought. He hadn't held anyone for over seven months, which, of course, no one would believe. His sisters had offered to fix him up with their friends and their friends' younger sisters, cousins and coworkers, but he wasn't interested.

He'd been waiting. He was thirty-five and he knew what—and who—he wanted. Maybe he'd get lucky and get his wish.

"I've driven past this house so many times," Grace said. "I always liked how it sat on the hill and looked over the road to the lake. I like all of the houses around here."

"Yeah, me, too." He was grateful for the automatic lights that lit the walkway to the back door and bathed it in a light bright enough to help him find the right key. "I'm going to set you down for a second, all right? But hold on to me. I just need to unlock the door."

"I'm okay." She clutched the plastic shopping bag and her purse in one hand, his sleeve in the other.

Al's excited barking began. The mutt didn't believe in barking at strangers, only people who had keys. The sound of a key in the lock sent him into raptures of joy.

"You have a dog!"

"I do. Does that surprise you?"

"A little," she admitted. "You don't seem like the type."

"I don't think you know what type I am," Nico replied. "Brace yourself. He might wag you off your feet." Al, his aging yellow Labrador mix, blocked the foyer. He woofed and wagged, torn between greeting Nico and his curiosity over the visitor. Nico noticed that Grace properly held her hand out for Al to sniff, but anyone could see that the dog wasn't the least bit aggressive.

"Hi, Al." Grace stroked the dog's head, but she kept hold of Nico's arm. "Are you glad to see us?"

"He spends most of his days, when I'm working, with my oldest sister. She lives farther up the hill, not far from here. She spoils him rotten. I hired my nephew to take him for walks after school." Very slow walks, since the dog had grown lame from arthritis. He preferred to hang out by the gas stove and sleep on his heated dog bed. "They bring him home after dinner and he spends his evenings sleeping."

"You are such a good dog," Grace told him, and Al wriggled as best he could in response to the compliment.

Nico managed to maneuver Grace onto the

bench by the door, next to Al's water and food bowls, and then helped her remove her coat and the one tennis shoe. She left her socks on, which looked adorably sexy with the sleek red dress.

"I'm going to carry you again," he said, lifting her into his arms, and for once she didn't protest. She looked paler than she had at the clinic, more fragile. He needed to get her settled, as he'd promised. They walked down the hall, past the laundry room and a bathroom, then into the kitchen. Al pattered behind them, staying close.

"Your favorite room, of course."

"Of course." The original dark wood cabinets stretched to the ceiling, the appliances were from the 1980s, the counter an old cracked white Formica. "I'll need to replace the countertop and the appliances soon," he explained. "But I don't want to change it too much."

A large battered pine farm table stretched along one side of the room under the expanse of windows, sixteen chairs around it. The table, which once belonged to a nearby summer camp, had been the first thing he'd bought for the house. His sister Marie had found an assortment of wooden chairs at estate sales and had painted them the palest shade of blue.

"Your house is beautiful," she murmured, gazing into the living area that faced the lake. "It looks like everyone's fantasy of the perfect Victorian summer home, only better."

"I haven't had time to buy much furniture." Al's enormous dog bed sat in front of the fireplace, a twin for the one that graced the lobby of the lodge. He owned one tan sofa—a reject from his parents—and an old round coffee table, which had been left there by the previous owners. Two plastic laundry baskets full of toys sat in one corner, an enormous and very bare Christmas tree in the other, though hills of wrapped gifts lined the wall under the windows. Seen through Grace's eyes, the place would seem pretty sparse. As if he wasn't doing it justice or something. Suddenly he doubted his wisdom in bringing her here. "Getting the restaurant back up to—"

"You don't have to explain," Grace interrupted, her voice soft. "You should take your time, buy only what you want, what feels right."

"Exactly," he said. That was the way he operated. He waited for exactly what he wanted, which might explain why Grace was here, in his arms and in his house. "It drives my sisters crazy. They're dying to decorate this place."

"You have a close family."

"*Close* would be an understatement. Three sisters, three brothers-in-law, a nephew, four nieces and another baby on the way. They are constantly in and out of here."

"Which explains the toys in the living room."

"And the jigsaw puzzle on the coffee table. Anna is eleven and she's crazy about them. It can get a little hectic." But he was never more grateful to his sisters than he was now. Marie and her three children, who lived less than half a mile away, took care of Al. Cathy came every Monday and cleaned, telling him she needed the exercise and the excuse to get out of the house with the kids, who were two and four. Beth, the sister with an MBA, oversaw his investments, handled his money and managed his manager. His parents ran Vitelli's, with the help of their three daughters, two excellent assistants, a head chef and an aging but devoted staff.

He headed past the living room to the master bedroom, a large white-walled room with a king-size bed and its own bathroom, complete with soaking tub and separate shower.

"Here you go," he said, setting Grace on the quilt-covered bed.

"This is your room." She frowned up at him. "I can't take your bed."

"I don't sleep here. My room and office are upstairs, along with two more bedrooms and two bathrooms."

"Really?" Those beautiful blue eyes held doubt.

"Really." He grabbed the neatly placed bed pillows and tucked them behind her. "Time for dinner and pain pills. And ice."

He handed her the remote control and pointed to the television set mounted on the wall across the room. "See? All the comforts of home."

"I just need my cell phone."

"I'll get it," he assured her, moving away from the bed. He hoped Patsy had handled any emergencies, though what could go wrong with pizza and raffles in the bar? He'd donated gift certificates to the restaurant and also to Vitelli's, as his parents supported every charity in town.

"Thank you." Grace winced as she stretched out her foot. "You didn't have to go to all of this trouble, but it feels really, really good to lie down."

"Good. I'll come back with your things and then you can tell me what you want to eat."

"I get to boss around the famous Nico Vitelli?"

"Not many people can say that," he said, fleeing the room before he said something stupid, like, *You can boss me around for the rest of my life if you want.*

"ARE YOU GOING to need any help getting your clothes off?"

Grace looked up from her tray of food. He'd brought her ravioli stuffed with some kind of wonderful cheese filling and drizzled with a light pesto sauce. He'd offered salad and an apple tart, but she'd politely refused. He'd left her to eat while he took Al outside, but he'd been in and out of the room making sure she had everything she needed.

"I think I can manage." She eyed the crutches propped against the nightstand. "I'm pretty sure I can get my nightgown on without falling over."

"Well, if I hear a crash I'll come racing in and pick your naked body up off the floor, so don't lock the door."

"Okay." She felt herself blush again and hoped he wouldn't notice. "Dinner was delicious," she said, changing the subject from nude bodies to food.

Al padded over and rested his chin on the mattress next to her hip, so she reached over and stroked his head. The dog closed his eyes and inched closer.

"He'll want to sleep with you," Nico warned. "Don't be too nice."

"I don't mind. There's plenty of room." She'd had a dog after her mother passed away, a little spaniel mix that followed her everywhere. He had died during her junior year of high school, and stepmother number three had refused to consider adopting another, which had left a pretty big gap when it came to having someone to love.

"Not a good idea. What if he rolled over on your foot?"

"It's my right foot. He can sleep on the left side. If he wants to."

"I usually carry him upstairs at night."

"You do?"

"His hind legs are bad. He can't do stairs."

That was a sweet picture, the fancy Hollywood chef carrying his old dog to bed. "Did he live with you in California?"

"Yes. He loved the pool."

"I'll bet." Al leaned closer and whined. Nico leaned over and removed the tray. "What else can I get you? Tea? Coffee? Cookies? My mother sent over a platter two days ago. She's obsessed with baking right now."

"I could eat a dozen cookies, so don't tempt me." She set her cell phone on the nightstand. The pain pill she'd taken before dinner was making her drowsy, and now that she'd checked her messages, all she wanted to do was crash. "I got interesting news from Julie Barrett."

"The runaway bride?"

"Don't call her that. She didn't run away. She just…changed her mind. Better than marrying the wrong man."

Nico perched on the edge of the bed and looked at her foot, now devoid of the boot and covered with an ice pack. "There would be nothing worse than marrying the wrong person. Have you ever been married?" he asked.

"No."

"Engaged?"

She hesitated. "No. I thought we were heading in that direction, but I was wrong. What about you?"

"No. My friends tell me I'm too fussy. My mother says I'm too old and set in my ways. And my father tells me not to worry, I'll know when I meet the right woman."

"My father has been married three times and engaged twice. He has a new girlfriend every year."

"And your mother?"

"She died when I was twelve. Cancer. They were divorced before that, though. But we all lived in the same small town north of Boston. She was a teacher."

"You must miss her. I'm sorry."

"Thanks," she said, taking a deep breath. "I was lucky to have my aunt Ellen. That's how I ended up working here, in upstate New York." Those summers with her aunt and cousins had saved her from cranky stepmothers and emotional scenes between her father and the women he loved and left.

"So, what was the message from Julie Barrett?"

"She's given her wedding to Noelle."

"Noelle? At the lodge?"

"Yes. She's engaged to Ted and they were planning a small, inexpensive wedding. I guess Julie and Noelle talked and Julie gave her the entire thing. Most of it had been paid for, and Noelle's wedding won't be as big, so it shouldn't cost Ted and Noelle anything, unless they have an open bar."

"Dinner for eighty-five people," Nico said. "Beef Wellington. The Barrett family wouldn't get much of their deposit back anyway."

"Now it won't go to waste. What do you think?"

"The food was never going to go to waste," he said. "Not in my kitchen."

"But the cake. And the decorations. And the flowers." She sighed contentedly. "All the beautiful flowers."

"I think it's a very kind and generous gesture."

Grace blinked back tears. "I think so, too. I mean, Noelle has that little boy, and Ted has to go back overseas, someplace dangerous—did you know he's a Green Beret?—and they will just *love* the fairy lights in the jars and the pinecone place-card holders and the little jingle bells, don't you think?" Her voice caught on a sob.

"Grace?"

"I love weddings," she whispered. "I always wanted to get married on Christmas Eve. You know, to make it special?"

He leaned forward and took her into his arms. "Oh, Grace. All weddings are special. Or should be. You make them that way."

She flopped against his chest and rested her head on his shoulder. "This is so embarrassing."

"What? Crying? I grew up with three sisters. I am totally used to it."

"I should have watched where I was going."

She'd been concentrating on avoiding Nico's smile instead of looking for dangerous, fallen Christmas decorations.

"I'm selfishly glad you didn't." He pulled back slightly and smiled down at her. "This has been a memorable first date."

"I'm only crying because I took Percocet," she sputtered. "Pain medication makes me emotional."

"Well, then," he murmured, folding her back into his arms. "Weep away."

CHAPTER FOUR

SHE WOKE UP next to the dog. He was a comfortable and warm weight stretched against her side, but he snored. Not that the noise had bothered her. It was after eight o'clock and she was due at work in an hour. She'd need every minute to get ready.

"Good morning, Al."

His tail thumped once and he wriggled closer, his eyes closed. Grace patted his rump and eased herself to a sitting position. Her foot throbbed, but not as painfully as last night. She'd managed to get into her nightgown without Nico's help— Patsy had selected her only flannel gown instead of one of her many cute pajama sets.

After her weepy breakdown, he'd offered to help her out of her clothes to make her laugh. She'd refused, making him laugh. He'd fixed her a cup of herbal tea and delivered it, with an assortment of his mother's cookies, to the nightstand while she was in the bathroom washing the tears from her face.

She would never, ever take Percocet in a man's

presence again. Not unless the man was her husband and she had just given birth to triplets.

She managed to climb out of bed and brush her teeth with the help of her crutches before she heard the knock on the door.

"Come on in." She was resigned to the fact that he would see her dressed like a ninety-year-old woman. He may as well see what she'd be wearing when she was ninety.

He opened the door and peered in. "Hey. How are you doing?"

"Okay." She sat on the bed and wished she could crawl back in next to Al, who was pretending to be asleep. Nico looked wide-awake, cheerful and heart-stoppingly handsome. The man looked ready to flip a thousand pancakes.

"Did you sleep?"

"Al and I both were practically comatose." She wished she'd put on makeup. Patsy had emptied the entire contents of her bathroom drawer into a gallon ziplock bag, so she had no excuse for not putting on lipstick and eyeliner, for heaven's sake.

"You look a lot better than you did last night." He reached out and touched her cheek. "You're not as pale. How's the pain?"

"Not bad at all," she fibbed.

"Can you walk?"

"With the crutches."

He looked over at her bed. "Al! Time to go out!"

The Labrador didn't budge.

"I know he's alive." Grace laughed. "He wagged his tail for me a few minutes ago."

"He's faking it. He hates snow." Nico looked at Grace. "Want some coffee before I haul him out of here?"

"Yes. Give me a few minutes to get dressed."

"Don't bother. I'll bring it to you. Cream, no sugar, right?"

"How did you know that?"

"The executive chef at The View knows everything," he informed her. "Stay right where you are. I haven't brought a woman coffee in bed for days."

"Very funny," she said to his back as he left the bedroom. Or maybe he wasn't joking. According to the tabloids, Nico's social circle had once included the Kardashians and *Sports Illustrated* models. She hadn't heard of him dating anyone in Lake Placid, but then again, there were plenty of beautiful women on the ski slopes and at the Olympic park. She wondered if any of them wore light blue flannel dotted with pink roses.

"Woof."

She heard the child's voice the same time Al did.

"Woof, woof!" Al finally raised his big head and turned brown eyes in her direction.

"Hey, Al! Wanna go for a ride?"

"Woof woof woof!" came the answer, just as a tall, thin boy ran into the room.

"Hey, Al, what are—"

The boy skidded to a stop, turning a pair of dark eyes toward Grace. He had the same head of thick dark waves as Nico, the same angular features and easy smile. He was dressed in a warm jacket and knitted cap, and his gloved hands held a bright blue leash.

"Whoa," he said, sounding exactly like his uncle. Grace assumed this child had to be Nico's nephew, the one who took his dog for walks and lived nearby. "Uncle Nico has company!" the boy called over his shoulder before returning to Grace.

"Hi," he said.

The dog suddenly came to life and let out another happy bark before easing himself off the bed to greet his friend.

"Hi. I'm Grace," she said, wishing she was dressed but glad she wore flannel at the very least. The boy's mother stepped into the room and stopped as soon as she saw Grace.

"Oh! I'm sorry," she managed to say. She was tall, with short dark brown hair and a handsome, angular face. Dressed in jeans and a puffy red vest with matching sweater, she looked as ready to take on winter as her son. "I didn't know Nico had company."

"I'm Grace Clarke." She held out her hand and attempted to get to her feet, but Nico's sister intervened.

"Marie O'Rourke. And this is Brian, my son. You're hurt." She put out a hand to stop Grace from moving. "Stay where you are." Her gaze darted to Grace's nightgown, then to her booted foot and on to the rumpled bed. "What happened?"

Nico came to the rescue. He stepped into the room and handed Grace a mug of coffee. "Grace works at the lodge. She slipped in the kitchen last night and I brought her home."

"Does it hurt?" Brian asked.

"Yes. But not as much as it did last night," Grace said. "And Al kept me company."

The dog leaned against Brian and licked his hand.

"I hung your clothes in the closet," Nico said, jerking a thumb to one of the wide doors opposite the windows.

"Thanks, Nico. And thanks for the coffee."

"Are you up to go in to work or do you want to hang out here for a few hours?"

"It's Secret Santa day," she reminded him. "Staff brunch at 10:00 a.m., remember?"

"Oh yeah, that's right. We drew names?"

Maria turned to him. "Isn't that why you asked Cathy to make you a—"

He put his hand over her mouth. "*Secret* Santa, big sister. They take these things seriously at the lodge." Nico turned to his nephew. "Come on, let's give Grace some privacy." He ushered the dog, his sister and his nephew out of the room and shut the door behind them.

"As soon as they leave I'll make you a frittata," he whispered. "With a crunchy potato layer that will make you weep with joy."

She thought of the calories. Her mouth watered. Her foot throbbed.

Her heart melted.

CHAPTER FIVE

"YOU'VE GOT IT BAD, little brother."

"I'm going to pretend you're not here." Nico didn't bother to argue. Once Marie decided something, the sun would have to fall out of the sky to change her mind. How her mild-mannered husband stayed sane was a mystery to the entire family. Ignoring the cold, he leaned against the back door's frame and waited for his sister to continue, as he knew she would.

"She's beautiful. And she spent the night."

"She slept with Al, not me."

"So you say." She eyed him speculatively. "Wait till Mom hears about this. She'll think Christmas came early."

"Mom doesn't have to know anything."

"What? Are you kidding? Brian's going over there to decorate cookies again this afternoon. You think he's not going to tell his grandma that Uncle Nico had a friend over? A pretty female friend with a boot on her foot, just like the one that Elizabeth in Mrs. Rayak's class had last year when she fell off the ski lift?"

"I could pay him. What's the going rate for keeping his mouth shut?"

Marie shrugged. "He's not motivated by money. Unfortunately. I offered him five dollars not to tell his father that I said three very bad words when that guy backed into me last week."

"Yeah? What happened?"

"Oh, his insurance company will pay for it. There was a witness."

"I meant with Brian." Nico liked the kid. For a nine-year-old, he pretty much had it together. He managed to tiptoe through the minefield of having an older sister and a younger one quite well. His ability to stay calm and detached in the midst of female drama made him more like his father than the Vitelli side of his family.

"He told me he had heard worse at school and to be cool."

"You are cool."

"I am," Marie said. "I'm forty-two and I'm definitely cool. Now, let's talk about you."

"I'm going to ask her to dinner Thursday."

"That's Christmas Eve."

"I know."

"That's big."

"I'm aware of that. I hope the family doesn't scare her off."

"Nico, we'll be on our best behavior." She frowned. "I mean, we'll do our best. Maybe 'best behavior' is a little optimistic. But for you to bring a woman to Christmas Eve? This is really big. How long have you known her?"

"Since I started work here. I see her almost every day at the lodge." *And I've been half in love with her since the first minute I saw her.*

Nico thought it wise not to say that aloud.

"She's why you wouldn't let us fix you up. How long have you been, uh, dating her?"

"I've been, uh, dating her since last night." He enjoyed the look of surprise on his sister's face. "I told you, she fell in the kitchen at work and hurt her ankle. I brought her home to help her out. To take care of her."

"And now we're back where we started," his sister said. "You've got it bad."

"I do," Nico admitted. "But it's not mutual. Yet."

"It will be," Marie assured him, giving him a quick hug. "Just be your charming self. And ply her with chocolate. Women like that."

"I don't think it's going to be that easy."

"You've never failed at anything you set out to do." She frowned. "Except when you tried out for football. That was pretty much a disaster."

"I've put on some muscle since then." But he would never be able to throw a ball fifty yards and actually hit a target.

"Don't be *too* charming," Marie warned. "That

California stuff was ridiculous." She gave him another hug. "I'm so glad you're home."

"Me, too." He waved them off, watched Al lift
his leg on his favorite holly bush and then turned
back to the house.

He would romance Grace with food and attention. She was a very private person, but she'd let
down her guard a little last night.

And she'd smiled at him when he'd brought her
coffee.

That was a promising start to the day.

THE FUTURE BRIDE was the happiest person in the
Wildwood event room, but Grace was the most
pampered. She sat at a table close to the fireplace,
her legs resting on the seat of another chair, her
narrow skirt tucked primly over her knees. On
one foot she wore a golden tan suede knee-high
boot. On the other was the decidedly unfashion-
able walking boot, with one of Nico's white athletic socks underneath it to keep her toes warm.

Nico Vitelli hovered over her, something that
did not go unnoticed by the staff attending the
Christmas brunch. Between Nico's interesting behavior and the news of Noelle's wedding, there
was plenty for the employees of the lodge to discuss over coffee and plates piled high with food.
Much to everyone's delight, Nico had arranged a
sumptuous buffet. Grace made sure the presents

were piled underneath the Christmas tree and a member of the housekeeping staff had a fire burning in the fireplace.

Those who were working the morning shift took time out to have a cup of coffee and a bite of food, wish everyone a merry Christmas and open their gifts. Those on later shifts stayed longer to visit. Because the lodge was too busy in December to have a big Christmas party, the owners held an enormous outdoor party in June for the staff and their families. Grace had organized the Secret Santa brunch when she was hired at the lodge and it had quickly become a holiday tradition.

Thanks to Grace, the background music was a rousing New Orleans Christmas compilation. Patsy had agreed to hold off on Bing Crosby until after one o'clock, but only because Grace was on crutches and therefore an object of pity.

Patsy was bursting with questions, so the second Nico returned to the kitchen, she leaned closer. "Okay, tell me everything. What's his house like? It's the big white one about half a mile down the street, right? With the big porch?"

"I didn't notice the porch, but the house is old and big and gorgeous." She took a bite of a cinnamon roll. Just one bite wouldn't hurt, would it?

"And where did you sleep? Did he make you dinner?"

"I slept in the guest room. He bought me candy.

And made me breakfast. And served me coffee in bed." She didn't want to admit she'd enjoyed every minute. She didn't want her friend to think she was crushing on the Hollywood chef. "By the way, why did you pack the granny gown instead of my pajamas?"

"In case you were in a cast. Can't get pants on over a cast, you know."

"I never thought of that."

"You've never had a kid with a broken leg. I looked for something silk, with lace, but all you had were jogging pants and T-shirts."

"I like silk and lace," Grace sputtered. "But it's winter. Silk and lace are stored with my summer things."

Patsy sighed. "Of course they are."

"How many calories do you think there are in one of these?" She held up a star-shaped sugar cookie frosted with pink-and-yellow icing.

"Zero. It's Christmas. Calories don't count. Were you surprised when you got Julie Barrett's phone call?"

"I was thrilled." Grace smiled. "It was absolutely perfect."

"This is a nice turn of events." Patsy took a bite of a star-shaped cookie. "Noelle deserves something good."

"It's going to be fun to put this together. This morning I showed her everything I had planned and she was thrilled with it all. She said she felt like she'd won the lottery. I left a message for Julie to tell her how kind that was." Grace wriggled in her seat, trying to ease a cramp in her calf.

"What's wrong?"

"The darn thing hurts more than I thought it would," she admitted. "It's just a simple sprain, but the doctor said it could be uncomfortable for quite a while."

"I'm sorry," Patsy said. "I know I've teased you about going home with Nico, but this really is a bad time to be limping around on crutches, even with Mr. Hollywood over there helping you out." They both watched Nico laughing with two blushing housemaids. "But at least the wedding was all planned. And if you have a lot of running around to do, I can take care of it for you."

"Thanks. I can put together the decorations while I'm sitting down. Noelle said she'd help in any way she can, but she has a lot of things to pull together in two days."

"She told me she had the dress, though, so that's one of the big things crossed off her list."

They saw Noelle and her son enter the room. Josh whispered something to his mother and then made a beeline for the buffet table. Noelle approached Nico, who seemed to be taking the role of host seriously.

"He's so darn cute. I've never seen a boy who

eats so much, but then again, I raised a girl," Patsy commented.

"Noelle says all of his friends are like that." She wondered what it would be like to raise a son by herself. But now Noelle and Josh had Ted, and the Green Beret appeared to be the kind of man a boy could look up to. They watched as Nico and Noelle talked for a moment. He gave her a quick hug and then turned to Grace and smiled.

"Please tell me he cooked for you," Patsy pleaded. "I have to know."

"He did." And now he was heading toward them.

"So you and George Clooney have something in common," Patsy teased.

"Who would have guessed?"

Nico, carrying a cup of coffee, joined them at the table. His white chef's jacket made him look terribly sexy, in a television star kind of way. He plopped into the empty chair next to Grace.

"Good morning, Patsy." He looked at the open box in front of her. "What'd you get?"

"Shower gel. Love it."

He turned to Grace. "Whose name did you have?"

"I can't tell you."

"Sure you can. I had Carol, in Housekeeping. I bought her gourmet birdseed. She has parakeets."

Impressed, Grace had to ask, "Does ten dollars buy a lot of fancy birdseed?"

"It does, surprisingly."

Patsy looked fascinated. "And you knew she had parakeets because…?"

"I went to school with her husband. I ran into him at the pet store. Al has a corn allergy."

"Who's Al?"

"His dog," Grace told her.

"Oh. I didn't know dogs could have allergies."

"It gives them skin conditions. Here's your gift," Nico said, setting a silver gift bag in front of Grace. "It was under the tree, in the back."

"Thank you." She'd meant to go over and find her gift, but the thought of hobbling over there on crutches had stopped her.

"Are you going to open it?"

"Grace always saves hers," Patsy said.

"I like to open gifts on Christmas morning." She savored the presents tucked under her little tree. Her father would send a check, but her aunt's and cousin's gifts were already there, waiting to be opened. She would add this pretty silver bag to the others. The tag dangling from the silver ribbon had Grace printed on it in a woman's handwriting. "Did you cheat again and take my name, Pats?"

"Nope." She chuckled. "I cheated and took Noelle's."

"Patsy is in charge of name distribution," Grace told Nico. "She volunteers every year so she can pick who she wants to give a gift to."

"And then it's random," Patsy insisted. "Totally up to fate."

Hmm. Fate had assigned Grace the challenge of buying a gift for Nico. With the stipulation that a gift could cost no less than five dollars and no more than ten, she'd struggled to come up with something remotely appropriate for a man who cooked professionally. She'd opted for a practical gift instead. Patsy had set her up and she knew it.

"Where's yours?" Grace asked. What had he thought of the telescoping ice scraper for his car? It was difficult to wrap, so she'd covered it in red tissue paper, tied a bow and a name tag on it and stored it in her office for the past week. She'd asked Patsy to sneak it into the room and prop it up near the tree.

"My fancy snow-removal tool is in my office where no one can steal it." He grinned. "I guess someone assumes I'm not prepared for winter."

"Or wants to make sure you're safe," Patsy suggested.

"Or saw you cleaning your windshield with a scraper from the dollar store," Grace added.

"Come to think of it, you did see me doing that once," he said. "And you loaned me yours. So thank you."

"That doesn't mean it's from me," she said, but she smiled at him.

"True." He pushed the silver bag closer to her. "Open it. I can't stand the suspense."

It wasn't from Nico, thank goodness. Patsy hadn't gone so far as to arrange that, which was a relief. He'd bought birdseed.

"I have something for you," her friend said. "You can take that home and add it to your pile."

"Don't you think it's more fun to wait?"

"Sometimes," Nico said. "When you don't have any other choice."

She lifted the tissue from the top of the bag and pulled out a fluffy knit scarf composed of blended shades of aquamarine and light blue.

"Oh, it's beautiful!"

Patsy agreed, touching the wool. "It feels like alpaca. Or mohair?"

"I don't know," Grace said, "but it's so soft."

"And matches your eyes," Nico declared. "Are you sure you don't have a secret admirer? Other than me, I mean."

"Stop teasing," she said, fingering the scarf. "It looks handmade."

"Someone must have made it especially for you," Patsy said, shooting Nico a suspicious look.

He ignored her. "Aren't you glad you opened it? You can wear it tonight when I drive you home."

"Home to my place," Grace said.

"Home to mine," he countered. "We have a wedding to organize, remember?"

"No, we don't. It's all done. We can finalize the details later this afternoon." She intended to dip ornaments in glitter and assemble the lights in the canning jars while she kept her foot elevated. The darn thing had already begun to ache more than she thought it would. Spending another night being pampered by Nico sounded more tempting than she wanted to admit to herself.

"Al will be heartbroken."

"There is one thing you two might need to consider," Patsy interjected.

"What?"

"A bridal shower."

"A bridal shower?" Grace hadn't even thought about something like that for this last-minute wedding, but why not? "When?"

"Tomorrow night," Patsy said. "Noelle's friends on staff have been talking. You know how close they are. We could invite Noelle's and Ted's friends, plus some of the family. They wondered if they could hold it here. A couples thing. They talked to me about it last night because they didn't want to bother you until they knew you were okay."

"This room is available," Grace said, considering the possibility. "It was originally reserved for the rehearsal dinner."

"The ex-groom said he hoped the preparations wouldn't go to waste," Patsy said.

"Yes. I got that message," Nico replied. " Mason

wanted Ted and Noelle to have whatever couldn't be refunded."

"So we use Wildwood for a couples shower?" Grace saw Noelle and her son near the Christmas tree. Josh found a present with his name on it—Grace had made sure there would be something for him—and held it up to his mother. "If Noelle and her fiancé agree."

"Or we could surprise them," Nico suggested.

Patsy nodded. "I think her friends would like that idea."

"Well," Nico drawled, looking at Grace. "The romance continues."

CHAPTER SIX

"You missed the movie," Nico said, stepping into Grace's office. He stopped, taking in the rows of red ornaments covering her desk and the folding table opened to its six-foot length. Grace sat with her leg propped up on a metal folding chair. She was attaching something to a jar lid with white duct tape.

"The snowboarding preview? Was it good?"

"I looked in a few times. The crowd was certainly into it." He came closer. "What are you doing?"

"Putting batteries in two dozen sets of lights." She held up a plastic box. "This holds the batteries. Then I tape one to the underside of the canning jar lid and put the lights in the jar. When they're turned on they make a pretty decoration."

"These are for the wedding, I assume?" She looked tired. And she had silver glitter on her chin and her right cheek. He suspected she was hurting, too. He wanted nothing more than to scoop her into his arms, haul her out of the office and put her to bed, where he would tuck pillows around her and feed her. Chicken medallions sautéed in white wine, with capers. A little pasta, perhaps.

"Yes. I spent the afternoon fixing the ornaments."

"I see that." He eyed the rows of glittered balls. "Don't you have any help? I thought you had an assistant." He was sure he'd seen a tall young woman following Grace around, assembling floral arrangements and guiding guests to various events.

"Just part-time. She's in college and she went to Mexico for the holidays."

"Not good timing."

"I didn't mind. After the wedding, the rest of the holidays will be fairly quiet until New Year's Eve. Then I have a wedding in the afternoon and one in the evening, remember? Both are fairly small. I'd offer you a seat, but—"

"You can have one of my interns," Nico said, frowning at the pain in those beautiful eyes of hers. "Jilly is never going to be a chef. She cried twice today, so I think she'd jump at the chance to, uh, light up jars."

"You made her cry?"

"Of course not." He was taken aback. "Not all television chefs scream at their employees. I may have lost it a few times with idiot guests, but never with the people who work for me. Jilly is just overwhelmed, I think. She'll do fine in her own kitchen at home. Or maybe with a small catering business. She'd jump at the chance to get off the line."

"Really?"

"Really," he assured her. "And the kitchen will be a better place without her. She's yours, but only if you will quit this madness and come home. It's after eight, dinner service has wound down and I'm free to get out of here."

She hesitated, just as he knew she would, but he was prepared.

"We're both tired, Grace. And all your stuff is still at my house. Patsy brought over your Tuesday, Wednesday and Thursday outfits." He didn't need to add that she was in pain, because he could see from her face that she was tempted to return to his house, where there were no stairs and that big guest bedroom awaited. He'd already put on his jacket—he was ready to get out of there for the night.

"I feel like I'm taking advantage of you." She sighed. "Patsy shouldn't have assumed I'd be staying with you for more than one night."

He wanted to laugh, but he managed to control himself. "It's my fault you hurt yourself."

"I blame the shoes."

He shrugged. "Come on, sweetheart." He retrieved her crutches from where they leaned against the wall by the door. "Gather your things together and I'll bring you to the car."

"I guess it really is easier this way." She winced as she moved her foot from the chair.

"It is," he agreed, carefully avoiding the ornaments as she stepped around the desk. "We can plan the shower tonight over dinner."

She groaned.

"What?" he asked. "You don't want to do the shower? Or is dinner a bad thing?"

"Dinner is a very bad thing." She sighed again. "I love your cooking."

"I'm glad. So what's the problem?" He lifted the blue scarf from its bag and placed it around her neck.

"Calories," she said. "Lots and lots of calories."

"Olive oil is good for you." He smiled down into her blue eyes. "And you don't have to worry about calories."

"You only think that because I do worry about calories," she pointed out. "Don't look at me like that."

"Like what?" She had the most gorgeous skin. The occasional dot of red glitter made her look like a Christmas ornament.

"Never mind." The pink in her cheeks deepened.

"Like I want to kiss you?"

She gave him that little frown, the one that he found so intriguing. She thought it hid her feelings, but he had learned to see through it. He couldn't resist leaning closer to touch his lips to hers for just a moment. A brief, satisfying moment.

His intentions were honorable, the kiss declared.

She was his, the kiss said.

Everything was right in the world, the kiss proclaimed.

Nico backed away as if nothing had happened.

"Is any of this stuff going back to the house with us?" He was pleased that he sounded so casual and normal when all he wanted to do was take her into his arms and kiss her for a week. Or a month. Maybe a year would be long enough.

"No." She cleared her throat and stared up at him for a long moment. "I'm done. For now."

"Great." He lifted her coat from its hook behind the door. "I had one of the kids bring my car around to the front."

"You really think ahead." She stood and held on to her desk.

"I do," he confessed. "Sometimes too much."

"Well," she said, putting her arms in the sleeves of the coat as he held it. "I would think that was a good thing. As a chef."

"I like to be prepared," he said. "To know I have everything I need when I want to cook. And then sometimes there's the challenge of having only a few items and needing to make a meal out of them. Do you cook, Grace?"

"I'm the queen of casseroles," she said, surprising him. "I learned early on that if I didn't make dinner I wouldn't eat anything but takeout or frozen fish sticks."

"Your father wasn't home?"

"He was dating. At first I thought he was just lonely. I moved in with him after my mother died, but I was in sixth grade and I wasn't the best company."

Nico thought of his niece, a sensitive child around the same age. He couldn't imagine her father leaving her alone while he ran after women. "And then?"

She picked up her huge bag and turned. "What?"

"You said 'at first,'" he explained, scooping her into his arms. "At first you thought he was lonely. What happened?"

"I felt sorry for him. And for myself. He'd take me to my aunt's on weekends, which was fine with me. I realized he just didn't have much interest in me. I hadn't even seen him that much when my mother was alive. My aunt told me he was a fool."

"I think I'd like your aunt." He stopped at the door so she could flick the lights off.

"She is a very blunt, very kind person. Everyone loves her."

"I'll look forward to meeting her. Has she been to the restaurant?"

"Several times," she said. "But that was before you came."

"When she comes again I'll make her something special."

Grace didn't protest as he walked down the hall with her in his arms. Several guests stared and smiled. The woman at the front desk waved. An incoming guest held the front door open for them. In minutes he'd tucked her into the front seat, driven her to his house and carried her into his kitchen.

Nico felt positively heroic. Now all he had to do was figure out how to convince Grace to stay forever.

CHAPTER SEVEN

AL SMILED AT HER.

Nico pampered her.

The wine in her glass warmed her.

Oh, my. The man was dangerous. That kiss, well, she'd yet to put it out of her mind. He'd surprised her, and she'd surprised herself by how much that brief, intimate contact had affected her. She'd had to pretend it was nothing, of course, as he had. And now, with aching foot propped up on a chair, Grace watched the most handsome man she had ever seen—well, apart from Bradley Cooper—fix dinner. It was late, after nine o'clock, but he seemed to have limitless energy. On his television show he'd created a whirlwind of enthusiastic food preparations—chopping, slicing, tossing things into pans and hauling dishes out of immaculate ovens, all while he talked and explained and gave measurements.

Why had he left Hollywood, or wherever it was in California that these things were taped? She'd asked him yesterday, but he hadn't answered the question. Grace reached down and patted Al's head. "What are you making?"

"Something light," he said. "Chicken medallions. With wine and lemon. You won't have to obsess over calories. And you can skip dessert."

"Dessert?" *Do not think about dessert*, she told herself. Her stomach growled. She hadn't eaten since the Santa brunch, deciding it was safer to sip herbal tea at her desk and avoid Marie's afternoon cookie offering.

"My mother left another platter of sugar cookies. She and the kids decorated them today. They're for Christmas Eve, but she'll never know if we eat a few."

"She sounds like a wonderful grandmother."

"She is."

"Why did you come back? Was it to help your family?"

He took a sip of wine, put a lid on the pan of chicken and walked over to the table, where he pulled out a chair and glanced at his watch. "We'll eat in just a few minutes, I promise."

"Sorry, it's none of my business," Grace said. "Tell me about your nieces and nephew."

"I came home," he said, fiddling with the stem of his wineglass, "because I missed them."

"You were homesick?" She tried to hide her surprise.

He winced. "I don't expect you to believe me,

but it's the truth." Then he looked at her, the expression in his dark eyes unreadable. "What's your definition of success, Grace?"

"A successful life or a successful job?"

"Life."

She thought about that for a long moment. "To be financially secure, I suppose. And I'd like to have a family." To love the same man until the day she died. To be a good mother. To surround herself with love.

"Are you happy with your work?"

"I love it. Don't you love yours?"

He nodded. "I do, sweetheart. But California was not where I wanted to be." Nico looked embarrassed. He reached over and caressed her hand but didn't seem to realize he'd done it. "I had it all. A little fame, a lot of money, people catering to my every need. Most people's definition of success, right?" He didn't wait for an answer. "And then my show was canceled. That should have devastated me."

"And it didn't?"

He grinned. "I was thrilled. I bought a very expensive bottle of champagne and drank it with Al at my feet wagging his tail. I told him we were going home and I swear he knew what I was saying."

He looked at the dog, who whined and wagged his tail.

"He wants dinner, too," Grace said.

"He cries and whines like that no matter what I'm cooking. He loves pasta." Nico shook his head. "He loves anything I put on a plate."

"So you left Hollywood?" she prompted. She'd always thought he'd come home in disgrace, having lost his shot at the big time.

"I realized I no longer wanted to be in LA. I wanted to be around my family. I wanted to cook in my own restaurant. I wanted to train kids to work in the kitchen. And I missed skiing." He hopped up and returned to the stove to lift the lid on the pan. "Ah," he said with satisfaction. "You're gonna love this. Are you hungry?"

"Starving." She watched entranced as he arranged the food on two plates, then chopped food for Al's bowl. She waited for him to return to the table before asking the obvious question.

"So," she said, inhaling the delicious aroma of lemon. He'd sprinkled freshly grated Parmesan on the buttered penne and arranged steamed asparagus to accent the chicken medallions. "This looks fantastic."

"Thank you. More wine?" He lifted the bottle.

"No, thank you." She placed the white cloth napkin in her lap, picked up her fork and knife and waited for him to finish topping off his glass. "Are you glad you came back? Do you miss LA?"

"In some ways, yes. I miss the weather. And a

few friends. But I'm glad I came back. It was the right thing for me at the time."

At the time. What did that mean? And why was it suddenly so important for her to hear that he was staying?

"You're frowning again," Nico said. "You haven't tasted anything yet."

His cell rang, saving her from having to answer. He got up and retrieved it from the counter and, with an apologetic shrug to Grace, turned it on. "Hi. What's going on?" He listened for a moment while Grace cut a bite of chicken and tasted it. "Of course. No problem." Pause. "No, not yet, but they look good." Pause. "Mama," he said, chuckling. "I will, if possible," Pause. "Of course. I will ask. And I will call you tomorrow." Pause. "Yes, yes, good night."

Still laughing, Nico returned to the table. "My mother has heard that I have a new woman in my life."

"Uh-oh. Your sister told her about this morning?" She took another bite of chicken. Heaven, she decided. The man was a genius in the kitchen.

"Marie couldn't wait to share the good news, believe me." He picked up his fork and stabbed at the pasta.

"I'm good news?" For some reason that struck her as funny. "Doesn't she know you're just helping me out for a couple of days?"

"My mother is hoping I'll fall in love with you and she won't have to worry about my being alone when I'm an old man."

Didn't his mother realize this man could have any woman he wanted? He'd charmed everyone on the staff and most customers. All he had to do was smile and women melted. Grace pushed her thoughts aside. If she wasn't careful, she was going to fall in love with him, and she couldn't risk that. She'd learned her lesson: stay away from men with charisma and commitment issues.

"That's what she worries about? You being alone?"

"That's one of many things." He made a face. "I love them all—my mother, my sisters—but they worry too much."

They sounded nice, Grace thought. "They care about you and they want you to be happy."

"This is true." He grinned. "You could make them—and me—ecstatic, you know, if you would do me a favor."

"What kind of favor?" She looked down at her empty plate. How had she eaten all of that?

His eyebrows rose. "You do owe me, sweetheart. For room and board."

Grace choked back a laugh. "Nice try, Chef Hollywood."

Nico groaned. "Cheap shot."

"That's what they called you in the tabloids.

Hot Hollywood Chef, Chef Hollywood, Naughty Nico."

"I'm not the man the media made me out to be. I never was," he insisted, taking a sip of wine. He waved his arm toward his vintage kitchen. "Does this look like Hot Hollywood Chef style to you? The stove is green, for heaven's sake."

She wasn't sure what the color of the stove had to do with Naughty Nico, but she remembered his mention of remodeling. "You're going to modernize the kitchen, aren't you?"

"Not exactly. I like its charm," Nico declared. "I've found a designer who understands what I want."

"A kitchen that looks like it belongs with the house but with high-end appliances and all the amenities."

"Exactly. How did you know?"

"I watch a lot of those house-remodeling shows on HGTV," she informed him. "I have the lingo down."

He looked at her empty plate. "You like my food."

"Of course."

Nico beamed at her, stood and quickly cleared the table. "You look happy. And relaxed. And you are not in pain."

"I took another ibuprofen." She'd removed the boot and Nico had draped her foot with one of those refreezable ice packs from the drugstore. "It doesn't hurt as much as it did a couple of hours ago."

"Then let's talk about this favor you owe me."
He returned to the table and refilled her wineglass.
Grace didn't protest. She was warm and content
and even though Chef Hollywood was flirting
with her again, she knew that was just part of his
personality. For a Tuesday night, this was pretty
darn good, as long as she kept reminding herself
not to take him seriously.

"It's Tuesday night," she said. "I usually watch
Hell's Kitchen. Or the show with the little kids
cooking. *Master Chef Junior*."

"Don't think I don't know that you're changing
the subject," Nico warned. "But I like the show
with the children, too. We could do something
like that at the lodge, you know. Just for a day. Or
maybe a weekend. With some local kids."

"Really?"

"For charity," Nico added. "This summer?"

"I like it." She took a sip of wine. The idea had
all sorts of possibilities, so many her head swirled.
Or maybe that was the wine.

"It's almost Christmas Eve," Nico said.

"So I've heard. We have a lovely wedding to
work."

"We do," he agreed. "But before that…" He
paused. "Well, actually before, during and after
that, is the Vitelli family Christmas Eve party."

"All afternoon and night?"

"Just about. We're Italian. The cooking and eating goes on for hours."

"And you're going to miss it?"

"Noelle's wedding's at seven, cocktails after and dinner at eight-fifteen, which leaves plenty of time for photographs. Michael is itching to prove himself and we'll have the prep done. I'll be at my parents' from one o'clock until five or so. I hate to miss dinner, but they understand. Everyone has commitments, the little kids have to go home and go to bed early, but somehow we'll manage to spend a few overlapping hours together in total chaos and with enormous amounts of food."

"All right," Grace said. "I can oversee the setup in Wildwood. I'll be decorating in the morning—the florist is coming early—and will have everything ready for the appetizers. Michael and I can manage without you. It's a simple wedding and the whole staff is pitching in."

"Sweetheart, that's not the favor."

She couldn't think what else he would need. And whenever he called her "sweetheart" her brain turned to bread crumbs.

"Quit frowning at me like that," Nico said. "I'd like you—I need you—to come to the family party."

"But it's Christmas Eve. It's *family*."

"Precisely. If I don't bring you they'll do nothing but ask me questions about you."

"Because I'm staying here." *Or because you've kissed me. Because sometimes you look at me as if you are totally enthralled with the person you see? Because I blush when you tease me and secretly adore it when you take care of me?* She eyed her ankle. Had a sprained ankle brought her a hint of romance? "You told them why, though?"

"Well, sure. And they'd like to meet you anyway." He smiled. "Come on, do me a favor. If they think I'm keeping you a secret, which they do, they'll never leave me alone."

"Nico…" She didn't know what to say. His family would think they were a couple. She was living in his house, for heaven's sake. And she needed to remind herself she was only there because he felt responsible for her. Assuming there was anything else going on could only lead to major disappointment. She needed to stop thinking about kissing him and start getting a grip on reality.

"Stuffed manicotti," he murmured, taking her hand in his. "Lasagna. Meatballs that will melt in your mouth. We don't always do the traditional fish courses, having been corrupted by three sons-in-law whose requests for meat have to be honored. Antipasto. Cheeses. Shrimp risotto. And wine." He stroked her palm with his thumb. "Lots of wine. Only the best Chianti. And Pinots, too."

She groaned, but she didn't remove her hand from his. He'd held her hand before and she'd discovered she liked that gesture. She liked that gesture very, very much. "You're trying to bribe me with food?"

"Tiramisu like you've never had it before, babe," he growled in a mock-sexy voice.

"They'll think I'm your girlfriend," she cautioned. "Instead of a clumsy coworker who can't climb stairs."

"They'll think you're lovely," Nico said. He released her hand. "You'll be doing me a favor, remember?"

"Tiramisu?"

"Tiramisu." They clinked glasses to seal the deal. "Now," Nico said, "let's talk about this shower. I'm thinking hot and cold appetizers, with red and white wines, some local beer and a chocolate dessert bar. A friend of Noelle's called me and said she'd bring chocolates from the Candy Man. How many people are coming?"

"Thirty, maybe a few more. I think it's mostly staff and Noelle's and Ted's friends. More of a party than a typical shower."

"No games? No bouquets made of ribbons?"

"I doubt it." Grace chuckled, and then stifled a yawn. "But Patsy's involved, so you never know. She has a wild side."

"Can I help you get to bed?"

"I think I'll use the crutch so I don't have to put the boot back on." Grace put her foot on the floor and wiggled her sock-covered toes. "I think it's getting better. I should be able to manage my stairs tomorrow."

"Give it another day or two," Nico said, handing her the crutch. "Don't risk hurting yourself before then. I'll help you move back home after the wedding."

She thought about that while he helped her to her bedroom and turned down the quilted comforter. She'd made her bed this morning by hopping carefully on one foot.

"Do you need help with anything?" He held her gently by the waist, ignoring the dog who had woken from his nap under the kitchen table and now pattered into the room.

"No. I'm fine." She'd hung the flannel nightgown on a hook on the back of the bathroom door, tucked her makeup and toiletries into two empty drawers by the sink. She didn't intend to be a messy or demanding houseguest.

"Okay, then." He hesitated, then leaned down and slanted his mouth over hers. Her arms went around his neck in the most natural way, her lips responded to the warmth of his. On a scale of one to ten, the kiss was a fifteen, with extra points for self-control, Grace decided, pulling back slowly.

"Good night," he whispered, touching his lips to her cheek, her earlobe, her neck.

Shivers.

"Good night," she managed to croak, though part of her wanted to grab him by the front of his shirt and haul that sexy mouth of his back to hers. She resisted, but just barely.

"See you in the morning," Nico said, giving her a quick hug before practically running out of the room.

Grace thought about that kiss as she brushed her teeth, washed her face and slipped the nightgown over her head. She thought about it as she lay in Nico's beautiful guest room bed, his dog snoring softly next to her. Her foot ached and her arms were sore from using the crutches, so she was content to be snuggled under the covers and nestled into mounds of down pillows.

He'd kissed her as if he meant it.

She was going to have to be very careful. He might intend to stay here in town and he might be perfectly content with running the lodge's restaurant, but would that last? She'd thought Josh was going to stay forever, too, and look what happened there. She'd been left alone, after being certain they had a future together.

No matter what Nico said, Grace didn't think Chef Vitelli was the domestic, small-town guy he thought he was.

CHAPTER EIGHT

NICO WAS PREPARED this time. Yesterday he'd been caught by surprise when his nephew and sister arrived for the dog, but this morning he expected visitors.

And visitors came, shortly after he'd checked in with his staff, taken care of a few minor staffing issues due to something called the Jingle Bell Run, arranged for one of the wedding guests to deliver breakfast to another wedding guest, discussed a frozen-blueberry shortage with Michael and okayed next week's meat order.

"Is she still here?" His middle sister, Cathy, followed her nephew into the living room. She wore jeans, a thick vest and hiking boots. Her long brown hair was wrapped into a braid that hung over one shoulder and her cheeks were pink from the cold. She was his most domestic sister; she baked bread, sewed quilts, knit and made sure that her younger brother's house was clean. Her two little ones, both girls, had their mother's cheery disposition and their father's red hair.

"She is. And she's in the shower, so don't go

barging into the bedroom wanting to meet her." He handed Al's leash to Brian. "Here you go, kid. He's all yours until tonight. I might be working late."

"That's okay, Uncle Nico." Al wagged his happiness and grinned at the boy. "He can sleep over if you want."

"I won't be that late," he said.

"Do you have a date?" Cathy arched her eyebrow at him.

"No, I have a bridal shower. A last-minute thing that was supposed to have been a rehearsal dinner," he explained. "Grace and I are putting together a wedding for tomorrow night."

"'Grace and I,'" she repeated, looking amused. "Interesting."

"Yes," he said. "It is. So get out of here. Where are my beautiful nieces?" As if he had to ask. No doubt she'd dropped them off at Grandma's house so she could accompany Brian to fetch Al. He half expected Beth to show up any minute, though his very pregnant sister might be too far along to feel like leaving her cozy home in town. He guessed she'd be waiting for an update from Cath via text, though.

"With Mom. You're making breakfast," Cathy said, pushing past him to peer at the kitchen counter. "Your famous French toast. And berries. You have fresh raspberries, for heaven's sake!" She turned an accusing eye on him. "You only make that for us on our birthdays."

"Out." Nico pointed toward the door from which

Brian and Al had just exited. "Now. Before Grace sees you and is embarrassed all over again. She's not too pleased about staying here, but her condo in town is on the second floor. And she's on crutches."

"That's what Marie said, not that we believe that for a second. She could have stayed at the lodge."

"All booked up," he said, pointing once again to the door. "It's our busy season."

Cathy didn't budge. None of the women in his family were easily bossed.

"Mom said you might be bringing her tomorrow."

"I certainly plan to." He was going to do everything in his power to make sure that she came with him. She was alone, with no family, on Christmas. But she had him, and she had the Vitellis. If he wanted her to know him as someone other than Chef Hollywood, she would have to see where he came from.

"That's serious."

Nico didn't reply. Instead, he took her elbow and guided her to the front door. "Think what you want, Cath. I have to get ready for work."

"Good luck." She gave him a quick hug before she left. "I hope she's worthy of you."

He couldn't help laughing.

"I CAN'T BELIEVE tomorrow is Christmas Eve already." Patsy handed Grace a cup of coffee and sat down in the chair across from the desk. "First things first, are we set for the Jingle Bell Run today?"

Grace looked at her list. "Yes. We donated three prizes—two spa packages and a Valentine's Day weekend stay. Seven of the staff are participating and there will be some celebrating in the bar afterward, I suspect. The guests received invitations to join or watch."

"I donated a couple of reindeer hats and one very ugly Mrs. Santa sweater. And I assume we're ready for the wedding?"

Grace waved a hand toward the stacks of boxes. "We *are* ready. Nico loaned me one of his interns—"

"I heard she was thrilled to get out of deveining shrimp."

"Yes. That's what she told me. And she— Jilly — follows directions beautifully," Grace said. "Noelle loved the little pinecone place-card holders, too."

"You have the names of the guests? That was quick."

"Our new bride gave me a list and the seating chart. That girl wasted no time getting this together, thank goodness. Ted's been helping any way he can. They make a good couple." She took a sip of coffee. "Thanks for this."

"The chef's special blend." Patsy grinned. "He seems quite smitten."

"That's an old-fashioned word."

"I'm an old-fashioned woman." She leaned back

in the chair and crossed one leg over the other. Today Patsy wore a black pantsuit, white blouse and a cluster of vintage Christmas pins on her left lapel. "He's crushing on you. Is that better?"

Grace had to laugh. "Ridiculous."

"Not so ridiculous," her friend pointed out. "You two have a lot in common. You both work in the hospitality business, you both like working with people and you're both good at what you do. You live in the same town, you're old enough to know what you want. The people you work with respect you both. Plus, he's very good looking and he comes from a nice family."

Grace thought about what Nico had told her last night. "He's very close to them."

"Another plus."

"You sound like a matchmaking service."

Patsy shrugged. "I'm just pointing out the obvious. Just don't tell me you're still in love with what's-his-name. And *don't* tell me your heart is still broken over that guy, because you're smarter than that."

"I'm not heartbroken," Grace declared. "But I am a little more wary that I used to be. You can't blame me for that."

"Blame you for what?" Nico, wearing his official chef's jacket and unofficial blue jeans, stepped into the office. He held a legal pad in his hand and smiled at both of them. "Should I come back later?

I just wanted to go over the menu for tomorrow night."

"Stay," Patsy said, giving Grace a quick wink as she rose from her chair. "I have accounts to deal with. You're staying for the shower?"

"Absolutely. Jilly has gone into town to get a gift certificate from the Adirondack Store for me. That'll be my gift." She eyed her foot. Still trapped in the boot, it peeked out from the hem of her swirly gold-and-green skirt. She'd chosen a deep emerald V-neck sweater and gold snowflake earrings to continue her holiday-themed week. "I'm glad my Christmas shopping is all done because I'm not in any shape to hit the stores now."

"Thank God for that," Nico said, moving aside for Patsy. "I'm a terrible shopper and I'd have to go with you to make sure you didn't trip on any of the Christmas decorations. How long do we have to stay?"

"We?"

"I go where you go, babe. Unless you want to try to drive with that boot on your foot."

She didn't.

"For an hour or so into the party," Grace said. "I need to make sure everything is set up the way her friends want it. There will be enough staff members there to take over for us after that. Do you need to stay late in the kitchen?"

He shook his head and plopped down in the chair across from her. "Michael can handle the dinner service. We expect it to be fairly light, so we can head home whenever you like." He looked down at his notes. "So, let's talk about our wedding, shall we?"

EVERY TIME HE saw Grace she was in motion. She'd organized the table arrangements, created a gift table and used some of those little lighted jars to decorate the buffet, all while propped up on crutches. Nico had kept the food simple, turning the formal rehearsal-dinner food for the Barrett guests into hearty appetizers. Maria had baked chocolate cupcakes and the interns had practiced their cake-decorating skills by frosting them. He'd had to demonstrate proper pastry bag technique, which meant the opportunity to show off a bit.

Just like on television.

It had all been worth it. The bride and groom had been completely surprised, having been tricked into thinking they were meeting friends for dinner. The mood in Wildwood was festive, with the groom's favorite blues track playing from the speakers and the bride's friends laughing and talking nonstop.

The interns, basking in the glow of compliments from their boss, continued to put out appetizers. He waved to Patsy, who gave him a thumbs-up and then made her way through the crowd to greet him.

"Nice job, Chef."

"Thank you." They both looked at the happy

couple. Grace was explaining something to them, waving one hand toward the gift table as she spoke. One of the EMTs who had taken her to the clinic approached, put his arm around Grace's waist and then whispered in her ear.

"What the—"

"He's no competition," Patsy said. "At least, I don't think so. He's been asking her out for a year and she hasn't said yes yet."

"There's always a first time," he grumbled. "The guy looks like Paul Bunyan. He could carry her off to the top of the mountain and we'd never see her again." Seriously, the guy had legs like tree trunks and a chest the size of Montana.

"But she's been spending all of her time with you," Patsy pointed out. "And in your house, no less. I hope your intentions are honorable."

"I'm taking her to meet my parents tomorrow. Does that count?"

"She said yes to that? Good."

"She did." He couldn't help sounding proud. "I told her she was doing me a favor."

"If you hurt her I will take all of your fancy, expensive knives down to the beach and use them to cut firewood."

"Yes, ma'am," Nico said. "Duly noted." He didn't have the heart to tell her that he locked them up at night.

HE MISSED HIS chance to help Grace to bed. He had to deal with seventeen text messages and nine voice mails. The texts, from his sisters and his nephew, involved food, dog care and requests for wine recommendations. The voice mails were from his father, his mother, three friends vacationing in Mexico and his agent in LA.

His cell phone rang again once he arrived back home with Grace in tow. She'd insisted on using the ramp and managed just fine by holding on to the railing. It was clear she was feeling better, which meant he'd soon have to let her go.

But maybe not for long. She'd kissed him last night as if she'd meant it.

He had hope.

A lot of hope.

She blew him a kiss before she limped down the hall, Al following devotedly behind her, just as Nico wished he could.

CHAPTER NINE

"MERRY CHRISTMAS EVE. Nice dress." He held out a cup of coffee as she hobbled into the kitchen.

"I try to match the wedding colors. Merry Christmas Eve to you, too." She sat down and leaned her crutch against her chair before taking the cup. "Thank you."

It was early, not quite eight o'clock, but Grace had set the alarm on her phone. She knew that the earlier she was at work today the better. She'd showered and dressed in a burgundy lace dress that she could wear all day. The shoes were an issue. She needed flats—well, a left one—for her one uninjured foot. The garnet Manolos she'd planned on wearing were not going to work.

"Wedding day," he said, taking a big gulp of coffee. "Got to get the caffeine working." He was dressed casually, in a black sweater and jeans. His hair curled, damp from the shower, and he looked sleepy. "I'm looking forward to it, but I am not a morning person."

"What should I bring to your parents' house? I

can't arrive empty-handed." She'd thought about that the moment she woke up: hostess gift!

"Not food," he said, looking at his watch. "I can make breakfast here or at work. It's up to you. Maria's doing muffins today, for the Christmas buffet tomorrow."

"Muffins. Well, half a muffin," she amended, thinking about the feast that awaited later at the Vitellis' house. "Nico, give me an idea for today. I woke up at five o'clock worrying about it."

"Women are strange creatures."

"Yes, we are. Strange creatures with manners."

"Get a bottle of scotch. My father loves single malts."

"Single malt," she repeated seriously. "Got it. And your mother?"

"Candle freak."

"Seriously?"

"Like I could make that up?"

"Any special scent?"

"For what?"

"The candles."

He frowned, stared absently into the distance. "Not that I know of." He reached for his cell phone and punched out a text. "Cath will know."

Sure enough, two minutes later he got an answer. Nico showed Grace the screen: Any. Bigger better.

So Grace would buy single-malt scotch and a humongous candle before one o'clock, along with preparing the rooms for the wedding and getting the staff set up with their assigned chores.

Piece of cake, even on one foot.

"Drink up," she said. "We have to get going. Do you mind stopping at my place to pick up some shoes? And drop off my things?" She thought about that for a second. Nico rummaging through her closet. It was clean and organized to the max, which would amuse him no end.

"No problem." He fiddled with his phone. "There's a storm coming. We're going to get some snow."

"A lot of snow?" She'd have to factor in more time for guests to arrive if that was the case. Snow slowed things down, wreaked havoc on tight schedules.

"'A significant amount,' according to Accuweather."

She'd need to wear boots. Grace hobbled back to her room, grabbed her bag, iPad and phone, put her suede boot on her left foot and wrapped the soft azure scarf from her Secret Santa around her neck. She'd packed everything, but Nico would have to put her clothes and suitcase into the car. She looked around the room to make sure she hadn't left anything behind. She wondered if Al would miss her.

She wondered if Nico would.

"I'll take those now," Nico said, stepping into the room. "Unless I can talk you into staying longer."

"I have tomorrow and the next day off," she said. "I'll stay home and rest. And then I think I'll be as good as new."

"All right. But Al is going to be devastated when he has to sleep on the floor tonight."

He took her things and left, the dog following him down the hall and outside. They returned quickly, Al shaking a dusting of snow off his fur and moving immediately to his bed by the fireplace.

"He'll sleep until Brian comes to take him to my parents'," Nico said, chuckling. He helped Grace with her coat. "He knows it's going to snow and he really hates this kind of weather. Why are you smiling?"

"I love weddings. I love big days like this when all of the planning and work pays off and everything is beautiful. And then something goes wrong but it doesn't matter because I can fix it." She grinned at him. "I live to organize."

"Wow." He took a step back. "The adrenaline's pumping already?"

"Don't tell me you don't know exactly what I'm talking about," she said. "You love parties. Everyone knows that. You sing while you cook."

Nico launched into a rendition of "Winter Wonderland" and ushered Grace out the door and into the cold.

SHE WAS ARMED with gifts. She'd called the gift-delivery company she worked with and had them send over a bottle of Highland Park scotch, a selection of fat candles from the Adirondack Company and a huge box of fudge for the children. She'd gathered gift certificates and lotions from the lodge's spa for Nico's sisters, then added an extra one for his mother. The brothers-in-law were a mystery until Lyndsie, her gift coordinator, suggested gift certificates to the new microbrewery.

It was all just too easy.

"We're set?" Nico poked his head into her office. "You can still get away?"

"I can," she pronounced, grabbing her crutch. "I have so many people who want to help that everything was set up by ten. The florist came early because of the storm. Noelle will check into her suite at three o'clock. She'll get dressed in the room and then she and Ted will stay there tonight. I need to be back here by five or five thirty. It's a small wedding, but everything needs to be perfect. How's the food coming along?"

"We're all set. My team knows what they're doing." He held out her coat. "Even the interns are getting smarter. They're overseeing the buffet in the dining room. How hard can it be to make sure everything is hot and plentiful and neatly displayed?"

"Christmas Eve," she mused. "It feels like it."

"That's because they're playing traditional carols in the lobby."

"Patsy stole my iPod last night."

"I heard it's in a safe place until Monday."

"That's what the note said." There would be no more bluesy holiday music in the lobby this season.

"Bundle up," Nico said, handing her the blue scarf. "It's snowing."

She didn't ask if he thought they'd have trouble getting back to the lodge later. He had a vehicle equipped for traveling in snow, plus the village of Lake Placid knew how to keep roads clear.

"I hope you're hungry. And feeling domestic. My family will probably put you to work stirring or mincing." His eyebrows rose at the shopping bags she handed him, but he didn't comment.

"I can stir," she assured him. "I can mince," she fibbed. She hoped she could avoid cutting her fingers or dropping something on the floor. "Don't they make you do that, being the fancy chef and all?"

"You forget I come from a long line of chefs, fancy and otherwise."

Nico drove along the lake, passing his house and then continuing along the road for another half a mile. "When I was growing up we lived in town, near the restaurant, but my folks bought this place about fifteen years ago. They decided they wanted to be closer to the water."

"This place" turned out to be a low-slung modern ranch-style house at the end of a long driveway. Nestled into the hillside, it had breathtaking views of the water and a massive deck.

"They downsized," Nico explained. "Mom wanted a newer home on one floor, so they bought this and completely redid it." He parked close to the door, in front of a detached three-car garage. "Stay put and I'll help you in."

The snow was coming down heavier now and it coated the circular driveway. Someone had shoveled a path to the house and cleared the three stone steps that fronted a large entry door. Nico helped her from the car. Leaning on him seemed natural now.

She had grown used to touching him, to leaning on him. They'd become friends, she realized. Friends who kissed.

The door opened before they reached the steps, revealing a short, handsome man with a head of curly gray hair. Dressed in a down vest, khaki pants and thick snow boots, he beamed at them and hurried down the steps to help.

Nico's father, obviously.

"Hello, hello, Merry Christmas. You must be Nico's friend. How is that ankle doing? Oh, watch out now. It's slick. One of the boys shoveled a while ago, but the snow is coming down hard, isn't it?"

"It is," she agreed. She liked the man immediately and some of her nervousness dissipated. She gripped her crutch and prayed she wouldn't fall over and embarrass herself in front of him.

"Dad, I'd like you to meet Grace," Nico said once they were inside and stomping the snow off their feet on the rubber mat inside the door. "Grace Clarke, from Mirror Lake Lodge."

"Yes, yes, I've heard all about you, Gracie. The wedding planner! I think I've seen you at the lodge, though we've never officially met. I'm so glad you came. Here, let me help you."

Nico touched Grace's shoulder. "I'll go back for the bags. You've guessed that this happy man is my father."

"It's nice to meet—"

He enveloped her in a big hug. "We're glad you're here at last. Now, let's get that coat off and let you sit down. Oh, you have one of Cathy's scarves! You should always wear blue."

Cathy's scarf? Did he mean Nico's sister had made it? She didn't have a chance to ask.

"I'll be right back," Nico said, fleeing the foyer as his mother rounded the corner.

Mrs. Vitelli was tall and lean, much like her son, and at least eight inches taller than her husband. She wore black pencil-thin slacks and a gold turtleneck sweater. Her hair was a rich dark brown highlighted with auburn streaks. It was cut in a classic bob that framed a beautiful face with high cheekbones and lovely gray eyes. Grace guessed she was in her early sixties. She looked nervous, but her smile was genuine.

"You must be Grace. I'm Terry, Nico's mother," she said, holding out her hand. Noticing that Grace was trying to get her coat off while negotiating the crutch, she stopped. "What can I do?"

"We've got it, honey," her husband assured her. "Nico went out to unload the car."

"My boot," Grace stammered. "I don't want to track snow—"

"Never mind that," Terry Vitelli said. "Come straight through and sit down. It's only snow."

Grace bit her tongue before she could say, "Yes, ma'am."

The foyer opened up into a large room that faced the lake. Floor-to-ceiling windows and sliding glass doors revealed the snowstorm whirling beyond them, while inside, a large chestnut sofa faced a gas fireplace whose flickering flames warmed the room. A huge Christmas tree sat in one corner, presents spilling out from underneath into the room. No one else was there.

"We're early," Grace said, letting Nico's mother lead her to a leather recliner placed strategically across from a large television. "I hope that's okay. I have a wedding tonight—"

"Everyone's in the kitchen," Mr. Vitelli announced. "Terry won't let them out until we meet you."

Nico's mother flushed. "I didn't want you to be overwhelmed when you first walked in. We're a big family. Besides, they're baking cookies and I don't want them to burn."

Mr. Vitelli winked. "We're a noisy bunch. Couldn't have Nico's girl running back to the car, you know."

"I'm not—" She started to explain that she wasn't Nico's girlfriend, but stopped. Maybe, just for this afternoon, she'd pretend to be exactly that. "I'm not easily scared," she said, bending over to remove her suede boot. She'd leave the support boot on, with one of Nico's wool hiking socks covering her toes.

"Of course you're not," Terry said. "I don't know how my husband comes up with these things."

"Nona!" A little girl tiptoed into the room. She eyed Grace before turning to her grandmother. "Mommy said I can have two cookies."

"Grace, this is Greta, my middle daughter's older child. Greta, say hello to Grace."

"Hi." She was tiny and round, with red curls and fair skin.

"Hi, Greta."

Nico joined them, scooping the little girl into his arms and tipping her upside down, releasing delighted squeals. Another little one ran into the room. She looked about two, with the same red curls and heart-shaped face.

"Me, too!" She held up her arms to her uncle. "Me, too!"

He gave the other little girl a turn hanging by his arm and she giggled wildly.

"This is the youngest. Delia. Their father is Irish." He winked at Grace. "Can you tell?"

A very pregnant young woman waddled into the living room. "She's only the youngest for two more weeks, Nico." She turned to Grace. "Hi. I'm Beth. The *pregnant* sister."

Terry laughed. "I think Grace figured that out for herself."

"Hi. I'm Grace Clarke. I work with your—"

"Oh, I've heard," she said, her eyes twinkling with good humor. She resembled her father, petite and with black curls tumbling down to her shoulders. She looked as if she could give birth any moment, especially in the giant red tent dress and black tights she was wearing. "You're Nico's friend from the lodge. We couldn't wait to meet you. You met Marie a few days ago, but Nico wouldn't let Cath bother you yesterday. Our brother has a woman living with him! It's all we've been talking about."

"I stayed in the guest room for a few nights," Grace said, laughing. "Your brother rescued me from having to go up and down the stairs to my condo."

Nico groaned. "Ignore her, Grace. She's been hallucinating since her fifth month. Where is everybody? I thought I'd have to rescue Grace from the hordes."

"Your mother locked everyone in the kitchen."

"Johnny, really." Terry shot him an indulgent look. "You tease too much. Grace will think you're serious."

Grace thought he was wonderful. She watched his daughter wrap her arm around his waist and give him a little side hug. Cute.

"I raised Nico with good manners," Terry said, patting Grace's arm. "I'm sure he's taken good care of you and behaved like a perfect gentleman. How did you hurt yourself?"

"I slipped on a set of jingle bells in the kitchen."

"My kitchen," Nico said. "At the lodge. They fell off a cookie tray. And I've been stuck with Grace ever since."

"He caught me before I hit the floor," Grace assured his mother. "And he went with me to the clinic, then took me home because I couldn't do the stairs and he had a ramp."

Beth's eyebrows rose and she and her father exchanged amused looks.

"Well," Johnny Vitelli said. "Thank goodness for Al's ramp."

"Al's ramp?"

Beth answered. "Al can't do steps, either, so Nico had it built when he bought the house."

"He did?" Grace gave him a questioning look, which he ignored.

His mother shook her head. "I'm still confused about the jingle bells."

"Grace was coming into the kitchen to boss me around," he confided to another sister who'd recently entered the room. Tall, built like Nico and his mother, she had big blue eyes and wore her brown hair in a long braid that was draped over her shoulder. Faded jeans and a stained long-sleeved T-shirt added to the image of a woman who preferred comfort to fashion. Her smile was friendly when she turned to Grace.

"Hi," she said, sticking out her hand to shake Grace's. "I'm Cathy, mother of the two female hellions." She looked at her mother. "I didn't tell them they could eat cookies. They lied to you."

Terry chuckled. "Fibbed," she corrected. "Those sweet little girls would never lie."

Cathy rolled her eyes at Grace. "Yeah, right. Did you like the scarf? Nico picked out the yarn."

"He did?"

"Yep. Secret Santa, right?"

Grace looked at Nico, who avoided her gaze. "What about the birdseed?"

"Birdseed?" Cathy looked at her brother.

"*Secret* Santa," he muttered, looking guilty. "Isn't that the point?"

Grace wanted to hug him because he looked so uncharacteristically embarrassed. She wanted to wrap her arms around him and kiss him until they were both breathless because he'd given her a scarf that matched her eyes and kept it a secret. He'd built a ramp for his elderly, lame dog and kept that information to himself, too.

She was in love with him. Despite her best intentions she'd fallen for Nico Vitelli, who dated models and cooked for movie stars. And had just introduced her to his family as his friend from work.

This wasn't good, she realized. Not good at all.

"Where are the guys?" Nico attempted to change the subject as he dangled a little girl from each arm. "Hiding from their snoopy wives again?"

"Jon and Mark are in the basement doing a project for Grandpa." Cathy frowned at him. "Birdseed? What's that about?"

"Never mind." He turned to Grace. "I put your bags in the kitchen."

"Thanks." Nico certainly didn't want to talk about the scarf.

"Where's Marie and her gang?" Nico released

the girls, whispering something in their ears that sent them running out of the room. Cathy chased after them.

"Running late." Everyone laughed at that, leaving Grace to assume that Marie was usually running behind schedule. Terry shook a finger at her youngest daughter. "You wait until you have three children to get out of the house on Christmas Eve. It's not so easy."

Beth patted her stomach. "I feel like I have three of them in here right now. Besides, little Elvis in here might be an only child."

"Elvis?"

"His due date is January eighth. Same day Elvis was born." Beth grinned. "Mom hates it when I call him Elvis."

"I keep wondering if you're serious," Terry sputtered.

Nico held out a hand to Grace. "Come on, Grace. I'll take you into the kitchen where the real action is." He turned to his mother. "We haven't had lunch. Or breakfast."

Terry's face lit up. "Good. I'll fix you something nice. Grace, do you like eggplant parmigiana? Or would you rather have lasagna? With a nice salad and some lovely Tuscan wine we ordered last month and fell in love with."

"That sounds lovely, but don't go to any—"

"Save your breath," Nico said, holding her tightly.

"She will feed you no matter what you say, and it will make her happy. After all, we're here to eat, aren't we?"

"You are, you are," Johnny Vitelli said. "We are all here together and what could be better than that?"

Nothing, Grace decided two hours later. Nothing could be better than spending the afternoon with the large and noisy Vitelli family. Maria, her husband, Danny, and their three children arrived while Grace was seated at the large farm table, sipping her first glass of wine and sampling rosemary focaccia with a peppery olive oil. They brought Al with them, since he'd been at their house again that morning. The dog greeted her like a long-lost friend and she sneaked him a piece of her bread. Brian gave Grace a shy smile, then let his grandmother hug and kiss him. His older sister, Anna, got the same treatment from both grandparents before hurrying over to say hello to Grace. She was eleven, she confided while eating a thick slice of bread, and the oldest grandchild.

"I remember you," Anna said. "You helped me when I was sad, remember?"

It took Grace a moment to realize what the girl meant. Last fall at the lodge Anna had been crying. Her parents were late and she was worried because her little sister had had to go to the hospital with a fever.

"The Girl Scout dinner," she said. She remembered dispensing hugs and tissues before returning the child to one of the Scout leaders, who'd informed her that Anna's parents were on their way. The little sister had an ear infection and would be fine.

Another child, a fragile little angel with the sweetest expression Grace had ever seen, pranced into the kitchen and declared she was "dying for risotto."

"That's Emily," Anna explained. "She wants to be an actress."

"I think she's a natural."

They sat around the huge dining table and ate more food than Grace would have ever thought possible. Johnny Vitelli continued to laugh and hug and beam at everyone. Terry organized the cooking and the presentation of the food. The brothers-in-law greeted Grace with great enthusiasm and teased Nico for being the last single Vitelli.

"Someday," Ben O'Rourke declared, "you, too, will be changing diapers and coaching soccer."

"Hopefully not at the same time," said Jon Nally, little Delia sprawled asleep in his arms, said.

"Though it can be done." Ben winked at Grace.

She blushed. Nico frowned and didn't look at all amused. He left her side shortly after that and went over to the stove to oversee the pasta.

Her hostess gifts had been a big hit. Terry gave her a warm hug along with her thanks for the spa time and the candles. Johnny immediately opened his scotch and took a "wee sip," pronouncing it the best he'd ever tasted. Nico's sisters were fun and welcoming, the children excited and friendly. Al hid under the table at her feet and Terry urged her to try every dish that was placed on the table. It was chaos and noise and laughter and love.

But the more comfortable she felt, the more she enjoyed his family, the more distant Nico grew. She'd overstepped, she realized. She'd read more into this week than was there.

He felt sorry for the lonely woman he worked with. He was kind and caring—he'd built a ramp for his dog, for heaven's sake—and that was it.

Here at the Vitellis' she felt as if she'd come home.

And that was the very worst thing that could have happened this Christmas.

CHAPTER TEN

"Nico." His mother was waiting for him when he came inside after cleaning the snow from the car. It was almost five o'clock—time to brave the storm and head down the road to the lodge—though Grace was busy learning how to make risotto with Cathy while Anna read Christmas poems to her.

He hated to leave, but there would be other holidays. Other Christmas Eve parties.

"Mom?" He stomped the snow off his boots. "What do you need?"

She gave him a quick hug. "You're trying to hide it, but your heart is in your eyes."

Nico didn't know what to say. He'd hoped no one would notice. There had already been too many arch looks, too much teasing and too many assumptions. He was afraid Grace would feel trapped.

"She seems lovely," his mother added.

"She is."

"Yes. We're happy you brought her today. When you were in California we worried—well, never mind about that." His mother patted him on the arm. "Is this serious? Will we see her again?"

"You will, I hope." He kept his voice low. "I've

been half in love with her since the first time I saw her."

Terry shook her head. "You are such a romantic, Nico. So it was love at first sight."

"Like you and Dad."

"We were very young," she said, leading him toward the sound of people laughing and talking over each other in the kitchen. "And very lucky to find each other."

"Then wish me the same luck," he said, throwing an arm over her shoulder.

"Always," his mother said. "And especially with that lovely young woman. I hope we didn't frighten her off."

"Me, too," Nico replied, worried that he'd rushed Grace into an intimacy she wasn't prepared for. He'd sped up the dating process this afternoon. Heck, he wasn't even sure if he and Grace were officially "dating," but in his mind they'd been a couple since she'd fallen into his arms four days ago. Four days. She'd lived at his house, slept with his dog, eaten meals in his kitchen and worked with him to plan a wedding and a shower. They'd also collaborated on events almost daily for months. He'd like to think that counted.

But what if he was wrong?

"IT'S PERFECT," GRACE assured the bride as she posed in her wedding gown. "You're perfect. Everything is going to go beautifully, but you absolutely must stop crying." She handed Noelle another tissue. "Blot, don't rub."

"The storm—"

"Hasn't changed one thing about your wedding."

"Just the maid of honor. My sister—"

"Is stuck because of the storm, I know," Grace said soothingly. "But it's all going to work out."

"And Ted—

"Is with Josh, in the Wildwood Room. And they both look handsome and nervous." Grace had checked the room ten minutes ago. And twenty minutes ago. And forty minutes ago. Lanterns were in place, flowers were where they were supposed to be and the guests were pouring in.

The fire in the fireplace looked picture-perfect. The music was ready.

"Time to go," she said, smiling at the recently substituted maid of honor. "She's all yours."

The next hour and a half was a blur, leaving Grace little time to run and hide, no spare moments to wonder what on earth she had been thinking, allowing herself to fall in love with Nico Vitelli. It wasn't until dinner was served and the happy bride and groom were being toasted by the best man that Grace had a chance to retreat to her office and sit down in the dark.

Nico had been busy in the kitchen and hadn't spoken to her since they returned to the lodge. They asked and answered each other's event-related questions through Brian, the good-natured waiter who hoped to be promoted next year.

The truth was that Nico had been a good friend and a helpful coworker. He'd kissed her a few times, but she assumed that was his nature. Kissing him and being kissed by him felt natural at the time, but now it just seemed idiotic.

He'd taken care of her when she'd hurt herself in his kitchen. He'd carried her and fed her and even returned her things to her condo. He'd seen her closet and found her red flats with the rhinestone toes. He'd brought her home to his family on Christmas Eve.

Maybe he felt sorry for her because she had no family around.

He'd been quiet on the short ride back to the lodge. He hadn't teased her about how much risotto she ate or asked her if she'd had a good time. He'd seemed thoughtful and a little tired. He probably wasn't thrilled to work on Christmas Eve, either, though that was part of the job.

What if he felt pity for the lonely event planner? What if he didn't like that his family thought he was serious about her? What if he was embarrassed by it? That thought made her stomach knot up. She took a deep breath.

Well, Christmas and its hoopla were almost over. She would return home, go to bed early, open her gifts in the morning and rest her foot. The doctor had asked her to return on Monday, after the holiday, so he could check it. But he said she'd know when she could put her weight on it again. He'd also told her to avoid high heels for the rest of the winter.

She'd have to avoid more than just dressy shoes. She'd need to hide her feelings and pretend to be friends with a man who made her heart ache.

But that wasn't going to be simple. Nico had offered to drive her home as soon as they were no longer needed at the wedding. Once the food was served, the wedding cake was ready to be cut, the hot-chocolate bar was in place and the coffee and tea were ready, he and Grace could leave Michael and Jilly to oversee the cleanup.

Grace had other plans. She'd leave him a note.

Wish him a merry Christmas.

Wrap the lovely blue scarf around her neck and limp away.

HE'D SCREWED UP. He didn't have to wonder any longer because now he knew. *Too soon, Vitelli. You rushed it.* And Grace wasn't a woman to be rushed. He should have known better, but he'd thought fate had stepped in with that foolish set of jingle bells to toss Grace right into his arms.

Now what? He checked with the staff to find out who drove her home, but no one knew what he was talking about. He caught up to Jilly as she was replacing peppermint sticks in the hot-chocolate bar.

"Grace isn't in her office," he said, trying to sound casual. "Is she around here somewhere?"

Jilly shook her head. "She left. Her foot was really bothering her."

"She was in pain?"

"One of the EMT guys had to leave early and Grace caught a ride with him."

"One of the EMTs?"

"Friend of the groom. I guess some of them were in the military together. But she told me to call her if there were any problems." She reached into her pants pocket. "And she asked me to give you this."

"Thanks, Jilly." So much for that mystery. He opened the folded paper and read what he already knew. Grace was holed up in her own little home. Alone at Christmas, which obviously was how she wanted it.

Nico went home to his dog.

GRACE CURLED UP in her blue-and-white bedroom, listened to voice messages from her father— "great weather, wish you were here"— her aunt— "great weather, the baby is gorgeous, wish you were here with us"—and Patsy, who'd attended the wedding ceremony but went home to her family afterward.

"Tell me everything," her friend said. "Unless it's after eleven. Then wait until tomorrow."

Did Patsy want to talk about her afternoon with the Vitellis or the success of the wedding reception? She returned none of the calls.

There was nothing from Nico, not that she expected to hear from him. He wouldn't be pleased that she'd left without telling him. He took his responsibilities seriously. She'd done him a favor, she told herself, reaching for a tissue. He wouldn't have to take care of her anymore.

They would be friends.

Grace wept.

"IF YOU WEREN'T interested you should have told me. You didn't have to run off with one of the bodybuilders."

It was seven-thirty Christmas morning and a rumpled, pale Nico Vitelli stood at her door. "Nico, what are you—"

"Breakfast." He handed her a plastic grocery bag. "I grabbed some things to make pancakes."

"Pancakes?" She stepped back and let him enter her small living room. She'd been up for two hours and had opened her three Christmas presents while drinking three mugs of coffee. At least she wasn't wearing a flannel nightgown, not that pink yoga pants and a white sweatshirt with the Mirror Lake Lodge logo was much better. She leaned on the crutch and waited for him to explain.

"Yeah. I need to apologize. And Vitellis apologize with food."

"I didn't run off with a bodybuilder." She took the bag. "I was saving you a snowy drive to town."

"Liar." He followed her into her tiny kitchen and leaned against the counter as if he owned the

place. "You were running away from me. Why?
Who hurt you?"

"That's not—"

"Really, Grace. Who hurt you and how long ago?
I heard you were dating someone for quite a while,
but he moved away. Was it an ugly breakup?"

"His name was Josh. He got a job offer in Houston and he left me." She poured a cup of coffee
and handed it to him.

"Thank God for Houston's booming economy,"
Nico muttered.

"The relationship was getting serious," she continued, her voice soft. "Or so I thought. I trusted
him and he walked away."

"You were in love with him."

"It felt like love at the time." Grace saw the hurt
flash in Nico's eyes and wished she hadn't been
quite so honest.

"He obviously wasn't the right man for you."

"No. I know that now. But at the time? I was
heartbroken. He wasn't ready to get married, he
said. He wasn't ready to 'take the next step.' That
was news to me, because he'd hinted at a future together and I'd believed him." She tried for a smile.
"I seem to attract men with commitment issues."

"No," Nico said. "Those men just weren't right
for you. If that guy, the one who moved to Houston, had been the right guy you'd be eating tacos
and drinking tequila right now."

"Nico—"

"Just so you know, I have zero commitment issues," he informed her. "I'm as loyal as Al."

Grace couldn't help smiling at that statement.

Nico continued. "I started to fall in love with you when I interviewed for the job here. The evening I asked you for a drink."

"But—"

"Not because you were gorgeous. And wearing that red dress. Or because your hair was coming undone in a very sexy way. I fell for you when I saw you comforting a little girl. You really cared about her feelings and you took the time to make her feel better. I loved that. It made me want to know you."

"I was talking to Anna."

"Yes. I didn't know who it was then—Marie told me later what had happened. If I'd only known it was her, I could have stepped in and been the big-hero uncle." He smiled ruefully. "I didn't see her face, but I saw yours."

"She was crying into a corner when I found her. It took a few minutes to get her to tell me what was wrong."

"I waited around until you came back, to ask you out. I was desperate to impress you, to convince you to talk to me."

"You were flirting." And she'd thought he was a well-practiced charmer and would have none of it. "I was a tongue-tied mess," he confessed. "I've been trying to get your attention ever since."

"You have not."

"I have," he insisted. "Ask Patsy. She arranged the Secret Santa gift. I bought the birdseed as a cover."

"It worked. I was totally fooled. She set it up so I got your name, you know."

"I suspected from the way you blushed."

"I did not."

"You did." He slipped his arms around her waist. "Could we start over? I rushed things, I know. I scared you."

"Only because I thought you seemed so…distant yesterday. I thought you were embarrassed that your family thought we were serious. The guys were teasing you about changing diapers and having kids."

"I was afraid they'd know how very serious I am," he admitted. "I didn't want to scare you off."

He kissed her then, and it was definitely not the kiss of a man who was just looking for a friend.

"Can we start over?"

Grace looped her arms around his neck, letting her crutch drop to the floor. "What did you have in mind?"

"We could go out on a date. To the movies. Eat popcorn. Hold hands."

"Okay."

"We'll have Sunday dinners with the family

once in a while. Watch the Super Bowl. Emily has a dance recital coming up. We could go and cheer." His hands tightened around her.

"We could."

"Then on Valentine's Day I come up with some clever way to surprise you with a great big diamond ring. I get down on one knee and beg you to marry me."

Grace blinked back tears as she looked up at him. He was serious. And he was nervous. "And when I say yes?"

He broke into a smile. "We plan a Christmas wedding, which I know from experience you are very good at." Nico pulled back from her, reached into his pocket and pulled out a little bundle of jingle bells. "I kept them for luck. What do you say?"

"They'll be perfect in the bridal bouquet," she managed to say.

"And we'll live happily ever after?"

"Of course we will." She sniffed. "You, me and Al."

"And maybe a couple of little Vitellis." His lips skimmed her mouth.

"The more the merrier," Grace whispered before she kissed him.

* * * * *

HER HOLIDAY
PRINCE CHARMING

CHRISTINE FLYNN

For the lovely ladies
who have made the "Hunt" happen,
and everyone who believes in the fairy tale.

Prologue

"What's on your Christmas list this year? No matter how big or how small, you're sure to find what you're looking for at Seattle's one-stop answer to all your holiday—"

With a quick flick of the dial, Rory silenced the cheerful voice suddenly booming from her car radio. In an attempt to drown out her worries while she waited to pick up her son from kindergarten, she'd turned the music to a decibel she'd never have considered had her five-year-old been in the vehicle.

The ad had just brought to mind the one thing she'd been desperately trying *not* to think about.

She'd hoped to make the holiday special for her little boy this year. Not just special, but after last year's unquestionably awful Christmas, something wonderful. Magical.

As of three days ago, however, she was no longer sure how she would keep a roof over their heads, much less put a tree under it. Due to downsizing, her telecommuting services as a legal transcriptionist for Hayes, Bleaker & Stein were no longer required. She'd needed that job to pay for little things like food and gas and to qualify for a mortgage.

Without a job, she had no hope of buying the little Cape Cod she'd thought so perfect for her and little Tyler. She had no hope of buying or renting any house at all. Since the sale of the beautiful home she'd shared with her husband closed next week, that left her four days to find an apartment and a job that would help her pay for it.

A quick tap ticked on her driver's side window.

Through the foggy glass, a striking blonde wearing studious-looking horn-rimmed glasses and winter-white fur smiled at her. The woman didn't look at all familiar to Rory. Thinking she must be the mom of an older student, since she knew all the moms in the kindergarten class, she lowered her window and smiled back.

Chill air rushed into the car as the woman bent at the waist to make eye contact. "You're Aurora Jo Linfield?"

Rory hesitated. The only time she ever used her full name was on legal documents. And she rarely used Aurora at all. "I am."

"I'm Felicity Granger." Hiking her designer bag higher on her shoulder, she stuck her hand through the open window. The cold mist glittered around her, clung, jewel-like, to her pale, upswept hair. "But please, call me Phil. I'm an associate of Cornelia Hunt. You've heard of Cornelia, haven't you?"

Rory shook the woman's hand, watched her retract it. "I've heard of her," she admitted, wondering what this woman—or the other—could possibly want with her. Nearly everyone in Seattle had heard of Mrs. Hunt, the former Cornelia Fairchild. She'd been the childhood sweetheart of computer genius Harry Hunt, the billionaire founder of software giant HuntCom. Rory recalled hearing of their marriage last summer, even though she'd been struggling within her fractured little world at the time. Media interest in their six-decade relationship had been huge.

"May I help you with something?"

"Oh, I'm here to help you," the woman insisted. "Mr. Hunt heard of your situation—"

Harry Hunt had heard of her? "My situation?"

"About your job loss. And how that affects your ability to purchase another home."

"How does he know that?"

"Through your real estate agent. Mr. Hunt knows the owner of the agency she works for," she explained. "Harry bought a building through him last month for his wife so she'd have a headquarters for her new venture. When he learned why you couldn't move forward with the purchase of the house you'd found, he remembered Mrs. Hunt's project and thought you'd be a perfect referral. So we checked you out." Her smile brightened. "And you are.

"Anyway," she continued, anxious to get to her point. "Cornelia knows of a property for sale that you might want to purchase. She's aware of your current unemployment," she hurried to assure her, "but she said you're not to worry about that little detail right now. Just look at the place. If you're interested, suitable arrangements can be made for you and for the seller.

"It's not exactly what you told your agent you want," she cautioned, reaching into a pocket of her coat. "But it could be perfect for you and your little boy. You really do need to keep an open mind when you see it, though," she warned. "Don't judge it as is. Look for the possibilities.

"You'll be met at the address on the back." She held out a white, pearlescent business card. "The owner's representative will be there at ten tomorrow morning. A man by the name of Erik Sullivan. He's quite knowledgeable about the property, so feel free to ask him anything that will help you decide whether you want the place or not. You should keep an open mind about him, too.

"I have to run now. Double-parked," she said, explaining her rush but not the warning. "If you like what you see, I'll see you tomorrow afternoon."

Rory took the pretty little card. Neatly hand-printed on the back was an address outside Port Orchard, a short ferry ride across the sound from Seattle.

With questions piling up like leaves in the fall, she glanced back up.

The woman was gone.

Seeing no sign of her in the Pacific Northwest mist that was closer to fog than rain, she looked back to the shimmery little card.

The past fourteen months had left her without faith in much of anything anymore. The sudden, devastating loss of her husband to an uninsured drunk driver who'd run a red light. The whispered and crushing comments about their marriage that she'd overheard at his funeral. The exodus from her life of people she'd once thought of as family and friends. Each event had been shattering in its own right. Together, they'd made her afraid to trust much of anything. Or anyone.

And that had been before she'd lost the job Harvey Bleaker had said was hers for as long as she needed it.

The lovely woman with the bookish glasses had appeared out of nowhere. As if by magic, she'd disappeared into the mist the same way, like some sort of a fairy godmother dressed in faux fur and carrying Coach.

Dead certain her sleepless nights had just caught up with her, Rory dropped the card into the open compartment on the console. Whatever had just happened had to be either too good to be true or came with a spiderweb of strings attached to it.

Probably, undoubtedly, both.

Still, she, Tyler and the for-rent section of the newspaper were going apartment hunting in the morning. Having just picked up a check for the small down payment she'd put on the house she hadn't been able to buy, less fees, she had enough for three or four months' rent and expenses. In the meantime, feeling a desperate need for either magic or a miracle, she figured she had nothing to lose by checking out the address on that card.

She just hoped that this Erik Sullivan would be as accepting of her circumstances as Mrs. Cornelia Hunt seemed to be.

Chapter One

"Are we lost, Mom?"

"No, honey. We're not lost." Parked on the dirt shoulder of a narrow rural road, Rory frowned at the building a few dozen yards away. "I'm just not sure this is the right address."

"If we can't find it, can we go to the Christmas place?"

"We'll see, sweetie. We're looking for a new place to live right now."

"I don't want a new one."

"I know you don't," she murmured. Freckles dotted Tyler's nose. His sandy hair, neatly combed when they'd left the house, fell over his forehead, victim of the breeze that had blown in when she'd lowered his window to get a better look at the address on the roadside mailbox.

Nudging wisps back from his forehead, she smiled. "But we need one. And I need you to help me pick it out. It's our adventure, remember?"

"Then can we go to the Christmas place?"

They had seen a banner for a holiday festival in nearby Port Orchard when they'd driven off the ferry. Tyler had been asking about it ever since.

Everything she'd read last night on the internet made the area around the shoreline community a few miles around the bend sound nearly idyllic. The part of her that didn't want to get her hopes up knew that could simply have been good marketing by its chamber of commerce. The part that desperately needed this not to be a wild-goose chase focused on getting them moving.

"Not today, I'm afraid." She hated to say no, but housing had to be their first priority. "We don't have time."

It was nine fifty-five. They were to meet the seller's representative at ten o'clock.

Reminding Tyler of that, and agreeing that, yes, they were still "exploring," she pulled his hood over his head and glanced to the structure surrounded by a few winter-bare trees, dead grass and a wet patch of gravel that, apparently, served as a parking lot.

The address on the mailbox matched the one on the card. The structure, however, bore no resemblance at all to a residence. The two-story flat-roofed rectangle of a building faced a partial view of a little marina two city blocks away and backed up to a forest of pines.

A long, narrow sign above the porch read Harbor Market & Sporting Goods. Signs by the screened door read Fresh Espresso and Worms and Closed Until Spring.

Mailboxes farther up the road indicated homes tucked back in the trees. The only vehicle to be seen, however, was hers. With no sign of life in either direction, she was about to pull out her cell phone to check the address with Phil Granger when she remembered what the woman had said.

She'd warned her to keep an open mind when she saw the place. To look for possibilities.

The potential goose chase was also, apparently, a scavenger hunt.

A narrow driveway curved around the back of the building and disappeared down a slight hill. Thinking there might be a house or cottage beyond the gate blocking it, she grabbed the shoulder bag that held everything from animal crackers to a Zen meditation manual and gamely told her little boy they were going to look around while they waited for the person they were to meet to show up.

The damp breeze whipped around them, scattering leaves in their path as they left the car. With a glance toward the threatening sky, she was about to reconsider her plan when the relative quiet gave way to a squeak and the hard slam of a door.

Tyler froze.

Across twenty feet of gravel, she watched six feet two inches of broad-shouldered, purely rugged masculinity in a fisherman's sweater and worn jeans cross the store's porch and jog down its three steps.

"Sorry about that." His apology came quickly, his voice as deep as the undercurrents in the distant water. "I didn't mean to startle you. I keep forgetting to fix the spring."

The breeze blew a little harder, rearranging the otherwise neat cut of his slightly overlong dark hair. He didn't seem to notice the wind. Or the cold bite that came with it. All lean, athletic muscle, he strode toward them, his glance shifting between her and the child who'd smashed himself against her leg.

That glance turned questioning as he stopped six feet from where she'd rooted herself in the driveway.

"Are you Mrs. Linfield?"

Surprise colored the deep tones of his voice. Or maybe what she heard was disbelief. His pewter-gray eyes ran from the wedge of auburn hair skimming her shoulders, over the camel peacoat covering her black turtleneck and jeans and up from the toes of her low-heeled boots. His perusal was quick, little more than an impassive flick of his glance. Yet she had the unnerving feeling he'd imagined her every curve in the brief moments before she realized he was waiting for her to speak.

"I didn't think anyone was here." The admission came in a rush. "I didn't see a car, so we were just going to look around—"

"I flew over. Floatplane," he explained, hitching his head in the direction of the water. "It's down at the marina.

"I'm Erik Sullivan." Stepping closer, he extended his hand. His rugged features held strength, a hint of fearlessness. Or maybe it was boldness. Despite its lingering shadow, the square line of his jaw appeared recently shaved. He looked hard and handsome and when he smiled, faint though the expression was, he radiated a positively lethal combination of quiet command and casual ease. "I'm handling the sale of this property for my grandparents."

"You're a Realtor?"

"Actually, I build boats. I'm just taking care of this for them."

Her hand had disappeared in his.

She could feel calluses at the base of his fingers. He worked with his hands. Built boats with them, he'd said. What kind, she had no idea. The white-gold Rolex on his thick wrist seemed to indicate he was successful at it, though. The words *capable* and *accomplished* quickly flashed in her mind, only to succumb to less definable impressions as she became aware of the heat of his palm, the strength in his grip and the deliberate way he held that strength in check.

What she felt mostly, though, was a wholly unexpected sense of connection when her eyes met his.

Everything inside her seemed to go still.

She'd experienced that sensation only once before; the

first time Curt had taken her hand. It had been a fleeting thing, little more than an odd combination of awareness and ease that had come out of nowhere, but it had dictated the direction of her life from that moment on.

As if she'd just touched lightning, she jerked back, curling her fingers into her palm, and took a step away. The void left in her heart by the loss of her husband already felt huge. It seemed to widen further as she instinctively rejected the thought of any sort of connection to this man, imagined or otherwise. Because of what she'd learned since Curt's death, it was entirely possible that what she'd thought she'd had with her husband—the closeness, the love, the very rightness of the life they'd shared—hadn't existed at all.

Having struggled with that awful possibility for over a year, she wasn't about to trust what she'd felt now.

Conscious of the quick pinch of Erik's brow, totally embarrassed by her abrupt reaction, she rested her hand on her son's shoulder. Just as she would have introduced her little guy, the big man gave the child a cautious smile and motioned her toward the building.

"The main entrance to the living quarters is around back, but we can go through the market. Come on and I'll show you around."

Whatever he thought of her reaction to him, he seemed gentleman enough to ignore it.

She chose to ignore it, too.

Living quarters, he'd said?

"There isn't a separate house here?" she asked, urging Tyler forward as the sky started to leak.

"There's plenty of room to build if that's what a buyer wants to do. The parcel is a little over three acres. Living on premises has certain advantages, though." He checked the length of his strides, allowing them to keep up. "Shortens the commute."

If she smiled at that, Erik couldn't tell, not with the fall of cinnamon hair hiding her profile as she ushered the boy ahead of her.

Mrs. Rory Linfield wasn't at all what he had expected. But then, the new owner of the building next door to Merrick & Sullivan Yachting hadn't given him much to go on. He wasn't sure what the elegant and refined wife of Harry Hunt was doing with the building Harry had apparently given her as a wedding gift—other than providing Erik and his business partner an interesting diversion with her total renovation of its interior. It had been his offhand comment to Cornelia, though, about a place he'd be glad to sell if Harry was still into buying random pieces of property, that had led him to describe the property his grandparents had vacated nearly a year ago.

The conversation had prompted a call from Cornelia yesterday. That was when she'd told him she knew of a widow in immediate need of a home and a means to produce an income.

When she'd said *widow,* he'd immediately pictured someone far more mature. More his parents' age. Fifty-something. Sixty, maybe. With graying hair. Or at least a few wrinkles. The decidedly polished, manicured and attractive auburn-haired woman skeptically eyeing the sign for Fresh Espresso and Worms as she crossed the wood-planked porch didn't look at all like his idea of a widow, though. She looked more like pure temptation. Temptation with pale skin that fairly begged to be touched, a beautiful mouth glossed with something sheer pink and shiny, and who was easily a decade younger than his own thirty-nine years.

He hadn't expected the cute little kid at all.

He opened the door, held it for them to pass, caught her soft, unexpectedly provocative scent. Following them inside, he had to admit that, mostly, he hadn't anticipated the sucker punch to his gut when he'd looked from her very kissable mouth to the feminine caution in her big brown eyes. Or the quick caution he'd felt himself when she'd pulled back and her guarded smile had slipped into place.

What he'd seen in those dark and lovely depths had hinted heavily of response, confusion and denial.

A different sort of confusion clouded her expression now.

He'd turned on the store's fluorescent overheads when he'd first arrived. In those bright industrial lights, he watched her look from the rows of bare, utilitarian grocery shelving to the empty dairy case near the checkout counter and fix her focus on a kayak suspended from the ceiling above a wall of flotation devices. Sporting goods still filled the back shelves. After the original offer to buy the place fully stocked had fallen through, he'd donated the grocery items to a local food bank. That had been months ago.

The little boy tugged her hand. "Why is the boat up there, Mom?"

"For display. I think," she replied quietly, like someone talking in a museum.

"How come?"

"So people will notice it." She pointed to a horizontal rack on the back wall that held three more. Oars and water skis stood in rows on either side. "It's easier to see than those back there."

With his neck craned back, his little brow pinched.

"Are we gonna live in a store?"

"No, sweetie. We're just..." From the uncertainty in her expression, it seemed she wasn't sure what they were doing at the moment. "Looking," she concluded.

Her glance swung up. "You said this belongs to your grandparents?"

"They retired to San Diego," he told her, wondering what her little boy was doing now as the child practically bent himself in half looking under a display case. There were no small children in his family. The yachting circles he worked and played in were strictly adult. Any exposure he had to little kids came with whatever family thing his business partner could talk him into attending with him. Since he managed to limit that to once every couple of years, he rarely gave kids any thought. Not anymore.

"They'd had this business for over fifty years," he explained, his attention already back on why the property was for sale. "It was time they retired."

The delicate arches of her eyebrows disappeared beneath her shiny bangs. "Fifty years?"

"Fifty-three, actually. They'd still be running the place if Gramps hadn't hurt his back changing one of the light fixtures." Erik had told him he'd change the tube himself. Just as he'd helped with other repairs they'd needed over the years. But the Irish in John Sullivan tended to make him a tad impatient at times. "He can be a little stubborn."

"Did he fall?"

"He just twisted wrong," he told her, conscious of the quick concern in her eyes, "but it took a couple of months for him to be able to lift anything. Grandma picked up as much slack as she could, but those two months made them decide it was time to tackle the other half of their bucket list while they could both still get around."

Her uncertainty about her surroundings had yet to ease. Despite her faint smile, that hesitation marked her every step as she moved farther in, checking out the plank-board floor, the single checkout counter, the old, yellowing acoustic tiles on the ceiling. Watching her, he couldn't help but wonder how she would do on a ladder, changing four-foot-long fluorescent tubes in a fixture fourteen feet off the floor. Or how she'd wrestle the heavy wood ladder up from the basement in the first place.

Since Cornelia had specifically asked if the business was one a woman could handle on her own, he'd also thought his prospective buyer would be a little sturdier.

Rather than indulge the temptation to reassess what he could of her frame, hidden as it was by her coat, anyway, he focused on just selling the place.

"The original building was single story," he told her, since the structure itself appeared to have her attention. "When they decided to add sporting goods, they incorporated the living area into the store, built on in back and added the upstairs.

"The business is seasonal," he continued when no questions were forthcoming. "Since summer and fall recreation provided most of their profit, they always opened in April and closed the first of October. That gave them the winter for vacations and time to work on their projects."

It was a good, solid business. One that had allowed his grandparents to support their family—his dad, his aunts. He told her that, too, because he figured that would be important to a woman who apparently needed to support a child on her own. What he didn't mention was that after the first sale fell through, the only other offers made had been too ridiculously low for his grandparents to even consider.

Because there were no other reasonable offers in sight, he wasn't about to let them pass up Cornelia's offer to buy it—if this particular woman was interested in owning it. He hadn't even balked at the terms of the sale that required his agreement to help get the business back up and running.

Selling the place would rid him of the obligation to keep it up. Even more important than ending the time drain of weekly trips from Seattle to make sure nothing was leaking, broken or keeping the place from showing well was that his grandparents had been the last of his relatives in this part of the sound. Once the place was sold, he had no reason to ever come back.

Considering all the plans he'd once had for his own life there, nearly all of which had failed rather spectacularly, that suited him just fine.

His potential project had yet to ask a single question. He, however, had a few of his own.

"Have you owned a business before?"

He thought the query perfectly reasonable.

She simply seemed to find it odd.

"Never," she replied, sounding as if she'd never considered running one, either. Still holding her little boy's hand, she set her sights on the open door behind the L-shaped checkout counter. "Is that the way to the living area?"

He told her it was, that it led into a foyer.

Wanting a whole lot more information than she'd just given, he followed her with the child looking back at him over the shoulder of his puffy blue jacket.

The instant he met the child's hazel eyes, the boy ducked his head and turned away.

With a mental shrug, Erik focused on the mom. She looked very much like the spa-and-Pilates type married to some of his high-end clients. Yet the car she drove was a total contrast—economical, practical. "Are you into outdoor sports?"

"We have bicycles," came her distracted reply.

"Mountain or street?"

"Street."

"For racing or touring?"

"Just for regular riding."

"Do you know anything about mountain bikes?"

"Is there a difference?"

That she'd had to ask had him moving on. "What about hiking or camping?"

"Not so much."

"Water sports? Do you windsurf, paddleboard, water ski?"

"Not really."

He took that as a no. "Do you know anything about sporting goods?"

Clearly on a mission of her own, she answered his last query with a puzzled glance and moved past the stairs, one set leading up, the other down, and into a spacious living room.

The empty downstairs space was interrupted only by the kitchen's long island near one end and anchored by a ceiling-high stone fireplace at the other. The bare walls all bore a pristine coat of latte-colored paint.

It was toward the kitchen that she motioned. "Mind if I look back there?"

Not at all pleased with her responses, he told her he didn't and watched her head for the glass-faced cupboards.

Her sandy-haired son darted straight to one of the large picture windows lining the opposite wall.

"Have you ever worked retail?" he asked her.

"Never," she replied once more.

"Wow, Mom. Look! It has a park!"

Rory's glance cut to where her little boy pressed his nose to the wide window near the fireplace. A large meadow stretched to a forest of pines. Between the dawning potential in the place and the feel of the tall, decidedly distracting male frowning at her back, she hadn't noticed the expansive and beautiful view until just then.

What she noticed now was her son's grin.

That guileless smile added another plus to her escalating but decidedly cautious interest in what surrounded her. "It sure does, sweetie. But stay with me. Okay?"

Yanking his unzipped jacket back over the shoulder of his Spider-Man sweatshirt, he hurried to her, his little voice dropping as he glanced to the man who remained on the other side of the white oak island.

"Does he live here?" he asked, pointing behind him.

She curled her hand over his fingers. "It's not polite to point," she murmured. "And no. He lives somewhere else."

"Where?"

"I don't know, honey."

"But it's a long way, huh?"

"Why do you say that?"

"'Cause he said he came in a plane. It floated here."

From the corner of her eye, she noticed the big man's brow lower in confusion.

"He came by *floatplane*," she clarified, easing confusion for them both. "It's a plane that can land on water. It flies just like any other."

"Oh." Tyler screwed up his nose, little wheels spinning. "Why didn't he make him a boat?"

He remembered what Erik had said he did for a living.

There wasn't much Tyler heard that he ever forgot. She'd come to regard the ability, however, as a double-edged sword. While her bright little boy absorbed information like an industrial-strength sponge, there were things she knew he'd overheard that she truly hoped he'd forgotten by now. Things certain relatives had said that had confused him at the time, hurt him and made her even more fiercely protective of him than she'd been even before he'd lost his dad.

Since no response came from the other side of the island, she told Tyler it was possible that Mr. Sullivan did have a boat, but that it was really none of their business. Right now, they needed to look at the rest of the house.

There were certain advantages to a five-year-old's short attention span. Already thrilled by the "park," Tyler promptly forgot his interest in the boat their guide did or did not have and, like her, poked his head into the pantry, the mudroom and downstairs closets.

There was no denying his attraction to the cubbyhole he found in one of the upstairs bedrooms. Her own interest, however, she held in check. A person couldn't be disappointed if she didn't get her expectations up to begin with.

The property was nothing she would have considered even a week ago. It had none of the little neighborhood atmosphere she'd looked for. None of the coziness she'd craved for herself and her son. It felt too remote. Too foreign. Too…unexpected.

Her option was an unknown apartment in an as yet undetermined area near a job she still had to find.

Her hopes rose anyway, her mind racing as Erik led her back down from the three bedrooms and two baths that would be more than adequate for her and her son.

Phil had said to keep an open mind about this place.

Despite its drawbacks, it was, indeed, full of possibilities. But it wasn't just Tyler's surprisingly positive reactions or the idyllic views from some of the windows that tempered her misgivings. What Phil hadn't mentioned was that this wouldn't just be a place to live. It would be her source of income.

She could have her own business. Be her own boss. That meant the means to support her son would be dependent on her, not on someone else with obligations or agendas of their own. It would be up to her if she succeeded or failed. And while the thought brought as much anxiety as anticipation, mostly it brought a surprising hint of reprieve.

She could start over here. She could finally, truly move on.

By the time they'd worked their way back downstairs, Tyler knew which room he wanted to be his. He wasn't quite so sure what to make of their tour guide, though. Every time he'd looked over his shoulder to see if Erik was still with them, he'd moved closer to her or tightened his grip on her hand.

Considering the man's easy self-assurance, it struck her as odd that he appeared equally undecided about Tyler. Because he'd yet to say a word to her son, she wasn't sure if he simply didn't know how to relate to small children or if he was one of those people, like her father-in-law, who felt a child was to be seen and not heard and otherwise ignored until they became of an age to engage in meaningful conversation.

Maternal instincts on alert, the moment they reached the foyer, she asked Tyler to see if he could spot deer in the woods from the living room window. He was barely out of earshot when she felt Erik Sullivan's disconcerting presence beside her.

"Your son seems to like the place," he pointed out, joining her by the mahogany newel post. "What about you? You haven't said much."

Erik would admit to not being particularly adept at deciphering women, even when they did speak. *No* often meant *yes. Don't* often mean *go ahead. Nothing* always meant *something,* though finding out what that something was could be akin to pulling an anchor out of dried cement. But this woman hadn't given him so much as a hint about any conclusion she might have drawn.

"Do you have any questions?" he prompted.

"When did you say the store usually opened for business?"

"April. The first or second week."

She lifted her chin, her thoughts apparently coming in no particular order.

"Phil Granger said you know I can't qualify for a mortgage just now."

"We're aware of that," he assured her.

"Were your grandparents planning to carry the mortgage themselves?"

"A second party will carry it. So," he prodded, "you're interested, then?"

She wanted to smile. He could see the expression trying to light the flecks of bronze in her deep brown eyes. She just wouldn't let it surface.

"That depends on what they want for it. And the terms. How much are they asking?"

He should have been relieved by her interest. Would have been had she been even remotely qualified to take on the store.

"That's...negotiable."

"But they must have a price in mind."

"Do you have *any* business experience?"

It was as clear to Rory as the doubt carved in his handsome face that he had serious concerns about her ability to make a go of the store his grandparents were selling. Unflattering as his obvious skepticism was, she couldn't fault him for it. They had run the business for decades. They'd probably poured their hearts and souls into the place that had defined them for years. This man hadn't had to tell her for her to know how much the store and their home had meant to them. The shelving in the spare room upstairs—his grandma's sewing room, he'd said—had been built by his dad. The beautiful, lacquered banister beside them had been lathed by his grandfather.

He'd casually mentioned those things in passing. With his big hand splayed over the grapefruit-size mahogany ball atop the newel post, his thumb absently rubbing its shiny finish, she realized this place mattered to him, too.

Her only concern now was that he trust her with it.

She took a step closer, lowering her voice so Tyler couldn't overhear.

"It's not that I've never had a job," she informed him

quietly. "I was a file clerk while I worked on an associate's degree. After that, I spent four years as a legal secretary before Tyler came along. I went back to work transcribing documents at another law firm ten months ago. I'd still be doing that if they hadn't let me go because the firm merged and they cut my job."

Skipping over the five-year gap in her résumé, she aimed for the heart of his concern. "I've just never owned a business. Or sold anything other than whatever the PTA was selling to raise money for school projects.

"I'll admit that when I got here," she hurried on, hoping he'd overlook that last part, "the last thing I expected was a store. But you said it's a good, solid business. If your grandparents didn't usually open it until April, that would give me four months to figure out what needs to be done and how to do it." All she had to do was get past the daunting little fact that she had no idea where to start.

"Look," she murmured, too tired after too many sleepless nights to care how much of herself she exposed. "I'll admit I don't know a…a…"

"A bivy sack from a bobber?" he suggested.

"Exactly. And until now," she said, muscling on, "I'd honestly never thought about owning anything like this. The only sports I know anything about are tennis and golf." And that was only because her husband had wanted her to fit in at the club. She was so not the rugged, outdoors type. "But I'll do whatever I have to do to provide for my son.

"This could be a good place to raise him. He could help me in the store. I think he'd love that. He'd even have his own park," she pointed out, thinking of how badly she wanted them gone from the exclusive community that had come to feel like a prison. She'd hoped for a normal neighborhood, but breathing room would be a good thing, too.

"I'll never be able to replace the security he had before his dad died, but it's up to me to give him as much stability as I can." Her voice fell with her final admission. "I think I can do that here."

Her last words were as soft as the utter conviction in her eyes. Erik saw a plea there, too. Quiet. A little raw. And a lot uncomfortable for him to witness in the moments before he glanced to where her son seemed to be counting something at the window.

He'd been about that age—five or so, if he had to guess—when his grandfather had put him to work stacking canned goods on shelves. After that, he'd practically begged to come over so he could help.

He'd once thought this would be a good place to raise a child, too.

"There's one other thing," she admitted, her voice still quiet. "Tyler has never lived anywhere other than in the house we're leaving. We have to be out in three days. Until the job thing happened, I'd thought we'd be settled in our new house well before Christmas. He didn't have a very good one last year and it would be really nice to find a place that I don't have to move him from again." Practicality, or maybe it was weariness, kept her tone utterly matter-of-fact. "So how much is it?" she asked. "And how do I make this happen?"

He didn't know which struck him more just then: her absolute determination to do whatever she had to do to care for her child or the naked vulnerability lurking in the depths of her eyes.

As if she knew what he saw, her glance hit the floor.

Her determination to hide that vulnerability pulled at something unfamiliar deep in his chest, even as he steeled himself against it.

He hadn't been told how she'd been widowed. Or how long she and her child had been on their own. He had no idea if her marriage had been as good as his parents', as much a failure as his own had been or some form of tolerable in-between. He knew only from what she'd said about her child's loss that it was entirely possible she still grieved the man she'd lost, too.

He wasn't a particularly sensitive or sympathetic man. Or so he'd been informed by his ex-wife and certain of the arm candy who trolled the circles he moved in. But he wasn't at all comfortable being privy to something so personal. It disturbed him even more to find himself wondering what it would be like to mean that much to a woman.

Equally unsettling was the fact that an hour ago, she hadn't even known the store existed. "I can't give you the terms."

She hadn't a clue what she was getting into.

He knew for a fact that he was no longer comfortable with what he'd agreed to do himself.

"My agreement with Cornelia...Mrs. Hunt," he corrected, "is that she or her assistant will discuss those details with you."

Reaching into the back pocket of his jeans, he extracted one of the same pearlescent cards Phil had given her yesterday. "Did you take the ferry or do the loop through Tacoma?"

"Ferry."

"Which one?"

"Southworth. It lands at Fauntleroy."

By land or water, either way it would take her a while to get back to Seattle.

"Then I'll give you directions to their office from the dock. I have another meeting in Seattle at noon." Card in hand, he pulled his cell phone from another pocket and keyed in a number.

With the instrument to his ear, he turned away, started to pace.

Rory glanced at her watch. It was already after eleven o'clock.

She was about to mention that when she remembered his mode of transport was infinitely faster than hers. He was already into his conversation with Phil, anyway. She couldn't hear what he said, though. She knew only that he looked oddly resigned when he turned a minute later to inform her that Phil wanted to talk to her.

By the time the woman who had appeared out of nowhere yesterday told her everything was ready to proceed with the sale and confirmed their meeting that afternoon, Rory couldn't shake the feeling that nothing could possibly be as simple as Phil had made it sound—and that Erik Sullivan had more of a role in the sale than anyone was letting on.

Chapter Two

The directions Rory had been given led her to the Ballard neighborhood in northwestern Seattle and a weathered, two-story redbrick building much like the others along an old business section of the waterfront. What distinguished the structure was the trail of plaster dust and debris leading from the open front door to the Wolf Construction Dumpster at the curb.

Inside, sheets of milky construction plastic masked two stories of interior scaffolding and what appeared to be something grand under construction. The filmy barriers did little to deaden the occasional clatter and boom of interior demolition. The noise was muffled considerably, however, behind the closed door of the only completed space—an unexpectedly feminine and elegant ground floor corner conference room in shades of ivory and pale taupe with a view of a marina, Shilsole Bay and snow-capped Hurricane Ridge beyond.

The long banks of ivory-draped windows caught Tyler's

attention the moment they'd walked in. Rory had thought the boats in the inlet had drawn him. Until she noticed Erik.

A walkway ran behind the buildings. She could see him outside, pacing past the rows of windows, bare-masted sailboats bobbing in the background. Apparently oblivious to the chill, he had one hand in a front pocket of his jeans, his head down against the breeze as he talked on his cell phone.

He did not look happy.

Logic told her he could be talking about anything. But the unease joining her curiosity and uncertainty over this meeting made her fairly certain his scowl had something to do with her.

"We're so glad you liked the place," said Phil, leading her across the floor, the click of her heels on polished oak suddenly hushed by the pale blue Aubusson rug. "With everything so unsettled for you, we didn't know if you'd see the advantages of taking on a business right now. Especially one that you might not ordinarily have considered."

Wearing a cream blouse and slacks slung with a thin gold belt, the woman Rory met yesterday took her and Tyler's coats and motioned to one of the Queen Anne chairs at the circular conference table. The light from the ornate crystal chandelier above it made the mahogany surface gleam like glass. "Cornelia did feel you'd consider it, though," she added, "given your circumstances."

"Which are very close to what mine were at one time," came a voice from a small alcove.

A statuesque, elegantly mature lady in pale lavender cashmere emerged from the washroom, carrying roses she'd just freshened. Her silver-blond hair was coiled in a chic chignon at her nape. Diamonds glinted from her ears. The rock on her left hand, a huge pink diamond surrounded by a dozen of brilliant white, flashed in its platinum setting as she set the vase on a marble credenza with a quiet clink.

"Please pardon the mess out there, Rory. We're a work in progress at the moment. I'm Cornelia Hunt," she said, intent on putting her guest at ease as she held out her hand. "It's a pleasure to finally meet you."

Feeling a distinct connection to Alice after she'd slipped down the rabbit hole, Rory clasped the woman's hand. She had dressed that morning in a casual black turtleneck and skinny denims to look at properties and apartments, not to meet well-dressed ladies in what could have passed for a drawing room in a palace.

"The pleasure's mine," she returned, fighting the urge to curtsy.

"You only met briefly, so I'll officially introduce you to Felicity Granger. Phil is my assistant. She's also an academic counselor at the university. She's really rather brilliant at helping others with their life decisions, so I brought her in to help me with my work." Her green eyes seemed to twinkle as she smiled. "What have you been told about the arrangements so far?"

"Hardly anything. The man who showed us around… Erik," she identified, still aware of him pacing, "wouldn't even give me the price."

"I don't doubt that you have questions," Cornelia conceded. "I'll have Phil start answering yours and explain the details while I get us some coffee. Or would you prefer tea?"

Rory told her coffee was fine, thank you. And that yes, cocoa for Tyler would be nice. Even as she spoke, she wasn't at all sure what struck her as more incongruous just then: that Cornelia Fairchild Hunt, the very pleasant wife of a reportedly eccentric computer-genius billionaire, was getting her coffee. Or the mound of dingy canvas mail sacks piled beside a delicate French provincial writing desk.

On the desk's surface, dozens of what appeared to be opened letters teetered in stacks.

Phil took the chair next to Rory. Seeing what had her attention, she adjusted her overlarge glasses and leaned toward her.

"There was an article in the Seattle *Washtub* recently about how Cornelia helped a young entrepreneur get the break she needed with her business. Ever since then, requests have poured in by email and snail mail for her in care of the newspaper and the offices of HuntCom asking for her help from other young women. And for them. Like you," she explained. "The reporter who wrote the article said she's bringing another sackful over this afternoon."

"A reporter is part of this?"

"Don't worry," Phil hastily assured. "Cornelia wants to stay under the radar with her project and she trusts Shea Weatherby to help her with that. As for anyone else we might need to talk with, we only identify our clients to those directly involved in her situation."

The assertion was hugely reassuring to Rory. She'd already supplied enough fodder for gossip in certain social circles to last a lifetime. Nearly every member of those circles would have sold their summer homes to mingle with a Hunt, too. But all that mattered to her just then was that this meeting was confidential. Her relationship with her in-laws was strained enough without word getting out and embarrassing them because their son's widow apparently needed to be bailed out by strangers. For Tyler's sake, she needed to make as few waves with them as possible.

Thinking about her in-laws reminded her that she needed to call them about Christmas.

"The volume of requests Cornelia is receiving," Phil continued, mercifully sidetracking her from the stomach-knotting thought, "is why she needed to hire help. I just love what she's doing."

"I really am at a loss here," Rory admitted. "What *is* she doing?"

"She's being what the first woman she helped called her," her assistant replied. "A fairy godmother."

She had a fairy godmother?

"On to the details." Phil pushed a pale blue folder toward her, the snowflake polish on her nails glittering. "If these terms are agreeable to you, Cornelia will purchase the property you saw from the owners and you will purchase it from her for the amount stated on line one. To keep everything legal and as simple as possible, your down payment will be one dollar. Your balance will be interest-free with the first payment due September first. You'll have had five months of cash flow by then."

Disbelief held Rory's tone to nearly a whisper. The number couldn't possibly be right. "The property has to be worth three times this."

"Oh, it is. And that's what Cornelia will pay the owners for it. But that's your price. Of course, there is more to the sale."

Ah, yes, Rory thought, unable to understand why Cornelia would take such a loss for her. The strings.

"Cornelia has added a few perks," Phil chose to call them. "She believes the best route to success is to have a good adviser. Since it's understandable that you'd know little about this particular business and since the Sullivan's grandson is reasonably acquainted with it, she arranged for Erik to be your mentor for the next six months. He'll help you with your inventory, suppliers, getting part-time help and whatever else it will take to get your new venture up and running.

"The two of you can determine how often you need to meet, but there will be a status meeting here once a month.

Of course, I'm available to both of you together or individually at any time. At the end of the six months, if you're on track with your business plan, Erik will have fulfilled his mentor agreement, and you'll be on your own. All we ask," she concluded, as if she'd rather expected the stunned silence coming from beside her, "is for your discretion in discussing the work we do here."

Phil sat back, smiling.

Rory couldn't seem to move.

Poof. Just like that. The property her little boy had fallen in love with that morning—and the business that came with it—could be hers.

The reality of it didn't want to sink in. Yet even in her disbelief what registered most was that her new life included a man who she strongly suspected didn't want to work with her at all.

"This Erik," she said, caution competing with amazement as Cornelia joined them with a tray of tall porcelain mugs. "May I ask the terms of his agreement with you?"

Taking the chair on the opposite side of her, Cornelia passed mugs to her and Phil. "It's nothing complicated. I just requested that he help you with the business if I buy the property for the Sullivans' asking price."

"But why did he agree to that?"

"Because he wants a decent price for his grandparents and I offered him one. He's been taking care of the property for them, so I also imagine he'd like to be free of that responsibility. I don't think he begrudges his grandparents his time. He sounds quite fond of them," she offered, approval in the soft lines of her face. "But he's a busy man."

Rory remembered his strong, workingman's hands, the calluses she'd felt brush her palm. Right behind the thought came the disquieting memory of what his touch had elicited. "He said he builds boats."

"Oh, they're more than boats. He and his business partner build world-class sailing sloops. Their boatworks is down past the marina, but their sales and rental office is next door. J.T., one of my stepsons," she said, identifying Harry's second oldest, "commissioned one from him years back. He said Erik is the only man he'd ever do business with on a handshake. If you knew my stepson, you'd know that respect for someone's character doesn't get any greater than that."

Her carefully penciled eyebrows arched as she offered cream and sugar. "Did you find him disagreeable?"

Disturbing, yes. Disagreeable? She couldn't honestly say they'd disagreed about anything. "No."

"Are you not wanting help?"

Rory shook her head. She'd be a fool to turn it down. "I'm sure he has far more information about how the market is run than anything I can even begin to find on my own."

The unguarded admission brought Cornelia's smile back. "Then it's a win-win for everyone."

Baffled by the woman, more uncertain than she wanted to admit about her mentor, Rory touched the handle of her mug. "Please don't think I'm not beyond grateful, Mrs. Hunt—"

"It's Cornelia," the woman said graciously.

"Cornelia," Rory corrected. "But I'm having a hard time making sense of all this. I understand from Phil that you helped someone else when she needed it. But why do you want to help *me* like this?"

"Because I can," she said simply. "My Harry gave me a ridiculously large amount of money for a wedding gift. Since I have the means, I decided to make it my mission to offer deserving young women a hand up when the going gets rough for them, or when they just need the right break.

"In your case," she admitted, "I know all too well what it's like to be financially strapped and the only parent. My first husband was a dear, but he left me in a real financial bind when he died. I had to sell my home, just as you've had to do. And I had to work hard to raise my girls."

She gave Rory's hand a pat, drew back her own. "From what we learned about you from your real estate agent—and other resources," she admitted, making it clear she thoroughly vetted the recipients of her largesse, "I don't doubt that you'll do what you must to make it work. Erik has proven himself to be an excellent businessman," she assured, as the opening door let in the back-up beep of a truck. "I'm sure you can trust him to help you succeed.

"Can't she, Erik?" she asked the man himself as he walked in.

Seeming oblivious to the way his presence suddenly filled the space, much less to the faint tension leaking from him in waves, Cornelia raised an eyebrow in his direction.

"Can't she what?" he replied.

"Trust your business judgment."

"It hasn't let me down so far."

The disarming smile he gave Cornelia and Phil seemed to come easily. The wattage, however, lowered considerably when it settled on her. Having met her eyes long enough to make her heart jerk, Rory watched him lower his glance to the older woman's coffee.

"Mind if I get some of that?"

"Not at all. The pot is fresh."

His heavy footsteps muffled by the carpet, Erik headed for the coffeemaker in the alcove. Behind him he could hear the elegant matron and the bookish blonde he'd met last week explaining that the paperwork for Rory's mortgage would be handled at a title company Monday afternoon. Since he had power of attorney for the sale for his grandparents, he and Cornelia had already agreed to take care of their business there that morning.

The Hunt name tended to eliminate delays.

He could hear the low, soft tones of Rory's responses, but he had no idea what she said. He was too busy telling himself that the next six months wouldn't be as bad as he'd feared.

They'd probably be worse.

He didn't question the sincerity of the rather shell-shocked-looking young woman reading the papers in front of her. Her determination to do what she had to do for her child had been nearly tangible to him. But her impulsiveness had raised about a dozen red flags.

Women spent more time making up their mind about buying a pair of shoes than she had about taking on something that would require a nearly 24/7 commitment. Especially at first. He knew. He ate, slept and breathed his own business. And that business was something he'd wanted since he was a kid. She'd only wanted the store since she'd learned about it that morning. She'd even admitted to knowing nothing about what she'd agreed to get herself into—which meant she'd take far more time than he'd planned on devoting to the care and feeding of her education.

It was that last part that he'd explained to his business partner when he'd called a while ago to tell him he'd still be tied up for a while. Pax had said not to worry about what he'd committed himself to. He'd cover for him if he needed time during the day to work with the store's new owner.

Though they'd never talked about the reasons for it, Pax knew how badly Erik wanted to be out from under that property. And why. They'd grown up together. Pax had been his best man. He'd also gone through the ugliness of his divorce with him by letting him take on however many projects it took to keep him too exhausted to think about anything else.

It had been seven years since the demise of his eight-year marriage, and Erik had long since recovered from what he had no intention of ever repeating again, but he already felt guilt about the time he'd be taking away from work. Especially with an April delivery date on their present work under construction, another client waiting for his final blueprints and two others hovering in the wings to get on their list.

Then there were their evening commitments with past and future clients. The holiday party season had just started—and Merrick & Sullivan Yachting never missed a business or philanthropic commitment.

With the women still talking, and feeling the tension creep up his back, he took his filled mug to the nearest window and rubbed at his neck. He'd do what he had to do where the woman behind him was concerned, and hope she wasn't the sort who required a lot of hand-holding to come up to speed. Heaven knew he wasn't a coddling sort of guy.

Erik took a sip of the coffee that was infinitely better than the sludge he and his partner had been brewing since their secretary had gone on maternity leave. It didn't help the situation that Mrs. Rory Linfield had a son. He'd made it a point over the past several years to avoid women with children. They tended to want more of a commitment than he was interested in. But that deliberate lack of exposure left him feeling less than capable when it came to anyone under four feet tall.

With his pretty little project deep in conversation, he looked out over the blue-tarped sailboats yawing in their slips. He and Pax had pulled their rental fleet out of the water last month, but farther up the shoreline, he could see the point that anchored the rest of their operation: the boatyard where they stored their boats over winter and the boatworks where they built their custom sailing yachts, one sloop at a time.

"How come that boat has a Santa on it?"

The little boy had walked over from two windows

down. Now, with his chin barely clearing the window-sill, the sandy-haired child pointed to a row of decorated sloops in the marina. Several had colored lights anchored fore and aft from the mainsail mast. One had a blow-up Santa at the helm.

Erik gave a shrug. "Some people just like to decorate their boats this time of year."

"How come?"

"Because they entertain on them," he said, thinking of the cocktail parties he and his partner had hosted on their respective sloops for their clients over the years. They had one scheduled next week. "Or maybe they're going to be in one of the boat parades." The floating parades were legend around the sound during the holidays.

The little boy's brow furrowed. Digesting what he'd been told, he said nothing else. For about five seconds, anyway.

"Do you have a boat?"

"I do."

"Do you decorate it?"

"I have."

"Do you put a Santa on it?"

"No."

"Oh," the child said.

He took another sip of coffee, waited for another question. When none was forthcoming, Erik tried to focus on the conversation behind him.

The small voice immediately cut in.

"I'm glad your house has a fireplace. So Santa can come down," Tyler explained, still looking out the window. "Mom said he can visit without one, but it's easier when he has a chimney."

It took a moment for the boy's conversational leap to make sense. Apparently since Santa was on his mind, any context was fair game.

"I've heard that about chimneys, too," he assured him. "And the house you saw isn't mine. It's my grandparents'."

The distinction apparently didn't matter.

"We have a fireplace in our house. But we didn't have a tree last time for him to put presents under." The small voice sounded utterly matter-of-fact. "Mom said this year won't be sad. We get a tree no matter what."

His mom had mentioned that he hadn't had a very good Christmas last year. Sad, the child had just called it. Yet Erik didn't let himself consider why that had been. Telling himself that her personal business was none of his, he murmured a distracted, "That's good," to her son and focused on the only business of hers he needed to be interested in. The store.

Cornelia had asked for his presence in case Rory had questions for him. He figured now was as good a time as any to see what those concerns might be.

The three females at the table glanced up as he approached.

It was Rory's dark eyes that he met.

"Is there anything you want to ask me about the property?"

Her shell-shocked look had yet to fade. With her ringless hand at the base of her throat, she slowly shook her head. "I don't even know where to start right now."

"Make a list as things occur to you," he told her. "I'll come by the market next week and we can go over it.

"The sale is being expedited," he told her, knowing now that part of the appeal of his grandparents' home, for her son, anyway, had been the fireplace his own family had gathered around at Christmas. "You can move in whenever you're ready. I'll check my schedule and Phil can set us up with a day and time next week to go over inventory."

He set his coffee on the table with a decisive clink and pulled his business card from his pocket. Walking around the table to give it to her, he watched her rise. As she did, his glance slid over what her coat had hidden earlier. The long black turtleneck she wore skimmed her feminine curves, molded the sweet shape of her hips.

She had the body of a dancer. Long, lithe and sexy as hell.

Masking his misgivings about having to deal with her, feeling them mount by the minute, he ignored the vague tightening in his gut. "Do you need help moving in?"

"No. I'm... No," Rory repeated, hating how flustered she felt. "But thank you." The last thing she wanted was to impose on this man. Considering what he'd been asked to do for her, she'd be obligated enough to him as it was. "I'd planned to be out Monday, so I've already arranged for movers."

She pushed back her bangs, revealing the pinch of her brow. "You really don't mind if I take things over before the sale closes?"

"You said you want to be settled before Christmas." He assumed now that that desire had something to do with putting up a tree. "The earlier you start, the sooner you can be."

Rory swallowed. Hard.

"Thank you."

He held out his card. "My office and cell numbers are on here. Call me if something comes up. I'll leave a key under the rock by the back porch. You'll get a full set at closing." His fingers brushed hers. Her skin felt cool to him, soft, and though he was trying not to notice anything in particular about her, he could have sworn he felt her trembling.

Without looking up, she palmed his card and clasped both hands in front of her.

"You're sure you're covered on the move?" he asked

"I'm positive. I arranged everything a couple of weeks ago."

Standing as close as he was, he caught the tremor in her

breath as she eased it out. He didn't doubt she felt overwhelmed with all that was happening for her. Yet she managed to maintain the composure that had her graciously
assuring Cornelia that she truly needed nothing else as far
as help was concerned. Something about that composure
seemed practiced to him, though. It was as if she'd found
herself in overwhelming or uncertain situations before and
wasn't about to let anyone see how unsettled she really was.

She wouldn't look at him again. She seemed to know
what he'd seen, and felt totally embarrassed being so exposed. A huge burden was being lifted from her slender
shoulders, but she wasn't letting herself feel the relief of
that weight. It appeared that admitting the scope of that
relief would be admitting how truly desperate she'd begun
to feel. So she just kept it all in, as if that was what she'd
become accustomed to doing anyway, and turned to the
women.

With a choked little laugh, she said she had no idea
how to thank them.

Leaving her to figure it out, he looked to the matriarch
running the show, thanked her for the coffee and headed
for more familiar territory.

He'd given his word that he'd help. And he would. He
never promised anything he didn't intend to deliver. But
when he showed up for the meeting Phil arranged for him
with Rory the following Wednesday, he discovered something about his charge that he hadn't anticipated.

The young widow with the sweet, sharp little boy might
have looked as fragile as sea foam, but she had a stubborn
streak as wide as Puget Sound.

Chapter Three

Erik hesitated at the store's front door. For years he'd simply walked in when the business had been open. After his grandparents had moved, he'd let himself in with his key. Since the sale had closed two days ago, he no longer had the right to come and go as he pleased from a place that had been part of his life for as long as he could remember.

The odd sense of having been displaced lingered as he rapped his knuckles on the frame of the screen door, and promptly disappeared the instant the inside door swung open. Even with her pretty features schooled into a smile of greeting, the unease in Rory's guarded expression made him suspect she was already having second thoughts about what she'd taken on.

Or so he was thinking when she let him in and his glance cut from the black hoodie and yoga pants molding her curves to the furniture behind her.

It looked as if every possession she owned sat piled in the interior of the market. Bedroom sets, tables, chairs, boxes.

"You said you didn't need any help moving in."

Good morning to you, too, Rory thought. "I didn't think I did," she said, stepping back for him to pass.

Deliberately overlooking the accusation shadowing his rugged features, she crossed her arms over her hoodie and the teal turtleneck and thermal undershirt layered beneath it. She wanted to believe her shiver had more to do with the chill in the large space than with the big man in the waffle-weave pullover and charcoal cargo pants. After all, the thermometer by the dairy case did read forty-nine degrees.

The man should wear a coat, she insisted to herself. It was easily ten degrees colder outside.

She turned on her heel to lead him inside where it was warmer. "The college kids I hired were only available long enough to drive the U-Haul over and unload it into the market," she explained, heading between the packing boxes that formed an aisle to the interior door. "It wasn't until we got here that they told me they wouldn't have time to carry everything to the rooms. They did take one of the beds upstairs, though." The thud of heavy hiking boots echoed behind her. In running shoes, her footsteps barely made a squeak. "A mattress, anyway," she qualified. "And a box of bedding." That had been huge.

Spending the past couple of nights on a hard floor would have guaranteed even less sleep than she usually managed. Even with a reasonably comfortable place to rest, she'd spent most of both nights trying not to disturb Tyler and listening to the building's unfamiliar creaks and groans while hoping to heaven she could make this store work.

"They'll come back to finish sometime next week," she continued, "so I've been taking in what I can by myself. Tyler's helping." Boxes too heavy to carry she'd emptied one armload at a time. The method wasn't the most efficient, but she now had one bathroom in order and the kitchen organized, except for the table and chairs. The old refectory table weighed a ton. She knew—she'd tried to move it last night.

She chafed her arms along her sleeves, winced a little when she rubbed a spot above the elbow that now sported the bruise she'd earned in the attempt. She had a matching one on the back of her shoulder. No longer hearing Erik's footfalls, she glanced around to see that he had stopped.

Across ten feet of worn plank flooring, she saw his dark eyebrows merge. "Isn't the furnace working?"

"It's working just fine."

"Then why is it so cold in here?"

"Because I'm not heating this big space until I have to. Fuel's expensive. By the way," she added, gratitude slipping into her voice, "thank you for having the tank filled. You saved me from running out of oil." She'd always had electric heat before. Not accustomed to an oil furnace, she hadn't realized the need for fuel until the man who'd performed the building inspection Sunday had showed her the tank and pointed out the gauge.

"The driver of the truck wouldn't leave an invoice," she told him. "So if you'll tell me what I owe you, I'll give you a check."

"You don't owe me anything."

"Yes, I do."

"No," he insisted, "you don't. Just think of it as a move-in present."

He obviously considered the matter settled. There seemed no doubt of that as he turned away to ponder the height and breadth of the obstacles blocking his view of the back of the store.

As appreciative as she was for his thoughtfulness, she couldn't accept his gift.

"Look." Hugging her arms a little tighter, she stepped in front of him. "I'm already not sure how I'll repay you for helping me get to know the store. I know you agreed to do it to help your grandparents sell this place," she conceded, which meant his benevolence definitely wasn't personal, "but I'd rather not be any more obligated to you than I already am. Or will be," she qualified, because other than make her acutely aware of his reluctant and very male presence, he hadn't done anything yet. "Okay?"

For a moment, he said nothing. He just let his deceptively easy glance slip over the quiet determination in her eyes before he headed to the checkout counter.

"Then don't accept it as a gift. Accept it because I'd rather work out here with heat."

Confusion preempted further defense. "I thought we were going to go over the inventory."

"That's the plan."

He carried a briefcase. A rather hefty one of scarred butterscotch leather and straps with buckles that had far more character than the sleek, unscuffed ones carried by other men she knew. As he set it on the scratched counter, she could see his burnished initials, worn shiny in places, above the equally worn lock. A section of stitching on the side looked new, as if it had recently been repaired. The case was old, she thought. It had history. And part of that history seemed to say that he'd rather keep and care for what he had than replace it.

Not appreciating how he'd dismissed her attempt to establish an understanding, she didn't bother to wonder why she found that so appealing.

"I thought we'd work where it's already warm. Inside," she pointed out, ever so reasonably. "We can sit at the island and go over the books in there."

"I meant the physical inventory. The stuff that's on the shelves and in the bins back there." He hitched his thumb over his shoulder. "I have a printout of what came with the sale, but those items have been sitting around for a year. You'll want to discount some of what you have and replace it with new merchandise. Things like sinkers, bobbers and leaders are fine, but creels and some of the stock that isn't packaged looks shopworn."

Rory hadn't a clue what he was talking about.

"Fishing gear," he explained, apparently sensing that.

Undaunted, she picked up a couple of the boxes from the cracked surface. She'd already decided the old laminate needed to go. "Then we'll work here at the counter."

The boxes had been emptied, Erik realized when she easily lifted two marked *Dishes* from where his grandfather had once kept displays of bug repellent and sunglasses. She removed two more, adding them to the only space available without blocking either doorway: the tops of three tall stacks of red-and-green bins marked *Christmas.*

She had to stretch to get them there. Jerking his glance from the enticing curve of her backside, he reached past her.

"Let me get that."

"Already have it," she insisted, and having placed the boxes, turned right into him.

Rock had more give to it.

The thought occurred vaguely as she bumped into his chest. Promptly bouncing back, she gasped a breath when his quick grip tightened on her upper arms. Her heart had barely slammed against her ribs when he pulled her forward to keep her from hitting the bins behind her and bringing the empty boxes down on their heads.

The freshness of soap and sea air clung to him. With her pulse scrambling, his grip tight on her bruise, she had no idea why the scents even registered. Her hand shot up, covering the back of his where it curved over the tender spot on her arm.

The pressure of his fingers eased.

With their bodies inches apart, she went as still as stone. Or maybe he froze first. She just knew that one moment she'd been intent on doing whatever she needed to do to make it clear that she wouldn't waste his time, and the next, the tension in his body and the warmth of his hands had seeped through to her skin, making her conscious of little more than…him.

Erik's eyes narrowed on hers an instant before she ducked her head. Slacking his grip, he dropped his hands. There'd been no mistaking the way she'd winced when he'd grabbed her.

Without thinking, he reached toward her again, touched the back of her hand where it now covered where his had been.

He hadn't thought he'd grabbed her that hard.

"Are you okay?"

At the concern in his voice, the caution in his touch, her head came back up. "I'm fine." Wanting to convince them both, she smiled. "Really."

His brow pinched as he drew his hand away once more.

Rory's breath slithered out. That small contact had been far too brief to elicit the loss she felt when he stepped back. Yet that sense of loss existed, sinking deeper into her chest with every heartbeat—unexpected, unwanted and feeling far too threatening under his quiet scrutiny.

A certain numbness had protected her since she'd lost what had felt like the other half of herself. Yet, as with the first time this man had touched her, something about him scraped at the edges of that barrier, made her conscious of things she truly didn't want to consider.

Out of nowhere, the need to be held sprang to mind. It was such a simple thing, so basic that she'd never truly considered it until it had been found and suddenly lost— that need for security, comfort, a sense of oneness. But she knew how rare it was to find that sense of belonging, and the need didn't feel simple at all. Not when she realized she was actually wondering what it would feel like to be folded against Erik's broad, undeniably solid chest. A woman would feel sheltered there. Safe from what troubled her. And for a few moments, anyway, free of the need to stand alone.

Shaken by her thoughts, by him, she started to move back, as much from the need behind the unexpected admissions as from the man who'd prompted them. The stacks behind her allowed her no escape at all.

His scrutiny narrowed. "If you're okay, why are you still holding your arm?"

She was holding in his touch. Realizing that, hoping he didn't, she promptly dropped her hand.

"It's nothing." Rattled, trying not to be, she shrugged. "It's just a little sore."

"Why?"

"Because I landed against the corner of a dresser." She was just tired. Tired and apparently in need of some downtime with her yoga mat. If she could find it. Or, even better, some fudge. The one thing she did not need was to think about this man's chest, his arms or the way he was scowling at her. "I was trying to move a table and lost my grip.

"So," she said, fully prepared to move on so he'd move himself.

He didn't budge. "Which table?"

Trapped between the counter, bins and boxes, she leaned sideways and pointed toward the eight-foot-long, solid oak-and-iron refectory table jammed between a bedroom set and the dairy case. "That one."

His scowl deepened as it swung back to her. "You tried to move that yourself?"

"It wasn't going to go inside on its own."

Forbearance entered his tone. "You said you were going to wait for the kids who moved you here to help with the heavy stuff."

"What I said," she reminded him, just as patiently, "is that they'd be back next week."

"When next week?"

"When they can fit it in."

"Meaning this could all be here a week from now," he said flatly. "Or the week after that."

She didn't particularly appreciate the cynical certainty in his tone. Especially since she was trying not to dwell on that discouraging suspicion herself.

"What about your friends?" he asked, clearly prepared to pursue other possibilities. "Have you asked any of them to help you?"

"I'm sure everyone's busy."

"Do you know that for certain?"

She could omit and evade. No way could she lie. Thinking of the few people she still thought of as friends, she muttered, "Not exactly."

"Then ask."

She started to say that she didn't want to. Fearing she'd sound like a five-year-old, not liking how he prodded at her defenses, she ignored the command entirely.

Since he had yet to move, she ducked around him. "I'll go turn on the heat."

She would do her best to cooperate with him for his help with the store. She could cut corners somewhere else to keep expenses down.

"I only took two bar stools inside, so there are a couple more back there we can bring up to sit on. I'm going to tell Tyler I'll be out here. He's watching a DVD on my laptop."

Erik watched her slip behind the counter, his focus on the resolute set of her shoulders as she disappeared inside. Her son was undoubtedly watching her laptop because her television was buried somewhere in the stacks beyond him. He also gave the guys she'd hired about a fifty-fifty chance of returning to finish their job.

He didn't care what she said. She did need help here. She just didn't want to ask for it.

Considering that she hadn't wanted to accept his little housewarming present, either, he couldn't help but wonder if the woman was always unreasonable, impractical and stubborn, or if some less obvious trait compelled her to refuse assistance when she clearly needed it.

What she needed now was some serious muscle.

Judging from the size of the decidedly upscale sofa and armchairs, sections of wall units, tables and a huge mirror sitting between the rows of shelving, there had been significant space in the house she'd left behind. The larger of two armoires was the size of a king-size mattress. He had no idea where she was going to put that. It might have fit in the largest of the bedrooms upstairs, but it would never make the bend at the top of the staircase.

He pulled his cell phone from his pocket, checked the time before scrolling through his contact list.

He'd just ended his call when she hurried back through the door.

"I have a friend on the way to help with the heavy stuff," he announced. "You and I can take care of the rest of it." Pushing up his sleeves, he motioned to an overstuffed, roll-armed, oatmeal-colored chair blocking a bedroom set. "Where does that go?"

Beneath a dusting of dark hair, his forearms were roped with sinew and muscle. They looked every bit as strong as she imagined them to be, but it was his left arm that had her staring. A silvery scar, hook shaped and wide, slashed from wrist to elbow.

"Just part of a collection. Caught a jib line when it snapped," he said, seeing what had her attention. "It couldn't be helped." His glance slid pointedly to the sore spot on her arm. "Unlike banging yourself up trying to move something you had to know was too heavy for you.

"So where do you want it?" he asked. "The living room?"

His presumption made her let the table reference go.

"You don't need to do this." *Part of a collection,* he'd said. He had more injuries like that? "And you definitely didn't need to call your friend."

Unease over what he'd done had collided with a hint of concern for the scar. Or maybe what he saw was embarrassment warring with interest. Whichever it was, he could practically see her struggling to decide which should take precedence as she moved with him toward the chair. The process, he thought, was rather fascinating.

"Yeah," he muttered, undeterred. At least she now had some color in her cheeks. "I did. I can't get those dressers up the stairs by myself."

"I meant, you didn't need to impose on him at all. I can't ask you to do this," she stressed, only to have him hand her the chair's seat cushion.

"You didn't ask," he pointed out.

"You know what I mean," she muttered back, arms wrapped around the awkward bulk.

"What I know is that there's no way to go over the inventory when we can't even get to it. So, yeah. I do need to do this." Challenge lit the chips of silver in his steel-gray eyes as he pulled one of her arms free and handed her the wide back cushion, as well. His glance slid to her biceps. "You're skinny, but you have more muscle than I'd thought. This'll go faster if you help."

Over the tops of the pillows, Rory could have sworn she saw challenge shift to a smile. Too disconcerted by him and what he'd done to stand there and make certain of it, she turned with the cushions and headed for the door.

She'd admit to having lost a couple of pounds in the past year or so, but no one had called her skinny since sixth grade.

"Which room do you want the twin bed in?" she heard him call.

"The one next to the master," she called back.

She had no intention of arguing with him. Not just because she didn't want to appear difficult. Or because he had a valid point about not being able to get to the inventory. As unsettled as her life felt—would always feel, she feared—getting the visible chaos under control would be huge. Tyler having his own bed that night would be nice, too.

Focusing on her son distracted her from the man carrying up her little boy's bed. For all of five minutes. The moment Tyler saw his bookshelf going up the stairs, he wanted to help. Wanting to keep him out of Erik's way, since she was trying to stay out of it herself, she waited until the piece was in place, then put him to work filling the shelves with his toys. While Erik moved on to tackle the living room furniture, she carried in lamps, pictures and, now that she could get to it, her box of potted herbs for the kitchen windowsill.

They didn't work together so much as they worked around each other. Erik clearly just wanted to get the job done so he could get on with the job he was there to do. Hating how she'd inconvenienced him, she just wanted to get it done, too.

An hour later, she'd returned to the base of the stairs for the rolled-up dinosaur posters she'd left there when muffled male voices drifted from inside the store.

"No way is this thing going up the stairs," she heard Erik insist. "Not without a saw."

"She might take exception to that," came the sensible reply. "How about through the bedroom window? Aren't there picture windows on that side of the house?"

"We'd have to take the window out and bring over a

crane, but it might be doable. The boys could load the EZ-Rig on a trailer and one of them can drive it over."

"That would do it." The unfamiliar voice paused. "There just isn't enough time to do it today. Not if you want the rest of this cleared out. That party starts at six."

Not totally sure what had the men talking about bringing in heavy equipment, equally concerned by mention of a prior obligation, Rory left the posters and poked her head inside the store. In the bright overhead lights, she saw Erik facing the large cherry armoire that blocked one of the grocery aisles. He stood in profile to her, his arms crossed over his broad chest, his wide brow furrowed.

He seemed totally occupied with logistics. She just couldn't see whom he was talking with. Whoever it was remained hidden by the sizable piece of furniture.

Needing to remove the apparent complication, she scooted past the checkout counter. "If it can't be carried up, just leave it. Or move it out of the way if you need to. I'll figure out what to do with it later."

Erik's glance caught hers as an athletic-looking male in worn denims and a plaid flannel shirt stepped from behind the armoire. The man had a scant inch on her mentor in height, which put him in the range of six-three or so, and the same imposing, broad-shouldered, leanly muscular build that spoke of intimate familiarity with hard physical work. Or a gym.

Beneath his wavy, wood-brown hair, his eyes narrowed an instant before he smiled. That smile seemed as easygoing as the man himself when Erik introduced him to her as Pax Merrick.

"My business partner," Erik added.

Pax reached out. "And partner in crime."

Shaking her hand, he gave her a quick once-over, the kind men who enjoy women often do, along with a rakish wink. "We go back a long way. You're Rory," he said, sparing his partner the introduction, along with whatever he could have added about their apparently extensive history.

Her glance bounced between the two unquestionably attractive, undoubtedly successful, probably rather fearless males. With the sense that their history might be rather intriguing, she offered Pax an apologetic smile of her own. "I'm really sorry to cut into your day like this."

"Not a problem. He'd do the same for me," he admitted, eyeing her with no small amount of curiosity. "You're really taking over this place?"

Something in the man's tone gave her pause.

"I am," she replied. "Why?"

"It'll seem really different, is all. I used to hang out here with Erik when we were kids. We built our first boat in Gramps's garage down there. And this store… It was just the Sullivans here all those years. They had sort of a mom-and-pop thing going," he explained, looking her over as if to verify some preconceived impression. "Down-to-earth. Comfortable, you know? I never thought about it being run by someone…"

Like you, she was sure he'd been about to say, only to be cut off by the quick-but-subtle slicing motion Erik made across his own throat.

"…else," he hastily concluded. "But if Erik's going to teach you the ropes," he hurried to add, "I'm sure you don't have a thing to worry about. The guy's got the patience of Job."

Meaning he thought she was going to require…what? she wondered, swinging her glance to Erik. Patience of biblical proportions?

Erik pointedly ignored her. "Are you going to help me move this, Merrick?"

"Absolutely. I'm on it."

As if wanting to muffle his partner, Erik motioned to the furniture the large piece blocked. "As soon as we get this out of the way, we'll take up your son's dresser," he told her. "Where do you want those bookcases?"

"In the spare room across from Tyler's." *Please,* she might have added, but his friend's insinuation still stung.

"Is there a bed that goes in there?"

"I don't have a spare bed anymore." She nodded toward the headboard and nightstands an aisle over with the same carving as the armoire. "That's a set we had in a guest room. I'll use it for my room now."

She'd sold the bed she'd slept in with Curt for so many years. Its new owner had picked up all the master bedroom furnishings the morning her movers had come. She'd sold the bulk of her other possessions to an estate broker she'd met at the country club to which she no longer belonged. Had it not been for Tyler, she'd have sold everything and bought only what she'd need to start over. But too much had changed for him already for her to indulge the need she felt to shed all the reminders of a life that no longer was.

Taking a deep breath, she pushed her hand through her hair and looked over to see Erik still watching her.

"I take it you've downsized."

"You have no idea," she murmured back.

She couldn't imagine what he saw in her expression, but she saw something in his that looked remarkably like understanding. It was as if he knew what it was like to walk away from the trappings and reminders of a former life. Whether he'd had no choice or the choice had been solely his, she had no idea. All she felt with any certainty as he shoved up his shirtsleeves to get back to work was that he wanted no part of those reminders now.

The realizations gave her pause. As she turned away herself and headed inside to pick up the posters, so did her disquiet over his partner's unwitting revelations. The fact that Erik had obviously implied to his friend that she would require considerable patience was merely annoying. She also questioned just how patient he actually was, given his steamroller approach to getting her things moved out of his way. But what truly troubled her was what his friend had said about her mentor's grandparents having been there for so long.

She hadn't even considered what her neighbors and customers would think of someone new running a business that might well be some sort of institution in the area. She'd already been wondering if she could keep it open year-round, and added that to her list of questions for Erik. Her newly heightened concerns about fitting in she'd have to add later, though, when she wasn't busy keeping Tyler out of the way of all the testosterone hauling bedroom furniture up the stairs.

Every time they clamored up the stairs and down the hall with another piece of something large, he'd dart to the door of his new bedroom to watch them go by.

Pax joked with him, noticeably at ease with small children. Erik, preoccupied, said even less to him than when he'd been around him before. He'd given him a half smile on their first pass, which had put a shy grin on Tyler's face, then barely glanced at him at all.

Because her little boy continued to wait in his doorway for "the man with the boat," it soon became painfully apparent that Tyler was hoping Erik would acknowledge him again—which had her feeling even more protective than usual when he asked if he could help him.

"I don't think so, sweetie. They're in a hurry," she explained, brushing his sandy hair back from his forehead. "When people get in a hurry, accidents can happen."

"If I be careful can I help?"

Erik heard the tiny plea drift down the hallway. Focused on getting Rory's possessions out of the way of the inventory, he'd paid scant attention to the child other than to make sure he wasn't where he could get something dropped on him.

But now they needed tools. Deciding to save himself a trip and do something about the dejection he'd heard in that small voice, he called, "Hey, Tyler. Can you do something for me?"

A nanosecond later, little footsteps, muffled by carpeting, pounded down the hall.

Tyler appeared in the doorway of the master bedroom, shoving his hair back from the expectation dancing in his eyes. Rory was right behind him, unmasked concern in hers.

Erik crouched in his cargos, his forearms on his thighs, hands dangling between his knees. Behind him, Pax continued squaring the bed frame to the headboard.

Rory's glance fixed on his as she caught her son by his shoulders. "What do you need?"

Whatever it was, she seemed prepared to do it herself. She had mother hen written all over her pretty face.

"Let him do it. Okay?"

The little boy tipped his head backward to look up at his mom. "Okay?" he echoed. "Please?"

For a moment, she said nothing. She simply looked as if she wasn't at all sure she trusted him with whatever it was he had in mind, before caving in with a cautious okay of her own.

It didn't surprise him at all that, physically, she hadn't budged an inch.

"There's a red metal box at the bottom of the stairs," he said to the boy. "It has socket wrenches in it. It's kind of heavy," he warned. "Do you think you can bring it up?"

With a quick nod, Tyler turned with a grin.

"No running with tools!" Rory called as he disappeared out the door.

"'Kay!" the boy called back, and dutifully slowed his steps.

Caught totally off guard by what Erik had done, Rory looked back to the big man crouched by her bed frame. He was already back to work, he and his partner slipping the frame parts into place and talking about how much longer it would take them to finish.

Not wanting to be in their way herself, she backed into the hall, waiting there while Tyler, lugging the case with both hands, grinning the whole while, made his delivery.

When he walked back out of the room moments later, his expression hadn't changed. She couldn't remember the last time her little boy had looked so pleased. Or so proud.

"Erik said I did good."

She knew. She'd heard him.

"Can I show him my boat?"

"Maybe some other time. He's really busy right now," she explained, then added that *she* really needed his help finishing his room.

Helping his mom wasn't nearly the thrill of helping the guys. Especially when Erik called for him again ten minutes later, this time to carry down the tools he'd had him bring up.

From where she stood on a chair adjusting the ties on a primordial-forest curtain valance, she watched Tyler walk by his bedroom door with both hands again gripping the handle of the red metal box. Right behind him came Erik, telling him he'd take the box when they got to the stairs so he wouldn't lose his balance with it.

Right behind Erik, Pax paused and poked his head into the room.

"I've got to run, Rory. No need to stop what you're doing," he called, because she'd done just that. "We have a client's Christmas party tonight or I'd stick around and help. Erik's going to finish up."

She'd forgotten they had plans. Groaning at the lapse, she left the last tie undone and headed for the door.

Erik had disappeared into the store. Tyler, now empty-handed, stood in the entryway as Pax passed him, ruffling his hair on the way.

"What can I do to repay you?" she called.

"Do you bake?"

"What's your favorite cookie?"

"Any kind that goes with coffee." Grinning, he disappeared, too.

Erik eyed his buddy as Pax walked into the store. "If she has any spare time," he insisted, setting the toolbox on the counter, "she'll need to spend it out here."

"Hey," his shameless partner said with a shrug, "if she wants to bake me something, it'd be rude to refuse. So how much longer will you be?"

Erik flatly rejected the odd sensation that hit out of nowhere. It almost felt like protectiveness. But just whom he felt protective of, he had no idea. The woman wasn't Pax's type at all. "Half an hour at the most."

"You taking a date tonight?"

"Yeah," he muttered, the word oddly tight. "What about you?"

"I'm leaving my options open. I'll cover for you if you need more time," he added, his smile good-natured as he headed out the store's front door.

Erik wished he'd left his options open, too. Though all he said to his partner was that he'd catch up with him at the party and turned back to what was left of his task.

The aisles were finally clear. The inventory visible. Except for the large armoire they'd moved to the empty space near the front door and the boxes and bins Rory had said she didn't need just yet, mostly those marked *Christmas*, nothing else needed to be carried in. Except for her monster of a dining table, which they'd put in place, he and

Pax had carried the rest of the furniture in and left it all wherever it had landed in the living room.

His briefcase still lay on the checkout counter's marred surface, its contents untouched.

Burying his frustration with that, he glanced up to see her watching him uneasily from the inner doorway. More comfortable dealing with logistics than whatever had her looking so cautious, he figured the furniture in the living room could be pushed or shoved into place. It didn't feel right leaving her to do it alone. It wasn't as if she'd call a neighbor for help with the heavier pieces. She didn't even know them. And she'd seemed inexplicably reluctant to call in a friend.

"Where do you want the sofa? Facing the window?" That was where his grandparents had always had theirs.

Rory wanted it to face the fireplace. She just wasn't about to impose on him any more than she already had.

"I'll take care of it," she insisted, because he had that purposeful set to his jaw that said he was about to get his own way. Again.

"What about the big cabinet?"

"It's fine where it is. For now," she conceded, not about to tell him she wanted it moved across the room to the stair wall. "I'm hugely grateful for your help with all this, Erik. And for your friend's. But I'd just as soon not feel guiltier than I already do for having used your time like this. You came to work on the business. Not to help me move in. You need to go now."

One dark eyebrow arched. "I need to go because you feel guilty?"

"You need to go because you have a date."

She'd obviously overheard his conversation with his partner. Not that it mattered. Like Pax's unveiled allusion to the care and feeding Erik had told him he was sure she'd require, nothing had been said that he'd rather she hadn't heard. He'd bet his boat she already suspected he wasn't crazy about being there, anyway.

"Right." He wasn't in the habit of leaving a woman waiting. "We'll get to the inventory later this week. I won't have time until Friday."

"Friday will be fine. I'll be here. And thank you," she added again, touching his arm when he started to turn away. The moment he turned back, she dropped her hand. "For letting Tyler help," she explained. "I haven't seen him smile like that in a really long time."

Thinking the cute little kid had just wanted to be one of the guys, he murmured, "No problem," and picked up the toolbox and his briefcase. There was no reason for her to be looking all that grateful. Or all that concerned.

Still, as he told her he'd call her later and turned for the door, adding, "Bye, sport," for the little boy who'd just appeared behind his mom, cradling a toy boat, he really wished he didn't have the date with the bubbly event planner he'd taken out a couple of weeks ago. He didn't know the striking blonde all that well, but she'd been easy on the eyes, into sailing and, had he been interested in pursuing her hints, not at all opposed to a little casual sex.

He just hoped she'd need to make it an early evening so there'd be no awkwardness at her door. His head wasn't into games tonight. He wasn't much up for a party, either, though he wasn't about to stand up a client.

For reasons he didn't bother to consider, what he wanted to do was stay right where he was.

Chapter Four

The last thing Rory wanted Friday morning was to be late for her meeting with Erik. Or for him to be on time.

As she turned her car into her gravel parking lot, she realized she wasn't getting her wish on either count.

She'd also just confirmed her suspicions about the gleaming white seaplane she'd seen tied to the dock at the bottom of the rise. It was Erik's. He was on her porch, leaning against a post.

The fact that her mentor flew his own plane meant that he hadn't had to queue up for the ferry or get caught in traffic the way she and the rest of the mortals had crossing the sound and navigating surface streets that morning. It also meant that it had only taken him minutes to make the flight that was now a ninety-minute-each-way expedition for her to Tyler's school.

Hating that she'd caused him to wait, she left her little car in the otherwise empty lot in front of the store rather than park it in her garage and hurried toward where he'd straightened from the post. "I'm sorry I'm late. I was the last car off the ferry," she called, praying he hadn't been there long. They'd agreed on eleven o'clock. It was only a few minutes after. Still… "How long have you been here?"

The ever-present breeze ruffled his dark hair as he pushed his cell phone into a front pocket of his jeans and picked up his worn briefcase.

"Long enough to figure out you weren't going to answer the back door or the one to the mudroom. I didn't realize you'd be gone. I was just going to call you."

His cloud-gray eyes slid from hers as a muscle jerked in his jaw. His skin looked ruddy from the chill. In deference to the cold, he wore a leather flight jacket—open, though, as if in defiance of the need for it.

She hadn't thought of him as defiant before. Or rebellious, or rash, or anything that might even hint at irresponsibility. He seemed too much in control of himself for that. Yet the finely honed tension surrounding him alluded to a sort of restiveness that implied far more than his impatience with her, and made her acutely aware of how restless a man with flying and sailing in his blood might be. Restless. Daring. Bold.

She couldn't remember the last time she'd felt anything that wasn't tempered by the numbness that lingered deep inside her. And she'd never felt bold in her life.

What she felt most was simply the need to keep pushing forward. Especially now. Forward was good. Looking back made it too easy to fall apart.

He didn't need to know that, though. As she crossed the porch planks, searching her crowded key ring for the unfamiliar key, she figured all he needed to know was that she would make this venture work. Exactly how she would do that was as much a mystery to her as the dawn of creation, but she figured the basics would be a good place to start. And basically, she knew she needed this man to help make it happen.

His footsteps echoed heavily as he came up beside her, his big body blocking the wind whipping at her hair. "Where's your son?"

"At school. He only has tomorrow and next week before winter break, so we're commuting."

"To Seattle?"

Conscious of him frowning at the top of her head, she tried to remember if the key she'd just selected was for the store's front door, its emergency exit, the door to the house or the side door to the garage.

"I don't want him to miss working on the holiday projects with the other kids. He already missed the first of the week because of the move and he really wants to help decorate the school's big tree." He wanted a big tree, too, he'd told her. A *huge* one. How she'd make *huge* happen currently fell in the mystery category, too. "Since he won't be going back there after Christmas, it's about the only thing keeping his mind off the need to change schools right now."

"How long does that take you?"

"An hour and a half, if you include queuing up for the ferry."

"You're spending three hours over and back in the morning, and another three hours every—"

"That's just today," she hurried to assure him. "I'll usually only make the round-trip once. Kindergarten is only four hours, so I'll run errands while he's there." And maybe see if she could slip into her friend Emmy's yoga class, since seeking calm seemed more imperative by the moment. "A friend is picking him up with her son this afternoon. He'll play at their house until I get there."

His tone went flat. "So you came all the way back just to keep this appointment."

"You said it was the only time you had this week."

"You could have told me you'd be in Seattle," he insisted. "I never would have expected you to come back here for this."

"You said we had to go over the inventory. We have to do that here, so there was no point in mentioning it."

The key didn't work. Her head still down, his disapproval doing nothing for her agitation, she picked out another.

Before she could try that one in the lock, Erik reached over and snagged the wad of keys by the purple rhinestone-encrusted miniflashlight dangling below them.

"That's to the garage." He paused at the practical bit of bling, chose one beside it. "You want this one."

He held a duller brass key by its blade.

"Next time something like this comes up," he continued, biting back what sounded a lot like frustration, "mention it."

All her rushing had left her jumpier than she'd realized. Or maybe it was the edginess in him that fed the tension she did not want to feel with this man. Taking the key, conscious of how careful he'd been not to touch her, she forced the hurry from her tone.

"My schedule is my problem, not yours. I'll make sure it doesn't interfere with what you need to show me here. Not any more than it has already," she concluded, since last time he'd wound up hauling in her furniture.

Trying not to give him time to dwell on that little failure, she slid the key into the lock.

As the lock clicked, he moved behind her. Reaching past her head, he flattened his broad hand on the heavy wood door.

His heat inches from her back, the nerves in her stomach had just formed a neat little knot when he muttered, "Then let's get to it," and pushed the door open.

Intent on ignoring the knot, disconcerted by their less-than-auspicious start, she hurried into the store to the warning beeps of the alarm system.

With the front display windows shuttered for the winter, the only light came from what spilled in behind them. Relying on that pale shaft of daylight, she headed straight for the checkout counter and the inner door behind it, mental gears shifting on the way.

Feeling his scowl following her, she deliberately sought to shift his focus, too.

"I'm going to start the coffee. While I do that, would you look over the floor plan I came up with? It's right here on the counter." Fluorescent lights buzzed and flickered as she snapped switches on. Punching the security code into the pad by the inner door, the beeping stopped. "I'll be right back."

In less than a minute, she piled her purse, coat and scarf onto the dining table, flipped on the coffeemaker she'd already filled and grabbed the tape measure she'd left on the island.

She'd barely turned back into the store when the hard line of Erik's profile had her freezing in the doorway.

He'd tossed his jacket over the far end of the U-shaped counter's now-bare surface. Without it, she could see *Merrick & Sullivan Yachting* discreetly embroidered in sky-blue on the navy Henley hugging his broad shoulders. Ownership, she thought. He had a definite sense of it. He had it stitched on his shirt. His initials, she'd noticed before, were on the latch of his briefcase.

On the scarred beige countertop lay the file she'd left open. His frown was directed to the new floor plan she'd come up with.

"You did this?" he asked.

With a vague sinking feeling she walked around to him. She might not know anything about the little doodads in the bins and on the Peg-Boards hanging in her new store, but she was a consumer with her fair share of shopping hours under her belt. If the interior didn't have some appeal, people might run in to buy what they needed, but they wouldn't stick around to browse and buy more.

"The store needs updating," she said simply, certain he could see that himself. "I thought it might make the space more interesting to have three shorter horizontal shelving units in back than that one long one down the middle. The floor space along here," she said, pointing to the front and back walls on the drawing, "would be a little narrower, but the endcaps would allow for ninety-six more inches of display space. I could use part of the longer piece—"

"I'm not asking you to defend this," he interrupted mildly. "I'm just asking if you drew it."

Erik's only interest when he'd first arrived had been in tackling the task they hadn't even started the other day. As far as he was concerned, they were already behind schedule if she was to open in April. Not wanting to fall further behind and risk her not making a success of the business, he'd just wanted to get in, get out and get back to work until the next time he had to meet with her. It had been that ambivalent sort of annoyance eating at him when he'd realized what she'd done to accommodate him.

The trip by air between the store and Seattle was nothing for him. Minutes from takeoff to touchdown, depending on head- or tailwinds and whether he left from his houseboat on Lake Union or the boatworks in Ballard. The drive and a ferry ride for her was infinitely less convenient. People commuted from the inner islands every day. But she had actually come back from Seattle just to meet with him, and would have to return later that day to pick up her son.

Even the time it would normally take her on other days seemed an enormous waste of time to him. She was right, though. How she did what she needed to do was her problem. Just as it was his problem, not hers, that he didn't want to consider changing the store from exactly as it had been for decades.

The need to play nice so they could reach their respective goals wasn't what had his attention at the moment, however. It was the detail in the drawing. It hadn't been generated using a computer program. The floor plan had been drawn with pencil on graph paper. While the layout was admittedly simple, the measurements and identity of the elements were all perfectly drawn and precisely printed. It had the touch of a professional.

"Oh," she murmured, apparently understanding. "I took a drafting class a few years ago. We'd thought about building our own home and I wanted to understand what the architect was talking about." She gave a shrug, the motion nowhere near as casual as he suspected she intended it to be. "We never got to the blueprint stage, though. We bought instead."

We.

The freshness of her soap or shampoo or whatever it was clinging to her skin already had him conscious of her in ways he was doing his best to ignore. He'd caught the light herbal scent of her windblown hair when she'd pointed out the walls on the drawing. He caught it again now. Whatever it was she wore seemed too subtle to define. But the elements managed to hit his gut with the impact of a charging bull.

Telling himself he didn't need to know anything about her that didn't apply directly to his reason for being there, he deliberately overlooked her reference to the man she'd married—along with the subtle havoc she wreaked on certain nerves—and indicated a rectangle she'd drawn by the front door.

"So what's this?"

"That's the armoire over there. It just needs to be moved

back against that wall and down a few feet and it'll be perfect. A couple of neighbors stopped by to welcome me yesterday. Actually, I think they came to check me out," she admitted, because their curiosity about the "single woman who'd bought the store" had been so obvious. "But one of them mentioned that she makes organic soaps and creams. She has a friend up the road who makes candles for craft shows. I thought I'd see what else is made locally and put a gift display in it."

He eyed her evenly. "This isn't a boutique."

"Are you saying it's a bad idea?"

He wasn't going to commit to anything yet. He was still back on her having taken a drafting class just because she'd wanted to understand her architect.

"When did you do this?"

Realizing he hadn't shot her down, a hint of relief entered her eyes. "After Tyler went to sleep in the evening. And between 1:00 and 3:00 a.m."

Sleepless nights, he thought. He'd once been there himself. Having one's world turned upside down did tend to promote a certain degree of restlessness. He figured it didn't help matters that she was trying to sleep in an unfamiliar house, in a bed she apparently wasn't accustomed to, either. She'd said the one she was now using had been in a guest room.

The thought of her in bed, tossing, turning or otherwise, had him reaching for his old briefcase.

"Let's get to the inventory. Once you know what you have to work with here, you'll know what you need to order and how much shelving space you can actually use."

"So you think this floor plan might work?"

The layout of the shelves his grandfather had built had served its purpose effectively for years. Changing anything about it hadn't even occurred to Erik. The old-fashioned footprint of the place was simply part of the store's personality. It always had been.

He'd thought it always would be.

He gave a mental snort, blocking his reaction to the change as irrelevant. No one knew better than he did how transient "always" could be. The store was hers now, he reminded himself yet again. She was free to do anything she wanted as long as she could turn a profit.

"It might. Probably," he conceded, because her plan would certainly better define the grocery section from the sporting goods. Using the big armoire to promote local artisans wasn't a bad idea, either.

Still, there was no denying the reluctance in his agreement. He could practically hear it himself. He also couldn't help but notice the small smile Rory immediately stifled.

It pleased her to know that her first instincts and efforts toward her new business were good ones. It didn't feel good to him, though, to know he'd deprived her of sharing that pleasure with the only person available. He was her mentor. He was supposed to be encouraging her. Showing a little enthusiasm.

Before he could tell her just how good her instincts probably were, she'd crossed her arms over the glittery designer logo on her hoodie and moved on.

"Before we start the inventory," she prefaced, "would you tell me about the customs your grandparents had here? One of the ladies I met said she hoped I'd have a farmers' market on the porch like the Sullivans did every summer. The other one said that the Harbor Market lighted walking kayak was missed in the Chimes and Lights parade last week."

She hadn't realized such an object even existed until Edie Shumway, the fortysomething community volunteer and, Rory suspected, neighborhood busybody, had explained what it was. Apparently Erik's grandfather and one of his cronies from the local lodge provided propulsion for the Christmas-light-covered kayak—which explained the two holes she'd finally noticed in the bottom of the one hanging from the ceiling in the back of the store.

"I'm going to call the lodge and see if I can get a couple of volunteers to walk it in the parade next year. I'll provide candy for them to throw to the kids, and get elf hats like Edie said they wore. But I need to know what else your grandparents did that I should do, too."

Erik hesitated.

"I'm not totally sure what you're after."

"Anything they did for holidays, or for community events. Or things they did every year that people looked forward to."

"Like the kayak and the elf hats," he concluded.

"Exactly. I want to belong here," she explained, as if that need meant as much to her as financial success. "I want us to fit in. The other day, your friend implied that this place was sort of an institution around here. If there are customs your grandparents had that their neighbors and customers looked forward to, then I'll keep them up the best I can."

"You want to maintain my grandparents' traditions?"

"If you'll tell me what they were."

Erik was not a man who impressed easily. Nor was it often that a woman caught him so off guard. Even as the businessman in him commended her approach to public relations, a certain self-protectiveness slipped into place.

Resting one hip on the counter, he crossed his arms over his chest, conscious of her honest interest as she waited for whatever he might be willing to share.

"They always gave suckers to the little kids." A few innocent memories would cost him nothing. And possibly help her bottom line. "And ice cream bars. Locals always got a free one on their birthday." His grandma had kept a

calendar under the cash register with the regular customers' birthdays written on it. Anniversaries were there, too.

He told her all that, ignoring an unwanted tug of nos-
talgia as he began to remember traditions he'd taken for
granted, then forgotten. Or noticed but overlooked.

"They always opened the week of the spring sailing re-
gatta in April, so they hung nautical flags along the porch
and a life preserver by the door. For the Fourth of July they
hung bunting and handed out flag stickers," he said, memories rushing back. He'd loved the Fourth as a kid. Lying
on his back in the grass to watch the fireworks over the
sound. Or better, being out on the water in a boat, watching them explode overhead.

"And every fall," he continued, thinking her little boy
would probably like it, too, "the porch would be full of
pumpkins and hay bales and they'd serve cups of cider."

With her dark eyes intent on his, she seemed completely
captivated by the small-town customs he hadn't considered
in years. She also appeared totally unaware of how close
she'd drawn to him as he spoke. As near as she'd come,
all he'd have to do was reach out and he would know for
certain if her skin felt as soft as it looked.

As his glance slid to the inviting fullness of her bottom
lip, he wondered at the softness he would find there, too.

Her lips parted with a quietly drawn breath.

When he looked back up, it was to see her glance skim
his mouth before her focus fell to his chest and she took
a step away.

"What about Thanksgiving and Christmas?" she asked,
deliberately turning to the file on the counter. "Aside from
the kayak."

Forcing his attention back to her question, he stayed
right where he was.

"Thanksgiving was just the fall stuff. But the day after,
Gramps would string lights along all the eaves and porch

posts and set up a Christmas village with a giant lighted snowman." There had been a time when he and his dad had usually helped. That was back when Thanksgiving dinner had always been here. Christmas had been at his parents' house, around the bend and in town a couple of miles. After the aircraft company his dad worked for had transferred him to San Diego a few years ago, he'd headed south for that particular holiday.

"The store was closed for the season by then, so I don't think they gave anything out. At least, not the past several years." He hadn't been around to know for sure. Seattle was only twelve miles as the crow flew, but he lived his life what felt like a world away. Unless his grandparents had needed something before they'd moved south, too, he'd given this place and the areas around it as little thought as possible. And he'd never given it as much thought as he had just now. "But a lot of people drove by to see the light display."

Whatever self-consciousness she'd felt vanished as she glanced back to him. "Where are the lights now?"

"They were sold."

"The snowman, too?"

"Everything. They had a garage sale before they moved."

For reasons he couldn't begin to explain, he wasn't at all surprised by her disappointment. What did surprise him was that he actually felt a twinge of it himself.

"Tyler would have loved to have a big snowman out there," she said. "And the village. He gets so excited when he sees Christmas decorations."

Threading her fingers through her hair, she gave him a rueful smile. "Unfortunately, I'd thought I was moving somewhere a lot smaller, so I sold everything for outside except a few strings of lights."

With the lift of her shoulder, she attempted to shrug off

what she could do nothing about now, anyway. "What else is there I should know?"

From the pensiveness in her voice, there wasn't a doubt in his mind that she was still thinking about how her little boy would have loved what his grandparents had done.

"I can't think of anything right now." Wanting to get her mind off what she couldn't do for her son, and his thoughts off her mouth, he rose from his perch. "But if I do, I'll let you know."

"One more thing," she said as he turned to his brief-case. "Everything I've heard so far tells me this will be a good place to live. But what do you think about it? The community, I mean."

Just wanting to get to work, he opened the case with the snap of its lock. "It is a good place. I grew up in town, but I was around here a lot, too. I even came back after college." Paper rustled as he pulled out a sheaf heavy enough for a doorstop. "Pax and I first went into business about a mile down the road." The stack landed on the counter. "You and your son should be fine here."

Considering that Erik had apparently lived much of his life there, it seemed to Rory that the entire area had to mean a lot to him. "Why did you leave?"

He pulled another stack of paper from his scarred brief-case. For a dozen seconds, his only response was dead silence.

"Didn't your business do well?" she prompted.

"The business did fine."

"Then if this is a good place to live and your business was doing well, why did you go?"

The defenses Erik had attempted to ignore finally slammed into place. He knew her question was entirely reasonable. It was one he'd want answered himself were he on the other end of their agreement. Yet as valid as her query was, it bumped straight into the part of his life that had led to an entirely different existence than he'd once thought he'd be living by now.

His plans had been unremarkable, really. No different from half the guys he knew: a good marriage, build boats, a couple of kids, maybe a dog. The one out of four he did have was 90 percent of his life. It was a good life, too. The rest he'd written off completely years ago.

"It has nothing to do with here."

"What did it have to do with, then?"

"Nothing you'd need to be concerned about."

"How can I be sure of that if I don't know what it is you're not telling me? If you were getting your life established here," she pointed out, "it's hard for me to imagine why you'd leave. You seem too much in command of yourself and everything around you to do that if you'd really wanted to stay. That's why your reason for leaving is important to me." She tipped her head, tried to catch his glance. "Was this place lacking something?"

She'd stated her conclusions about him more as fact than compliment. As if she saw his influence over his surroundings as basic to him as his DNA. He'd have been flattered by her impression of him, too, had it not been for how much control he'd actually given up to save the marriage that had ultimately ended anyway. He could see where she deserved something more than he'd given her, though. After insisting his business had been fine there and that she would be, too, he did feel somewhat obligated to explain why he hadn't stuck around himself.

"It didn't lack for anything," he admitted. At least, it hadn't as far as he'd been concerned. "I left because my ex-wife wanted to teach in the city for a few years before coming back to raise a family. Those few years led to a few more and she changed her mind. About coming back and about the family," he admitted, making a long story as short as possible. "When we left here, the business had barely gotten off the ground. But by the time I realized we weren't coming back, Pax and I were established in Ballard. We had a good location. We had good people working for us. So it made sense to stay there. Like I said, my leaving had nothing to do with anything around here."

Thinking he'd covered all the bases, he added two more stacks of papers to the first.

"She was a teacher?"

"Kindergarten," he said without looking up. "She was great with kids."

Her voice went soft. "You wanted children?"

A folder landed on the pile. "Let's get to this, shall we?"

He'd said as much as he was going to. He'd closed the door on all the excuses Shauna had come up with to delay having a baby, and on how he'd hung in there because he'd promised to be there for better or worse. She'd kept asking him to bear with her on the baby thing. Especially after his business took off. She'd eventually changed her mind about a baby, but only after they'd divorced and she'd remarried. He'd realized then that it wasn't that she hadn't wanted children. She just hadn't wanted his. She'd had no problem, however, keeping the house and a hefty chunk of their assets.

Frowning at his thoughts, he turned the whole stack of what he'd unloaded toward Rory. The past was just that. Past. Over. Done.

Rory saw a muscle in his jaw jerk.

The demise of his marriage evidently hadn't been his choice.

She thought that an incredibly sad thing to have in common. She'd had no choice in hers ending, either.

"I'm sorry about your wife."

"Ex."

"Ex-wife," she corrected. She spoke quietly, feeling bad for having pushed, worse for what she'd discovered. He'd once had plans to build his life in the fiercely beautiful surroundings where he'd grown up, but circumstances had forced him to move away, and move on. Just as circumstances had forced her in an entirely different direction than she would have chosen, and led her to the very place she strongly suspected he truly no longer wanted to be.

"Marriage can be complicated," she said, beginning to appreciate the roots of his restiveness. "That must be why it's never easy no matter how it ends."

The furnace kicked on with the rattle of the floor vent behind the counter. His head down, his hand on the printout, Erik slowly ruffled a corner of the pages with his thumb.

He'd heard understanding in her voice, suspected he'd see it in her fragile features were he to look up. She seemed to think they shared the same kind of pain.

He didn't want that kind of sympathy. He didn't want to poke around at what he'd finally grown so far beyond, or into what was undoubtedly fresher and more painful territory for her. And he definitely didn't want to be as curious as he couldn't seem to help being about her, or the man she'd married. She'd once spoken of her child's loss. There'd been no doubt in his mind at the time that she hurt for her son. He just hadn't considered how the boy's pain could easily compound the depth of the loss she felt herself.

Mostly, though, he didn't want her getting so close, or to get close to her. Emotionally, anyway. Physically would be just fine. Heaven knew he was aware of her in ways he had no business considering. But she didn't seem anything like many of the women he knew, those looking for a good time, no commitments involved. Not that he'd been intimate with anyone in longer than he cared to remember. He didn't want any commitments, either. Still, he'd grown tired of the games, the shallow conversations and walking away feeling little more than...empty.

He gave the top folder a nudge. "I'm sorry about yours, too," he admitted, because he didn't need to know the details to feel bad for her. "And you can have a good business here," he assured, because it was his job to help her make that happen. "We just need to get to work so we can make sure of it.

"This is my grandfather's business plan," he said, opening the folder. "Since you're new to all this, it'll be your bible. We can tweak it as we go, but to get you up and running, it'll be simpler not to deviate from it too much at first. This—" he pulled the top printout forward "—is a stock list of the groceries they kept on hand, divided by type and vendor. Dairy, produce, snacks, staples, that sort of thing.

"This printout," he said, indicating the tallest stack of paper, "is your sporting goods department. There are certain vendors you'll need to order from weeks or months in advance. Others can ship in twenty-four hours. You'll want to get their new catalogs. Gramps said they're all online, but some will mail hard copies. You'll need to establish accounts in your name with all of them."

He handed her a CD. "It's all on here for ordering and bookkeeping purposes. Look through it, list your questions and we'll go over them later. I want to get you started on the physical inventory. You need to know what you have on hand, so it's as good a way as any to get your feet wet."

The change of subject was as subtle to Rory as the slam of a door. He would share anything that would help her make a success of the business. But his personal life was now off-limits. Despite how deftly he'd closed off his past, however, he'd revealed wounds that might well have taken years to heal. Family mattered to him. His dreams had mattered. Once.

She'd give anything to know how he'd survived knowing that the woman he'd married had no longer loved him.

For her, even harder than Curt's death was the knowledge that he might not have ever loved her at all.

The deep tones of Erik's voice somehow overrode the sick sensation that inevitably came with the thought. Or maybe it was simply his no-nonsense presence that managed to keep that awful feeling at bay.

"We can start with things you can probably identify even if you've never used them. Camp stoves, lanterns, backpacking gear," he said. "Or go with something that might be more of a challenge. Your choice."

He was there to teach her what she needed to know to reopen the store, not about how to live with questions that could now never be answered. From his deliberate allusion to her lack of knowledge about certain outdoor activities, she had the feeling, too, that he intended his baiting to pull her out of her thoughts. If not for her sake, definitely for his own.

Since he had far more experience with both the store and self-survival, the least she could do was follow his lead.

"More of a challenge."

He said he wasn't surprised.

First, though, she brought them each a cup of coffee, his black, hers with milk, which they took with a section of the printouts and a notepad to the back of the store. It was there that he told her he needed to leave by two o'clock, which, thankfully, was a few minutes before she needed to leave to catch the ferry to pick up Tyler. So for the next hour, she learned to identify lures, hooks, rods, reels, creels, the difference between a bobber and a sinker and the different weights of leader—which would be important to know, he told her, if a customer came in asking for twenty-pound test. At least now she'd know they were asking for fishing line.

"If someone wants fish, wouldn't it be a whole lot more convenient to buy it from a grocery store?"

Towering beside her, he remained focused on a column of item numbers. "Might be convenient, but it wouldn't be nearly as much fun."

"I take it you've never been to Pike Place Fish Market." She focused on a page of her own. "You pick out the fish you want and the guys behind the cases toss it down the line to the scale. You get it wrapped, packed, you don't have to gut it and the show is free. That's fun enough for me."

With that even-eyed way he had of looking at her, he slanted her a tolerant glance. "You're missing the point."

"The point being?"

"Being in the great outdoors. The thrill of landing a thirty-pound salmon, or pulling an eight-pound rainbow trout from a freshwater stream."

"The guilt of taking Nemo from his mother," she muttered.

"What?"

"Never mind. I doubt that you know him."

"Please tell me that's not the approach you're going to take with your customers," he muttered back, just before his glance dropped to her mouth—which had the odd effect of shutting her up and getting her back to verifying counts.

They didn't have time to move on to the modest sections of hiking, camping or boating equipment before she noticed the time. Since she had to drive right past the marina at the end of the street, and he'd tied his floatplane there, she asked if she could give him a ride and save him the two-block walk in the misty rain.

Conscious of the time himself, he told her that would be great. She could go over the rest of the inventory on her own and call him with any questions. They'd meet again next week after she'd gone over the business plan. He also asked if he could take the drawing of her new floor plan with him.

Thinking he intended to give the layout she wanted some thought, she handed it over, along with a travel mug of coffee since he seemed to like hers. Minutes later, he'd just tossed his briefcase into the back of her fuel-efficient little car and folded his big frame into the passenger seat when her cell phone chimed.

One glance at the caller ID had her bracing herself an instant before she dropped the phone back into her bag, started the engine and backed up. The phone continued to chime as she pulled onto the wet two-lane road and headed down the rise.

Erik's glance cut from her purse to her profile.

"I'll call her back," she said. "It's Audrey. My mother-in-law. She's calling about plans for Christmas." The woman was actually returning Rory's call, something it had taken her three days to do. The conversation would be short, but it wasn't one she wanted to have with Erik in the car.

"She *was* my mother-in-law," she corrected. Technically, Rory was no longer related to the Linfields. Audrey had apparently pointed that out to Lillian Brinkley, the wife of the country club president, who had ever so thoughtfully shared it in the ladies' room with two other members of the socially connected among the mourners at Curt's funeral. Rory had been seeking a few minutes of quiet while closed in a stall at the time.

According to Audrey, via Lillian, Rory's vows with her son had been "until death do them part." They'd parted, however sadly. End of legal relationship.

As strained as her relationship with Curt's parents had always been beneath the polite manners and civility, Rory hadn't doubted the remarks at all.

"She's really only Tyler's grandmother now." That was the only part that mattered, anyway.

The wipers swiped at the heavy mist on the windshield. Through the veil of gray, the little marina came into clearer view. Erik barely noticed. For a couple of hours he'd caught glimpses of a woman whose guard with him had begun to ease, a smart, savvy woman who possessed no small amount of determination, ingenuity and a remarkable willingness to step beyond her comfort zone.

What he saw now was a woman doing her level best to mask disquiet. He'd seen her do it before, for her son's sake. Her attempts seemed to work fine on her five-year-old, but Erik recognized strain when he saw it. With her eyes on the road, he watched her take a deep breath, slowly ease it out.

Whatever was going on with Tyler's grandmother had her hands going tight on the wheel.

The heater whirred in its struggle to produce warmth, gravel crunching beneath the tires as she pulled to a stop by the wooden stairs that led to the long floating dock. In the choppy, chill water of the sound, his white Cessna Amphibian floated and yawed where he'd secured it at the end of the pier, well away from the few sport boats moored there this time of year.

He almost always felt better flying from this place than toward it.

"Thank you for your help today," she murmured, her hands now tucked at her waist, her shoulders hunched against the still-cold air. "I'll come up to speed on everything as fast as I can. I promise."

The bravado behind her smile pulled at protective instincts he'd rather ignore. He knew she wanted to belong there, in a place she'd known absolutely nothing about until last week. He knew she wanted to make a good home for her son. He suspected, too, that she could use a little reassurance on both counts.

After all, she was pretty much on her own here.

"I'll pass that on to our benefactor," he promised back, wanting to keep his purpose there in perspective. "And for what it's worth, Rory, you and your son really should do well here." He hesitated, perspective faltering. "I'd always thought it was a good place to raise a child."

He reached for the door, cold salt air blasting in as he opened it. "I'll call you next week. In the meantime, call me if you have questions." He climbed out, then ducked his head back in to retrieve his case from the backseat. "Thanks for the ride."

Rory had barely opened her mouth to tell him he was welcome before the door closed. In the space of a heartbeat she'd swallowed the words and was staring at his broad, leather-covered shoulders as he headed for the weathered stairs.

He'd made it halfway down the dock, his long stride sure and certain despite the drift and roll beneath his feet, when she finally put the car into gear. Even with the surface beneath him shifting with the unpredictable current, the man seemed as steady as a rock.

I'd always thought it was a good place to raise a child.

The admission had cost him. She felt as certain of that as she did of her gratitude for his having shared it. He knew his opinion mattered to her. She'd told him so herself. But sharing that particular thought had also demanded a hasty retreat back to the world he now lived in, back to a world so different from what he'd once wanted.

What stung, though, wasn't how anxious he'd been to retreat to the life he'd created for himself. It was the sharp, undeniable feeling that he had quite deliberately retreated from her.

Chapter Five

Rory returned the call to Curt's mother within a minute of dropping off Erik at the dock. When Audrey didn't answer, she left a message saying she was sorry she'd missed her and asking her to please call back as soon as it was convenient.

Despite two other attempts to reach her, it apparently hadn't been "convenient" for four days.

The conversation they'd had still had Rory reeling three hours later. Thanks to the distraction a text from Erik provided, however, at that particular moment she didn't have to struggle to mask the resentment, offense and indignation she wasn't about to impose on her little boy, anyway.

"Is Erik at our new house now, Mom?"

Following the beam of her headlights through the steady rain, she murmured, "Probably, honey."

"Can I help him again?"

"We'll have to see. I'm not sure why he's coming."

The text she'd received from Erik that morning hadn't given her a clue.

Am in mtgs. Need to know if you will be home around 6.

She'd texted back that she'd be there by 6:15 p.m.

His reply had been a wholly unenlightening See you then.

Since he'd indicated he'd be in meetings, she hadn't called to see what he wanted. She hadn't talked to him at all since he'd closed her out at the dock last week, even though he'd told her to call if she had any questions.

She had dozens. Between online catalogs and searches, she'd figured out the answers to most of them, though, and talked herself out of contacting him about the rest. Those she simply added to her list to ask at their next meeting. Partly because they weren't urgent. Mostly because she suspected that what she really wanted was more of the relief she'd so briefly experienced when he'd assured her that she and Tyler would be all right. The sensation hadn't lasted long enough to do much more than tease her with the hope of finding the security she hadn't truly felt in forever, but she desperately needed to feel something positive about the more personal aspects of her life—and that wasn't something she should be seeking from him at all.

There also existed the unnerving little fact that she'd just wanted to hear his voice—something she insisted she shouldn't even be thinking about, considering that she was nothing more than an obligation to him.

That glaring bit of reality mingled with her turmoil over her in-laws as she turned onto the gravel drive just past the store. Through the silvery drizzle, her headlights illuminated a black, bull-nosed pickup truck loaded with something large covered in plastic.

She'd barely pulled into the garage and gathered her

groceries from the backseat when Erik strode up and plucked the heavy sack from her arms.

"Anything else back there?" he asked.

Raindrops glistened in his dark hair, beaded on his leather jacket. His impersonal glance swept her face, his brow pinching at whatever it was he saw in her expression.

Not about to stand there trying to figure out what that something might be, she turned away. "Just one bag. I can get it."

Ignoring her, he reached into the car as Tyler raced around the back bumper and came to a screeching stop.

One strap of his green dinosaur backpack hung over his shoulder. The other dangled behind him as he looked up with a shy "Hi."

Erik straightened, looking down at the child looking up at him. "Hi yourself, sport."

Anticipation fairly danced in her little boy's hazel eyes.

As if unable to help himself, Erik smiled back and held out the bag of apples he'd snagged off the seat. "Do you want to take this?"

At Tyler's vigorous nod, he waited for the child to wrap his arms around the bag, then nudged him toward the warmth of the house. With Tyler doing double time to match Erik's long strides, Rory punched the remote to close the garage door and hurried to catch up, clutching her shoulder bag and keys.

She couldn't believe how pleased Tyler looked to see him.

"Were you on the ferry?" she asked, torn between her son's growing fascination with the man and trying to imagine why he was there.

"I took the long way around. I had a meeting in Tacoma," he told her, speaking of a town at the south end of the sound, "so I drove. Jake was on it, though. He should be right behind you."

"Jake?"

"One of our craftsmen." Rain glittered through the pool of pale yellow light that arced from the neat back porch. Even in that spare illumination, Erik could see strain in the delicate lines of her face, could hear it in her voice. "I'll explain when we get inside."

He watched her hurry ahead of him. Her head down, she unlocked the door and ushered Tyler inside, reminding him to wipe his feet on the way.

The mudroom, with its pegs for coats, cabinets for storage and the double sink his grandmother had used for repotting plants, opened into the kitchen. The warmer air held the same welcome it always had, but no longer did it smell of the pine disinfectant his grandmother had used with abandon when mopping the floors. Now lingering hints of lemon soap gave way to scents of cinnamon and orange as Rory distractedly flipped on lights and told him to set the bags anywhere.

The island of the neatly organized kitchen seemed as good a place as any. As he set the bags on the laminate surface, his glance cut to where she'd left on a lamp at the far end of the long, open space.

She'd just moved in last week, yet everything appeared to be in order. Furniture had been pushed, pulled or shoved into place. Drapes and pictures were hung. Not a box remained in sight.

Not a hint of what had once been familiar remained, either.

The walls had been bare for over a year. Having walked through that empty space a dozen times, it no longer felt strange without the chaos of floral patterns and knick-knacks his grandparents had acquired living there. But with that blank canvas redecorated, the sense he'd had the other day of no longer belonging there, of having lost a piece of himself, threatened to surface once more. He didn't doubt that it would have, too, had the unexpected ease of what she'd created not distracted him from it.

The well-defined spaces now bore his student's decidedly understated stamp. The heavy wood pieces he'd carried in were dark and substantial enough to make a man feel comfortable, but balanced by shades of ivory and taupe that felt amazingly...restful.

The rustic refectory table with its high-backed chairs held a large pewter bowl filled with glittered pinecones and cinnamon potpourri. Beyond it, the deeply cushioned sofa faced the stone fireplace at the end of the room. A long, narrow sofa table behind it held a trio of thick cream-colored candles. The two armchairs he'd brought in had been positioned to one side, a heavy end table stacked with books and a chrome lamp between them.

He turned to see that she'd left her raincoat in the mudroom. The apples and her shoulder bag had landed on the desk by the now child's-art-covered refrigerator—mostly red-and-green construction paper bells. Sinking to her heels in front of her little boy, she worked his jacket's zipper.

"You've been busy."

Oblivious to what had his attention, conscious only of his presence, Rory understated considerably.

"A little," she replied, thinking of the day she'd had and how desperately glad she was for it to be nearing its end. "I had a meeting with the probate attorney." Now that the house had sold, she'd had more paperwork to sign. "And I had to go to the bank to close the safe-deposit box, then go straighten out my medical insurance."

The good news was that she could pay the attorney's fees and increased insurance costs from the proceeds of the sale of the house. The not so good part was that both cost more than she'd expected—which meant she'd have to forgo the new sign and new shelving she'd hoped to have for her store's grand opening. And buy a considerably smaller Christmas tree than a version of the megadollar, floor-to-ceiling noble fir that had so mesmerized Tyler at his school. She'd already ruled out buying more outdoor lights to pay for the ferry rides.

Budget concerns, however, had taken a backseat to the varying degrees of anger and hurt she'd been busy stifling all afternoon. Thanks to Curt's mother.

"After I picked Tyler up from school," she continued, "we dropped off library books and went grocery shopping before we caught the ferry."

"And saw Santa ringing a bell at the store," supplied Tyler, still in Christmas mode. "Not the real Santa," he explained. "Mommy said he was a helper." He gave a sage little nod. "The real Santa has lots of helpers."

"Be tough to do all he does alone," she explained. Her little boy's zipper now freed, she rose and headed for the bags. "I hope the milk stayed cold."

Erik had never seen her in a suit and heels before. A crisp white blouse peeked from beneath the black jacket that curved at her waist and hugged the hips of her slim pencil skirt. Black tights covered the long, shapely line of her legs. As he glanced up from her spike-thin heels, he had to admit he hadn't seen her truly upset before, either. Though she definitely was, and trying hard to hide it.

"I meant you've been busy around here."

Apparently realizing the extent of her preoccupation, she met his eyes and promptly closed hers with a sigh.

"Can I have an apple?" Tyler asked.

She forced herself to brighten. "You'll ruin your appetite, sweetie." Taking his head between her hands, she kissed the top of it, hard, and tipped his face to hers. "Hang up your jacket and empty your backpack. Dinner will be ready in a few minutes."

With Tyler dragging his jacket into the mudroom, she reached into the nearest bag to unload groceries. She'd just put the milk in the fridge and grabbed two boxes of cereal when she turned on her stylish heel.

The boxes landed on the counter three feet from where Erik watched her with his hands in the pockets of his cargos. The stance pulled the sides of his jacket back from the navy pullover covering his chest and made his shoulders look broad enough to bear the weight of the world.

It seemed terribly unfair just then to be taunted by the memory of how very solid his chest had felt. Especially when she so badly wanted to be held against it. But fair hadn't been a big part of her day.

"I'm sorry." She shook her head, the neat wedge of her hair swinging. "You didn't drive all the way here to watch me put away groceries." She tried for a smile. "May I get you something? Juice? Milk?" Neither sounded very adult. "Coffee?"

He took a step toward her. "I didn't come to interrupt. I just want to drop off your shelving."

"My shelving?"

"The three units for the back of the store. I had a couple of the guys work on them with me over the weekend. With Christmas coming, they were up for the overtime. One of the units is in the back of my truck. Jake is bringing the rest."

Disbelief cut through the anxiety that sat like a knot beneath her breastbone. They'd barely discussed her layout to update the market. Though he'd said it would probably work, he hadn't even bothered to tell her whether or not he liked the idea. All she'd done was show him her sketch, explain why she wanted it and all of a sudden the shelving she'd felt certain would now have to wait had materialized. He made it happen just like that, as if he was some sort of…fairy godfather.

The man fairly leaked masculinity. As utterly male as he was and so *not* fatherly in the way he'd checked out her legs, the thought would have made her laugh had she not felt like crying.

"You made my shelves?"

"You wanted them, didn't you?"

She wanted world peace, too, but that didn't mean she expected it to happen.

She raked her fingers through her hair, wondering if they were a gift, which she couldn't accept without reimbursing him. Wondering, too, how much he'd paid his men, since it was undoubtedly more than she could afford.

"Yes. Absolutely. I'm just…" *Speechless,* she thought. "Thank you," she concluded, because she had no idea what else to say before the ring of his cell phone had him pulling the instrument from his pocket.

After two short beeps and a glance at the text, he muttered, "Jake's out front," and dropped the phone back into his pocket. "I'll be back in a few minutes. Then you can tell me what's wrong."

Certain he was referring to her less than gracious reaction, she said, "Nothing is wrong. You just caught me off guard. I never expected you to make the shelves—"

"I meant what was wrong with you when I got here."

Oh. That.

Thinking him far too astute, uncomfortable with that, too, she turned for the cereal. "It's nothing."

Moving with her, Erik stopped scant inches from her back. With Tyler just around the corner, he lowered his voice to nearly a whisper. "Lying is a bad example to set for a child."

Conscious of his warm breath moving her hair, her head still down, she lowered her voice, too. "Then how about it's nothing I can talk about in front of him?"

"That's better." Taking a step back, he indicated the door near the stairway. "I need to get into the store. Mind if I go in through the living room?"

Since he tended to do what he wanted to do anyway, she was a little surprised that he'd asked. Mostly, she was just conscious of how close his muscular body still was to hers. All she'd have to do was turn around...

She shook her head, swallowed hard. "Not at all."

"Give me half an hour. I'll be back."

Twenty minutes was actually all the time it took him and his employee to unload the sections of the three shelving units from a company vehicle and the back of Erik's truck. It wasn't long enough, however, for Erik to question why he couldn't leave well enough alone with the woman he'd spent the past few days trying not to think about at all. Not beyond her needs for the store, anyway. He'd told her to call him if she needed anything. Since she hadn't, he'd assumed she was doing fine.

Except she clearly was not. Even when he let himself back inside, greeted by the scent of something delicious, there was no mistaking the disquiet she was still trying to hide.

Tyler smiled from where he sat on the dining room side of the island. Beyond him, light glowed through the glass-paned white cabinets, revealing neat stacks and rows of plates and glasses.

"Mom's making mac and cheese. It's my favorite. You want some?"

"Mom" had shed her jacket and heels. She stood across from them in her stocking feet, stirring a pot on the stove. The cuffs of her white blouse had been folded back. A green dish towel had been tied into an apron at the waist of her skirt. Erik knew she'd heard him come in, but it was her son's innocent invitation that had her looking over her shoulder with apology in her expression.

"I told him you probably already had plans," she said,

sounding as if she fully expected his refusal and had already prepared her son for it. "But he wanted to ask anyway."

Had this been any other woman, any other child, Erik knew without a doubt that he'd have done what she obviously expected and come up with some excuse for not being able to stick around for dinner. With just the three of them, the beat of the rain against the windows and the cozy warmth of the kitchen countering the cold outside, the scenario felt entirely too domestic for him.

He wanted to know what had upset her, though. If for no reason other than to be sure it wouldn't impede her progress with the store. Or so he told himself. He also knew she wasn't going to say a word about whatever it was as long as her son was present.

Then there was the little boy himself. With Tyler looking all hopeful, he simply didn't have the heart to say no.

"Mac and cheese, huh?"

Again, the quick nod. "It's really good."

"Then I guess I'd better stay." He looked to the woman at the stove, caught the strain countering the softness of her smile. "That okay, 'Mom'?"

Her hesitation held uncertainty, and collided with something that looked suspiciously like gratitude for indulging her child. "Of course it is. Tyler?" she asked. "Let's move your place mat to the table and get another one from the sideboard for Erik."

Erik tossed his jacket across the stool next to where Tyler sat. As he did, the boy scrambled down and grabbed his pine-green place mat from the island. Intent on his mission, he laid it on the heavy oak table, then pulled a matching one from a long drawer in the printer's cabinet his mom had pushed to the wall by the stairs.

He'd just set the mat across from the other when he looked back to the man tracking his progress. "Do you want to see my boat?"

Erik hadn't a clue what had prompted the question. Seconds ago they'd been talking about food. With a shrug, he said, "Sure," and the little boy was off.

Wondering if the kid's energy ever ran low, he walked over to where Rory spooned dinner into two shallow pasta bowls.

"What can I do?" he asked.

"You've already done it," she said quietly. "He's wanted to show you that boat ever since you said you build them. After you told him about the boats outside Cornelia's office, it was nearly all he talked about." She turned, a bowl in each hand. "But if you want, set these on the table for the two of you while I slice another tomato. That would be great."

Handing them over, she slipped past him to take two salad plates from the cupboard.

"Where's yours?"

"I'm not hungry. What do you want to drink?" she asked, pointedly avoiding his scrutiny as he set the bowls on the table.

Walking toward them with his toy, Tyler announced that he wanted milk.

Rory told him she knew he did. As she set salads of tomatoes, herbs and olive oil above their place mats, she also said she knew he really wanted to show Erik his boat, but right now he needed to sit down and eat his dinner before it got cold.

She appeared as calm and unruffled to Erik as he'd always seen her with her son. Still, he recognized restlessness when faced with it. There was no mistaking the nerves that had her too keyed up to sit down herself. She seemed to be using motion as a means to keep that tension under control as she started pulling measuring cups, flour and a big wooden spoon from cabinets, cupboards and drawers.

Intimately familiar himself with the cathartic effects of

movement, specifically his usual morning run or sanding teak until his arms ached, he said nothing about her joining them. While she moved about the kitchen side of the island, he turned his attention to the boy who'd docked his little blue plastic boat on the table between them.

His fork in his fist, Tyler stabbed a noodle. "It's my Christmas boat."

It certainly was.

The miniature ski boat held a hunk of clay middeck. A peppermint-striped straw stuck up from the little blob like a mast. More clay anchored a bit of pencil-thin neon-green tinsel from bow to mast and mast to stern.

He'd rigged the tinsel on it just like the lighted boats they'd talked about in Cornelia's office.

Erik couldn't believe how deeply touched he was by the boy's innocent desire to share something of his with him. Or how humbled he felt by the innocent expectation in the child's eyes.

The silence coming from the table had Rory nearly holding her breath as she waited for Erik to acknowledge what her son had shared.

He finally picked up the toy, turned it in his big hands.

She could have hugged him when he said, "Now that is one awesome sailboat."

Tyler beamed.

Rory felt her heart squeeze.

Setting the child's handiwork back on the table, Erik pointed his fork at the bow. "Do you know what that's called?" he asked.

"The front?"

"That, too," came his easy reply. "But in nautical terms, the front of a boat is called its bow."

"What's 'not-cul'?"

"Nautical," Erik emphasized with a smile. "It means things relating to boats and sailors," he added, which led

Tyler to ask what the back was called. That led to a discussion of stern, port, starboard and keel, the latter of which his ski boat didn't have, but which Erik fashioned out of a paper napkin just so Tyler would get the idea of what one looked like.

When Rory casually mentioned that she was going to have to reheat their dinner if they didn't start eating, conversation turned to the merits of shell-shaped pasta over elbow while they cleaned their bowls. Over pudding for dessert, talk then turned back to the boat—specifically the differences between sail and motor.

Her child ate up the attention her mentor so generously bestowed while she put cranberry muffins into the oven to have with breakfast and cleared their dishes. By the time she'd finished cleaning up the kitchen and removed the muffins from the oven twenty minutes later, it was nearing Tyler's bedtime, and she didn't want to impose on Erik any further.

"It's time to put the boat away," she finally told him. "Say good-night to Erik now, okay? And go brush your teeth. I'll be up in a few minutes to tuck you in."

She'd thought he would do as she'd asked and simply say good-night. Instead, with his toy under one arm, he walked to where Erik stood by the island and wrapped his free arm around the man's thigh. "'Night, Erik," he said.

She wasn't sure who was caught more off guard by the unexpected hug—her or the man who went completely still a moment before his big hand settled on Tyler's head.

"'Night, sport," he murmured back. "Thanks for showing me your boat."

Tyler tipped back his head, gave him a smile. "You're welcome."

Her conversation with her former mother-in-law already had Rory's maternal instincts on high alert. Torn between allowing the draw her child obviously felt toward someone who would be out of their lives in a matter of months and the need to protect him from it, she took him by his little shoulders and eased him back.

"Teeth," she reminded him, and turned him around to get him headed in the right direction.

"Can I read?" he asked on his way.

"Until I get there," she called after him.

"'Kay," he called back and disappeared up the stairs.

"He's a neat kid." The admission came almost reluctantly, as if he hadn't wanted to be as impressed—or touched—as he was by a five-year-old. "I don't know how long it's been since he lost his dad, but you seem to be doing a great job with him."

It had been fourteen months that sometimes felt like mere weeks. Sometimes, strangely, as if it had been years.

"It was a year ago in October. And thank you," she offered at the compliment. "Thank you for being so nice to him, too. I'm sure you had other things to do tonight, but you just made his week. He's not around men very often," she said, compelled to explain why her son had monopolized his evening. "And he really misses his dad."

"I imagine he does." The agreement brought a frown. "What about relatives? Grandfathers? Uncles?"

She shrugged. "My parents are in Colorado." This month, anyway. Heaven only knew where they'd be this time next year. "I'm an only child. So were my parents. So that's it for my side. Curt's family is in Seattle, but his parents aren't…available." Pushing her fingers through her hair, she could practically feel the hurt building in her chest. Even with Tyler out of earshot, her voice sank at the heartlessness of what had been said. "Actually," she conceded, "they don't want anything to do with him."

He took a step closer, his brow dropping right along with his voice. "Why wouldn't they want to see their grandson?"

The need to restrain her resentment pushed hard. The

hurt pushed back. It was Erik's expression, though, the unquestioning disapproval in it, that urged her on.

"Until a few hours ago, I'd thought it was just because of me," she admitted, pride biting the dust. "I don't care about having a relationship with Curt's parents for myself. I gave up wanting their acceptance a long time ago. But they're family. Tyler's, anyway," she clarified, reminded again of how succinctly her change in status had been pointed out to Audrey's friends. "For his sake, I did want him to have a relationship with them. I wanted him to have traditions.

"Especially this time of year," she hurried on. "Curt and I barely had time to start our own and my parents never had any." None that counted, anyway. None she wanted to pass on. "But as much as anything, I'd hoped he'd have a sense of being part of more than just him and me."

This wasn't the first time she'd mentioned traditions to him. The last time he'd been there, she'd made learning those his grandparents had maintained over the years a huge priority. But discovering why she apparently lacked those bits of history herself—and, if he had to guess, the sense of belonging that came with sharing them—would have to wait. He was far more interested in what had her looking agitated enough to pace the walls.

Until a few hours ago, she'd said.

"Does this have something to do with that call from his grandmother when you dropped me off last week?"

It had everything to do with it. It also surprised her that he remembered it.

"I finally talked to her this afternoon. I already knew she didn't want me to be part of their Christmas Day," she told him, hating how she'd even let that matter to her. "But I'd hoped I could stop by for an hour or so with Tyler on Christmas Eve so he could spend some time with them. Audrey hadn't sounded thrilled with the idea when I first asked," she admitted, understating considerably, "but she'd said she'd get back to me. She called while I was on my way from the lawyer's to pick up Tyler at school."

Rory would be forever grateful that Tyler hadn't been in the car at the time. She had known for years that the senior Linfields hadn't approved of her. She'd just had no idea until that call how little they'd cared about the child their son had so dearly loved. "She and Curt's father decided it best that there be no further contact between us. She said it was just too painful for them to see me or 'the boy.'"

The hurt she felt for her son shadowed her eyes, filled her hushed voice as slights of past years could no longer be ignored.

"I should have seen this coming." She turned toward the rack of muffins cooling on the counter. Turned right back. "Nothing about this ever came up while Curt was alive, but since his death they haven't wanted to spend any time with Tyler at all." Twice she had arranged to meet them. Once for Curt's father's birthday so Tyler could give him the present he'd made for him, a collage of photos of Tyler and his dad. Once for a trip to the zoo. Both had been canceled by last-minute calls from Audrey. "I'm just glad I hadn't told him we'd be seeing them at Christmas. It's so much easier on him to not get his hopes up at all than to have him be disappointed all over again."

She turned back to the muffins, brushed a couple of crumbs from the counter into her palm, took two steps to the sink.

"What are you going to tell him if he asks about seeing them?"

"I don't know. I haven't had time to figure that out."

"Maybe they'll change their minds."

With a glance toward him, the crumbs landed on white porcelain.

"Only if you believe in hell freezing over."

The rush of water in pipes told her the child under discussion remained occupied in the upstairs bathroom. Still, her voice grew quieter as agitation had her turning away, turning back once more.

"Audrey said that they feel no bond with him." She spoke bluntly, as Audrey had. "That they never have. She said they tried while Curt was alive, for Curt's sake, but with him gone, there was no need to keep up the pretense. He's not their son's blood, so they want nothing to do with him. Apparently, they already amended their will to delete Curt's 'legal offspring.' Heaven forbid 'the boy' should get a penny of their precious money."

Caution crossed the hard angles of Erik's face.

"Not their son's blood." He repeated her words slowly, as if to make sure he hadn't misunderstood. "He's not Curt's child?"

As upset as she was, as insulted and offended as she was for her son, that caution barely registered. "Not biologically. We adopted him. We've had him since he was two days old," she explained, going with the bonds that really mattered. To her, anyway. "We didn't know until after a year of trying that Curt couldn't have children. It wasn't anything we ever discussed with anyone," she added in a rush. "We just said that the opportunity to adopt came up and we couldn't say no. After nearly four years and no other children, I'm sure his parents figured the problem was with me.

"Not that it matters," she muttered, hugging her arms around her waist. "And not that I'll ever tell them otherwise. They hadn't liked me the minute they found out I was Curt's secretary and not a lawyer myself. You could actually *see* them withdraw when they found that out. It got even worse when they found out my 'people' weren't the right pedigree. But Tyler's a *child*," she insisted, only to forget whatever else she'd been about to say when she realized all that she'd said already.

Erik looked as if he wasn't about to interrupt her. Though one dark eyebrow had arched significantly, at which detail she couldn't be sure, he was clearly waiting for her to continue.

Appalled by the scope of personal detail she'd just dumped at his feet, she closed her eyes and turned away. Rubbing her forehead, she muttered, "I cannot believe I just told you that."

His hand curved over her shoulder. The comforting weight of it barely registered before he turned her back around.

"Which part?"

"About Curt's…"

"Inability to father a child?" he asked when her voice drifted off.

She gave a nod, not at all sure how she felt having divulged something that, until moments ago, had been only between her, her husband and their fertility doctor. She felt just as uncertain about the odd sense of loss that came as Erik's hand slid away. "And about how his parents felt about me."

He didn't seem terribly interested in that. "Curt was a lawyer?"

Of all the questions he could have asked, he'd gone straight for what had been so hugely important to the Linfield family status. "Corporate. His father's a litigator."

"His mother?"

"She's into charities."

"What about brothers, sisters?"

"A brother. He took after their dad. His life is the firm and his wife is from money. She and Audrey adore each other."

"So they had a problem with you not being equal, or whatever the hell it was?"

Among other things, she thought, though she wasn't

about to get into everything she'd overheard in that bathroom stall before she'd opened the door and watched Audrey's friends go pale.

She'd said more than enough already.

"Seems so," came her embarrassed agreement.

Quick, assessing, his glance swept her face. As if looking for where the problem might lie, apparently finding nothing in what he knew of her, utter certainty entered the low tones of his voice.

"Then this is their loss. Not yours." Lifting his hand as she lowered her head, he caught her chin with one finger, tipped her head back up. "And for what it's worth, everything you've said stays right here." He brushed the back of his finger along the curve of her cheek, only to catch himself and still the motion scant seconds later. Drawing back, he settled both hands on his hips. "All of it."

At the gentleness in his touch, her shoulders had risen with her indrawn breath. They now fell with a soft "Thank you" that had as much to do with his unexpected defense of her as his assurance that her secrets were safe with him.

She couldn't deny how good his support felt. She was also rather horrified by how badly she wished he would stop looking at her as if he wanted to touch her again, and just do it. She felt terrible for her child. Totally powerless to give him the family he'd once had, imperfect as parts of it had been. Knowing what she knew now, she didn't want him around the Linfields anyway. Yet what made her ache the most just then was what Erik had so inadvertently done.

Simply by touching her, he'd reminded her again of how long it had been since she'd been held. There had been brief hugs at Curt's funeral, many of them awkward, most of them part of the blur that awful time had become. She couldn't remember the last time she'd felt any measure of comfort from a man's touch. She couldn't even remember the last time she'd been in Curt's arms. Or the last time they'd made love. She could easily recall the last kiss Curt had given her, though. She'd played it over a thousand times in her head. As rushed and preoccupied with work as he'd been in the mornings, it had been little more than his customary peck on her cheek on his way out the door.

After what she'd overheard, she couldn't think of that kiss without wondering if it hadn't been tolerance more than preoccupation underlying those absentminded good-byes. But the awful possibility that the man she'd adored had merely endured living with her had existed since the day she'd buried him.

She shoved back the memories, fought the threatening ache.

"This is so not what you signed on for, Erik." She shook her head again, tried to smile. "Thank you for listening. And for your help. And for the shelves. I still can't believe you did that. Just tell me what I owe you." She'd add it to what she owed him for the oil. "And thank you for having dinner with my son," she hurried on, because that had been huge. "I'm sure you'll think twice about sticking around for a meal in the future, but if you do happen to stay, I'll make a point of not burdening you with my baggage."

Despite her attempt to brush off the pain of what she'd shared, she looked as fragile to Erik as the thin silver chain resting below the hollow of her throat. He didn't want her thanks or her money. What he wanted was more detail, not less. He especially wanted to know what she felt about the man whose privacy she still protected. He didn't question why that mattered to him, or ask anything about Curt now. He was too busy hating how the man's family had rejected her and the child she clearly cherished.

He'd never have guessed Tyler was not biologically her own. He'd just figured the boy had come by his fairer coloring from his father.

"What I signed on for was to make sure you can make

a success of the business. I'll do what I have to do to make that happen. I'm not taking your money, Rory. The shelves are just part of the service."

He could see her protest forming even as he lifted his hand to her cheek once more. It was as apparent as her disquiet that she didn't want to feel more obligated to him than she already did. Yet that protest died as he curved his fingers beneath her jaw and touched his thumb to the corner of her mouth.

"As for your son, he doesn't need people in his life who don't appreciate him." Having made her go still, he drew his fingers toward her chin. "And you have too much else to do to waste any more energy on people who don't appreciate you, either. Got that?"

She swallowed, gave him a small nod. Other than that questionable agreement she simply stood there, looking very much as if she was afraid to move for fear that he would.

He'd been physically aware of her since the moment they'd met. Knowing she wanted his touch made that awareness tug hard. She looked very much as if she needed to be held. Needed to be kissed. It was that stark vulnerability that drew him as his hand cupped the side of her face.

Lowering his head, he brushed his lips over the soft part of her mouth.

He heard her breath catch, felt it ease out, the warmth of it trembling against his cheek.

Rory wanted to believe it was just anxiety catching up with her as she slowly leaned toward him. Longing curled through her, a subtle yearning to simply sink into the incredible gentleness in his touch and let it take away the ache in her chest.

But that ache only grew.

So did the need for him to make it go away.

She leaned closer, drawn by that need, by him. As she

did, his fingers eased through her hair, tipping her head and causing her to cling a little more tightly, to kiss him back a little more deeply.

It was kissing him back that turned the ache to something less definable. Shattering sweetness gave way to confusion. She craved the feel of this man's arms, his strength, his self-possession. She just hated how needy she felt, and how badly she wanted him to make all the hurts and the doubts go away.

The pressure of her nails pressing into her palm suddenly registered. So did the realization that all that kept them from cutting into her flesh was the fabric wadded in her fists.

Beneath his own hands, Erik felt tension tightening the slender muscles of her entire enticing body. Before he could ease back himself, she'd released her death grip on his sweater and ducked her head.

Her quiet "I'm sorry" sounded like an apology for everything from the desperation he'd felt building in her to the way she'd bunched the front of his pullover. To remove any possible wrinkle she might have left, she hurriedly smoothed the fabric with the palm of her hand.

As if suddenly conscious of her palm on his chest, or possibly the heavy beat of his heart, she jerked back her hand and stepped away.

Erik moved with her, canceling that negligible distance. There wasn't a doubt in his mind that he'd just added to the chaos of all she was struggling with. That hadn't been his intent at all. Not totally sure what his intention had been, feeling a little conflicted himself, he lifted her face to his.

"Hey. It was just a kiss," he murmured, attempting to absolve them both. Just a kiss that had done a number on his nervous system, he qualified, but her decidedly physical effect on him was beside the point. "No apology necessary. Okay?"

Unlike her unease, her nod was barely perceptible.

"I'll call you in a couple of days." Aware of how she barely met his eyes, he consciously lowered his hand. He shouldn't be touching her at all. "Can you finish the inventory by Friday afternoon?"

As segues went, he knew his was positively graceless. All he wanted at the moment, though, was to get past the awkwardness that had her protectively crossing her arms as she pulled composure into place.

"I'll have it finished."

A wisp of her shiny bangs had fallen near the corner of one eye. Instincts that still wanted physical contact with her had him starting to nudge it aside. More prudent senses had him dropping his hand an instant before the small voice coming from the top of the stairs would have had him dropping it anyway.

"I'm ready to tuck in, Mom."

She took another step away. "I'll be there in a minute," she called toward the stairs. Brushing at the taunting wisp, she looked back with an uncomfortable smile. "He has to be up early in the morning."

"Then I'll get out of your way so you can take care of him. I'll let myself out," he said, stopping her as she started for the door. "Just say good-night to him for me."

His jacket lay on the stool behind her. Reaching around her, careful not to touch, he snagged it and backed up. "Thanks for dinner," he added, and walked out the mudroom door, wondering what in the hell he thought he'd been doing when he'd reached for her in the first place.

He had no one but himself to blame for the tension that had his entire body feeling as tight as a trip wire. He was messing where he had no business going. Even if she wasn't so obviously not the sort of woman a man could have a brief, casual affair with, she was just now moving on from a loss that had affected her in ways that went far beyond anything she'd shared with him.

He couldn't even pretend to understand how she felt, or to know what she needed. Whatever it was, he couldn't give it to her anyway. He didn't know how. Even if he did, he suspected she wouldn't let him close enough to try. She didn't want to rely on anyone she didn't absolutely have to. He could appreciate that. He'd been there himself. As it was there were only a handful of people he truly trusted— and not one of them was a female he wasn't related to or who wasn't in his employ. He suspected, though, that her walls weren't nearly as thick as those he'd erected around his heart. There was no denying how vulnerable she was right now.

He wasn't about to take advantage of that, either. He also wasn't going to do anything else to potentially screw up his relationship with her as her mentor and jeopardize his agreement with Cornelia.

That was why he'd told his lovely protégée that he'd call in a couple of days instead of meeting with her. If he wasn't near her, he wouldn't be tempted to touch.

That didn't stop him from being touched by her, though. Or by the little boy who'd strung Christmas tinsel on his toy boat.

He knew Rory wanted her son to have traditions. Knowing how tight her money was, and how badly she wanted this season to be special for the child, he decided there was no reason he couldn't give them one of the traditions that had long belonged there anyway.

Chapter Six

She never should have said she'd have the inventory fin ished by Friday. She should have asked for another day at least. As much as she required his expertise, she'd just made it a point to accommodate Erik's schedule any way she could.

Had she been thinking, she would have realized how impossible that deadline was. But she'd been too rattled by the needs she'd felt in his arms and the kiss he'd dismissed as inconsequential to consider everything else she'd committed to do before Friday—which happened to be Tyler's last day at his current school.

Given the occasion, guilt over not having kept her word to Erik would have to wait. Her little boy was not taking this latest transition well at all.

The familiar faces and routines at Pine Ridge Day School were the last constants in the life they were leaving behind. As a child, she'd had considerable practice dealing with such separations. Her parents' nomadic lifestyle had made a new school or two every year her norm, and they'd tried to ease those transitions. But her little boy had never known that sort of instability. Even after his father had died, she'd managed to protect him from the biggest upheavals and keep his routine as consistent as possible. Until they'd had to move, anyway.

As she'd feared he would, he started missing his playmates the minute he'd fastened himself into his car seat in the back of their car and they'd pulled out from the portico.

A quick glance in her rearview mirror caught his pensive expression. He looked the way he had driving away from their old house a couple of weeks ago. Solemn and a little uncertain.

"We can always come back for a visit, Ty," she assured him, heading for the freeway and the ferry. "Just because you'll be going to a new school doesn't mean you won't ever see your old teachers or classmates again."

"They'll still be there?"

"They'll still be there," she promised. It wouldn't be like when he'd lost his dad. There wasn't that sort of finality to this parting. She needed him to understand that. "We can come back after the holiday to say hi, if you want."

"Will the tree be there, too?"

The tree. Ten feet of pine studded with a thousand white lights and draped with paper chains and cutouts of students' handprints. It graced the main building's foyer.

"The tree won't be there, honey. Everyone takes Christmas trees down after the holiday. But everything else will be the same."

"Nuh-uh," he replied, picking at the knee of his khaki uniform pants. "I won't be there anymore."

No, she thought with a sigh. He wouldn't be, and the silence that followed hinted at how very much that new change disturbed him.

Thinking the Christmas carols playing on the radio

might distract him, she turned the volume up over the hum of the heater and encouraged him to sing along.

That didn't work. Neither did any of her other attempts to console, cajole or otherwise ease away his dispirited expression.

Fighting discouragement herself, she finally conceded that she had no idea just then how to make everything better for her little boy.

That disheartening fact had just registered when her eyes widened on what should have been nothing more than the dusk-gray shapes of the road, the woods and the distant rectangle of Harbor Market & Sporting Goods.

Peering past the headlights, she heard Tyler's sudden "Oh. Wow!"

Wow, indeed.

The market stood glittery bright in the encroaching dark. Every pillar, post and eave, its roofline, even the chimney had been outlined with twinkling white lights. The bare branches of the apple tree at the near end had been wrapped in peppermint stripes of white lights and red. It was the snowman beyond it, though, that had her attention. Glowing blue-white, his top hat cocked at an angle, the tall, grinning Frosty stood as bold and impressive as the only person she knew who would have put it there.

The light on her answering machine was blinking when she finally coaxed Tyler out of the cold and into the kitchen. Hitting Play, she heard Erik's recorded voice say he was checking to see if she'd finished the inventory and ask when she'd be available to discuss the business plan. He mentioned nothing about the dazzling Christmas lights that hadn't been there when she'd left that morning.

She hit Redial. Apparently taking his cue from the number on his caller ID, he answered with an easy, "You're home."

"We just got here. Erik," she said, her tone half laugh, half hesitation, "I can't believe what you've done."

"Is that good or bad?"

"I don't know." She honestly had no idea how to weigh her son's reaction against her next electric bill.

"Does Tyler like it?" he asked while she figured it out.

"Like it?" *This is* ours, *Mom?* he'd asked, his eyes huge. "He hasn't stopped grinning since we got here. He's practically stuck to the window right now watching the icicle lights."

The sequential lights strung along the overhangs looked like dripping ice. Even the back of the house had been decorated. They'd noticed the lights wrapped around the side of the building the moment they'd driven up the rise. "He loves the snowman."

"You said he would have liked the one my grandparents had," he reminded her over the drone of what sounded like an electric saw. "My grandfather always put theirs facing the sound, but I had it put farther back on the lot, thinking Tyler could see it from the window."

Truly torn by what he'd done, she dropped her scarf on the phone desk and unbuttoned her coat. When they'd talked about his grandparents' traditions with the store, he'd seemed to see maintaining them mostly as a good approach to business. Yet her mentor's gift clearly had less to do with marketing than with the little boy pressing his nose to the glass.

She didn't want his thoughtfulness to mean so much. She just wasn't able to help it. Not with her little boy so totally captivated.

"How did you get it done so fast?"

The drone beyond him grew quieter. Nearer, voices rose, then faded.

"This close to Christmas, lighting companies are usually finished putting up decorations and are just waiting to take them down. I called a company a client uses, told them what I wanted, gave them the building measurements and they did their thing."

Just like that. With one phone call, he'd managed to do what she hadn't been able to do no matter how hard she'd tried and totally distracted her son from his dejection.

"It's just lights, Rory."

The man had a serious gift for understatement. He'd used the same think-no-more-of-it tone right after he'd proved that the shell of control she fought to maintain around her life was about as thin as paper.

It was just a kiss, he'd said.

He was only being kind when he'd reached for her. Just as he was only being kind when he'd overlooked how she'd practically crawled inside his shirt when she'd kissed him back—shortly before he'd pointedly minimized the moment of comfort, security and whatever else she'd felt in his arms.

He, on the other hand, apparently hadn't felt much of anything at all, other than anxious to get out of there.

But this wasn't about them. Not that there *was* a them, she insisted to herself. This was about what he'd done for her child.

"It's more than lights, Erik. To us, anyway." He had to know that. "And Tyler loves them." That was all that she would let matter at the moment. For her son's sake, she wasn't even going to panic over the electric bill. Yet. "So thank you. From both of us."

"You're welcome. Listen," he continued over the thud of heavy boots on metal stairs, "I have to get back to the payroll right now, but we need to discuss your business plan and address inventory. I have to be in Tacoma before noon tomorrow, so let's do it over the phone. Are you okay for an eight-thirty call? That'll give us a couple of hours.

"You there?" he asked when she hesitated.

"Can we make it Sunday?"

"Sunday's not good for me."

"Actually," she began, wondering if Sunday involved the woman he'd taken out last week, "I'm not quite finished with the inventory." She hated telling him that. "I'd have finished last night, but we had to bake cookies."

With the bang of a door, the noise and conversations beyond him died.

"*Had* to?"

"I told Tyler's teacher I'd bring treats for his class today. And I'd promised him he could help. So, yes," she insisted. "I had to."

She'd also brought cookies for the staff—which meant she'd spent the past two afternoons and evenings baking and filling tins and decorating twenty-two gingerbread girls and boys. With Tyler's help, the project had taken twice as long as it might have, but she'd wanted something for him that she'd never had as a child, holiday memories of flour on noses, sugar sprinkles, the air scented with vanilla and spice. Her mom's idea of baking had been heating a muffin in the microwave.

"What about tomorrow? Will you have it finished by then?"

Juggling guilt and priorities, she rubbed the ache brewing beneath her forehead. "I told Tyler we'd get our tree tomorrow. I'm going to work in the store tonight after he goes to bed," she explained, hoping to minimize the delay to Erik's schedule. "After we get the tree decorated, I'll finish whatever I haven't done in the store. I've been working out there after he goes to sleep, but I ran out of hours in the past couple of days.

"Since Sunday isn't good for you," she hurried on, easily

able to imagine a scowl etched in his too-handsome face, "I'll be ready Monday for sure." That would also give her time to read the business plan she'd tried without much luck to study on the ferry and after Tyler had gone to bed. Having to look up terms like *gross margin, inventory turns* and *marketing mix* had also slowed her down considerably. So did being so tired her eyes blurred.

She hated the plea that entered her quiet "Okay?"

Leaning against the edge of his desk, Erik stared past the schematics on his drafting table to the black-framed photos of Merrick & Sullivan racing sloops lining the pearl-gray wall. To his left, the windows of his office, like those of the other offices lining the catwalk, overlooked the production floor a story below. Those on his right exposed the lights of other industrial buildings lining the night-darkened waterway.

The pleasure he'd felt knowing the snowman had been a hit with Tyler had rapidly faded to something far less definable.

When he'd left her place the other night, his only thoughts had been about doing what he could to make the kid's Christmas a little better, and his need for physical distance from the boy's mom. He'd wanted to focus on his work and his world and to get her out of his head for a while. He was good at that. Focusing his thoughts, his energies.

He usually was, anyway. His days were crowded enough to prevent more than a fleeting thought of her undeniably feminine shape, or the way her bottom lip curved when she smiled. But she was messing with his nights, too, driving him from his bed to pace the floor or exhaust himself with his weights before sleep would finally drive her from his mind.

He never should have kissed her. If he hadn't, he

wouldn't know the sweetness of her mouth, the feel of her satin-soft skin, how perfectly her body fit against his.

Now, frustrated on a number of levels, he pushed from his desk, jammed his fingers through his hair.

"Forget Monday," he muttered. Just because he would have preferred she keep her focus on his schedule didn't mean she could make it her priority.

In roughly two weeks she'd lost her job, sold her home and was settling into a place that hadn't even been on her radar until his amazingly generous neighbor had decided to help them both out. In between, she seemed to be doing everything she could to ease the transition for her son while dealing with the former in-laws from hell and getting a business she knew nothing about back up and running.

No way could he justify pushing her just because he wanted his obligations there over and done with.

"The store can wait for now. We'll pick up after Christmas."

Pure skepticism shaded her quiet "Seriously?"

"Seriously," he echoed. "You and Tyler have a good time picking out your tree. There's a great tree lot on Sydney Road. It's only a few miles from you. Old family operation. Tell them you bought John and Dotty Sullivan's store. I imagine they'll give you a good price on a little one."

"I'll do that. And thank you. Thank you," she repeated, sounding relieved beyond belief by the reprieve he'd offered. "But the tree can't be little. Tyler has his heart set on the tallest one we can fit into the room."

Erik's voice went flat. "The ceilings in there are nine feet high."

"Then I guess we're getting an eight-foot tree. That'll leave room for the angel."

"And you're hauling it how?"

"The only way I can," she replied, ever so reasonably. "On my car."

The thought of eight feet of freshly cut conifer atop twelve feet of rounded, lime-green Bug drew his quick frown.

"Have you ever driven with a tree strapped to your roof?"

"Not exactly. No," she finally admitted, leaving him to assume that her husband had been behind the wheel. He also figured that the guy had transported prior trees on something considerably larger than what she drove now. Or they'd had it delivered, given what she'd said about the sort of family she'd just shed.

"Then you need to know that the weight affects the way a car handles. Especially if it's windy, and we have a wind advisory for the weekend. Make sure they net it for you. It'll be easier to manage that way. And take a blanket to protect your roof. Have someone help you secure it, too. You want it tied tight so it doesn't slip."

She hadn't thought about the weather. Rain at least part of the day was a given. It was the Northwest. She didn't like wind, though. It made inclement weather that much more miserable.

"Did you *promise* Tyler you'd have it up tomorrow?"

"It was the only thing I could think of to take his mind off having to change schools."

"Did it work?"

Her little boy hadn't budged from the window. He hadn't even taken off his jacket.

"Not as well as your lights did."

The admission would have made him smile, had he not just caught the hint of defeat in her voice. Or maybe what he heard was simply fatigue.

"Tell you what." Totally sabotaging his plan to stay away, he did a quick reschedule. "I'll only be a half an hour away from you tomorrow. What time will you be at the lot?"

"About the same time you said you have to be in Tacoma."

"I'm just picking up parts from a machinist. I'll leave earlier and be at the lot about twelve-thirty." It would take an hour to pick up the tree, an hour plus to get back. That left him plenty of time to drop off the parts at the boatworks, get home, shower, change and get to yet another client's holiday party. At least this time he didn't have to pick up a date. He didn't have one.

"You don't have to do that, Erik. You've done enough," she insisted, obviously referring to the lights. "We'll manage."

"We? You mean you and Tyler?"

"We're the only we here."

"Look." He was really getting tired of the I-don't-want-to-be-obligated-to-you tone that had slipped into her voice, but he had neither the time nor the inclination to argue with her. "You've said you want this Christmas to be good for your son. I assume that means you don't want him to have memories of his mom having a meltdown because his tree fell off the car and the car behind her hit it and turned it into kindling. Or because the thing weighs a ton and she can't get it into the house. Or into the tree stand, for that matter. You have a tree stand, don't you?"

"Of course I do. And I don't have meltdowns," she replied. "Especially in front of my son."

"No. You probably don't," he conceded, not at all sure whom he was annoyed with. Her. Or himself. "You just suck it up and try to deal with everything on your own. It's fine if you want to be independent, Rory. I'm sure you have your reasons for being that way. But this isn't about creating an obligation, or you owing me if I help you. It's about Tyler. All I want to do is help with the tree. For him. Okay?"

Silence.

About the time he thought she might simply hang up, she said, "Okay. For Tyler."

"Good. I'll be at the lot tomorrow with my truck." With a glance at his watch, he winced. "Right now I've got to get to this payroll. I'll call you when I'm on my way."

He should probably apologize.

The thought crossed Erik's mind every time he noticed the wary way Rory watched him the next afternoon. He just wasn't sure exactly what he should apologize for. He hadn't said a word to her that wasn't absolutely true. And she'd definitely needed the help.

The rain came in fits and starts. The weather was cold, the temperature dropping, the wind blowing, and the tree Tyler had selected after carefully checking out the small forest under the huge canvas tent was not only the eight-foot maximum she'd given him, but rather wide. Even tied up to make it more manageable and tarped to keep it dry, with the heavy wind gusts, getting it to her place on the rounded roof of her car would have presented a definite challenge. So would the task of her and Tyler unloading the thing and carrying it into the store to get it into its heavy iron stand, a task that involved sawing off a couple of lower limbs and trimming the thick trunk to make it fit before tightening the screws into place.

Mother and son wrestling it into the house on their own would have presented its own set of frustrations. Especially since carrying it into the house through the store—which had been easier than putting it in the stand in the garage and carrying it through the mudroom—involved hoisting the stand end of the eighty-plus pounds of bushy branches, trunk and iron to his shoulder while she brought up the rear with the top end and Tyler ran ahead of them to open the door.

He said nothing about any of that, though. It wasn't necessary. The process proceeded far easier with his truck and his help, and that was all he'd wanted: to make something a little easier for her and her son—and to offset his guilt over having pushed her about the store to the point where she'd given up sleep.

"Where do you want it?" he asked.

"In the corner by the fireplace. On the towel so the stand doesn't stain the carpet."

"Can I help?" called Tyler.

"Just stay back for a minute, sport. I've got it." He told Rory, "You can let go."

Behind him, Rory stepped back as the weight lifted from her shoulder. With a quiet whoosh of branches and the thud of heavy metal on towel-covered broadloom, the stand hit the floor and the tree popped upright.

The whole room suddenly smelled like a pine forest.

Beside her, her little boy grinned. "It's really big, huh?"

Not just big. For the space, it was huge, definitely larger than what they would have wound up with had Erik not been with them. Fuller, anyway.

She'd realized within minutes of arriving at the tree lot that what she'd promised her son would have been a nightmare to manage on her own. On their own, they also would have wound up with something more in the five-foot range.

"Thank you," she said to Erik's back.

He turned, pushing his windblown hair back from his forehead.

"No problem. This is the fourth tree I've hauled this month." He wanted her to know that what he'd done wasn't a big deal. Not to him, anyway. Certainly nothing she needed to feel obligated to him for. "The one at work, a neighbor's and one of Pax's cousins'."

"Do you have a tree?" Tyler wanted to know.

"I don't usually put one up."

"How come?"

"Because I'm not home in the evenings much this time of year and I go to my folks' for Christmas."

Her little boy's brow pinched. Before he could voice whatever had him looking so concerned, Erik motioned to the single green bin sitting near the fireplace.

"You want the rest of those?" he asked her, referring to the others still stacked in the store.

She started to tell him she could bring them in herself. Thinking it wiser to accept his help than risk resurrecting the tension that had ended their phone call last night, she said, "Please," and hurried after him to help.

Tyler wanted to help, too, so she had him carry in their new two-foot-high, red-velvet-clad Santa with its price tag still attached while they brought in the bins filled with the lights and ornaments she'd need for the tree.

The only other thing she needed, other than for the heavy caution between them to ease, was to start a fire in the fireplace to take the deepening chill off the room. While Erik went back for the last bin, she crumpled newspaper under some of the kindling she and Tyler had found by a cord of split logs in the lean-to behind the garage.

Erik had barely walked back in when he shot a narrowed glance at the parka she still wore. Tyler hadn't taken his off yet, either.

"Did you turn off the heat?" he asked, hoping she hadn't gone that far in her efforts to conserve.

"I turn it down when we leave, but it's always colder when the wind blows. It just hasn't been this windy. Or this cold. It's freezing out there."

The house had always been drafty. As his grandmother had done on especially cold days, Rory had closed her heavy drapes over the big expanses of glass to insulate from the chill. With the wind that blew the rain against the windows stirring the fabric, he figured he should probably check the weather stripping.

Just not now. For now, all he'd do was make sure she had enough firewood and get out of there.

"There's plenty," she assured him when he said he'd bring some in. "Tyler and I carried a load into the mud-room this morning."

"Can we decorate now?" Tyler asked. "If you don't have a tree," he said to the man checking his watch, "you can help decorate ours. Mom said she'd show me her magic ornaments. You want to see 'em?"

"Magic ornaments?"

"Uh-huh. They're in here." With his arms still wrapped around the Santa, he bumped his little boot against a bin she'd brought in that morning. "She showed me a heart and a bell. I get to see the rest when we put them on the tree."

He looked eager and hopeful and was still running on a sugar high from the hot cider and big candy cane he'd been given at the tree lot.

"We've kept Erik long enough, honey." She hated to burst his little bubble, but with Erik frowning at the time, it seemed apparent he was anxious to go. She felt anxious for him to go now, too. Every time she met his glance she had the uncomfortable feeling he was wondering how she would ever manage there on her own. Or thinking about how much longer the project had taken than he'd probably planned. "He said he had to leave by four," she reminded him. "Remember?"

"But he doesn't have his own tree, Mom. We're s'posed to share."

They were indeed, which left Rory at a loss for a rea-sonable rebuttal. She didn't doubt her child's disappoint-ment. Yet that disappointment didn't seem to be only for himself. It was as much for the man she sincerely doubted needed anything from them at all.

"I suppose I could stay a little longer," he said to Tyler,

touched by the child's concern, ignoring her. "How much do you think we can do in thirty minutes?"

"We have to put the lights on before we can do anything," she pointed out to them both. Thirty minutes would barely get them going.

"Then I guess that's where we start." He looked to where she suddenly stared back at him. "Unless you hadn't planned on doing this right now."

He had accomplished his mission: delivering the tree. It hadn't occurred to him that he'd even want to stick around and decorate the thing. Especially with Rory stuck somewhere between grateful for his help, not wanting to have needed it and uncomfortable with his presence. Her little boy's excitement with the process, though, and his innocent desire to share that experience with him held far more appeal just then than heading home to get ready for yet another evening of schmoozing and champagne. Even if he didn't leave for another half hour, he'd barely be late. He just wouldn't stop by the boatworks.

Both males expectantly waited for her reply. That Erik seemed to want to stay caught her totally off guard. Considering how he'd practically bolted out the back door the last time he'd been there and how annoyed he'd sounded with her on the phone yesterday, she'd thought for sure that he'd be on his way as soon as he'd delivered Tyler's tree.

Not about to deliberately disappoint her son, and determined to not upset the precarious equilibrium between her and her mentor, she lifted both hands in surrender. "If we're doing lights, we need a chair," was all she had to say before Tyler started pulling off his coat and Erik started heading toward the dining room table.

On his way, he pulled his cell phone from the front pocket of his jeans.

"I need to tell Pax I won't be in today," he told her, punching numbers. They didn't need the parts until Monday, but his partner would be expecting him. "Just give me a minute."

Taking her animated little boy's jacket, she slipped off her own and headed into the mudroom to hang them up. As she passed Erik, she heard his easy "Hey, buddy" before he relayed his message, told him where he was and added that he'd see him "later at the party."

Marveling at the man's social life, and unsettled to find herself wondering yet again about the woman he'd taken out last week, she walked back into the kitchen moments later to see him still on the phone.

"No, I'm not 'seriously preoccupied,'" he good-naturedly defended. "I've just been getting a tree into a stand. What are you talking about?

"You're kidding," he muttered, and headed for the dining room window.

The moment he pulled back the closed drape, she heard a soft ticking against the glass. Little was visible in the gray light beyond. Blowing rain obscured the view.

His brow furrowed. "Turn on the TV, will you?" he asked her.

"What's going on?"

"Everything's closing down," was all he said before she grabbed the TV's remote.

With Erik joining her on her left, still listening to Pax, and Tyler smashed against her right leg, hugging Santa, the three of them watched the churning weather map on the screen while the authoritative voice of the weatherman warned everyone to stay off the roads. The ticker on the bottom of the screen listed temperatures in various degrees of freezing in Seattle and surrounding areas as the voice went on about predicted accumulations of freezing rain or sleet. Another voice took over as the picture switched to a weather cam with a blurry image of a multicar pileup on I-5.

A viewer video showed the sleet-shrouded image of a ferry rocking at its landing.

"What about the Narrows Bridge?" she heard Erik ask Pax.

The furrows went deeper. "Got it. Sure. You, too, man," he concluded, and ended his call.

Sensing the adults' concern, Tyler pressed closer as he looked up. "Is this a bad thing, Mommy?"

It wasn't good. "It's okay, honey. The weather is just causing a few problems," she explained even as more personal complications dawned.

"Nothing you need to worry about, sport."

Peering around his mom, Tyler looked to the man smiling over at him.

"All you need to worry about is finding a place to put that big guy." Erik nodded to the Santa that was nearly half Tyler's size. "Then we can start on the lights."

His concerns appeased, Tyler plopped his Santa on the floor beside him. Suggesting he put the decoration somewhere a little more out of the way, Erik turned to Rory.

"Pax said they're closing the airport, bridges, ferries and freeways. The roads are all iced." His partner had gone over to their client office. The one by Cornelia's. Now he was stuck there.

Given that the bridge he himself needed to take to get back was closed and that the ferry would be down, he seemed to be stuck where he was, too.

He could usually roll with anything. He just wasn't quite sure how the woman who'd just drawn a deep breath and turned away felt about having him there for a little longer then she'd expected. She didn't say a word as she knelt beside one of the bins and popped off the lid to reveal dozens of neatly wrapped strings of lights.

"We're having soup and sandwiches for dinner," she finally said.

Lifting out two strings, she stood up, turned to face him. "Since it seems you're here for the night, you can stay in my room."

His left eyebrow arched.

Mirroring his expression, determined to prove she could hold her ground with him, Rory added, "I'll sleep with Tyler."

Chapter Seven

Rory left the door to Tyler's room halfway open and paused at the top of the stairs. Her little boy had fallen asleep within seconds of his head hitting the pillow. No surprise considering how exciting the day had been for him and how hard he'd fought to stay awake after supper to finish the tree.

From downstairs, the television's barely audible volume told her Erik had switched from *How the Grinch Stole Christmas* to the news.

She hated the ambivalence creeping back as the low tones mingled with the beat of the sleet on the roof, the muffled sound of it pinging against the upstairs windows. The thought of riding out the ice storm in a still unfamiliar house would have had her anxious on a number of levels, had it not been for Erik.

She felt safe with him there. Physically, anyway. And there wasn't a single part of her being that didn't want exactly what he had just helped her provide for Tyler: an afternoon and evening of moments he might always remember as special.

That, in a nutshell, was her problem. His presence provided as much comfort as it did disquiet. Tyler had turned to her every time he'd had a question about where an ornament should go, but it had been Erik's assistance or advice he'd sought if he couldn't get it on a branch, and his approval he'd wanted with nearly every accomplishment.

She didn't want him being so drawn to the man.

She didn't want to be so drawn to him herself.

Wishing she still had her chatty little boy as a buffer, she headed down the steps, stopping when she reached the foyer.

Erik stood with his back to her, his heavy charcoal pullover stretched across his broad shoulders, his hands casually tucked into the front pockets of his jeans as he faced the talking head on the television. The size of the blaze in the fireplace indicated that he'd added another log. Strewn around him were empty bins and ornament boxes. In front of the sofa, the large, square coffee table held a red candle in a beribboned glass hurricane and the last of the crystal icicles waiting to be hung on the brightly lit tree.

As if sensing her presence, Erik turned toward her. She immediately turned her attention to cleaning up the mess.

"Is he asleep?" he asked.

"We barely got through brushing his teeth."

"I'm surprised he made it that far." Seeing what she was doing, and how deliberately she avoided his eyes, he picked up a bin that had held the faux evergreen boughs now draped over the stone fireplace mantel, set it in the entry and put another on the coffee table for her to fill with what she collected.

"Thanks," she said quietly.

"Sure," he replied, and finally found himself faced with what he'd managed to avoid the past few hours.

It had felt strange decorating her tree. Partly because he'd never helped decorate one with a small child buzzing around his knees, partly because the feel of the room with her understated touches in it was completely different from what it had been years ago. What he'd felt most, though, was the need to get past her guardedness with him. That caution still tempered her smiles, and made him more conscious of little things like how her animation had died when she'd opened a bin to see a Christmas stocking embroidered with *Dad.* Her wariness with him wasn't anything overt. It wasn't even anything someone else might notice. Probably something even he wouldn't notice, if he hadn't known he was responsible for it.

He never should have kissed her. The thought had crossed his mind a thousand times in the past few days, usually right behind the memory of how she'd practically melted in his arms. He'd yet to forget the sweet taste of her, the perfect way she'd fit his body. It was as if the feel of her had burned itself into his brain, leaving nerves taut, distracting him even now.

He shouldn't have gotten so annoyed with her on the phone last night, either, though he was pretty sure that same sort of frustration had been at least partially to blame. But the storm wasn't letting up anytime soon, the thickening ice made escape next to impossible and he didn't want this evening to be any more difficult than it needed to be. Short of apologizing to her, which he had the feeling would only make matters worse, especially for the kiss part, he'd do his best to put her at ease with him some other way.

She'd just reached up to hang a fallen ornament high on the tree. As it had every other time she'd reached that high, the motion exposed a thin strip of pale skin between the hem of her short white turtleneck, shorter green vest and the dark denims hugging her sweetly rounded backside.

"So," he said, forcing his focus to something he wanted

to know, anyway. "What's with the 'magic' ornaments?" He nodded toward the empty shoe box on the end table. "You told Tyler all those you took out of that box appeared out of nowhere."

The tiny crystal ice skates, the little Eiffel Tower stamped *Paris, Texas,* the miniature pink-and-white cupcake—all the ornaments in her "magic" collection looked much like the other decorations sparkling on the tree. Yet she'd even handled them differently, more carefully, he supposed.

"That's because they did," she replied, lowering her arms to pack up more empty boxes. "It didn't matter where my parents and I were, every Christmas morning I'd open the door and there would be a package with a gold box tied with a red bow. Inside would be an ornament that had something to do with where we were staying. Or something I was into at the time."

"Did your parents leave them there?"

"They had no idea who sent them. There was never a return address."

"So that's why you call them magic," he concluded.

"It was more than that." Conscious of him watching her, she packed the boxes into the bin he'd set on the coffee table. "It was what I felt when one of those little packages appeared. That's what made them magic. At that moment, no matter what town we were in, with Mom and Dad mine for the day and that gift in my hands, I had the feeling that everything was right in my little world." That was the feeling she wanted Tyler to know. He deserved that. Every child did. "I wound up with fourteen of them."

"It sounds like you moved around a lot."

"We did. Mom and Dad still do." Their mailing address was their agent's. "They're musicians."

His brow furrowed. "So what's wrong with that?"

The question brought a quick frown of her own. "I didn't say anything was wrong with it."

"I didn't mean you. You said the other day that Curt's parents had a problem with you being his secretary instead of a lawyer. That things got worse when they found out your 'people,'" he repeated, making air quotes, "weren't the right pedigree. What's wrong with being a musician?"

Her instinctive defense eased with his mystified tone. Marginally.

Apparently he had her a little edgier than she'd realized.

"There wouldn't have been anything wrong with it if they'd played the violin or French horn in a symphony, but Dad plays bass guitar and Mom is a singer in a rock band. That was not the image Audrey wanted their friends to have of their son's wife." She closed the lid on the now full bin and moved to fill another. "On the rare occasion mention of my family came up, she said they were in the music industry and changed the subject."

Unlike nearly everything else she'd exposed about herself the last time Erik had been there, she'd forgotten she'd even alluded to her parents. She'd be the first to admit that their decidedly bohemian lifestyle hadn't provided the most stable environment, but it wasn't as if they'd tattooed her forehead and named her Moonbeam or Thistleweed. They were good people who just happened to be creative, extroverted free spirits who'd never figured out which of them possessed the recessive "conventional" gene each accused the other of passing on to her. They were her mom and dad. She loved them. She didn't understand them, but she loved them.

"Are they any good?"

"They're very good."

"Where do they play?"

"Sometimes they get a gig doing backup for tours," she told him, grateful for the ease of his questions as they worked. Relieved, too, that he wasn't letting her dwell on her former in-laws' biases.

Trying to appear as comfortable with their present situation as he did, she looked around for anything she'd missed. "Mostly they're on a circuit where they play small venues for a few weeks at a time."

"That had to make for an interesting childhood," he muttered, and handed her the stack of boxes from the sofa.

"I suppose it was." After adding what he'd given her to the last bin, she snapped on its lid. "I just never knew where we'd be next, or how long we would be there." *Fluid,* her mom liked to call their lives.

"But a little gold box showed up everywhere you went." The container now filled, Erik picked it up to stack with the others. "Just trying to get the rest of the story," he explained, and waited for her to move so he could carry it to the door.

She stepped aside, pretty sure he would have moved her himself if she hadn't.

With him carrying away the last bin, she scooped up a few of the crystal icicles and snowflakes still on the coffee table, started hanging them on the tree. "They showed up every year until I stopped traveling with my parents," she told him. "Mom and Dad had been playing in Seattle and I didn't want to move around anymore. I'd just turned eighteen, so I stayed here when they left for their next engagement. That was the first Christmas a package didn't show up. We finally figured out it was their booking agent's wife who'd been sending them. Apparently, he represented a few other artists who traveled with their kids and she did it for all of them."

"Nice lady." Erik came up beside her, pulled one of the icicles from her hand. "So where will your parents be this Christmas?"

"Colorado. They're booked through New Year's."

He glanced at her profile as she lifted another bit of crystal above her head to hang on a high branch. She wouldn't have family around, he realized. Not liking that thought, not questioning why, he took the icicle from her and hung it below the white angel on top. As he did, he caught the clean scent of something herbal mingling with pine. Her shampoo.

The fragrance was subtle. Its effect on him was not.

Intent on ignoring both, he took one of the snowflakes. "So what will you and Tyler do? Go to a friend's house? Have friends over?"

He was just making conversation. Rory felt certain of that. And the question seemed casual enough. It was his nearness, and the answer, that gave her pause.

"We'll just stay here. My girlfriends from Tyler's school will both be out of town."

"What about other friends?"

"Except for work and Tyler's school, I wasn't involved in much the past year. Most of the other people I socialized with were in Curt's circle. Members of the firm and their spouses," she explained. "I don't belong in that group anymore."

For a moment Erik said nothing. Beyond them, the low voice of the weatherman droned on, the fire snapped and crackled. He could let it go, move on to something less personal. His mention before of the man she'd married— his relatives, anyway—had dented the calm facade she'd worn for her son the past few hours. But her guard with him had finally slipped, and his curiosity tugged hard.

"You said Curt had a different area of practice," he reminded her, "but was he in the same firm as his father and brother?"

With a faint frown, she handed him the last two ornaments she held and turned to pick up more for herself.

"Different firms. Both firms belong to the same country club, though. It's where the guys play racquetball and squash and wine and dine their clients. For the most part," she qualified, moving back to the tree. "Curt liked us to entertain at home." He'd seemed proud of her skills as a hostess, too, she thought, only to banish the memory before others could take hold. The moment she'd seen his stocking a while ago, the old doubts had rushed back, adding a different sort of disquiet to an already challenging day.

"You lived in the same circles as his parents?"

"It's not like we saw them all the time," she replied, hearing the frown in his voice. "But the wives of some of the partners in Curt's firm were on the same committees as Audrey and her friends. The ones who don't work outside their homes, anyway. Symphony. Heart Ball. That sort of thing."

"And you?"

"I was on them, too. For a while." She'd done her best to help Curt's career any way she could. They'd been a team that way, a more intimate extension of the partnership they'd developed when he'd been her boss and she his secretary. Or so she'd thought. "Our personal friends were more into getting together for dinners, or taking the kids out for lunch after T-ball."

"What about them?"

"What do you mean?"

"Why don't you ask them over? I bet Tyler'd be up for it."

She was sure he would. It just wasn't that simple. And what Erik was asking was really quite sweet. Surprising. Unexpected. But sweet—if such a word could be applied to the six feet plus of disturbing male quietly messing with her peace of mind.

It seemed he didn't want her and her son spending Christmas Day alone.

"That's the group I don't belong to anymore." The other one, the country club set, she'd never really had. "I was part of a couple with Curt," she explained, wondering how long it had taken the man beside her to think of himself as an *I* rather than a *we* after his wife had gone. "After he died, the guys didn't have their colleague and I was a reminder to the wives of how their lives would change without their husbands. Or how their lives might not even be what they'd thought they were," she concluded, only to find herself in the one place she hadn't wanted to go.

The place where so many questions begged for answers that would never come because the only person who could provide them was no longer there.

She wasn't at all sure how their conversation had taken such a swerve.

"What part wasn't what you thought it was?"

Her eyes met his, old pain quickly masked as she glanced away.

"All of it." She gave a brave little laugh, tried to smile. "So any advice you have about how to move beyond something I can't do a thing about would be greatly appreciated. Something more immediate than a five-year plan would be nice."

Perspective. That was what she needed. Since she couldn't imagine how she'd ever have it where her marriage had been concerned, the least she could do was maintain some about the too-attractive man who'd kissed her senseless four days ago and now acted as if nothing had happened at all—which she would be eternally grateful for, if she could somehow forget it herself. He was her mentor. Granted, he was her business mentor, but maybe the more she reminded herself of his place in her life, the less she'd be affected by things like the swift concern lowering his brow. Since his place in her life was to provide advice, she might as well take advantage of his counsel.

"Do you want to be a little more specific?" he asked.

Pretty certain the tensions of the day had just caught up with her, she dropped her glance to the slender ornament between her fingers. What she wanted had nothing to do with the store. But Erik did have a certain amount of experience in this particular area. He'd lost someone who'd once been important to him, too.

"I overheard some things at Curt's funeral that I can't seem to forget. About our marriage," she explained, her voice quietly matter-of-fact. "Since he's not here for me to ask about them, I think what I really want is to know how long it will take before the answers don't matter so much."

Erik watched her blink at the ornament, her eyebrows knitted as she stared down at what she held.

She'd never told him what had happened to her husband. Neither Phil nor Cornelia had mentioned it, either. And he hadn't wanted to ask. It had seemed to him that the less he knew about her, the easier it would be to keep her pigeonholed as a project, a duty. Something with a start and end date that required nothing of him in between but a little business advice and elbow grease.

It would have helped enormously if her little boy had been a brat.

It would have helped even more had she not been trying so hard to move on.

"What happened to your husband, Rory?"

Her focus remained on the light reflecting off the crystal. "He was on his way home from work. It was late and a drunk ran a red light." The twin slashes between her eyebrows deepened. "He was dead at the scene."

The unnatural calm in her voice belied how totally her world had shattered at that moment. That same stillness held her there, motionless except for the movement of her finger along the spiral facets.

"And what had you heard that you couldn't ask him about?"

She barely blinked. "That he'd married me to spite his parents.

"It was after Curt's funeral," she added quietly. "At the reception." His parents had wanted the reception after the service at the club. She hadn't cared where it had been held, had been fine with going in whichever direction she'd been pointed. Other than Tyler, she hadn't cared about anything at all.

"I was in the restroom when some other women came in. They didn't know I was there because I overheard one of them ask how long Curt and I had been married. One of Audrey's friends told her, then said I was nothing like the women he'd usually gone out with. Refined women, she'd called them. I heard someone else say that everyone knew he'd married me just to spite his parents. Apparently, not long after Audrey heard we were dating, she started setting him up with women she thought more appropriate. The more polite consensus was that he'd married me to get her off his back."

That was the only clear memory she had of that entire day. So much of it had been a fog of hugs, sympathetic murmurings and just wanting to find the friends watching Tyler and get her son out of there.

She absently hooked the icicle she held onto the nearest branch. "He'd never told me his mother was doing that. But it could certainly explain why he'd wanted to elope." She'd thought at the time that his idea to run off to Lake Tahoe had sounded wonderfully romantic. But at barely twenty-one, what had she known?

"I'd been happy. I'd thought he was, too." Her hand fell, her voice along with it. "He'd always put in long hours. But that last year he'd put in even more. He'd been trying to make partner," she said, though she had no idea why the detail even mattered now. "After hearing those women, I couldn't help wondering if he was really away so much because of work. Or because he just didn't want to be there with me and I'd been too naive to realize it."

Her throat felt oddly tight. It had been well over a year since she'd verbalized that fear. She'd found out later that some of their friends had heard the rumors that day, too. Audrey, grieving herself, and in an apparent effort to save face for both of them, had even called her the next day to apologize for her friends' "lack of sensitivity at such a time." She had not, however, denied their conclusions.

Rory swallowed. Hard.

Feeling nearly as bewildered and betrayed as she had that awful afternoon, she pushed her fingers through her hair, trying desperately to force a smile. "I think now would be a really good time for you to give me the estimate I'm looking for. Six more months? A year? Please just don't say 'never.'"

For long seconds, Erik said nothing. He remained an arm's length away, his thoughts about the women's thoughtlessness anything but charitable, and fought the instinct to pull her into his arms.

He'd had closure when his marriage had fallen apart. He'd had answers to his questions. After he'd divorced, there had been no doubt in his mind that his marriage had been irreparably broken. The way this woman's had ended, she was left with questions that could never be answered.

Not by the man she'd married.

He seriously questioned Curt having had any ulterior motive when he'd married her. There was far too much about her to be attracted to, too much to truly care about.

Since the guy wasn't around to tell her what all those things were, he'd just have to enlighten her himself.

"Come here."

Taking her by the hand, he led her toward the wing chair by the sofa, muting the television on the way, and nudged her to the cushion. With his side to the fire, he hitched at the knees of his jeans and sat down on the heavy hassock in front of her.

Resting his forearms on his thighs, he clasped his hands loosely between them. "You want my take on this?"

Her arms crossed protectively at her waist, she murmured a soft, "Please."

"For starters," he began, being as objective as possible, "it's far more logical to conclude that he married you not to spite his parents, but *in* spite of them. You're beautiful, smart and easy to be with. For the most part," he qualified when she blinked at him in disbelief. "You can be pretty unreasonable at times," he pointed out, mostly so he wouldn't have to consider how unwillingly drawn he was to her himself. "But, trust me, he was attracted to you. He had to be." Especially if she'd showed up at the office looking the way she had the other night in that suit and heels.

"As for what those big mouths in the bathroom said about you being different," he continued, "you probably were. If he'd been going out with society types or old money or whatever his mother considered 'refined,' you'd have been a breath of fresh air."

A few years out from leaving the mobile nest of her fairly unconventional parents, there probably hadn't been an ounce of pretension about her. Even now, the polish he suspected she'd acquired in her husband's circles seemed as understated as her quiet sensuality. There was something about her that defied definition. It was almost as if her desire for permanence had forced her from her parents' artistic, nomadic lifestyle to seek stability in the urbane and conservative and she'd yet to find where she was comfortable in between. What truly impressed him, though, was the strength that pushed her past what many would see as totally daunting obstacles, along with a seemingly innate ability to nurture, to ease and to make a man feel as if every word he uttered mattered.

The way she made him feel just then.

"He might not have even realized how constrained he

felt until you came along." Thinking of the emotionally vacant relationships he personally limited himself to, he cleared his throat, glanced from the quiet way she watched him. "You went to work as his secretary. Right?"

Looking a little doubtful about his assessment, she gave a small nod. "He'd been there four years."

"So even before you came along, his career choices made it pretty clear he had a mind of his own. It sounds like he was willing to follow the family profession, but on his own terms. When he did meet you, I doubt he gave a second's thought to what his mom and dad would think. By the time he realized he wanted you in his life, their opinion might have mattered to him, but not as much as you did."

He knew for a fact that the physical pull between a man and a woman tended to lead the way where the sexes were concerned. If Curt had been half the man Erik suspected he was, he'd have had as hard a time as he was at that moment keeping his hands to himself. On the parental objection front, he couldn't imagine his own folks finding any fault with her at all.

"As for eloping," he continued, not at all sure where that last thought had come from, "he probably knew his parents wouldn't be willing participants, so it just made sense to avoid the problem. Most guys I know prefer to duck all the big wedding plans, anyway. Unless that's what his fiancée really wants," he qualified, because he'd given in on that one himself.

A bit of red glitter clung to one knee of her jeans. With the tip of her index finger, she gave it a nudge. "I didn't care about anything big, Erik. I just wanted to marry him."

He had no idea why that didn't surprise him. What did was how a while ago, he'd wanted details. Now, he did not.

"A little more insider info here," he offered, despite a stab of what felt suspiciously like envy. "Men aren't that complicated. If Curt was like most of us, if he was working longer hours, he was just doing what he needed to do to get ahead in his field and provide the kind of life he wanted for his family. It's what a guy does," he said simply. "Our egos tend to be tied to what we do for a living. But our work is also how we take care of the people we care about."

As if he'd just touched on something familiar, her glance lifted, then promptly fell.

She'd forgotten how often Curt had told her that he wouldn't be putting in those hours forever. That soon he'd be a partner and they could afford a bigger house, better cars, the kinds of vacations he wanted them to take. So many times he'd told her he was doing what he was doing for them.

She'd loved him for that. But she also remembered telling him she couldn't imagine living in a house larger than the one they had. She'd been fine—more than fine—with everything they'd already possessed.

"I think he needed bigger and better more than I did."

"That's entirely possible." Erik watched her nudge again at the bit of sparkle, the rest of her fingers curled into her palm. "A lot of people measure their success by their acquisitions. Especially if the people around them do the same thing." He wouldn't be in business himself if there weren't people who wanted to own the exclusive sailing sloops he loved to build. "That doesn't mean he wasn't thinking of you. And Tyler. And don't forget, he also cared enough about what you had together to work through the...ah... baby problem you two had," he decided to call it, "and adopt that great little guy upstairs."

What she had recalled moments ago had put a microscopic tear in the doubts that had caused her to question nearly every memory. Erik's conclusions had just ripped that hole wide.

She had no secrets from this man, she realized. There was nothing of any import about her he didn't know and, in some inexplicable way, seem to understand. Because of that he had just reminded her of a time when she had known without a doubt that her husband loved her. Curt had been so worried about losing her, of her thinking less of him because he couldn't give her the child they'd both wanted so much. Yet the struggles, disappointments and finally the joy of Tyler had only brought them closer.

So many details of her married life had faded in the past months. So much had been lost or skewed by second-guessing and uncertainties. But that much she remembered with crystal clarity, and while the memory was a bittersweet reminder of what she had lost, it also felt mercifully…healing.

"As for the rest of it," he said quietly, "if you were happy and if he seemed happy with you and Tyler, that's all that matters." Without thinking, he reached over, traced his finger over hers. "If you'd stop looking for ways to explain what you heard, I think you'd probably know that."

The tip of his finger moved over her knuckles, his touch gentle, reassuring. His strong hand looked huge next to hers, and she wanted badly to absorb his certainty as he uncurled her fingers and rested his palm on the back of her hand.

"Do you think you can do that?" he asked.

Watching his fingers curve around hers, she gave another little nod.

"That's a start, then," he murmured.

He had no idea how far beyond a start he'd led her.

At that moment, with Erik doing nothing but holding her hand, she couldn't help but think of how Curt would have really liked this man. She could have hugged him herself for defending Curt the way he had—had she not already been wishing he would hold her.

He tipped up her chin, curved his hand to the side of her face. "Are you okay?" he asked.

Her heart gave an odd little bump. "Sure."

"You're a really lousy liar."

She had no idea what he saw in her expression. She just knew her throat felt suspiciously tight as his dark eyes narrowed on hers.

"You'll be all right, Rory. I don't know how long it will take for you," he admitted, surprising empathy in the deep tones of his voice. "It was a couple of years before I realized I was having a good time again. But you'll get better before you even realize it's happening."

Her head unconsciously moved toward his palm. The heat of his hand felt good against her cheek, warm, comforting. Grounding. At that moment, she just didn't know if it was that anchoring touch or his confident assurance that she needed most. She felt relieved by that contact. It was as if he was letting her know she wasn't as alone as she so often felt. She craved that security as much as she did his disarming gentleness when his thumb brushed the curve of her jaw and edged to the corner of her mouth.

His eyes followed the slow movement, his carved features going taut as he carried that mesmerizing motion to her bottom lip.

Her breath caught. When she felt his thumb give a little tug, her heart bumped hard against her ribs.

An instant later, his jaw tightened and his hand fell.

At his abrupt withdrawal, disappointment shot through her. Swift and unsettling. She wouldn't have pulled away, wouldn't have done a thing to stop him had he moved closer. Knowing that, embarrassingly certain he did, too, Rory rose before he could and reached for an empty mug on the end table.

"Sorry," she murmured. "I said I wouldn't do that again. Dump on you like that, I mean."

When she turned back, Erik had pushed himself to his feet.

Beyond his broad shoulders, a log broke in the fireplace, embers spraying upward. The tick of ice blowing hard against the window grew more audible with another gust of wind.

The storm added yet another layer of unease.

"I asked," he reminded her.

"That's true." Hoping to shake how he unsettled her, she tried for a smile. "So it's your fault."

She was talking about his uncanny ability to uncork her most private concerns. From the way his glance dropped to her mouth, he seemed to be thinking more of the seductive pull snaking across the six feet of tension separating them.

Or maybe it was just her own tension she felt.

"Just part of the service."

He'd only been doing his job.

The reminder had her ducking her head as she turned away. It didn't matter that she'd wanted his kiss, or how badly she'd wanted him to hold her. It didn't even matter that she didn't trust what she'd felt when she'd been in his arms before, that almost desperate need to hide in his strength.

He'd offered her his help, a little comfort and his experience. What he wasn't offering was a refuge, and she had no business thinking of him as one.

"If you don't mind, I think I'll just say good-night now," she murmured. "You're welcome to stay down here and watch TV if you want. My bedroom is the one—"

"I know where your bedroom is, Rory."

Of course he did.

"The sheets are clean and I put clean towels in the master bathroom." Her bathroom wasn't very big, but he already knew that, too. "I set out a new toothbrush for you."

"I'll figure it out," he assured her. "Is there anything you want me to do down here?"

"Just bank the fire."

The rest could wait until morning.

The telltale muscle in his jaw jerked. "Consider it banked. I'll take care of that," he said, taking the mug from her. "You go on up. I'll catch the news for a while and turn off the lights."

He obviously felt the need for a little space, too.

More than willing to give it to him, she started for the stairs.

The silence behind her and the faint ticking of ice against glass had her turning right back.

"Is the roof up there okay? It can handle the weight of the ice, can't it?"

"The roof should be fine."

She lifted her chin, turned back again.

Another step and she turned right back. "Is there anything I can get you before I go up?"

He'd barely met her eyes again before he shook his head and turned away himself. "I don't need a thing," he assured her. "Just go to bed. I'll see you in the morning."

Chapter Eight

For Rory, sleep rarely came easily. When it did, it was usually fitful, an often futile exercise where the loneliness she could sometimes mask with activity during the day reared its ugly head at night to haunt her. But she must have been asleep. Something had just wakened her, a distant, cracking sound followed by an odd, heavy silence.

With Tyler's back tucked against her, she blinked into the dark. Realizing that it shouldn't be that dark since his night-light should have been on, she reached for her robe at the foot of the twin bed.

She had no idea what time it had been when she'd heard Erik come up the stairs and close the door at the end of the hall. She'd lain there listening to the sound of water in the bathroom pipes and the heavy creak of floorboards as he'd moved around her room. When silence seemed to indicate that he'd gone to bed, she'd attempted to block further thought in that direction by listening to her son's deep, even breathing and the wind gusting like muffled cannon blasts against his bedroom wall beside her.

The ice pelting the window had no longer sounded as sharp, as if the buildup had muffled it. The only thing that had allowed her to not feel as anxious as she might have about the fury outside had been thinking about the man down the hall being so near.

Now she heard nothing at all.

There was no clock in Tyler's room. Quietly, so as not to wake her sleeping child, she pulled on her robe and found her way to the door.

The moment she opened it, she realized the electricity had gone out. The night-light in Tyler's bathroom across the hall wasn't on. Neither was the one in the outlet down by her room. The hall was as black as pitch.

She kept a flashlight in her nightstand, another in a drawer in the kitchen. Without questioning why she didn't head for her room, she edged toward the stairs, her hand sliding along the wall to guide her to the handrail.

"Rory?"

Her hand flattened over the jolt behind her breastbone. "Erik," she whispered, turning toward his hushed voice. "Where are you?"

"By your bedroom door. Where are you?"

"By the stairs," she whispered. "What was that noise?"

"It sounded like a tree went down. My guess is that it took out a power line." Across twenty feet of dark came the soft, metallic rasp of a zipper. "Do you have a flashlight up here?"

It seemed he'd just zipped up his jeans. Thinking he could well be standing there shirtless, she murmured, "The nightstand on the left. In the drawer."

She heard him move inside, and his mild oath when he bumped into something, the end of the bed, probably. Moments later, shadows bounced around the room and a flash of bright light arched low into the hall. Following that blue-white beam, he walked up to her, his undershirt and sweater in his free hand, and handed her the light.

She kept the beam angled down, the pool of it at his feet. Still, there was more than enough illumination to define every superbly sculpted muscle of his chest.

Deliberately, she moved her glance to the heavy sports watch on his wrist. "Do you know what time it is?" she asked.

"Almost seven."

It would be getting light in less than an hour.

He dropped the sweater. In two quick motions he shoved his beautifully muscled arms into his long-sleeved undershirt.

"When you did the walk-through with the building inspector, did he say anything about the generator? It should only have taken seconds for it to take over."

The generator? "He said it was set to come on for a few minutes once a week," she told him, scrambling to remember as she watched him pull his shirt over his head. "To make sure it'll be available when I really need it," she added.

Erik's dark head popped out, rearranging his already sleep-mussed hair. His jaw was shadowed, hard and angular in the dim light. "Has it been working?"

"I don't know." The gray metal generator on the slab at the back of the building hadn't been on her priority list. It hadn't been on her list at all. Until now. "I think he said it's set for either Tuesday or Wednesday mornings. We haven't been here then."

He swiped the sweater from where it had landed near her beam-lit, glittery-red toenails. Rising, his glance skimmed the length of her pale robe, only to jerk away before he met her eyes.

She'd barely realized he looked nearly as tense as he

had when she'd left him last night before he dragged the sweater over his head and tugged it down. "I'll check the transfer switch. Then I'll get a fire going.

"I just need this." He took the flashlight from her. "Give me a minute and you'll have enough light to do whatever you need to do up here. The hall light won't work, but the bathroom lights will. Did he explain how the standby works?"

A transfer switch sounded familiar. The guy who'd inspected the building a couple of weeks ago had pointed it out. It was in one of the electrical panel boxes in the basement.

"I think so. I don't remember everything he told me," she admitted. "We looked at a lot around here that day." There'd also been Tyler to calm. He hadn't liked the huge, shadowy space. "There was a lot to take in."

Something shifted in Erik's expression. She knew he'd been aware of how overwhelmed she'd been by Cornelia's intervention, and by how suddenly she'd found herself in a place she'd known nothing about at all. It stood to reason there were a few things she might have missed, or had forgotten. As it was, she could have managed on her own to start a fire to keep Tyler warm. She just had no idea what to do about the generator—which meant, right now, she couldn't fix this particular problem without him.

She didn't doubt that he knew that, too, as he followed the beam of light down the stairs, pulled on the heavy boots he'd left at the bottom and disappeared into the dark.

Feeling at a distinct disadvantage where he was concerned, and hating it, she turned in the dark herself, working her way first to Tyler's bathroom, then back to his room. She'd just started to put on the clothes she'd left on his play table last night when she heard his bedclothes rustle.

"Mom? I'm a-scared."

"It's okay, honey. I'm right here. The power went out," she explained, her voice soft, "but it'll be back on in a minute." Leaving her robe on, she found her way to him, hugged his warm little body to hers. "You don't need to be afraid." Forcing a smile into her voice, she murmured, "You know what?"

His response was the negative shake of his head against her neck.

"I have a big surprise for you."

"Is the tree all done?"

"It is. But that's not the surprise."

She felt him pull back. "Is he here?"

He. Erik.

The man's presence was not at all the news she'd hoped would get his morning off to a better start.

"He's downstairs," she told him, and felt certain he'd have scooted off the bed that very moment had he been able to see where he was going.

She'd thought to tell him her surprise was the big adventure the day might be, since making an adventure of uncertainties, for the most part, had taken his mind off his fears and insecurities before. Since Erik had unknowingly just accomplished that for her, she told him they'd just wait right where they were while his idol turned the lights back on.

Instead of electric lights, however, it was the beam of the flashlight that illuminated the hall outside the open door.

The beam swung inward, causing Tyler to bury his head in her chest at the momentary brightness and her to block the sudden flash with her hand.

"Sorry," Erik muttered. He aimed the beam at the rumpled bedding on the trundle. "It's not the switch. I'll have to wait until it's light out to see what the problem is."

The circle of light bouncing off the cerulean sheets

filled the room with shades of pale blue. Along the far wall, he watched Rory cuddling her son on the higher bed, her hair tousled, her hand slowly soothing the child's flannel-covered back as Tyler turned to smile at him.

It hit him then, as they sat huddled in the semi-dark, that all they really had was each other. He'd realized that on some level last night when he'd prodded her about where they'd spend Christmas. But seeing them now, realizing how much she'd lost and how vulnerable she could easily feel being that alone here, drove that reality home.

The troubling protectiveness he felt for her slid back into place. That same protectiveness had been there last night, protecting her from him.

He'd had no business touching her last night. All he'd wanted when he'd met them at the tree lot yesterday was to make sure she could give her little boy the Christmas she wanted for him.

All he'd wanted last night was her.

There hadn't been a trace of defense in her pretty face when he'd touched her. Nothing that even remotely suggested she would have stopped him if he'd pulled her to him. He'd known when he'd left there a few days ago that distance was his best defense against complications with her. Especially since the not-so-subtle needs she aroused in him simply by her presence had a definite tendency to sabotage objectivity where she was concerned.

Having sabotaged the distance angle himself simply by showing up, it seemed like some perverted form of justice that distance was going to be deprived him for a while.

"Do you have another flashlight up here?" Objectivity now appeared to be his only defense. And objectively, she truly needed far more help from him than a little tutoring with the store. "Something stronger than this?"

"The only other I have is just like that one. It's in the kitchen in the phone desk drawer."

"You need something brighter. I'll get one of the camp lamps from the store and bring it back for you to use up here."

She didn't know she had camp lamps. But then, she hadn't finished her inventory, either.

"We'll wait," she told him, then watched him leave them, literally, in the dark.

There was something he wasn't telling her. She would have bet her silk long underwear on that, had she not needed to wear it under her favorite gray fleece sweats to keep warm.

She couldn't believe how quickly the house had cooled. She turned the thermostat down every night, but without the furnace running at all, the temperature inside had dropped ten degrees within the hour.

She'd compensated by bundling Tyler in long johns, fleece pants, heavy socks, slippers, an undershirt, thermal shirt and sweatshirt and parking him under a blanket in front of the blaze Erik had built in the fireplace.

The only layer Erik had added was his jacket when he'd gone out a few minutes ago. He'd already left it in the mudroom when the thud of his heavy-treaded work boots announced his return.

"This is the last of the wood you brought in yesterday. I'll get more from the shed in a while."

The drapes were still closed, but the edges of the room were no longer dark. The fire had grown to throw flickering light into the room. The camp light that now occupied the dining table illuminated from that direction much like a table lamp.

Tyler smiled up at him.

"Can we turn on the tree?" he wanted to know.

He hadn't been talking to her. "We don't have electricity yet," she reminded him anyway. "Why don't you read

Frosty?" With the suggestion, she handed him his new favorite picture book. "And I'll get you something to eat."

Concern suddenly swept his little face. Dropping the book, he shoved off the blanket and headed for the wall of drape-covered windows.

"Is there a problem with the furnace, too?" she asked Erik, wondering what her little boy was up to. Wondering, too, if a problem with the furnace was what the larger male wasn't sharing. "It's oil. Not electric. Shouldn't it be working?"

Tyler pulled back the living room drapes. Dawn lightened the window, but the coating of frost and ice on the glass made it impossible to make out anything beyond it.

The logs landed with quiet thuds at the far end of the hearth. "The furnace is oil, but the fan and pump are electric. You need power to pump the oil and push out the hot air."

Great, she thought. "Oh," she said.

Tyler let go of the drape. The heavy fabric still swung slightly as he ran to the dining room window next to it and pulled back the drape there.

"How come I can't see it?" he asked.

"See what, honey?"

"The snowman. He has lights."

"Hey, Tyler. I heard your mom say she'd get your breakfast. How about we get that out of the way before we tackle anything else?"

At the obvious change of subject, Rory's glance darted to Erik. It was met with the quick shake of his head and the pinch of his brow.

He moved to her side, his voice low. "I don't think you'll want him to see it yet. Give me time to fix it first. I haven't been all the way around the building, but some of those gusts last night were pretty strong. You might want to take a look from the store porch.

"So," he continued, brushing off his hands as he walked over to the child smiling up at him. "Why don't you show me what kind of cereal we're having?"

Totally distracted by his friend's attention, Tyler dutifully led the way to the pantry while Rory grabbed a flashlight and headed for the door into the store. On the way, she could hear Erik asking questions about flakes versus puffs and Tyler answering like an expert before she closed the inner door and hurried by flashlight beam to the outer one.

She'd barely opened the store's front door and screen and crossed her arms against the freezing air when she froze herself.

The world outside had been transformed into a wonderland as disheartening as it was beautiful. In the pale twilight, the stubbles of her lawn appeared to be a blanket of clear marbles. Across the ice-glazed street, every bough on every tall pine, every branch of every winter-bare tree, every leaf on every bush had been encased in a robe of ice.

In between, the ice-coated electric line sagged heavily from pole to pole—except for where it dangled loose a few feet from the tangle of branches of an oak tree now uprooted from her yard and lying across the road, blocking it completely.

Near the entrance to her driveway, half of the maple tree that would shade it in summer lay squarely in it.

Clouds filtered the cold sunrise, but the sky to the east was lightening enough to add hints of color to the gray when she carefully edged her way over the icy boards to the end of the porch and looked toward the meadow. It was there that she saw the snowman that now rested in parts not far from the still upright and remarkably unbroken apple tree. The white chicken-wire, light-encrusted balls had separated when they'd blown over and were now frozen in place with boughs that had flown in from the grove of pines beyond.

Erik had suspected that seeing the dismembered decoration would have upset her little boy. He was right. And though what she saw distressed her, too—especially when she thought of what had to be an identical mess of toppled debris on the other side of the building—she wouldn't let herself think about how she was going to clean it all up right now. Mother Nature froze it, and she'd thaw it, too. She'd worry then about taking care of the scattered and broken boughs, branches and trees. Right now she couldn't let herself think about anything beyond going back inside, making sure the guys were fed and figuring out how to make coffee without any power.

The rest of it was just too daunting.

"Thank you," she said softly on her way past Erik the moment she walked back in.

He stood at the island, Tyler a few feet away at the silverware drawer. "No problem." He searched her face quickly, looking to see how she was taking what she had seen.

Not sure what to make of the deceptive calm she diligently maintained around her child, he turned with two boxes in his hands. "Cereal?"

"Sure." Doing her best to ignore the knot of anxiety in her stomach, she reached for bowls and bananas. "What kind are you having, Ty?"

"Both," her son announced.

"We're mixing 'em," Erik explained.

The camp light now stood on the kitchen counter. In that relative brightness, Tyler's eyes fairly danced.

The dark slash of Erik's eyebrow arched. "Is that a problem?"

For a moment she thought the suggestion must have been Erik's, until she considered that Tyler could have come up with the idea and Erik had decided to let him think the notion a good one. Looking between the two of them, she decided it could go either way. And either way, as protective as Erik had been of her son's feelings moments ago, and sensing that what that mountain of muscle really needed was to be outside and moving, she couldn't think of a thing to say but, "Of course not."

Being deprived of his usual five-mile morning run did nothing to help Erik escape the restiveness nagging like a toothache as he headed into the early morning light. The bracing air felt good, though. He didn't even mind that the ground felt like a skating rink beneath his boots. His balance on it was as sure as on a yawing sailboat—managing that shift and roll was second nature to him.

Where he was out of his element was figuring out how to stay objective about the woman inside when he'd been kept awake half the night by her scent on her sheets and thoughts of her tantalizing little body playing havoc with his own.

When he had first agreed to help her, he hadn't considered how much her education would require beyond a business plan and inventory. But the scope of his responsibility had finally hit him. It had taken both of his grandparents to maintain their store and their home. For her to make it here, she'd need to be as self-reliant as they had been.

What he also hadn't considered until a while ago was how much more difficult her tasks might be because part of her focus would almost always be on her child.

Ten minutes and another trip to the basement later, she had power—which was one less thing he needed to be concerned about before he headed back upstairs to see her by the light switch in the dining room.

"You fixed it." Relief lit her guarded smile as she pushed the toggle. "I heard the refrigerator come on. And the furnace."

From where he'd stopped in the entryway, he watched her glance up at the still dark fixture above the long table.

"That light is off circuit right now," he told her. "The only overhead light you have up here is in the kitchen. Besides the bathroom lights upstairs, you have one live outlet in each bedroom. All the appliances up here have power. So does the water heater in the basement, but the washer and dryer don't."

The minor inconveniences barely fazed her. "What was wrong with the generator?"

"The fuel line valve from the propane tank had been left in the off position. It could have been turned when the servicing company filled it, or by the inspector when he checked it out. Either way," he said, conscious of her concentration, "it would be a good idea for you to check it the next time it's filled. I'll show you later how to thaw the valve in case it ever freezes in place again. Right now there are a few things I want to show you in the basement."

"I wanna go to the basement," Tyler announced.

Rory looked to where he had just jumped to his feet. "I thought you didn't like the basement."

With a small shrug, he walked up to Erik.

"It's okay," was all Tyler said, but it was infinitely more obvious than Erik's faint smile that it was only okay because of the big guy.

With more immediate concerns to deal with, she knew she couldn't afford to worry about that growing attachment now. His new hero had the vaguely impatient look of a man on a mission as he led them down the steep stairs and across the concrete floor.

Because Tyler wanted to see what he was talking about, he scooped him up, catching his small hand to keep him from touching anything, and proceeded to describe how the transfer of the power between the generator and the grid took place and how this system had a double-pole,

double-throw transfer switch gear as a safety feature because it was the best way to prevent shock or electrocution.

Her son looked fascinated by what the big man holding
him so easily was saying about currents, shutoffs and sen-
sors. And while she grasped the basics of what she needed
to know, much of the detail escaped her just then. She had
no problem, however, recognizing when something could
be dangerous. As the day wore on, she even found herself
wondering if there was any double sort of safety feature
a woman could use to protect herself from the effects of
a man who had the disturbing ability to draw her to him
even as he pushed her away.

"I just want to know how to use a regular saw. Okay?
The one you used to trim the trunk on the Christmas tree
would work fine."

"It would work on the smaller branches," Erik agreed,
the icy breeze carrying away the fog of his breath, "but
not for those you need to cut to get something this size
moved. If you're serious about this, a chain saw is faster
and a lot less work."

Concern clearly battled her determination.

"If I'm using that, I won't be able to hear Tyler if he
needs me. And I can't have him right with me, because I
don't want him anywhere near that thing."

"I'll show you how to use the handsaw." He didn't hesi-
tate to offer the assurance, aware himself of the child on
the porch, breaking ice off the fir boughs she'd collected
for a wreath. "But you should know how to use this, too.
We'll be where you can keep an eye on him."

He watched Rory look from the wicked-looking chain
saw blade to the long tangle of ice-coated limbs that had
split away from the maple on the far side of the drive. A
slash of exposed, raw wood on the heavy trunk mirrored

the ragged tear on the thick branch where it had fallen from the tree's side.

He'd already cut up the branch that had fallen atop it with the now-silent saw he'd borrowed from her neighbor. He'd heard the saw's droning buzz when he'd come outside a couple of hours ago to fix Frosty and put a little physical distance between himself and his charge. Being near her in the confines of the house had left him too edgy, too restless. Outdoors, he at least had the buffer of space.

His glance slid from her burgundy fleece headband and jacket to the hem of her jeans. Since she'd kept herself occupied away from him for the better part of the morning, he suspected she'd been after a little distance, too.

Apparently having reassessed her options, and with her immediate concern addressed, she anchored the toe of her black boot in the loop of the saw's handle. "So," she gamely began, "I start it by putting my foot here?" she asked. "And pulling on this?"

Catching her arm as she reached for the starter pull, he turned her in the churned-up gravel to face him. "You start by putting on these."

He tugged off his heavy leather gloves, then slipped the clear safety goggles Ed Shumway also loaned him from around his neck.

Teaching her how to use a saw hadn't been on the agenda he'd outlined for himself that morning, but she'd wanted to know how to use one to clear the property after it thawed. Since he didn't much care for the thought of her outside sawing and hauling limbs by herself, he'd already planned to have the mess cleared for her. This wasn't the only storm she'd likely ever encounter, though. And he wouldn't be around once she was on her financial feet. If she was going to be self-sufficient, it was his job to give her the tools she'd need to make that happen.

Reaching toward her, he looped the goggles' wide elastic strap around the back of her head. Not giving her time to take off her gloves to adjust the bright orange band, he did it himself and settled the clear skilike goggles in place.

"Keep in mind that the barter system still works for a few things around here, too," he informed her, tucking back a strand of the dark hair he'd dislodged from the fleece covering her ears. "Someone should be willing to take care of all these trees for you in exchange for a load or two they can sell or use for firewood."

Far too conscious of the softness of her skin, the silk of her hair, he deliberately dropped his hand.

Pulling his gloves from where he'd tucked them under his arm, he jerked them back on and nodded to the saw. "Now you can start it."

Rory braced herself. Not so much for what she was about to do, but because everything about this man had her feeling so off balance.

He'd given her his jacket a while ago. He stood there now in his heavy charcoal pullover and jeans, seeming totally unfazed by the cold and the almost familiar ease with which he'd touched her.

"Hold the blade straighter," he called over the din of the idling motor. With his broad chest pressed to her back, he reached his arms around her, placed his gloved hands over hers and adjusted her angle.

"Ready?" he asked, his breath warm through the soft knit covering her ear.

Conscious of his body enclosing hers, she gave a tense little nod.

She wasn't sure which disconcerted her more, the thirteen pounds of suddenly screaming machine, or the man surrounding her, making sure she didn't hurt herself with it. With the blade engaged, metal teeth spinning, the chain bit ice. A quick spray of what looked like snow and wood chips flew.

"Keep your grip steady." He spoke near her cheek now, his body still at her back as he eased his hands to her shoulders. "You need to keep it from bucking back if you hit a knot. Keep it under control."

Control, she thought. She hadn't felt "in control" in ages.

"Like this?" she called, handles in a death grip, her eyes glued to the blade sinking into the wood.

"Just like that," he called back and, just like that, the weight of the free end of the limb cracked it downward and the blade went through.

A second of disbelief was replaced with a grin as she swung toward him.

"Don't!" His hand shot forward, the side of his face bumping the corner of her goggles an instant before his hand caught hers to hold the saw in place. Bent against her, he'd turned his head to hers, his lips inches from the startled part of her own.

"The brake," he said. With a small movement of his hand, the throttle dropped back to idle. "You need to set it as soon as you finish your cut. It's safer that way."

She realized now why he'd stayed behind her. Had she swung around, she could have caught him with the blade in his thigh.

Taking the idling machine from her, he shut off the motor, set the saw on the ground.

In the sudden silence, she could hear her heart hammering in her ears. Shaken from the start he'd given her, horrified by what she could have done to him, she dropped her glance to the short placket on his pullover as he rose and turned to her.

"Erik, I'm so sorry."

His forehead furrowed as he pulled her hand from her mouth and lifted the orange band at her temples. Removing the goggles, he looped them over the fabric covering his forearm.

"Hey. It's okay." Hating how he'd killed her quick smile, he touched his gloved finger to her high cheekbone. It was there that the goggles would have bumped. "We hadn't gotten to that part." Another second and they would have, he thought, searching her pale features. He just hadn't expected her to get excited about felling a limb. "Next time you'll remember."

He couldn't feel the smoothness of her skin through the thick suede. He could imagine it, though. Just as he could too easily imagine so many other things he knew he shouldn't be thinking about her.

Detachment wasn't an option at the moment. Not with her looking so frightened by what she could have done. "Right?"

Beneath his hand, he felt her faint nod. What he noticed most, though, was how her head turned toward his hand, as if somewhere in her subconscious she craved that unfettered contact, too.

She'd done the same thing last night, right about the time he'd been thinking about reacquainting himself with the feel of her mouth. Heaven knew how tempted he'd been to do just that. But he acknowledged now what he hadn't then. It hadn't just been complications with her he wanted to avoid. He hadn't wanted her thinking of anyone but him when he kissed her. And last night had been far more about easing the doubts that had haunted her for so long than whatever it was that kept him from caring about how easy she was to touch.

Rory watched his glance shift over her face. She had no idea what he was thinking, what it was vying with the concern so evident there, but from the way his eyes narrowed on her cheek, he seemed to be looking for a bruise.

"It didn't hurt," she told him, praying she hadn't caused him one as she unconsciously lifted her hand to his temple.

"I don't see a mark," he murmured. "But that doesn't mean you won't have a bruise later. You should get some ice on it." He gave her an encouraging smile. "There's plenty of it."

She felt far too concerned to smile back. "I don't see one on you, either," she told him, tipping her head to get a better look. "Not yet, anyway."

Erik's smile faded. He couldn't remember the last time a woman had touched him simply to make sure he was okay. There was caring in that touch, a hint of worry, a little gentleness. As complex as it seemed, it was really such a simple thing. Something basic. Yet her unveiled concern pulled hard at something deep inside him. Something he hadn't been sure still existed, and which would have felt decidedly threatening had he had time to consider what it was.

"Mom? Come help me?"

At her son's request, Rory's hand fell. Only now aware of how she'd reached to be sure Erik was all right, and of how they must look standing there checking each other out, her glance darted to where Tyler stood by a stack of pine on the porch.

He wanted help with the wreath.

Taking a step back, she called that she'd be right there.

Erik met her lingering disquiet.

"Stop worrying. You're quick. You'll get the hang of this," he insisted. "We'll give it another try later. In the meantime, you did fine. Really."

"Except for the part where I nearly disabled you," she muttered, half under her breath.

"I had you covered, Rory. You were a long way from anything like that."

A split second was hardly a long way. She'd have

pointed that out had his assessment of her capabilities not just registered. It was like last night, she thought, when he'd talked her through the doubts and turmoil of the past year. It seemed he didn't want her doubting her abilities, or herself, about anything.

He clearly expected her to challenge his last claim. The quick part, probably. She couldn't. Last night he had called her beautiful, smart and stubborn. The stubbornness she would concede. That he thought her beautiful and smart still left her a little stunned. But what mattered to her most was that for him to feel so certain about her meant he might actually believe in her himself.

Until that moment, she hadn't realized how badly she wanted that sort of faith—that trust—from him.

"I'm going to go help Tyler now."

His eyes narrowed on hers. "You're good, then?"

He wanted to know if she believed what he'd said.

I had you covered, Rory.

"I'm good," she said, and with him already turning to his task, she headed for the porch to rescue the boughs and her rosy-cheeked child.

He had her back. He wasn't going to let anything bad happen as long as he was there.

He couldn't begin to know how much that assurance mattered to her.

Chapter Nine

Erik had told her not to worry.

Rory wasn't sure she knew how to do that. The unwelcomed trait had become second nature. Yet what concerned her far more than her lack of skill with gas-fueled equipment was how she found herself wishing Erik's solid presence could be part of the community that encouraged her with its potential.

Ed Shumway, the neighbor who'd loaned Erik the saw, was married to Edie, the loquacious neighbor who'd first welcomed her to the neighborhood. He had come to repay Erik for his assist moving a limb from his garage that morning. Having heard on the news that it would be at least two days before crews could get in to restore power, he'd brought his bigger saw to help him clear the uprooted oak from the road that was their main access to town.

Even for her neighbors who didn't have access to TV news, word traveled fast by cell phone. Crystal Murphy, her laugh infectious and her carrot-red hair clashing wildly with her purple earmuffs, brought her four-year-old son to play with Tyler while her husband, Tony the roofer, joined the men. Her mom was at their house a quarter of a mile away with their two-year-old. They didn't have power but that seemed just fine with them. They had a woodstove and kerosene lamps and Crystal confessed to liking the throwback lifestyle. She turned out to be the candle maker Edie had told Rory about.

Jeremy Ott came for the same reason as Tony and Ed. Talia, his wife, who taught riding lessons at the stables a mile farther up, had braved the cold with her five-year-old twins because Edie had mentioned that Rory had a son their age.

Edie herself showed up with her two children, twelve and six, and a half gallon of milk. With all the children, hot cocoa went fast.

Even with all the activity, Rory found her attention straying to the man who stood just a little taller than the rest.

It was nearing four o'clock when the women stepped out onto the porch to see how much longer the men would be. The kids were warming up in front of the TV, under Edie's preteen's supervision, and it would be dark soon. There were suppers to prepare.

Rory doubted that Erik had taken a real break since lunch. All she'd noticed him stop for was to stretch his back or absently rub his neck before tossing aside another log or attacking another limb on the downed oak.

She was standing by the railing between Crystal and Edie when he made a V of his arm and hitched his shoulder before putting his back into hefting another chunk of tree. He and Tony were hauling cut sections of limbs to the side of the road while the other two men continued decreasing the size of what had blocked it.

Seeing who had Rory's attention, Edie flipped her braid

over her shoulder and tipped her dark blond head toward her. A navy Seattle Seahawks headband warmed her ears.

"He's an attractive man, isn't he?"

"Who?" asked Talia, leaning past Crystal.

"Erik," the older woman replied.

Rory gave a noncommittal shrug. "I suppose." *If you like the tall, dark, unattainable type,* she thought. Suspecting her neighbor was fishing, she glanced to Edie's nearly empty mug. "More coffee?"

"I'm good. Thanks." The loquacious woman with the too-keen radar kept her focus on the men methodically dismantling the tree.

"He and his business partner have done quite well for themselves, you know."

"I'd say they've done extremely well," Crystal emphasized. "Pax—his business partner," she explained helpfully to Rory, "is from here, too. I've heard they're both millionaires."

"I've met Pax. Nice guy," Rory admitted. What she didn't mention was that she already knew that Erik had means—that he even had friends among the very rich and famous.

She had been surrounded by the well-to-do, and those intent on joining their ranks, from the moment she'd married until she'd moved mere weeks ago. The understated way Erik used his wealth and the way he didn't balk at getting his own hands dirty just made her forget that at times.

Edie gave her a curious glance. "Would you mind a personal question? I didn't want to ask when I first met you," she explained. "I mean, I did, but it didn't seem appropriate at the time."

Rory smiled, a little surprised by the request for permission. "Ask what?"

"How long you've been widowed."

"A year and two months."

"That's too bad."

"It really is," Crystal agreed. "I'm sorry, Rory."

"That has to be so hard." Talia placed her gloved hand over her heart. "I don't know what I'd do without Jeremy."

Edie shook her head. "I meant it's too bad it hasn't been longer. I was just thinking how nice it would be if you two hit it off. I'm sorry for your loss, too," she sincerely assured Rory. "But I imagine you need a little more time before you start thinking in that direction."

"I don't know about that," Talia piped in. "My uncle remarried six months after my aunt passed."

"I think men do that because they don't know how to take care of themselves," claimed Edie.

Crystal frowned. "I thought that the men who married fast like that were the ones who'd had good marriages, so they weren't afraid to jump back in."

"If that's true," Talia said, leaping ahead, "then the opposite could explain why Erik hasn't remarried. I've never heard what happened with him and...what was her name?"

"Shauna," the other two women simultaneously supplied.

"Right. She wasn't from here," she explained to Rory. "They met one summer and she moved here after they married, but they left for Seattle after a year or so. My point, though," she claimed, getting to it, "is that maybe his experience has put him off women."

"Oh, I wouldn't say he's off women," Rory admitted. "We've had a couple of meetings where he had to leave because he had a date."

Talia shrugged. "Well, there goes that theory."

"That doesn't mean he's not gun-shy," Crystal supplied supportively.

"True. But Rory's not looking right now," Edie reminded them. "Anyway, I was just thinking it would be nice if Erik would come back. I can't imagine that he ever would," she insisted, certainty in her conclusion. "Not with his business so well established over in Seattle. But he still seems to fit in so perfectly here."

The woman who'd brought up the subject of her potential availability had just as abruptly concluded it. Relieved to have escaped matchmaking efforts, for a while at least, and not sure how she felt having reminded herself of her mentor's social life, Rory found herself silently agreeing with her well-intentioned neighbor.

Erik did seem to fit in. But then, he'd been raised there. Without letting herself wonder why, she'd also wondered if there was ever anything about this place that he missed. Or if his emotional barriers kept him from even noticing.

It hadn't sounded to Rory as if the women knew the other, more personal reasons why he wouldn't be coming back. The dreams he'd buried there. Still, Edie was right. Everything Erik cared about was in Seattle.

And everything she now cared about was here, she thought, and went back to looking a little concerned about him again.

"Why didn't you stop?"

"Because we were almost finished."

"You were out there another two hours, Erik."

"That's close enough to almost. I'll be fine after a hot shower. How did it go with the neighbors?"

The man was hopeless.

"It was nice." You escaped the part where Edie wanted to make us a couple, she thought, but other than that... "Crystal is going to bring me samples of her candles to see if I'd be interested in selling them. And Talia's twins go to the school I enrolled Tyler in. We're going to carpool."

She frowned at the way he cupped his neck as he sat down at the island. He'd said he'd be fine, though. The man had a scar as wide as Tyler's tired smile on the inside of his forearm. It was visible now where he'd pushed up his sleeves. He knew how much discomfort he could handle.

"What are you grinning about, bud?" he asked, tired but smiling himself.

Tyler took a deep breath, gave a decisive nod. "This was the best day ever."

"Wow. That's pretty cool." Forearms resting on either side of his heaped and steaming bowl of stew, he looked over at the little guy who'd mimicked his position. "What made it so good?"

Tyler looked over his shoulder at the white lights softly illuminating the room behind them. The fire in the stone fireplace crackled and glowed.

"My tree. And the ice on everything. And my new friends." He wrinkled his little brow, thinking. "And Mom, 'cause I got cocoa two times. And you."

"Me?" Erik exhaled a little laugh. "What did I do?"

"Well," he began, pondering. "You fixed things. And you made Mom laugh."

Erik's glance cut to where she sat at the end of the island, back to the child between them. "I did?"

"Uh-huh," Tyler insisted, his nod vigorous. "When you dropped your coat on her."

Though Erik looked a little puzzled, Rory knew exactly what Tyler was talking about. The two of them had just gathered boughs for the wreath. She'd been sorting them on the porch, her head bent over their project, when Erik had walked up behind her and asked if she'd take his jacket. With her back to him and him in work mode, she'd no sooner said she'd be glad to when he'd unceremoniously dropped it over her head.

He'd meant it to land on her shoulders. But she'd looked up just then. Heavy and huge on her, she'd practically disappeared under the soft black leather.

She'd already been smiling at what he'd done and gone

still at the unexpectedness of it when he'd lifted the back of the collar and peeked around at her.

"You okay in there?" he'd asked, and the smile in his eyes had turned her smile into something that had sounded very much like a giggle.

She hadn't giggled since she was sixteen.

Erik apparently remembered now, too.

Looking over at Tyler, he gave his little buddy a knowing nod. He remembered the bright sound of that laugh, of hearing a hint of lightness in it he suspected she hadn't felt in a very long time.

"She needs to do that more often," he decided, and after arching his eyebrow at her, suggested Tyler finish his stew before he went after it himself.

Rory glanced away, stabbed a piece of carrot. She wished he wouldn't do that—arch his eyebrow at her that way. Something about the expression seemed teasing, playful and challenging all at once. Except for the challenging part, it also tended to disarm her and she'd been having a hard enough time remembering why she needed to keep her emotional guard in place with him pretty much since he'd strong-armed her into trying Ed's saw. Or maybe the problem had started last night, when she'd unloaded on him. Again. Or yesterday, when he'd sided with Tyler about the size of the tree.

There were reasons. Compelling ones, she was sure. She just couldn't remember them as she gave him her most charming smile and told him there was more stew if he wanted it.

He had seconds, told her it was great, then finished the bit in the pot before she carried his and Tyler's bowls to the sink.

"What Tyler said about it being a good day," he murmured, handing her his milk glass when she came back for it. "It was." He kept his focus on the glass and her hand, his tone thoughtful, as if he was a little surprised by that perception. Or perhaps by the admission.

"Now," he continued, moving past whatever had prompted it, "if you don't mind, I'm going to get that shower. You wouldn't have a spare razor, would you?"

She told him she did. A small package of them was in the drawer below where she'd left the toothbrush on the counter for him last night. She didn't bother telling him they were hot pink.

It did Rory's heart good to know her little boy had had such a good time that day. It did something less definable to it to know Erik had somehow appreciated it, too. Something that fed an unfamiliar bubble of hope that common sense told her was best to ignore. But with Tyler pretty much worn out and in need of a bath, she gave it no further thought. By the time she'd helped him with his bath and his prayers, it was all he could do to keep his eyes open.

Erik seemed to have had the same problem. When she finally came back down the dimly lit stairs, the fire was nearly out and Erik had fallen asleep in front of the television.

He lay stretched out on the sofa in his jeans and pullover, one leg angled with his bare foot on the cushion, the other foot on the floor. With his dark head propped on the curved arm of the sofa, one arm thrown over his eyes, his other hand splayed on his stomach, it looked as if he'd intended to catch something more entertaining than the weather report before turning in for the night.

The volume on the detective series had been muted, though.

They hadn't talked about it, but there had been no question that he would stay again that night. The negligible melt that afternoon had started refreezing the lower the sun had sunk and, last they'd heard, it was taking forever to get anywhere on the roads. Those that were open, anyway.

That was why he'd followed the Otts home in his monster of a truck, because they'd made the drive on balding tires, and dropped off the Shumways since it was dark by then and they'd all walked earlier.

His breathing was deep and even as she picked up the television's remote and turned off the set.

As exhausted as she suspected he was, she didn't want to wake him. She shouldn't stand there thinking about what a beautiful man he was, either. Or how kind and generous he truly seemed to be even when he didn't want her getting too close. There was something terribly intimate about watching him sleep. Something that might almost have felt intrusive had she allowed herself to remain there any longer.

She lifted the soft throw blanket from the arm of the chair, moved back to lift it over him. Smiling a little at his freshly shaved face, she eased the covering over him. When he didn't move, she let out the breath she hadn't even realized she'd been holding and carefully lifted her hand to his head.

Her fingers had just skimmed the barely damp hair he'd combed back from his forehead when she went still. She hadn't been thinking. She'd simply started to do what she always did with Tyler when she tucked him in and brushed back his hair. The gesture was one of simple affection, of taking care.

As oblivious as he remained to her presence, she let her fingers slip over the soft strands, then curled her fingers into her palm as she stepped away and quietly headed for Tyler's room. Since she felt pretty certain Erik would wake up at some point and head for bed himself, she left the tree lights on so he'd be able to see.

It was to that soft light that he awoke a little after midnight, along with a cramp in his neck and an ache in his back that, he realized an hour later, made sleep impossible.

* * *

Rory heard the faint tap on the door, blinked into the shadows. It had been raining for a while now. She'd lain there, listening to the steady sound of it, imagining the drops taking all the ice away, before the new additions to her usual anxieties about what she'd taken on ruined the little exercise. Everything always felt so much more overwhelming alone at night. With Erik there, she'd at least been able to manage the more restful thoughts for a while.

Hearing the tap again, she slipped from the trundle by the night-light she'd moved to the only working outlet in the room and opened the door.

Her glance collided with Erik's solid, shadowed and bare chest. Down the hall, light from her bathroom filtered through her bedroom door, too dim to reveal more than curves and angles and the shadow of his forearm as he gripped his neck.

He stepped back as she stepped out and pulled the door closed behind her.

She hadn't grabbed her robe. Shivering a little, she crossed her arms over the sleep shirt that barely hit her knees. "Are you just now coming up to bed?"

"I came up a while ago. Do you have anything I can rub on my shoulder?"

He still hurt. Pretty badly, she assumed, to have come seeking help. Feeling guilty that he'd hurt himself helping her, feeling worse because his discomfort was bad enough to keep him from sleep when she knew how tired he must be, she headed for her bedroom door and the bathroom right inside.

The light above the vanity cut a swath across the near edge of the queen-size bed that had once occupied her guest room. If the rumpled purple comforter and sheets were any indication, whatever sleep he had managed had been as fitful as hers tended to be. As she turned into the bathroom, she noticed his nearly dry socks, his long-sleeved undershirt and a pair of gray jersey briefs on the towel rack above the heater vent. With the washer and dryer off circuit, he'd had to improvise.

Realizing what he wasn't wearing under his jeans, she quickly opened the medicine cabinet, pulled out a tube and turned to hand it to him.

He'd stopped in the doorway beside her.

The light was infinitely better here. There were no shadows to hide the broad expanse of his beautifully formed chest, the flare of dark hair, the impressive six-pack of his abdomen or the fact that while he'd zipped his pants, he hadn't bothered with the button.

Her glance jerked up. His hand still clasped his shoulder, his fingers kneading the tight muscles there. But it was his cleanly shaven jaw that held her attention. The hard line of it looked tight enough to shatter teeth. The way he arched his back and promptly winced made it evident his shoulder wasn't the only problem.

His frown of discomfort shifted to the pastel tube he took from her.

"What is this?"

"Herbal cream. I bought it when I pulled a hamstring."

"When?"

"It wasn't anything I did here," she assured him, since she had been known to acquire a bump, bruise or strain herself during her move. "It was in a yoga class. It'll help," she insisted, pretty sure he'd had something more industrial strength in mind.

The skepticism carving deep lines in his face remained as he held up the tube and backed into the bedroom to let her pass. A gravelly edge of fatigue roughened his voice. "I appreciate this. Sorry to wake you."

She didn't bother telling him that he hadn't. Or that she

was actually grateful for the reprieve from her sleeplessness. All that concerned her now was that he was in pain.

"Where do you need that?"

He'd moved to the foot of her bed, away from the narrow shaft of light spilling across the bedding at the corner. Her bare feet soundless on the carpet, she stopped three feet away.

"By my right shoulder blade."

He wouldn't be able to reach there. Not very well, anyway, as stiff as he appeared to be.

"Do you want me to do it?"

He didn't look as if he thought that a very good idea. "I'll manage."

"You're sure?"

"Yeah. I've got it," he insisted, only to wince again the instant he moved his hand in that direction.

Not allowing herself to overthink the situation, she took back the tube. Twisting off the cap, she squeezed a hefty dab of the white cream onto her fingertips and handed the tube back to him.

"You have no business calling me stubborn, you know that?" With him filling the space in front of her, she added, "Turn around," and after a second's hesitation on his part found herself faced with his broad and sculpted back.

In the filtered light, the view of him half naked was no less unnerving, but at least he couldn't see how hard she swallowed before she reached up and spread the cream between his shoulder blade and the long indentation of his spine. His skin felt as smooth and hard as granite when her fingers slipped upward.

Traces of rosemary and mint mingled with the scents of soap, shampoo and warm, disturbing male.

Silence didn't seem like a good idea.

"Why is it that when I came literally a split second from wounding you, you said I wasn't even close? You actually did hurt yourself," she pointed out, rubbing the cream over a knot the size of an egg, "and your 'almost' is two hours."

He lowered his head, gave a small groan with the movement.

"It had to do with circumstances."

She was about to tell him he'd have to do better than that when he sucked in a breath.

She went still. "Did I push too hard?" she asked instead.

His breath leaked out, the tightness in his back audible in his voice. "In a good way."

She'd smoothed her fingers alongside the wide curve of his shoulder blade, the long muscle there as unyielding as the bone beside it. Repeating the motion, keeping the same pressure, she felt his broad back rise as he drew another deep breath, then slowly released it.

What she was doing felt good to him. So she did it again, slower this time. It felt good to her, too, she realized, easing her motions even more. Though she'd tended to fight his efforts, he had been taking care of her in one form or another since the day they'd met. As little as there seemed to be for her to do for him in return, as little as he seemed to want from her beyond what centered on their professional relationship, the least she could do was take care of him now.

"What about the other side? Is it sore?"

"Not as bad."

Meaning it hurt there, too.

Reaching around him, she held out her hand. "I need more cream."

"You don't have to do this," he told her, but even as he spoke, he uncapped the tube and squeezed the analgesic onto her fingers.

"You hurt yourself helping me," she pointed out. "So, yeah, I do." As tall as he was, her elbows were even with her eyes as she raised her arms to work on the other side.

He seemed to realize how far she had to reach.

The bed was right there. "So it's guilt motivating you," he concluded, and sank to the nearest corner. He straddled it, his legs planted wide.

She sat down a little behind him. With one leg tucked under her, the other dangling over the foot of the mattress, she rested her hands on his shoulders to knead the knots with her thumbs.

"Must be," she conceded as he lowered his head again. "Especially since I know this isn't how you'd planned to spend your weekend."

She'd thought before that there were reasons she needed to keep her guard in place with this man. She just hadn't bothered recalling them at the time. With the feel of his big body relaxing beneath her hands, her palms tingling as much from the feel of him as from friction and herbs, it seemed wise to recall those points now.

Reminding herself of the subtle but definite distance he'd put between them last night helped her remember why that need was there. Recalling her comment to the girls about his dates helped, too. There were other reasons, she knew. Even more compelling ones. But for the moment, the last one served her purpose perfectly.

"I'm sorry you missed your party."

"Everybody missed it."

That would be true, she thought, now working her fingers up the cords at the back of his neck. "I'm sure your date was disappointed."

For a moment Erik said nothing. Her fingers were making slow little circles at the base of his skull, reversing their motion to follow the rigid cords to where they met the equally taut muscles in his shoulders.

"I didn't have a date," he finally muttered.

She kept moving down, past the sore spot on the right,

but before he could wish she'd stayed there, she'd continued lower, working her magic along the sides of his spine.

What she was doing felt like pure paradise. She had
wonderful hands. Soft. Surprisingly strong. Yet incredibly gentle as she lightened her touch to soothe away the
worst of the soreness, then gradually increased the pressure again.

He'd felt a different sort of gentleness in her touch before. He'd thought he'd been dreaming, that he'd only imagined her touching him with even more tenderness—until
he'd opened his eyes to see her turning away. The brush
of her fingers over his forehead had brought something
he couldn't remember ever experiencing from a woman's
touch. A feeling of ease, of comfort.

There had been a disturbing contentment to the feeling
that didn't coincide at all with the direction his thoughts
headed now, but something in him craved that kind of caring. Something undeniable and essential and that should
have felt far more threatening than it did with the feel of
her small hands unhurriedly working over his back.

The ache running from his neck to the bottom of his ribs
had started to ease, the tightness there no longer threatening another spasm. An entirely different sort of tension replaced it as her fingers methodically moved over his skin,
massaging toward the base of his spine.

His breath slithered out when she stopped well above the
waistband of his jeans. Still, the thought of her dipping her
hand lower had every other muscle in his body going taut.

"I thought you might be taking the woman you'd gone
out with before," she said into the quiet. "Is she someone
you've been with a long time?"

There was nothing deliberately sensual about her touch
as she worked her way back up. Nothing provocative in
the quiet tones of her voice. Yet the question added a certain strain to his own.

"I haven't been with anyone in a long time, Rory."

Her hands had reached his shoulders. Feeling her go still at the status of his sex life, or maybe the fact that he'd so frankly admitted it, he turned as he spoke, catching her wrist as her hand fell.

"Why the questions?"

Beneath his grip, her pulse jumped.

Rory wasn't sure how to answer. She hadn't expected him to tell her how long it had been since he'd slept with a woman. That hadn't been what she was asking. Or maybe it had been and she just hadn't let herself acknowledge her need to know. The queries had started out simply as a defense against the undeniable emotional pull she felt toward him. She hadn't allowed herself to consider why his being in a relationship with someone should even matter to her. But it had. And he wasn't. And all she could do now was scramble for an explanation that wouldn't betray how very much he already mattered to her. And he did, in ways she was only beginning to comprehend.

"I guess I wanted to know if you were involved with anyone." She lifted her shoulder in a shrug. "Just curious, you know?"

In the pale light, she looked impossibly young to him. Incredibly tempting. Mostly, she looked much as she had last night. Far more vulnerable than she wanted to be, and trying hard for a little bravado.

He saw weariness in her guileless features. He'd heard that same drained quality in her admission. It was almost as if as late as it was, as long as the day had been, she was simply too tired to keep the bravado in place.

"I'm not," he assured her. "I haven't been involved with anyone in years." Involvement implied an attachment he'd avoided for the better part of a decade. A need to be there for someone. A need to let that someone count on him to be there for her. A need to know she'd be there for him.

He'd had absolutely no interest in that sort of commitment. Until now.

"Just curious, huh?"

"A little."

If she'd been trying for nonchalance, she failed miserably.

"You know, Rory," he murmured, self-preservation fighting the need to tug her toward him. "Now would probably be a good time for me to let you get back to bed."

"Probably," she agreed softly. "But I think I'll just go downstairs and read for a while. Seems like a good night to tackle the business plan." She lifted her chin, gave him a tiny smile. "I tried, but I can't sleep."

The simple admission pulled at him, the helplessness in it, the weary frustration of trying to escape what kept a person from rest. What got him, though, was the loneliness she tried to hide with the quick duck of her head.

She'd made no attempt to reclaim her hand, and he couldn't quite make himself let go. Unable to shake the thought of how alone she'd seemed cuddling her son on the boy's bed that morning, realizing how she undoubtedly spent many of her nights, he put self-preservation on hold.

"So what kept you awake? Old worries?" he asked, because he knew how long she'd struggled with them. "Or new ones?"

"Both."

"Today probably didn't help."

He probably hadn't helped. He just wasn't sure how else he could have accomplished what they'd both needed for her to know. Yet while he'd been busy making sure she was aware of everything that needed to be done around the place to keep it up and how to take care of the problems she could expect, the weight of even more responsibility had piled on her shoulders.

"Today was actually a good day." He and Tyler weren't

the only ones who'd thought so. "The worry part is just always there. It's okay during the day when I'm busy, but at night…"

"You can't shut it off," he concluded for her.

"I managed for a few minutes tonight. But then it all came right back."

"What was it about tonight that helped?"

She lifted her glance.

"You," Rory said quietly. Of everything he had done for her in the past two days, everything he'd done in the weeks before, what he had done since yesterday had mattered to her the most. "You being here."

Especially tonight, she thought. Tonight, for a while, anyway, because of him she'd been able to shut everything out and concentrate on nothing but the soothing sounds of the rain still pattering on the roof. Because he was there, because he had her back, because he had everything under control, for the first time in well over a year she'd had a day when she hadn't had to make every decision on her own. She hadn't had to worry about how she would get a tree home for her son, or get one out of her driveway. Or remove the one that had blocked the street. Because of him, they had heat and lights. And for that day, anyway, she hadn't had to handle everything thrown at her alone.

Erik brushed the back of her hand with his thumb, conscious of the small weight of it where he held it on his thigh. The thought that he had somehow given her some measure of relief had just made it that much harder to let her go. Not until she was ready, anyway.

"Do you want to go downstairs?" he asked.

She met his eyes, looked away with a small shake of her head. "Not really."

"Do you want to go back to Tyler's room?"

Another small shake. "Not yet."

"Are you cold?"

"A little."

He knew what she needed even before he asked. He asked anyway. "Could you use a pair of arms?"

That was all he was offering. Just to hold her. This wasn't about wanting her between her sheets. Heaven knew it wasn't about self-protection. It was about giving her a break.

She didn't have to say a word for him to know that his arms were exactly what she needed. But her quiet "Please" was all it took for him to rise and turn out the bathroom light. The night-light now filtering through the doorway cast the room in shadows.

"Come here," he said, and tugged her to her feet.

Leading her to the side of the bed, he pulled the comforter over the sheets and propped both pillows against the headboard. He didn't want her in the bed, just on it.

The distinction seemed just as clear to her as she snagged the wadded throw blanket from the foot of the bed and sat against the far pillow, hugging her arms around her knees when the mattress sank beneath his weight. With his back against his pillow he drew the throw over them both and pulled her knees toward him, his arm low around her back, his hand at the curve of her waist.

"How's this?" he asked, coaxing her head to his shoulder.

He felt her sigh, the long, quiet leak of air leaving her nearly limp against the side of his body.

For a moment, Rory couldn't say a word. She could barely believe she was actually where she had so badly wanted to be. It didn't matter that his jeans felt rough against her bare calf, or that the contrast of his heat and the cool air against the back of her neck made her shiver. She could hear the heavy beat of his heart beneath her ear, could feel it where her hand rested on his hard, bare chest. It didn't even matter that for some strange reason her throat had suddenly gone raw, making her quiet "Good" sound a little tight.

His chin brushed the top of her head as he settled himself more comfortably.

"Good," he echoed, slowly skimming his hand over her upper arm.

She swallowed, then made herself take a deep, even breath. "Erik?" she finally said.

"Yeah?"

"Thank you."

A tired smile entered his voice. "For holding you?" It was hardly a hardship, he thought. She felt wonderful curled up against him. Small, feminine, trusting. The only difficult part was trying not to think of how curvy she truly was with his hand at the dip of her waist, inches from the curve of her hip.

Wanting distraction, he smoothed his hand back up her arm. The herbal scent of her hair teased him, filling his lungs every time he breathed.

"For all of it. But yes." Her tone grew muffled. "For this, too."

He wasn't sure what all she meant. It could have been anything. He just forgot to wonder what might have meant so much to her when he caught the hitch in her voice.

He started to tip up her chin.

She wouldn't let him. Instead, he cupped his hand to the side of her face, brushed it with his thumb and caught the moisture gathered at the corner of her eye.

His heart gave a strange little squeeze. "Hey." *Don't do that,* he thought. He could handle anything but tears. "What's wrong?"

"Nothing. Honest," she insisted, keeping her head right where it was. "Absolutely nothing is wrong." She tried to draw a deep breath, made it halfway before it caught. Swallowing, she tried again. "For the first time in…forever," she said, because that was how it felt, "right now there really isn't a thing wrong."

Which was what had brought the sting behind her eyelids, she realized. Not because of sadness, fear or grief. But because of an amazing, unfamiliar and totally unexpected sense of relief. She knew it wouldn't last long. That it couldn't. It was just for now. While he held her. So just for now, relief was what she felt.

"Then why tears?"

Because of what you let me feel, she thought. "Because I'm tired," was easier to admit to him.

She felt his lips against the top of her head. "Then go to sleep."

"I don't want to."

The slow shake of her head brushed her hair against his chest. Letting his fingers sift through that dark silk, he gave a small chuckle. "Why not?"

"Because I don't want to miss you holding me."

It had to be the hour, the lateness of it, the need for sleep himself. Or maybe it was his need to let her know he'd be there for her in the morning if she'd just let herself rest, but he didn't question what he did as he slipped down, bringing her with him.

His lips grazed the spot on her cheek where they'd literally bumped heads that morning. "You shouldn't say things like that."

Turning her face to him, she whispered, "Why not?"

He'd been about to tell her to go to sleep, that he wasn't going anywhere. But with her sweet breath filling his lungs, the feel of her supple little body playing pure havoc with his intention, he leaned closer.

"Because you'll make me forget why I shouldn't do this," he murmured, and brushed his mouth over hers.

Once.

Again.

"Or this." He carried that gentle caress between her eyebrows, to the space where the twin lines formed when she was worried.

He cupped his hand at the side of her face.

"Or this."

The admission vibrated against her mouth a faint second before he increased the pressure ever so slightly. His lips were firm, cool and far softer than anything that looked so hard had a right to be, but it was the feel of him tipping her head to gain the access he wanted that had her reaching for him herself.

Relief gave way to something infinitely less soothing. It barely occurred to her that this was exactly what she *hadn't* wanted when she found herself opening to him, flowing toward him, kissing him back. She'd known what she would feel if she ever got this close to him again. And she'd been right. She felt everything she had when he'd kissed her before: that deep, awful longing, the yearning to simply sink into his compelling strength, his incredible gentleness, and have him take away the ache in her chest. To relieve the void, the emptiness. Only now with her fingers curling around his biceps and his hand slipping to the small of her back, pulling her closer, the hollowness inside her seemed to be receding, and the emptiness felt more like...need.

When he lifted his head long moments later, his features had gone as dark as his voice. "I think you'd better remind me."

Her own voice came as a thready whisper. "About what?"

He touched the first of the short line of buttons on her nightshirt. His fingers trailed down, found her soft breasts unrestrained beneath thermal cotton.

His lips hovered over hers. "Why we should stop."

Surrounded by his heat, that warmth gathering low in her belly, her voice went thin. "I don't remember."

She didn't know what he saw in her shadowed face when he lifted his head. Whatever it was caused his body to go beautifully taut before his hand slipped over her hip.

"Me, either. But if you do," he warned, the low tones of his voice sounding half serious, half teasing, "stop me."

She was about to tell him that wasn't going to happen, but he lowered his mouth to hers just then and she almost forgot to breathe.

There was no demand in his kiss. Just an invitation to a heady exploration that was deep, deliberate and debilitatingly thorough.

Winding her arms around his neck, she kissed him back just a little more urgently. With him, because of him, she finally felt something other than alone and uncertain, or the need to be strong.

She'd been so frightened by her doubts, so afraid that what she'd thought had been real in her marriage hadn't been at all. If she'd been so wrong about all of it, that meant she couldn't trust her judgment about anything, or anyone, else. But he'd helped her see that she hadn't been wrong about what had mattered most. And more important than anything else he'd taught her, he was teaching her to trust in herself.

She could love him for that alone.

The thought had her clinging a little more tightly, kissing him a little more fiercely. It hurt to know how much of herself she'd let others take away from her. But he was taking that pain away, too, allowing parts of her to come back, allowing feelings she hadn't realized she still possessed to finally surface. For the life of her she had no idea why those thoughts made the back of her eyelids start to burn again. She just knew that at that moment, nothing mattered to her so much as the sense of reprieve she was only now beginning to feel. And the fact that it was he who had finally allowed it.

Erik caught her small moan as she pressed closer. Or maybe the needy little sound had been his own. There wasn't a cell in his body that wasn't aware of how beautifully female she was, and of how badly he wanted her beneath him. To him, she was perfect. Small, supple and infinitely softer than his harder, rougher angles and planes.

He would have just held her if that had been what she'd wanted. It would have about killed him, but he'd have done it. Yet, incredibly, she seemed to hunger for the feel of him as much as he ached for her.

Stretched out beside her, he drew his hand over the nightshirt covering her belly, letting it drift upward, pulling soft cotton away with it. He kissed her slowly, tracing her soft curves, allowing himself the sweet torture of finally knowing the silken feel of her body, the honeyed taste of her skin. He didn't know what to make of the tears he tasted again at the corners of her eyes when he kissed her there, or the almost desperate way she whispered, "No," when he started to pull back to make sure she was all right. Slipping her fingers through his hair, she drew him back to her, meeting him in a kiss that nearly rocked him to his core.

Gritting his teeth against the need she created, he skimmed the bit of silk she wore down her long legs. It landed somewhere beside the bed, along with his jeans.

He'd left his billfold on her nightstand. Some miracle of common sense made him drag himself from her long enough to fumble for the small packet inside. He'd barely rolled their protection over himself when she curled into him, seeking him as he sought her.

The intimacy of gentle exploration had created its own tormenting heat. What they created as they moved together now, his name a whisper on her lips, had him thinking he'd never be able to get enough of her before that heat turned white-hot and he was barely thinking at all.

Chapter Ten

Rory burrowed deeper under her comforter. A delicious lethargy pulled at her, coaxing her back toward sleep. But she heard voices. Male ones. One sweet, the other deep.

Sleep was suddenly the last thing on her mind.

Tyler was awake. Erik was with him. Through the two-inch-wide gap he'd left between the door and the jamb, she could see the light from Tyler's bathroom faintly illuminating the hall. The gap in the curtains next to the bed revealed a thin sliver of gray.

It was daylight. That meant it was somewhere after seven-thirty. She couldn't remember the last time she'd slept that late.

She threw off the covers. Nearly tripping over her nightshirt, she snatched it up and moved to the door. They were just disappearing down the stairs, Tyler in his pj's, Erik in his undershirt and jeans. From the conversation, it sounded as though they were discussing breakfast. Specifically, which one of them got to slice the bananas.

Minutes later, thoughts of how she'd practically fallen apart in Erik's arms adding to the anxiety of wanting to hurry, she'd pulled herself together enough—in the physical sense, anyway—to head into the hall herself.

Slipping a blue corduroy shirt over a cotton turtleneck and yoga pants, she could hear her little guy as she reached the first step.

"Can I help you work today?" he asked. "An' can you help put my train around the tree?"

The low tones of Erik's voice drifted up the stairway. "I think all I'm going to do out there this morning is check the gutters. It's too dangerous for you to help."

"Why?"

"Because it's a long way up there."

"How come you need to check 'em?"

"Because I need to see if the weight of the ice pulled them from their brackets."

"Why?"

She heard a deep, indulgent chuckle. "Because if they're not lined up right, the rain will pour straight off the roof instead of draining to the downspouts and get you and your mom all wet."

Her foot hit the bottom step just as she heard a pondered little "Oh."

Tyler hesitated. "Can we do the train after, then?"

Across the entry, she could see Tyler sitting in front of the lit tree, the blanket she'd covered Erik with last night wrapped around his shoulders. Expectation beamed from his little profile.

Erik sat on the edge of the hearth, his gray undershirt stretched across his broad shoulders as he closed the glass doors on the growing fire.

"I'll have to see how it goes, but I don't know that I'll have time for that, Ty." He picked a stray bit of bark from the stone beside him, tossed it onto the logs in the curved wood basket. "Now that the rain's melted the ice, I need to finish here, then get to my own place."

"You're going home?"

There was no mistaking her son's disappointment at that bit of news. She heard it in his small voice, could practically feel it in him as she watched Erik look up at her an instant before Tyler turned and looked up himself.

Shoving her fingers through her hair, partially undoing what she'd managed to arrange with a few random strokes of a brush, she found it infinitely easier to meet Tyler's sad little face.

"Good morning, sweetie," she murmured, bending to give him a hug. "How did you sleep?"

"Good," came his usual, though decidedly disheartened, reply.

She nudged back his hair, wanting to ease away his sudden seriousness. What Erik had done hadn't been deliberate. There had been nothing but kindness in his voice as he'd explained why he wouldn't be staying. But the painful proof of how her little boy could come to rely on him, could even come to love him, only added to the confusion of wants and uncertainties tearing at her as she kissed the soft, tousled hair at the crown of his head.

"I'll help you with your train later, okay?"

"'Kay," he reluctantly replied.

"So, what's up down here?" she asked him and, as casually as she could, straightened to meet the caution in Erik's smile.

He rose himself, all six feet plus of him, and came to a stop in front of her.

His gray gaze skimmed her face. Slowly assessing. Unapologetically intimate. "The plan so far was to turn on the tree, then build a fire." His eyes held hers. "Then what, Ty?" he asked, since the child hadn't answered his mom.

"Breakfast," came the slightly more enthused reply. "And cartoons?" he added hopefully from below them.

"And coffee?" Erik asked with that disarming arch of his eyebrow.

"Definitely coffee," she agreed.

Grabbing the remote, she punched in the channel she usually only let Tyler watch as a treat. With him on his way to the sofa with his blanket, she headed for the kitchen, Erik's footfalls behind her matching every heavy thud of her heart.

She pulled the carafe from the coffeemaker, turned to see him watching her from beside the sink.

Holding the carafe under the faucet, she turned the water on.

"Why didn't you wake me?" she asked, her hushed voice muffled further by the sound of running water.

"Because I was already awake. When I heard him in the bathroom, I figured he'd come looking for you, so I intercepted him before he could. I thought you might not want him to find us in bed together.

"Besides," he added quietly, "you were out. You barely moved when I pulled my arm from under you."

The reminder of how she'd fallen asleep tucked against his side, their bare limbs tangled, had heat rising in her cheeks.

"I can't believe I didn't hear him." It was so unlike her not to hear her son. "I never sleep that hard." Except with this man beside her, she obviously had.

"Thank you for the rescue," she all but whispered.

He turned off the water for her. With Tyler hidden by the sofa, he lifted his hand, curved his fingers at the side of her neck.

"I'm going to leave in a while," he told her, brushing his thumb over the lobe of her ear. "Pax said everything was okay at the boatworks yesterday, but I have some things I need to do. There's something here I want to check first, though. Is there anything you can think of that you need me to do before I go?"

In the past eight hours, his touch had become as exciting to her as it was calming, as disturbing as it was comforting. He had reawakened her heart and her senses and she'd never felt as confused as she did now, standing there desperately wanting him to pull her to him and hoping he wouldn't.

He'd said he needed to leave, that he had things he needed to do. He'd already talked with Pax, asked about the condition of their properties, their business. She'd heard him tell Tyler that he needed to check on his own place. She knew his entire life was on the other side of the sound. In her need for the temporary escape he'd offered, she'd forgotten that for a few critical hours last night.

"You don't need to check my gutters, Erik."

"Yeah, I do," he said, thinking of her lovely, long limbs and how perfect they'd felt wrapped around him. He'd really prefer that none of them got broken. "It'll save you having to do it yourself."

"I'd have to do it if you weren't here."

The hint of defensiveness in her tone sounded all too familiar.

"But I'm here now," he pointed out, looking a little more closely to see the unease he'd missed in her moments ago.

"You can just tell me what I'm supposed to look for. I'll need to know, anyway."

Caution curled through him. "It's raining out there."

"So I'll wait until it stops."

"That could be June."

He had a point. She just wasn't prepared to concede it. "Is there a particular bracket you noticed?"

There was. The one at the front of the garage that would keep water from pouring over her and Tyler when they came and went from the car. He'd noticed it yesterday and had meant to walk around the garage and the main building to see if any other gaps were visible. But this wasn't about a bracket. It wasn't about a gutter. From the uncertainty underlying her quiet defensiveness, he'd bet his business this wasn't about anything but what had happened between them last night.

Not totally sure what he felt about it himself, not sure what to do about any of it with Tyler wandering over in search of cereal, Erik decided it best to just go do what he'd planned to do anyway.

"I'm going to get the ladder from the basement. I'll be back when the coffee's ready."

It took eight minutes to brew a full pot of coffee. It was another ten before she heard the rattle of the ladder being propped against the wall in the mudroom and the faint squeak of the door to the kitchen when it opened.

Tyler had just handed her his empty bowl and was on his way past the island to go get dressed when she heard him tell Erik he'd be right back.

"Take your time, sport." Ruffling the boy's hair as he passed, Erik looked to where she again stood at the sink.

Still holding the bowl, she watched his easy smile fade to something less definable as he pushed back the navy Merrick & Sullivan ball cap he'd taken from his truck. It looked as if he'd shaken the rain from his cap and swiped what he could from his leather jacket. Beneath it, the charcoal pullover he'd pulled on before he'd gone out was dry, but the darker spots on the thighs of his jeans and the hems looked damp.

"You have two broken brackets," he told her, conscious of Tyler still moving up the stairs. "I'll pick up new ones and be back with them in the morning. I leave for my folks' house in San Diego tomorrow afternoon, so that's the only chance I'll have."

She set the bowl in the sink, picked up the mug she'd taken out for him and poured him his coffee.

Tomorrow was Christmas Eve.

She held the heavy mug out to him.

"You know, Erik," she said as he took it, "you really don't need to come all the way over here to fix those brackets."

The mug settled on the counter beside her.

"I know I don't. And I don't need you telling me that," he insisted, and skimmed her cheek with his knuckles.

The small contact compounded the anxiety knotting behind her breastbone.

Taking a small step back, needing to break his touch as much as the hold he'd gained on her heart, her voice dropped to an agonized whisper. "I can't do this."

Even as his hand fell, his shoulders rose with a slow, deep breath. His hard, handsome features were suddenly impossible to read.

"By 'this' you mean the sex."

"No. Yes." Shaking her head, she shoved her fingers through her hair. "I mean, it's not just that. Making love with you was amazing," she admitted, because it had been. "It's that I can't let myself feel what I'm starting to feel for you." What she already did feel, she thought, and which totally terrified her. "I can't let myself count on you to do things for me. Or for you to be around to talk to. Or for you to be here. If I do, it would be too easy to rely on you even more."

Apparently nothing she'd said explained why she was withdrawing from him. If anything, Erik just looked a little mystified. She figured that was because of what she'd admitted about the sex part. But then, she always had had a problem filtering what she said to him.

His eyes narrowed on hers. "Why not?"

Crossing her arms over the knot in her stomach, her voice dropped another notch. "Because I'm not going to set myself up to lose something I don't even have. It doesn't make sense to do that," she admitted, not sure she was making sense to him. "I can't do that to myself. And I definitely can't do it to my son. It will only hurt Tyler if I let him grow any more attached to you than he already is, Erik. I know people will come and go from his life. People already have, but I've never seen him take to anyone the way he has to you." She'd done a lousy job of protecting herself. That failing would not keep her from protecting her son. "Since the arrangement between us is temporary anyway, it just seems best to back away and keep business…business."

Her heart hurt. Rubbing the awful ache with her fingertips, she watched his jaw tighten as he stepped back.

Erik wasn't at all sure what he felt at that moment. He wasn't even sure what he felt for this woman, beyond an undeniable physical need and a sense of protectiveness he wasn't familiar with at all. All he knew for certain was that they had stepped over a line she clearly had not been prepared to cross.

Recriminations piled up like cars in a train wreck. He'd known all along that it would be a mistake to get involved with her. He'd known from the moment he'd met her that she was dealing with far more than he'd gone through when his marriage had ended. What he didn't understand was how he could have forgotten that his sole goal in agreeing to help her was to have no reason to return to this place once his obligation to Cornelia had been satisfied.

The fact that he hadn't considered any of that last night had his own defenses slamming into place. Having done enough damage already, he wasn't about to complicate their relationship any further. Or let her push him any farther away.

"Just answer one question for me."

"If I can."

"Last night. The tears. Were they because you were thinking of Curt?"

He figured he had to be some sort of masochist for wanting to know if that was what really had been going on with her while they'd been making love. No man wanted to think a woman had another man on her mind while he had her in his arms. Still, for some reason he couldn't begin to explain, he needed to know.

For a moment, Rory said nothing. Partly because the question caught her so off guard. Partly because it was only now that she realized her only thought last night about the man she'd married was how Erik had lessened the void he'd left.

She couldn't begin to explain everything she'd felt last night. Or what she felt now because of his question.

It seemed easiest to just go to the heart of what he really wanted to know.

"The only person in that bed with me was you, Erik."

He heard something a little raw in her quiet reply, something that made her look as if he'd just totally exposed how absorbed she'd been in only him—which was no doubt why she stood there with her arms crossed so protectively and her eyes begging him to go.

He could hear Tyler racing down the stairs.

"We're supposed to meet with Phil after the first of the year." He spoke the reminder quietly, as conscious of the child coming toward them as he was of the definite need for distance. "I don't remember the date, but I'll get it from her. We can figure out our work schedule from there."

"Can we do the train now?"

Tyler had stopped at the end of the island, his expectant glance darting from one adult to the other. He'd pulled on pants and a green thermal shirt and held a red flannel shirt in his fist.

"I have to go now," Erik told the grinning little boy. "But I heard your mom say she'd help you."

His smile fell. "You have to go?"

"Yeah, bud. I do." Unprepared for how the child's disappointment affected him, not sure what to make of the strange hollow in his chest, he tousled his sandy hair one last time, gave him a smile and let himself out through the store.

"Erik! I was just going to call you!"

Erik turned from where he was locking the front door of Merrick & Sullivan's client office. Phil had just emerged from the silver Mercedes parked behind the construction Dumpster in front of the building next door. The tails of her white scarf flew in the breeze as she hurried around to the sidewalk. "Do you have a minute?"

He didn't feel particularly sociable. What he did feel was defensive, edgy and impatient to be on his way. Still, he made himself smile. "Sure," he called back, pocketing his keys. Hunching his shoulders against the chill, he headed to where she'd stopped by Cornelia's building's front door. "What's up?"

"Let's get out of the cold. I'll make us some coffee."

"A minute is really all I have, Phil. I'm leaving to see my folks in a couple of hours."

"Oh. Well, then." Hitching her bag higher on her shoulder, she crossed her arms over her furry white coat. Beneath her matching hat, her eyes smiled through the lenses of her bookish, horn-rimmed glasses. "Rory said you were there when I called the other day. The power being out everywhere had us concerned about her and her son," she explained, "but some neighbors were visiting so I knew we didn't have to worry. We didn't have a chance to really talk, though. Is everything all right with the property?"

Realizing she was checking up on Cornelia's investment

threatened to turn his mood even more restive. "There are a few downed trees and a loose gutter, but no structural damage," he told her, thinking that was about all she'd be interested in. "I heard the power was restored a while ago."

He'd learned that from Ed, who'd done as Erik had asked him to do and called when the area had gone back on the grid. Since he'd told his old friend about Rory's unfamiliarity with the generator when he'd borrowed his saw, Ed hadn't questioned his concern about wanting to make sure there were no other glitches.

Erik hadn't let himself question his concern, either. He'd tried hard to keep thoughts of her and Tyler to a minimum.

"That's good to know. Just one other thing, then, and I'll let you go." She flashed him a smile as she crossed her arms tighter, anxious to get out of the wind. "I take it the two of you were working when the storm hit," she said quickly, making it apparent that Rory hadn't mentioned his insistence about helping with their Christmas tree. "So, how do you think she'll do? Or is it too soon to tell?"

He wanted to say she'd do just fine. She certainly didn't lack for aptitude or the determination to succeed. She even had the incentive of keeping a roof over her son's head pushing her. It would be a challenge doing it on her own, but she'd make a living there. With the connections she was establishing, she'd probably even make a life.

He brushed past the thought that she'd be making that life without him. He had a life of his own right where he was. He had work he loved, a great business, good friends. He had money and the freedom to come and go pretty much as he pleased. His obligation to the woman messing with his carefully constructed status quo ended once they had the business established. Once it was, he could walk away and never go back there again.

"Is there a problem, Erik?"

"No. No," he repeated, waiting for the quick shutdown

of feeling that normally reinforced his last thought. "I'll make it work."

I will. Not *we.*

Phil apparently heard the distinction.

"Isn't she cooperating?"

Not when she was giving him grief about helping her, he thought.

"She just needs a break right now," he decided to say. "With her little boy and the holidays, it just seemed like a good thing to do."

"Was that your idea?"

Initially, it had been. For the business part, anyway.

"The decision was mutual."

"So when do you meet again?"

"Whenever we're scheduled to be here."

"That will be the fifth."

"That soon?"

"At two," she added, and cocked her head. "Do we need to meet before then? We certainly can, if there's ever a problem," she hurried on, having caught his lack of enthusiasm for the meeting. "Part of what we do for our ladies and their mentors is help them work through challenges. Differences of opinion can arise over anything from creative priorities to scheduling—"

"It's nothing like that."

"May I ask what it is?"

It was clearly too late to deny a problem even existed. But all he would admit was, "It's complicated."

"I see." Adjusting the frame of her glasses, she peered at him with interest. "Do you have a solution to the problem?"

He wasn't sure there was one. Not for the two of them. "Not yet."

"Can you work together?"

"Yeah. Sure. There's always email and the telephone." He'd given his word. He'd hold up his end of the deal. For his grandparents. For her. "She wants the business to work. That's what I want, too."

She considered him for a moment, her head tipped thoughtfully, the fine fibers of her white hat fluttering. "You know, Erik, when I gave Rory the address of your grandparents' property, I suggested she look for the possibilities. We knew what she would see when she got there, and that it would be nothing she could have imagined she would want.

"What she'd been looking for was a small home for herself and her son," she confided, "but her needs changed when she lost her job. To see the potential in that property, she had to let go of a mind-set that focused on what she had been looking for and what she now needed. To find the solution to your problem, maybe you should look at the possibilities, too."

She smiled then, gave a little wave of her white-gloved hand. Crystals shimmered on its cuff. "I've kept you long enough," she said. "You have a plane to catch. And I need to get inside before I freeze. Have a safe trip. And merry Christmas."

He thanked her. Added a quick "You, too" and started to turn away.

As he did, his glance caught on the gold plaque engraved with three letters above their doorbell. He'd been curious about it ever since it had gone up last week.

"Hey, Phil," he called, catching her unlocking the door. "What does FGI stand for?"

"It's who we are," she called back. "Fairy Godmothers, Incorporated."

His forehead furrowed. As near as he'd been able to figure out, he'd thought they were in some sort of mortgage business. "Fairy Godmothers? Don't they have something to do with pumpkins?"

"And helping dreams come true." With a charming smile, she disappeared inside.

Mentally shaking his head, he strode toward his truck at the curb in front of his office. He had no idea how anyone over the age of ten could possibly believe in fairy tales, happily ever afters or that other impossibility that Rory had once imagined, Christmas magic. As for dreams, they died by the thousands every day. Reality simply wore them down, if it didn't kill them outright. He knew. He'd spent years in the emotional limbo that remained after his vision of his future had turned to ash. But he'd glimpsed those dreams again, and what Phil had said about possibilities now gave him pause.

She'd said Rory had to let go of a mind-set that focused on what she had been looking for and what she needed now. She'd had to be open-minded enough to see what would be possible living in a place she'd have never considered, rather than writing it off as not what she'd had in mind.

He certainly hadn't considered any sort of personal relationship with her when they'd first met. But one had evolved in spite of him. To see the possibilities in it, he'd need to get past the defenses he'd spent years honing before he could be open to what those possibilities were.

Part of the problem there was that he had no desire to give her a chance to push him any farther away.

The other part would be getting Rory to see past whatever it was holding her back from him to see their potential, too.

Rory had hoped for snow. For Tyler's sake, because that was what he'd said he wanted for Christmas. But Christmas morning had dawned with a gray sky that promised little beyond more rain.

Until a week ago, every other time she'd asked him what he wanted Santa to bring, all he'd wanted was a big tree.

The day after Erik had left, he'd told her he'd changed his mind. Since he already had the tree, what he wanted Santa to bring was Erik.

She'd explained that Erik would be with his parents for Christmas, so Santa wouldn't be able to bring him. Though decidedly let down by that bit of news, he'd decided later that he wanted snow.

All he seemed to want as far as a gift was concerned were things beyond her power to give him.

Without any sort of hint for something that Santa could bring down the chimney, she, being Santa's helper, had left him a mini kick scooter that he could ride between the counters in the store while she worked to get it ready. He'd been excited when he'd come downstairs a couple of hours ago to see it by the tree. He'd been tickled to see that Santa had eaten all but a few crumbs of the cookies they'd left out for him, and awed and delighted by the small tuft of faux-fur trim that appeared to have snagged on one of the fireplace stones when the jolly old guy had departed.

What had truly thrilled him, though, had been discovering the present from Erik among the others from her and her parents beneath the lit and glittering branches. It had been delivered yesterday with a note asking her to please put it under the tree for him to find Christmas morning. Except for the "Thanks" he'd scrawled at the bottom, that was all the note had said.

Tyler had declared the huge pop-up book about sailboats his "very favorite" and gone through every page with her while they sat on the sofa.

It had been only two days since Erik had left her standing in the kitchen feeling as if the world was falling out from under her all over again. Two long nights of missing him more than she'd thought humanly possible. The man was a rock. A truly decent guy. And while she suspected he was fiercely loyal to those he cared about, he held back from needing anyone himself—from needing her, anyway—in the way she now knew she needed him. It wasn't about survival. She could survive on her own. It was about the need to share, and he had worked his way into her life and into her heart as if he was simply meant to be there.

That had only happened with one other man.

Too unsettled to stay still any longer, she left Tyler with his book and cleaned up the bright paper wrappings and ribbons from the carpet.

She had no idea how to repair the damage done to their relationship. He was her mentor. He'd become her confidant. His voice had been one of experience and his advice had been invaluable where other situations were concerned. She just didn't know how to ask what she could possibly do to make things right between them when he was part of the problem, even though she'd picked up the phone a dozen times to try. He had no responsibility to her beyond the agreement he'd made with her benefactor, and now even that part of their relationship had been jeopardized.

The two-tone chime of a bell startled her from her painful thoughts. She'd only heard the chime ring twice before: the first morning she'd met Edie, when the woman had stopped by to welcome her to the neighborhood, and two days ago when Talia had brought the twins over to play. Erik had explained that the service bell was used for after-hours deliveries. A few of the locals obviously used it as a doorbell to save themselves from having to walk around back.

Thinking it might be one of the neighbors she and Tyler had delivered Christmas cookies to yesterday, she headed through the store and opened its front door.

No one was there.

Stepping out, the cold breeze tugging at her hair, her

glance caught on a small package on the weathered plank boards.

The little gold box was tied with a red bow.

Now conscious of the dark truck in the parking lot, her heart beating a little too fast, she picked it up.

The neat print on the back of the gold tag read "I want you to find it again."

She knew exactly what *it* was. It meant the inexplicable feeling of magic she'd told Erik she'd once known every Christmas. The feeling of everything being right in her world. He knew it was the feeling she'd wanted her son to know and something she'd given up hope of ever experiencing again herself.

Yet that sense was what she felt now as she lifted the lid on the box to find a glittery little life preserver on a thin gold cord.

She had the feeling he was only letting her know he'd help her stay afloat with the business. And that was huge. But the way he'd done it had her closing the box and holding it with both hands to her heart.

It was only then that she looked to where Erik unfolded his arms and stepped away from his driver's side door.

Gravel crunched beneath his hiking boots as he moved past the bits of storm debris still strewn over the wet grass. Dark plaid flannel hung open over a navy Henley shirt, his broad shoulders looking impossibly wide as he climbed the steps and stopped in front of her.

He hadn't been at all sure what to expect when he'd left the box for her. He'd just wanted her to discover it the way she had the others she'd told him about. They seemed to have appeared out of nowhere, she'd said, so that sense was part of what he'd wanted to give her, even if only for a moment.

He knew he could have just left it for her. But that would have defeated another part of his purpose. He'd needed to see her reaction to his gift so he'd have some idea of what to do next. It was so unlike him not to have a clear plan, but he felt much as he suspected he would setting sail without a compass or preparation. He wasn't totally sure how to get where he wanted to go, or if the waters he'd face would be calm, rough or totally unpredictable.

Encouraged by the way she held his gift, he quietly said, "Merry Christmas."

"Merry Christmas," she echoed, still clutching the little ornament. Caution merged with disbelief. "What are you doing here? I thought you were in San Diego."

"I was. I spent Christmas Eve with my family and caught the first flight out this morning. I don't want to keep you from Tyler. I just wanted you to have that."

Rory watched him nod toward her clutched hands. She could have hugged him for his gift. The reserve carved in his expression held her right where she stood.

Considering the hated relief she felt at his presence, her "Thank you" seemed terribly inadequate. "Do you want to come in? Tyler loves his—"

Erik was already shaking his head. "There's one other thing." More than one, actually, but he wanted them alone right now. "The other day, you said you didn't want to set yourself up to lose something you don't even have. You said it would be a mistake for you to count on me. I understand the need to protect yourself," he insisted. He'd mastered that one in spades himself. "And I get the reasons you don't want Tyler to start believing I'll be around for him. But I'm not all those other people who've let you down, Rory.

"You seem so certain the only way you can create stability for yourself is to keep anyone who could rock your boat at arm's length. But you've rocked mine, too. You already have me," he admitted. "I figure the least we owe each other is a little time to reconsider our positions before we totally blow something that could have a lot of potential."

She looked at him warily, a betraying glint of a smile in her eyes. "You think we have potential?"

"Yeah," he said. "I do."

She'd rocked his boat. The thought made relief harder to suppress. His admission that she already had him made it nearly impossible.

She took a step closer. "If I let myself count on you," she began, already wanting that more than he could possibly know, "what are you offering to reconsider?"

"Are we negotiating?"

"Apparently," she replied, holding his gift even tighter.

She couldn't begin to identify what she felt as the tension left his handsome features. Reprieve, for certain. But something that felt suspiciously like hope had risen right behind it. He didn't want them to close any doors.

Lifting his hand toward her, he curved it to the side of her face.

"In that case," he said, more relieved than he could have imagined when she tipped her cheek toward his palm, "you should know I've already considered how much my hangups were getting in the way of possibilities where we were concerned. I've spent years thinking I just wanted to be away from here. But once I moved past thinking about what I'd wanted and considered what I might need, I realized that what I needed was another chance with you.

"You made me realize how much I still want a family. And a home here. It's not just the place," he assured her. It was how she made it feel. Comfortable. Familiar. As if he belonged there. "It's you. And Tyler."

He knew he already had a good life. Until he'd met her, he'd just refused to let it matter that he didn't have anyone to share it with. He'd work or play late so that he was too tired to care that he had no one to come home to who actually cared that he'd had a great day or a bad one, or whom he could care about in return.

"We're good together. If we want to make this work between us, we can. I'm in love with you," he confessed, finally acknowledging what he'd denied to his partner well over a week ago. Pax had somehow known that she was the woman he'd been waiting for, though he hadn't realized he'd been waiting for her at all. "All I'm asking is if you're willing to try."

Rory knew his walls had existed far longer than hers. Yet he'd just put his heart on the line for her. Her own heart feeling full enough to burst, she went up on tiptoe, curved her arms around his neck and hugged him hard.

Folding her to his chest, his hold just as tight, he chuckled against the top of her head. "That's a yes, then?"

"Absolutely."

"Are you okay?"

She nodded against his shoulder. "I'm falling in love with you, too, Erik. I think that's what scared me. I knew the day we met that it could happen, but I wasn't ready for it. It happened so fast."

Drawing a deep breath, she lowered herself to her heels and let her hands slide to his chest. Still holding the little box, she met his eyes. "I think I panicked," she explained.

He brushed back the hair the breeze fluttered across her cheek.

"I know you did." She'd been no more prepared than he'd been to put a name or label on what had seemed to be growing more complicated by the moment. A little apprehension on her part hadn't been surprising at all. He hadn't dealt with it all that fearlessly himself. "We'll take it slow now. Okay? No pressure. No rush. We'll just take our time and stay open to possibilities."

"Possibilities," Rory repeated. "That's what Phil told me I should look for here." She'd only been thinking about the property, though. As Erik smiled into her eyes and drew his hand to the back of her neck, Rory remembered that the woman had also warned her to keep an open mind about him.

"She told me that, too," he told her, and lowered his mouth to hers before she could say another word.

There was relief in his kiss as he pulled her closer, and promise, hunger, possessiveness and need. It was the need she felt most. His, definitely, but her own, too, in the long moments before he lifted his head and eased back far enough to release her hands from where they'd been trapped against his chest.

"What?" he asked, seeing the question in her flushed features.

She looked at the little gold box, lifted off its lid. Suddenly she felt certain the little life preserver didn't represent what she'd thought.

Erik's voice was quiet. "You said there was a time when you could always count on something like that being there for you Christmas morning."

Her smile came easily at the reminder. "I thought this had something to do with the store. Something about keeping it afloat. But it's a lifeline, isn't it?"

"It is," he murmured, touching his lips to her forehead. "I'm just not sure which one of us I thought needed rescuing."

"Erik!"

In a flash of maroon fleece and gray denim, Tyler bolted through the door onto the porch.

"Hey, buddy!"

"You're here!"

"I'm here," Erik agreed, and pulled him between them for a hug.

It was then that Rory felt what Erik had wanted her to glimpse again.

At that moment, all felt truly, completely and utterly right in their little world. That was the magic, and it was the most wonderful gift of all.

As they headed in from the cold, it started to snow.

Epilogue

"Why are we waiting in here, Erik?" Confusion shadowed Rory's smile. "We've said hi to Phil and Cornelia," she pointed out, their purpose at the FGI office accomplished. Or so she'd assumed.

"We'll go in a couple of minutes. This is just some of that year-end stuff I need to take care of."

He'd been busy with work off and on for the past week. That afternoon, though, he was going to show her and Tyler where he built boats.

As if anxious to get business behind him, he tugged her closer to where he stood by a gold filigree chair. "Do you want to spend tomorrow night on my houseboat? Tyler might get a kick out of the fireworks."

Tomorrow was New Year's Eve. "He'd love that. I'd love it," she stressed.

She hadn't seen his place yet, though he had warned her it was small. By land-standards, anyway.

"Then that's what we'll do."

Looking more preoccupied than impatient, he glanced to the open door of the room the elegant older woman presently used as her private office. The space off the lovely conference room wasn't much bigger than a closet, but it apparently served her purpose until the major construction behind the sheets of heavy plastic in the entryway would be completed.

Beyond them, Phil and a petite, honey-gold blonde sat beneath the crystal chandelier at the mahogany table. On its surface, hundreds of letters from the mailbags mounded by the delicate French writing desk teetered in stacks. Others had been sorted into piles as the women carefully read each one.

Cornelia had introduced the pretty woman with Phil as Shea Weatherby. She was the reporter who'd written the article that had resulted in the continuing deluge of mail from prospective Cinderellas, or "Cindies," as Rory had just learned her fairy godmothers called the ladies they sponsored. She'd also just learned she'd been their second success.

As focused as Shea appeared to be on her reading, she seemed even more intent on ignoring Pax. Erik's business partner had come over with them after Erik had showed her and Tyler around their client office next door. Pax had used the excuse of needing a decent cup of coffee, something he apparently mooched off the women with some regularity. Yet it was as obvious as the charmingly devilish smile that clearly wasn't working on Shea that she was the reason he was hanging around with Tyler by the pretty little Christmas tree, checking out the boats beyond the window.

"Do you mind if I ask what we're waiting for?" Rory ventured.

"Not at all," came Erik's easy reply. "I just need to give Cornelia a check and pick up a deed from her. I'm paying off the mortgage on your property so you can stop worrying about it."

He was paying off her mortgage? "I never said I was worried."

The look he gave her said she couldn't possibly be serious. "Honey." Brushing back her bangs, he planted a kiss on the furrows between her eyes. "You've never had to tell me when you were concerned about something. I can see it. This way, the pressure's off."

"You're giving me the place?"

"Consider it a pre-engagement present."

She opened her mouth, closed it again.

"Pre-engagement?" she finally asked.

"Yeah. You know. It comes before an official engagement. If you want, I can hold off titling it to you until then. Either way, the property is yours to do with as you please."

He'd figured they could eventually live together there or he could have a bigger house built back by the woods. Whichever she wanted. With the boatworks here, he'd commute by plane most of the time. If she decided to sell or lease the place, that was her call, too. He just wanted them together. But he'd already gotten way ahead of where he figured she mentally was with their relationship.

Seeing that he'd left her a little speechless, he figured it best to change the subject. He'd told her they wouldn't rush. That they could take their time.

"Hey. Ignore me. I was just in business mode," he explained. "I hadn't intended to bring that part up until you got used to me being around." He hitched his head toward the open door. "I'm going to see what's holding up Cornelia."

He gave her a kiss, quick and hard, and turned away.

Catching his arm, she turned him right back. "I'm getting used to you," she assured him. "How long an engagement are you talking about?"

"However long you need."

Christmas morning, he'd given back to her a feeling she'd thought she'd never know again. Now he was ready to offer himself, along with the gift of time, to accept what, in her heart, she already knew.

"Then, I have no problem discussing it now." Some things, simply felt, simply were…right. "All you have to do is ask."

His eyebrow arched. "Seriously?"

"Seriously," she echoed.

With now familiar ease, he slipped his arms around her, drew her close. "In that case, I'm ready if you are."

The teasing in her expression met the smile in his. Narrowing her eyes, she tipped her head as her hands flattened on his chest. "That's a proposal?"

"It's due diligence. I don't want you to shoot me down."

"Never," she murmured. "I love you too much."

"I love you back, Rory." There'd been a time when he couldn't imagine ever saying anything like that again. Or, ever feeling what he felt with her. "And just for the record," he said, glancing toward Tyler before lowering his head to hers, "you made me believe in the magic, too."

* * * * *

THE RANCHER'S WIFE

APRIL ARRINGTON

Dedicated to Jason. "Keep going."

Chapter One

Almost. Two syllables with so much promise and no damn reward. The most disappointing word in existence.

Logan Slade stifled a grimace and spun the ring on his left hand with his thumb. The silver band glinted with each twist. He eyed the nervous movement, willing it to stop. It was an absentminded habit. One he'd almost managed to quit.

His mouth twisted. *Almost…*

"We'll almost have snow," the white-haired man at his side chided again. "Yes, siree. Just needs to be a few degrees colder. They're predicting sleet tonight instead. Strange, huh? November ice in Georgia? Guess the angels left the fridge open." He laughed.

A shaft of frozen air abraded Logan's forearms and he clutched the door of Hartford Insurance Agency's lobby against the whipping wind. Crumpled leaves swept across the walkway outside in a violent flurry. Logan began to regret his impulse to jump up and assist the elderly man out. The chill pierced his skin but he kept his grip, willing the man to shrug into his coat a little faster.

"My Pearl loved the snow," the man mumbled. His

jubilant expression melted away. "We almost had some here last Christmas." Gnarled fingers struggled to fasten the top button at his neck.

"Here. Let me." Logan tucked his heel against the door and gingerly threaded the button through its hole.

"Almost…" the man whispered, his gray eyes lifting.

Logan stilled. It was impossible to count the regrets haunting the depths of his gaze. They pooled in the corners of his eyes, seeping into the crow's-feet and coating his white lashes.

Almost. Logan had almost not come today. Was no more than two thoughts away from calling the trip off when he finally twisted the key in the ignition and allowed his truck to haul him from his ranch.

And, after arriving, he'd almost left. Empty-handed, but with a heart crammed full of a thousand more regrets than he already carried.

Logan straightened, renewing his hold on the door. *Almost* be damned. He wasn't leaving until he did what he'd come here to do. What he should've done a long time ago.

He wasn't leaving until he saw his wife. And he wasn't leaving until she left with him.

The man's eyes still hovered on him. Logan summoned up a polite smile.

"Thank you, son," the elderly man said, shrugging further into his coat and edging out. "Yes, siree. Just a few degrees…"

The arctic blast receded as the door closed and Logan returned to his chair by the exit. He pressed his palm against the thick fold of papers stuffed inside the pocket of his jeans. They cracked under the pressure of his touch, shooting chills through him.

The massive grandfather clock in the corner sounded the five o'clock hour, doling out bellows and chimes. Each lilt of the bells pierced his ears and dropped into the hollow of his gut.

"How much longer do we have to sit here?"

Logan jerked his head to the side. The teenager beside him slumped further into a crumpled heap on the wide lobby chair. A thick hood obscured her face.

"Please sit up, Traci," he said.

"This is stupid." The hood shifted with her grumble. "Why can't we wait at her apartment?"

Logan shifted in his seat, heat spiking up his neck. "We're in public." He clenched his teeth, his knee bouncing with agitated jerks. "Sit up, please."

The hood dropped back. Emerald eyes flashed up at him. Eyes the same shade as those of her older sister, Amy. *His wife.*

Logan snatched in a breath. Dear God, Traci reminded him of Amy. Made it impossible for him to forget how much he missed her or how much he'd failed her. As a husband and a friend.

Amy had been his best friend long before she'd been his wife. That was how it should've remained. He'd never wanted to jeopardize their friendship by clouding it with lust. But that was exactly what he'd allowed to happen. When he found out she was pregnant, the only option he was willing to consider was marriage. And damned if that wasn't exactly what Amy had planned on.

"I can show you where her apartment is, you know?" Traci smiled. "It's not that far. Only five or ten miles."

Logan ducked his head and dragged a hand through his hair, the searing heat engulfing his face. He didn't need directions to Amy's apartment. He'd memorized her address four years ago. One day after she left.

He'd spent each morning counting the miles between them and each night adding more hours to her silent absence. The simple fact was, she'd never issued him an invitation to visit.

Logan had known better than to expect it. Amy had always been stubborn. Still, he'd hoped time would work its magic. Help her heal and bring her around to reaching out to him.

And she had finally reached out. But in a different way entirely.

Logan's fist clenched. His knuckles dug deep into the denim covering his thigh, driving a dent in the packet of papers filling his pocket. He wished he hadn't signed for them. Wished he hadn't taken the manila envelope from the mail carrier's hands, opened it and read them. Wished this ice storm would've changed direction and missed Georgia altogether.

Then, he wouldn't have been forced to leave Raintree and make the six-hour drive to Augusta. He could've continued to remain on the ranch, reminding himself why things were better left alone.

"We're waiting here," Logan muttered through stiff lips.

"But the apartment complex is right down the road." Traci perked up, straightening and sliding to the edge of her seat. "It's next door to a coffee shop and there's a rec room in the main hall that has a pool table. We could get a latte and shoot a round or two while we wait for her." Her slim hand latched on to his forearm, voice rising. "They have a sub place, too, if you're not in the mood for coffee." Her nose wrinkled. "It's different in the city. It's not like back at the ranch. Everything's right around the corner. You can find anything you want."

Yeah. He could find anything he wanted here. Anything except the friendship he'd once shared with Amy. The only place he had any hope of resurrecting that was back at their childhood home. At Raintree Ranch, the memories were rich. They grew out of the ground and wrapped around you on the wind.

"No," he said. "We're waiting for Amy here."

Amy. Logan's mouth tightened. *His wife. His best friend.* Alone. Hundreds of miles away from her family.

No doubt she could hold her own in a big city full of strangers. Otherwise, he never would've agreed to her decision to leave four years ago.

At the time, he'd thought it was for the best. A chance for her to experience life somewhere else. Shake the depression she'd fallen under after the loss of their daughter. Learn and grow. Mature into a woman who knew the value of honesty and loyalty. Then, she'd choose to come back. Only, she hadn't come back.

Logan sighed. He just needed to get Amy home. Back to her family. The sooner they returned to Raintree Ranch, the better.

"It's not a big deal," Traci continued. "Amy won't mind if we wait for her at the apartment. She told me I could use it whenever Mama and I visited. Even if she wasn't there." Her eyebrows rose. "It's better than sitting here—"

"I said, no."

"You heard that man. It's gonna sleet. The sign says they close at five and it's five," she stressed. "There's no one here but us now. She's not coming and if we're not going to her apartment, we're better off leaving without her. Before it sleets and we get stuck here. Let's head back now."

"I said no." Logan shot her a firm look. "Now, that's the end of it."

Traci released her death grip on his forearm and flopped back in an indignant heap. "I swear, if I miss Mama's turkey and dressing tomorrow, I'll never forgive you, Logan." Her lip curled. "Never."

Logan tensed and cast his eyes up to trace the popcorn patterned ceiling. *Teenagers.* Any other day Traci wouldn't utter two syllables strung together. Today, though, the endless chatter had begun the second the kid jumped into his truck insisting she take the trip with him. It had continued in a never-ending stream since.

Logan shot to his feet. "Wait here." Taking swift steps to the reception desk, he tossed over his shoulder. "Quietly."

A rough exhalation was her only response. *Thank God.*

"Excuse me, ma'am." He placed his hands flat on the reception desk to still the tremors running through them.

The young receptionist looked up, smiled and eased closer to the counter.

"Your daughter sure is talkative," she giggled. "I don't think she's drawn a breath in the last hour."

"She's not my daughter." Logan's throat tightened, a sharp pain ripping through his chest. "She's my sister-in-law."

"Oh." Her smile slipped. "I'm sorry. I just assumed—"

"I don't mean to be a pest but I was wondering if Amy Slade has come in yet?"

Her forehead scrunched, confusion clouding her features. "Amy Slade? You mean Ms. Johnson, right?"

Logan swallowed hard, the wad of papers in his pocket burning through his jeans.

He nodded, forcing out, "Johnson. Amy Johnson."

"Well, she had a lot of claims to document today. She was trying to squeeze in as many as she could before she left for vacation." She grimaced in apology. "I thought she'd be back by now but it looks like she may not make it in. I'm sorry. I know you've been waiting a long time."

"Can you give me her cell number?" His face flamed. "I'd like to give her a call. Let her know I'm here."

"Sure," she stated quietly. She held a business card out between pink nails. "I could…"

Johnson. Logan's hand halted in midair. There it was. Her maiden name. In bold, black ink stamped in the center. Plain print. Thick paper. Such a harmless item. But it cut to the bone.

"Sir?" Concern contorted the receptionist's features. "I could give her your number, if it's an emergency? Ask her to give you a call tonight? Or tomorrow?"

"No," he choked, ripping his hand away from the card.

He'd let four years of tomorrows slip by. He should've been here yesterday. His shoulders slumped. *Four years of yesterdays.*

"No, thank you," he repeated. "I'd like to wait a little longer."

A push of cold air swept in from the hallway, fluttering the papers on the desk. The receptionist glanced over her shoulder at the muffled clunk that followed.

"Back entrance," she said, rising from her seat. "That might be her. I'll go check."

Logan strode around the desk to the mouth of the hall.

"Please give me a moment, sir."

He drew to a halt at her raised hand and pleading expression. She cast anxious glances behind her.

"Just let me tell her you're here. Please?"

Logan managed a stiff nod. She dropped her hand and moved down the hall, disappearing into a room on the left.

His legs tensed and his torso pitched forward. *Wait.*

He glanced back at Traci still slouched in the lobby chair then found himself inching down the hall despite his polite promise. His ears strained to capture the receptionist's hushed tones and low words.

"...been here for hours. Very insistent on seeing you."

"Who is he? Is he filing a claim?"

Logan faltered, his breath catching. *Amy.* There was no mistaking her soft, questioning tone. His steps quickened, the tips of his fingers slipping inside his pocket and curling around the papers in a crushing hold.

"I don't think so. I think he might be..." Hesitancy coated the receptionist's words. "I think he's your—"

"Husband." Logan clamped his lips together and flexed his finger against his wedding ring.

He'd reached the threshold. The view of the room remained obscured by the receptionist. She swiveled to face him, hands twisting at her waist.

His earlier reminder to Traci returned. *We're in public.*

He issued a tight smile. "I apologize for not waiting. I didn't mean to rush you but it's important that I see her."

Floorboards creaked. That quiet voice returned. It drifted around the receptionist's tense frame. "It's okay, Kimberly."

The receptionist blinked and glanced back over her shoulder. "Would you like me to stay, Ms. Johnson?"

"No. You go ahead and start your holiday. I'll lock up."

The receptionist hovered briefly then nodded and slipped past Logan, the click of her heels fading.

A thousand thoughts had clamored in Logan's head on the ride up here. A million words had vibrated on the tip of his tongue as he drove. He'd sifted through each one, preserving or discarding them with precision until he'd carefully arranged a select few that were the most important. The ones that needed to be delivered first. Ones that would give him a fighting chance.

One glimpse of Amy and every one of them dissipated. Just as they always had.

Amy had been a pretty girl from the start. Eight years old to his twelve when she'd first arrived at Raintree, she'd been all daring smiles and impish expressions. At nineteen, she'd been beautiful. That shiny length of black hair, and tanned legs that seemed to stretch on forever.

Now, as a woman of twenty-four, she was breathtaking. Curves replaced the coltish angles and a relaxed strength resided in her lithe frame.

"Logan."

His attention shot to the lush curves of her mouth and the deep jade of her eyes. Both opened wider with surprise.

"I needed to…" His blood roared, his tongue clinging to the roof of his mouth.

Needed to see her. Touch her. Hold her.

Amy's expression cleared. She regained her composure and took slow steps toward him, stopping when the toes of her shiny heels were an inch from the scuffed toes of his boots.

At well over six feet, Logan found it rare that anyone met him on his level. Amy, however, never failed to do so. Wearing heels, her slender frame reached almost the exact same height, her gentle breaths dancing across his jaw.

"It's good to see you," she whispered.

It was the last thing he'd expected her to say.

She rested her palms loosely on his shoulders, her smooth cheek pressing gently against the stubble of his. Her sweet scent enfolded him and soothed his senses. He closed his eyes and breathed her in, sliding his hands over her back to draw her closer.

She felt the same. Soft and strong. Only, now, the mature curves of her body met the hard planes of his, filling each hollow and reminding him of exactly how much he'd missed.

How the hell had he ever managed to accept her decision to leave? Encouraged it, even? And why had he waited so long to come? When all he had to do—

"You look well," she said, drawing back.

She crossed the room to the other side of the desk and removed her jacket to hang it on the back of the chair. Smoothing a hand over the collar of her sweater, she adopted a welcoming stance. A patient countenance.

It wasn't the empty expression she'd had years ago after the loss of their daughter. Or the defeated one she'd shown for months after several failed attempts at getting pregnant again. And it was a far cry from the rebellious one she'd worn as a girl, intent on challenging him at every turn.

This was something different. This was worse. It was the professional posture a claims adjuster assumed with a client. The polite demeanor a woman assumed with a stranger.

Logan balled his fists at his sides, his chest tightening with the familiar sting of regret. He'd waited too long.

"What can I do for you, Logan?"

She continued running her fingers over the sweater's neckline. The movements remained small and graceful. Not erratic or anxious. Certainly not an action that should draw attention.

A flush bloomed on the skin of her neck. A fraction of an inch above the tips of her fingers. Her bare fingers.

Logan's eyes burned. This trip was a mistake. Like so many others. There was nothing left of their marriage to salvage here. He should walk away, get back in his truck and leave. It was the sane, sensible thing to do.

He jerked his head to the side but couldn't force his stare to follow. It clung to the small motions of her fingers, causing the pink shade on her neck to spread and deepen to a fiery shade of red.

Logan clenched his jaw. He'd already lost a child. Hell if he'd lose his best friend, too. The girl he remembered was still there. Buried beneath the sophisticated veneer. And he wasn't leaving without her.

Reaching deep into his pocket, Logan withdrew the thick wad of papers and tossed them onto the desk. They bounced, slid across the mahogany wood and drew to a precarious halt on the far edge.

"I'm here to bring you home."

LIES VARIED. Amy knew that. They could be as white as a consoling whisper. Or as dark as a secret never spoken. As a girl, she'd only lied to Logan once but it had been dark enough to follow her for years.

Amy curled her fingers tighter into the collar of her sweater and refused to look at the papers balancing on the edge of the desk. Instead, she focused on Logan, lingering over the dark depths of his eyes, the strong line of his jaw and the sensual curve of his mouth.

He hadn't changed much in the four years since she'd last seen him. His lean length was still as sculpted as ever. His broad chest and shoulders were just as wide and impressive. And the familiar attire of jeans, collared shirt and boots were still the same.

A deep rush of longing enveloped her, making her ache to reach out and wrap her arms around him. To draw him close and hold on. Just as she had so many times over the years as a friend and, eventually, as a lover.

Dear God, she'd missed him. Missed his smile, his strength. Even his tight-lipped frowns of disappointment. Most of which had been directed at her over the years.

Her stomach churned. Figured the one thing she'd always admired most about him was something she had never been able to possess as a girl. Something she'd always found so elusive and so foreign.

Honor. Logan lived and breathed it. Even when it cut deep.

Amy smiled, hoping the slight quiver of her mouth didn't show. "I told Mom on the phone that I'd drive home as soon as I got off work today. I promised I wouldn't miss Thanksgiving dinner this year and I won't. I'm already packed and—" she flicked her sleeve back and glanced at her wristwatch "—it's time to close up. I'm about to swing by my apartment, grab my bags and head out. There was no need for you to make such a long trip."

A muscle in his jaw jumped. His left hand moved, his thumb twisting the ring on his finger. The same one she'd slid there years ago when she was a selfish girl of nineteen. A girl who had lied and purposefully gotten pregnant with Logan's child, knowing his honor would demand he marry her.

The memory conjured up shame. It scorched a path from her soul through blood to muscle, then sizzled on the surface of her skin.

There were so many things she couldn't change. But one thing had changed. She was no longer that selfish girl. No longer reckless or relentless in her pursuit of Logan. Always pushing for more than friendship and stealing his freedom from him.

She'd ruined his life back then. Hurt him more than she'd ever hurt anyone, and she'd never hurt him that way again.

Amy squared her shoulders and wrapped her hands around the chair in front of her. *End this fast. Make it clean and painless.*

"It may have been a while since I've made the drive," she said, trying for a small laugh. "But I can manage to find my way back on my own."

The tight grooves marring Logan's face deepened.

She longed to reach up and smooth the lines away with her fingertips. Cup his jaw and press her forehead to his. She'd done it so many times over the years it had become second nature.

But things were different now. She wasn't that naive girl anymore.

Logan moved, taking long strides across the room to reach the desk. The dark waves of his hair weren't cut quite as short and the lines beside his mouth were deeper. But, the slight changes only enhanced his rough-hewn appeal. If possible, he was more handsome now, at twenty-eight, than he'd ever been.

"Your mom was worried," he said. "Betty knows it's a long drive and she's concerned you'll get caught in the weather." His mouth tightened. "I was worried, too. They're calling for sleet. Driving in ice is dangerous. Especially when you're not used to it."

"Maybe." Amy tossed her hair over her shoulder and straightened, firming her tone. "But it'll be a good experience for me. I need to get used to driving in extreme winter conditions."

Logan frowned. "Why?"

She smiled. A real one that untied the knot in her chest.

"I've accepted a job in Michigan. There's a new insurance branch opening in Detroit and I'll have a management position. That means higher pay and more opportunities for advancement." She shrugged. "The winters are a lot harsher up there. Wouldn't hurt to get a little taste of it now before I move in January."

"Michigan?" Logan's frown deepened, his voice strained. "That's damned far, Amy."

He cut his eyes to the window, remaining silent for

a moment. The wind outside strengthened and tumbled bits of trash across the parking lot. A tree branch scraped across the glass pane, its shrill squeak breaking the silence.

"You've stayed here longer than I thought you would." Logan faced her again. "You used to say you loved Raintree. That you never wanted to live anywhere else."

Amy forced her features to remain blank. The only thing she'd missed as much as Logan and her family over the past four years was Raintree Ranch. Her mother and her younger sister, Traci, came to Augusta to visit every summer, but it wasn't the same as being together at Raintree. Their childhood home had always been her safe haven.

Even now, Amy could feel the warmth of Raintree's spacious kitchen. See her mother flipping pancakes on a wide griddle and humming happy hymns over the stainless steel stove.

Having secured a position at Raintree as head chef, the widowed Betty had brought her two young daughters with her to the beautiful guest ranch. And Logan's family had welcomed them all from the moment their feet touched the dirt drive.

As a girl, Amy had spent thousands of hours racing across Raintree's green fields on her favorite stallions, Thunder and Lightning. She'd helped Logan deliver both foals on the same stormy day. Logan had laughed at her choice of names, but at the time it had seemed like fate to her tender heart.

It had always surprised her how far and fast she could ride across Raintree's acres and still have ground to cover. And the gallop back had always been just as exciting knowing Logan would be watching and waiting for her safe return. The endless acres, beautiful horses and interesting visitors had made Raintree Ranch her favorite place in the world.

Amy had never known a more peaceful place. Until her selfish actions changed everything.

"I said a lot of things back then," she stated. "When I wanted something."

She'd wanted Logan. Marriage. *A family.*

Amy swallowed hard. That dream was gone. Logan had never loved her the way she'd loved him. Pushing him into marriage had destroyed their friendship and complications from pregnancy had almost taken her life. They'd been told she'd probably never be able to get pregnant again. That had been proven in the barren months that followed.

Amy shook her head. "All of that was a long time ago."

"Four years," he said.

"Yes."

Logan spun and crossed the room. The planks of the hardwood floor vibrated beneath her feet as his heavy steps carried him to the window. His spine grew rigid and he shoved his hands into his pockets.

She'd never met a stronger, more dependable man. But her deceit and their broken marriage seemed to have dented his armor. Cracked his bravado. And their stillborn baby girl—

Amy's lungs burned, sharp pain searing in all directions. That dark day had seemed like retribution. A justifiable punishment for her grievous sin.

Amy curled her toes and looked down at her shoes. She'd refused to give up on her dream of being a mother, though. But several failed attempts had forced her to finally accept that it was never meant to be.

She raised her head and straightened. That was all in the past. She'd moved on since then. She no longer mistook her admiration for Logan as love and she had let go of her dream of becoming a mother. All she wanted was to proceed with her respectable new life and continue giving Logan back his.

"The move to Michigan is why I decided to come home for the holidays this year," she said, working the words through her constricted throat. "I'm using some vacation time I have saved up to visit the ranch for a few weeks, see everyone and—"

"Say goodbye?"

Logan's accusing rasp shot across the room. He turned, yanked his hands from his pockets and rubbed them over his denim-clad thighs. The action seemed nervous and hesitant. Both emotions uncharacteristic of him.

"You sure are making a lot of decisions for everyone else," he said. "Doing a lot of assuming. As usual."

Amy rolled her lips and bit hard, a spark of anger lighting in her chest. One she hadn't felt in years. A product of the impulsive nature she'd worked so hard to shed.

Logan's dark eyes roved over her face, peering deep. He nodded toward the papers on the desk. "You gonna look at those?"

She held his sharp gaze, tensing and tempering her tone. "Later."

"Now's as good a time as any."

"I know what they are," she forced out.

The corner of Logan's mouth lifted. "I don't think you do. Take a look."

"You came all this way to boss me around?" Amy wrapped her fingers tighter around the chair. She tried to stop. She really did. But the words kept spewing. "I'm not a little girl anymore, Logan. You can't stroll into my life, toss orders about and demand I do things your way. Matter of fact, that never worked out for you back then, either, did it?"

"No, it didn't." Logan crossed the room, leaning into his palms on the desk and drawing close. "But it can work this time with the right persuasion."

Amy hissed and lifted her chin. "You think so?"

"I know so." A broad smile broke out across his lean cheeks, warming his expression. Logan lifted his hand, the blunt end of his finger smoothing over the tight line of her mouth. "There's my girl," he whispered. "I miss you, Amy. I miss *us*."

Amy sagged against the chair, shoulders dropping. "Us fighting?" She shook her head. "Because that's all we're good at anymore."

His big palm cradled her jaw, calloused thumb sweeping gently over her cheek. "We're good at a lot more than that. We just need to work at it. Do things right this time."

Amy drew back, slipping away from his touch. "No. That's not why I'm coming home. And I don't plan on staying permanently. You already knew that." She nudged the papers with her fingertip. "That's why you signed these."

His eyebrows rose. "Did I?"

"Good Lord, I'm glad you're here."

Traci rushed into the room, sweeping past Logan

and barreling into Amy's middle. Grateful for the distraction, Amy wrapped her arms tight around her sister's waist. The bulk of Traci's coat made it difficult to pull her close.

"We've been waiting out there for hours," Traci mumbled against her neck. "It's cold, I'm bored and Logan refused to go anywhere. He wouldn't do anything but sit there and wait."

Traci's frantic whisper tickled her ear. Amy laughed, drawing back to say, "Why did you ride out here anyway? You knew I was coming home today."

Traci shrugged, stepping back and tugging at her hood. "You know Mama always starts cooking the night before Thanksgiving. If I'd stayed home, I'd have had to peel all the sweet potatoes for the soufflés." She curled her lip. "A girl can get carpal tunnel doing that." Her fingers picked at the cuffs of her jacket. "And I missed you." She shrugged. "Besides, there were too many people stuffed in that house. I needed to get out of there for a little while."

Amy smiled. "I take it Raintree's packed for the holidays, as usual."

"Oh, you don't know the half of it. I spend one summer visiting you in Augusta and munchkins invade while I'm gone." Traci shook her head. "When I got back to the ranch last August, six-year-old twins were tearing up the place."

"Twins?"

"Yeah," Traci said. "Dominic married their aunt last fall. They're seven now and I swear those boys got wilder. You'll see what I mean."

Dominic, Logan's younger brother, had been Amy's friend the moment she'd arrived at Raintree all those years ago. She couldn't imagine Dominic getting married and settling down. He was a nomadic bull rider, living in the moment and always searching out adventure.

"Dominic got married?" Amy glanced at Logan for confirmation.

Logan nodded, a small smile appearing. "He came home for good last year and he's happier than I've ever seen him." His smile slipped. "You've missed a lot."

Amy tensed, looking away from the sad shadows in Logan's dark eyes.

"We're really glad you're coming home for a visit," Traci said, squeezing Amy's arm. "It'll be nice for us all to be together again." She withdrew, moving around the desk to tug at Logan's elbow. "Can we start back now?"

"Soon." Logan nudged Traci toward the door. "Go on out and warm up the truck. We'll swing by Amy's, load up her bags, then head out."

Amy watched Traci leave then cocked her head at Logan. "Who's doing the assuming now?" she asked. "I never said I was riding back with you."

"No. You didn't." Logan walked to the door. "But I promised Betty I'd get you home safely, and I always keep my promises. Plus, your sister's been looking forward to catching up with you and there's no way I'm letting the two of you ride back alone in this weather. We'll follow you back to your place, get your stuff and you'll ride back with me. So lock up and meet us out front."

He left, leaving her glaring at the empty doorway. Amy huffed. It looked like Logan was getting his way again. At least, for the moment.

She firmed her mouth. Her plans hadn't changed. Not really. She'd accepted the new job and was moving to Detroit. Just as intended.

This trip home would still serve its purpose. She'd spend some time making amends, visit with family and find a gentle way to break the news of her move to her mother. Then, she'd move on to a new life and a fresh start.

It didn't matter what mode of transportation she took to the ranch. The path she'd follow would still be the same and her ticket to a new life was now in her possession.

Relaxing, Amy glanced down at the folded papers balancing on the corner of the desk, their ivory shade a stark contrast to the deep tones of the wood. She retrieved them, unfolded the pages, and slid her thumb over the bold heading.

Divorce Settlement Agreement.

She scanned the papers, each glimpse of blank space tightening her chest to the point of pain. Her fingers flipped up the corner of each page with a more violent flourish than the one before.

"If you're looking for my signature, you're not gonna find it."

Her head shot up. Logan stood in the doorway, his wide shoulders and lean length obscuring the exit. His grin widened into a firm curve, sparking his dark eyes with intent.

"Not now. Not ever," he said. "I never break my word."

Amy's breath caught. This was the Logan she knew. A bold, decisive man. One who never faltered once his mind was set on something.

He stepped into the hallway, tossing over his shoulder. "Go on and lock up. We need to start back soon. Before the storm hits."

The papers cracked in Amy's hand, crimping into a wrinkled heap before she dropped them to the desk. She stared ahead blankly, listening to the heavy tread of Logan's boots and the bell chiming on his exit.

The room was empty, her rapid breathing the only sound. Amy lifted her hand and slipped her fingers beneath the collar of her sweater to tug the silver necklace out. It dug into the back of her neck as she threaded her finger through the ring hanging from it. The weight of the silver band was familiar and comforting.

She squeezed her eyes shut. Only a few minutes with Logan and she'd reverted to old sins. She'd lost control, lashed out and goaded him into action.

The dig of the necklace turned painful, her finger straining to reclaim the ring. Amy gritted her teeth, slid the ring off her finger and shoved the necklace back beneath the cover of her sweater.

There was no way she was slipping back into old habits. Always trailing after Logan, begging for whatever attention he deigned to throw her way. What she'd felt for him all those years ago had been exactly what he'd called it. Ill-begotten hero worship. Nothing but a young girl's ridiculous fantasy. Something cynical– Logan would never deliver.

No. She'd come too far and worked hard to change. No way would she ever be that selfish girl again. She'd gotten over her obsession with him long ago.

Amy jerked open a drawer, yanked out her purse and shoved the wad of papers deep inside. This wasn't ending here. Like it or not, Logan was signing that agreement. And they were both going to shed the past and begin new lives.

She made her way through the lobby, flicked off

the lights and hovered by the window. The gray clouds grew thicker and the furious sweep of leaves through the parking lot whispered to a halt. Small white pellets plummeted from the sky in scattered patterns, slamming into the concrete and pinging against the glass pane.

Logan stood at the foot of his truck. Eyes fixed on hers, he crossed his muscular arms over his broad chest and leaned back against the tailgate. He didn't shiver or waver. Just stood there. A solid pillar of heat in the freezing onslaught of ice, not heeding its vicious bite.

Amy clenched her jaw. A sharp ache throbbed in her head at the tight press of her teeth. There was no need to rush. No need to try to outrun the storm. It had already hit.

Chapter Two

He'd come on too strong. Had pushed Amy too hard.

Logan shifted to a more comfortable position in the truck's cab and eased his foot off the accelerator. He glanced to his right, finding Amy in the same position she'd adopted an hour ago. Perfect poise, legs crossed at the ankles and eyes straight ahead. Her hands shook in her lap.

"Cold?" He stretched over to cut the heat up and angle the vent toward her.

"No. I'm fine, thanks."

She didn't look it. The closer they got to the ranch, the tenser she became.

"How much longer?" Traci asked from the backseat, removing her earbuds. "I'm getting stiff."

Traci rearranged her long length in the back of the cab, stretching her legs out to prop her boots on the console. Logan's mouth twitched at the sight of the muddied heels. A few clumps of dirt dropped from them, tumbling into the front seat by his jean-clad thigh.

He eyed her in the rearview mirror. "You got two floorboards back there, Traci."

"And a lotta leg," she drawled, raising her voice

above the deep throb of music from her cell phone. "I'm starving. We haven't missed dinner, have we?"

Logan shook his head. "Nope. We're right on time. Not much farther now."

Traci stuck the earbuds back in, settled against the seat and closed her eyes.

Logan faced the road again and they traveled in silence for a couple of miles before he glanced at Amy. The brash glow of the low-hanging sun flooded the cab and highlighted the pinstripes in her pantsuit. Her black hair was pulled up, giving him a clear view of her pale cheeks and blank expression.

Logan opened his mouth to speak but shut it quickly. He used to be able to talk to Amy about anything. Never even gave a thought to what he would say. Knew she'd be as eager for his thoughts as he'd always been for hers. But over the past twenty-four hours, he'd discovered that even though they were no longer separated by miles of road, a distance still remained between them. One he had no idea how to cross.

"Is dinner still at six?" Amy's green eyes flicked to the clock on the dashboard.

"Yeah. Betty runs a tight ship." It was almost 5:30 p.m. They'd cut it close. "We'll make it."

Barely. Despite his best attempts last night, they'd been unable to start home before the storm hit. Instead, the ice fell fast once they'd arrived at Amy's apartment and by the time he'd loaded Amy's bags in his truck, the roads were too slick to drive on. They decided it would be best to spend the night and start back in the morning after the ice began to melt. Traci had slept in the guest room and Logan had slept on the living room couch.

He winced and rubbed the kink in the back of his

neck. Or better yet, he'd tried his damnedest to sleep. It'd been hard to do with his legs dangling off one end of the sofa and his head the other. It didn't help matters that Amy's bedroom had been only a few feet away. He'd heard the rustle of sheets every time she'd tossed and turned. Apparently, she hadn't been able to sleep either.

He rolled his shoulders and tightened his hold on the steering wheel. At least they were almost home now rather than holed up in that suffocating apartment. It'd been obvious that Amy had already begun preparing for her move to Michigan. The stacks of boxes lining the living room walls had glared at him from the moment he'd entered. He'd done his best to ignore them but they'd loomed over him all night.

Logan's mouth twisted. No wonder sleep had eluded him. He hated this. Hated how quickly he'd become fixated on Amy again. How every thought running through his mind centered on her and excluded common sense. It made him feel weak. Vulnerable.

"Tell me about Dominic."

He turned his head to find Amy studying him. Those emerald eyes traveled slowly over his face and lingered on his mouth, warming his cheeks. Her lips trembled slightly.

She looked away, asking, "Who did he marry?"

"Her name's Cissy. He met her one night on his way back to Raintree. She was stranded by the side of the road with her nephews."

"Are those the twins Traci mentioned?"

He nodded. "Cissy's sister died early last year and the twins' father didn't want them. Cissy took the boys in but had a hard time providing for them. Dom brought the three of them to the ranch and we set her up with a job." A smile stretched his cheeks. "Dom fell hard for her. He loves those boys, too." He released a low laugh. "We all do. They're great kids, Amy. You'll love 'em. And Dom and Cissy are expecting—"

Logan bit his lip, cutting off his words. *Babies. Twin girls.* Nausea flooded his gut. He couldn't say either of those things to Amy. Could barely say them out loud himself.

Red blotches broke out on Amy's neck, marring her clear skin. She smoothed her hands over her blouse and sat straighter in the passenger seat. "I'm happy for him," she whispered.

She would be. When she'd first arrived at Raintree, Logan recognized right off that Amy shared the same wild streak as Dominic. It hadn't taken long for Amy to begin regarding Dominic as a brother and Dominic was equally fond of Amy.

Logan frowned. He'd always been pleased with Amy's close connection with Dominic but after his own friendship with Amy eroded, Logan found himself envious of her bond with his younger brother. Which was ridiculous. More of the irrational behavior Amy inspired in him.

"I called Dom last night," Logan said. "Asked him to let everyone know we were running behind. He said Betty was excited to see you. Said she couldn't stop smiling."

Amy tucked a strand of raven hair back into her top-knot. "I'm looking forward to seeing her, too. It'll be a good visit."

Logan glanced in the rearview mirror at Traci. She bent deeper over the cell phone in her hands and her fingers flew over the screen. Her music blared, the rhythmic bass pumping past the earbuds.

"Betty never mentioned anything to me about you moving to Michigan," he murmured. "You haven't told her your plans, have you?"

"Not yet." Amy twisted her hands in her lap. "But I will. There's plenty of time. I don't want to upset her at Thanksgiving."

He scoffed. "You think Christmas would be a better occasion?"

"No." She sighed. "But I couldn't bring myself to tell her over the phone. I will, though. When the time's right."

"Augusta is far enough. Michigan will feel like the other side of the world to her. You're gonna break her heart, Amy," he said, ignoring the tightness in his chest. He eyed Traci again. "Your sister's, too."

"They'll understand. They'll be happy for me."

"Knowing you're thinking of moving clear across the country won't make them happy." Logan grimaced. It sure didn't sit well with him. "No one that cares about you would be happy hearing that."

"What would you have me do, Logan?" Amy glanced over her shoulder at her sister before whispering, "Stay in limbo with you forever? The opportunity came and I took it. I have to move on at some point. We both do."

Her argument was sane and sensible. The kind he should agree with and understand. But he couldn't bring himself to accept it.

Logan palmed the steering wheel roughly and took a right turn onto the long dirt drive of Raintree Ranch. He lifted his foot from the pedal as the truck dipped into a pothole, sloshing muddy water against the sides of the cab. Fragmented patches of white speckled Raintree's sprawling fields. The late-afternoon sun that had melted most of the ice hung low on the horizon and night loomed closer with every minute.

Amy's pants legs rustled as she sat taller, craning her neck and looking out at their surroundings. Logan took the next turn through a gated entrance and she braced her hands on the dash, swiveling to glance over her shoulder at Raintree's wooden sign as they passed. The sweet scent of her shampoo released with her movements, lingering around him and making him ache.

They traveled past the large stables, barn and paddocks lined with white fencing and the multi-storied main house emerged into view. Logan smiled. The white columns and wide front porch were already adorned with garlands, wreaths and bows for the holidays. Betty must have decided to decorate early for Amy's return.

A tender expression crossed Amy's features. Logan's chest warmed. No matter what she said, Amy had missed Raintree. Her longing for their childhood home showed in every sweet curve of her face.

"It still looks the same," she said.

The gentle look in her eyes faded as the truck drew closer to the house. Her mouth tightened. She eased back in the passenger seat, shoulders sagging.

"Nothing's changed." Amy trailed her hands away from the dashboard and dropped them in her lap, fingers twisting together.

A heaviness settled in Logan's arms. "Yes, it has. Everything has been different since you left. For all of us." He covered her smaller hands with his palm and squeezed. "Please think this move over. Before you make a final decision."

She slid away from his touch. "The decision's already been made." Her voice lowered to a whisper. "It's for the best."

"Amy—"

"The twins are out," Traci shouted over her music, perking up and dragging her feet from the console.

Logan released a harsh sigh, bringing the truck to a halt and removing the keys from the ignition. Two blond boys scrambled over the ground at the end of the drive, gathering up what was left of the sleet and packing it into muddy balls.

"Hide everything you value and get your armor on, Amy," Traci said, yanking out her earbuds and shoving them along with her cell phone into her bag.

"Are they that bad?" Amy asked, a hesitant smile peeking through her tight expression.

Logan grinned. "Nah. They're just being boys."

"Yeah, right," Traci drawled. "Tell me that the next time they break my phone. Or take my bras and use them for slingshots. Or draw plans for their fort on my homework—"

"All right, Traci." He laughed, muscles relaxing. "I know they've done you wrong a time or two but they do it with love."

Traci harrumphed and shoved her door open.

"That's one warped way to look at it," she grumbled good-naturedly, jumping out and taking swift strides up the dirt drive.

The boys noticed Traci approaching and stilled. A huddle, quick whisper and nod later, they advanced, surrounding her and pelting her with their icy bundles.

"Stop it, squirts," Traci squealed, "or I'll smooch you into oblivion."

Traci swooped down with open arms, bag flopping over one shoulder, and chased them. One twin escaped but she caught the other, scooping up the wriggling boy and plastering noisy kisses all over his face.

"Yuck!" The escapee ran several feet across the mud and jerked to a halt at Logan's open door. He scowled, jabbing a dirty finger in Traci's direction. "Look what Traci's doing to Jayden, Uncle Logan. Tell her to stop."

Logan stifled a laugh. Leave it to Kayden. He was always the first to point the finger of blame.

"Come on, now," Logan said. "You can't go on the attack, then cry for help. Don't dish it out if you can't take it."

"I ain't did no dishing," Kayden argued. He paused, forehead scrunching before saying, "I *didn't* do *any* dishing."

"That sounds better," Logan praised.

Kayden nodded. "Aunt Cissy don't like us using no double negatives." He climbed onto the truck's running board and leaned into his hands on Logan's thigh. "Anyways, I ain't did no dishing. We were just throwing snowballs."

"There's no snow out here, buddy." Logan ruffled his golden hair. "Y'all were throwing ice."

"So." Kayden shrugged. "It's white."

"Unlike a friendly snowball, ice hurts and I'm sure Traci felt a twinge or two. Both of you owe her an apology."

"Yes, sir." Kayden rolled his eyes, the blue pools skimming over Logan then narrowing on Amy. "Is that her?"

Logan turned, absorbing the warm look Amy directed at Kayden, and smiled. "Yeah. This is your aunt Amy."

Amy frowned but quickly adopted a polite smile when Kayden leaned in for a closer look at her.

Logan helped Kayden jump from the running board back to the ground. "Why don't you go around and introduce yourself properly?"

Kayden took off, his blond head bobbing out of view as he rounded the front of the truck.

"It's not a good idea introducing me as their aunt, Logan." Amy unbuckled her seat belt. It snapped back with a clang. "I'm leaving for good soon."

"Maybe." Logan met her hard stare with one of his own. "But you're here now."

She shook her head, grabbed her purse and climbed out of the truck. Logan followed, strolling to the other side of the truck to find Kayden tipping his head back and staring up at Amy.

"Gahlee, you're tall," Kayden said, mouth hanging open.

Amy's grin faltered as she teetered, her high heels sinking into the mud of the driveway. Logan stifled a laugh. The combination of melted ice and dirt had turned the path into slick mush. She yanked against it, attempting to jerk her shoes free, but the sludge won out.

Kayden stepped closer, studying her sinking shoes, then observing the rest of her. He blushed and stuck out dirty fingers. "I'm Kayden. And that's my brother, Jayden, over there. Good to meet 'cha."

Amy lowered with care, braced with one palm against the truck for balance and shook his hand. "It's very nice to meet you, too, Kayden."

"Boys," a deep voice called.

They all turned. Dominic ambled down the wide front porch steps of the main house and crossed the lawn toward them.

"Uh-oh." Kayden smirked.

He tore off toward the house, Jayden and Traci following. Dominic swept the boys against his thighs as they passed, kissing their heads and shooing them toward the porch with a pat on the butt.

Logan held Amy's elbow and helped her regain her balance. "You gonna ditch those shoes now?"

"No need."

She steadied herself by holding his forearms and yanked her heels from the suck of the mud. They broke free with a deep slosh. She lifted onto her toes, released her grip on his arms and straightened her purse strap on her shoulder.

"Well, I'll be damned," Dominic drawled, smiling wide and knuckling his Stetson higher on his brow. He strutted over, landing a heavy pat on Logan's back, then edging past him. "My partner in crime has returned."

Dominic wrapped his burly arms around Amy's waist, lifting her in a tight hug and spinning in a wide circle. She laughed, pure contentment shining on her face and eyes welling with happy tears. Logan savored the sight briefly then shoved his fists in his pockets and looked away.

"It's about time your butt moseyed back, kid," Dominic murmured. "Where the hell you been?"

"Around." She struggled to catch her breath.

"I've missed you." Dominic leaned back and studied her. "We've all missed you."

Logan's skin tingled under the weight of Dominic's

stare. He glanced over, eyes locking with his younger brother's.

"Haven't we?" Dominic asked.

Logan nodded, dragging a hand from his pocket and kneading the back of his neck. That kink was back, the pain streaking from the base of his skull down between his shoulder blades.

Amy cleared her throat, tapping Dominic's ankles with the toes of her shoes. "You can put me down now."

Dominic's lip curled, his tone teasing. "Don't know if I should. Doubt you'll make it to the house in those city-girl contraptions." He frowned at Logan. "You let her run around in these things?"

Logan opened his mouth but Amy beat him to it.

"He doesn't need to *let* me do anything." She popped her knuckles against Dominic's shoulder. "I do what I want when I please. Now, put me down."

Dominic chuckled. "Yep." He nodded with pleasure at Logan. "This is damn sure our girl you brought back with you."

"Almost as good as new," Logan said, voice catching.

Amy's cheeks flamed cherry-red and she shoved harder at Dominic's broad shoulder until he lowered her to the ground. Logan stepped forward, keeping a close hold on her elbow until she steadied on the mud and shrugged away his touch.

Amy nudged the bobby pins holding her updo into a more secure position and asked, "Were those your two misfits I saw earlier?"

The pride in Dominic's face was unmistakable. "Yep. Those are my boys. I adopted them last year after I married their aunt. Wished you'd been here for it, Ames."

He smiled. "Can't wait for you to meet my wife. I know you'll love Cissy as much as I do. And we're expecti—"

"That's enough for now, Dom." Logan's throat tightened at the quiver in Amy's chin. "It's been a long drive back. Let her rest before you yap her ear off."

Dominic nodded, his smile dimming. "Sun's dropping." He waved a tanned hand toward the horizon. "It'll be dark soon. 'Bout time I started rounding up the horses."

"I'll help," Amy said.

She squeezed Dominic's arm and brushed between them, making her way toward the paddocks grouped near the massive stable.

Dominic crossed to Logan's side, watching Amy's slow progress across the field. "How is she?"

"Better than she was four years ago," Logan said, trying to ignore the hollow in his gut at the memories assailing him. Amy, pale and unconscious, lying in a hospital bed while he sat by her side praying she'd wake up. His relief at her pulling through had been short-lived. After losing their daughter, she'd become a shadow of her former self. Each failed effort at becoming pregnant again had caused her to grow more listless and depressed over the following months.

Logan studied Amy's careful steps toward the paddock. "She seems physically healthy at least but she's still not herself."

The sun dipped sharply and an orange glow of light flooded the fields, silhouetting Amy's lithe figure. The outline of her curvy form turned black, becoming a stark contrast to the fiery light bathing the landscape.

"Y'all made any decisions about the future?" Dominic asked.

Logan sighed. "Amy has. Says she's moving again."

"Where to?"

"Michigan."

"Damn." Dominic shook his head, kicking the ground with his boot and squinting at the glare of the setting sun. "You talk her out of it yet?"

"No." Logan cut his eyes to Dominic. "And don't go bringing it up. Betty doesn't know yet, and Amy only told Traci she was moving to a new apartment, not where. Amy hasn't had time to settle in. She gets to feeling cornered, she'll pack up and leave. Then I won't have a chance in hell of getting her to stay."

"Well, if you ever do need me to talk to her, just say the word."

Logan scoffed. "She's *my* wife. If anyone talks to her, it'll be me."

Dominic stilled, a slow smile spreading across his face. "Well, hell, bro. You're getting hard-core in your old age, yeah?"

A burst of laughter broke from Logan's chest and the tension faded from his limbs. He loved having his brother back home again. He grabbed the back of Dominic's neck and squeezed, giving him a playful shake.

"Old? If you know what's good for you, you'll cut that shit out."

Dominic laughed and shoved him off. "I'll believe that when I see it."

Logan smiled and led the way over to the paddock to join Amy. She leaned further over the top rail of the fence as several horses milled around the enclosure. She pointed at a golden stallion standing a head taller than the rest, his white mane rippling with each movement of his broad neck.

"Is that my Lightning?" she asked.

"Yeah." A wave of pleasure swept through Logan at the eager expression on her face. "You're welcome to tuck him in for the night." He lowered his voice to a teasing tone. "That is, if you can make it over the fence and across the field in that stuffy getup."

Dominic chuckled at his side and Amy smirked, a hint of her old spirit shining in her eyes.

"That won't be necessary," she said.

She inhaled and whistled around two fingers. The melodic sound traveled across the expanse of the paddock, perking up the horses' ears and rebounding off the stable walls. Lightning shot to attention, spun and galloped toward the fence. He drew to a halt, dipping his broad head over the top rail and nuzzling his nose against her shoulder.

"Good boy," she crooned, kissing Lightning's forehead and resting her dark head against his thick neck. "You're still a beauty."

"He oughta be a beauty," Dominic said. "Logan's been babying him for the last four years."

Logan grunted, rubbing Lightning's back. "There's nothing wrong with a little extra attention. And he deserved it. He's pulled his weight on the trails. Every new guest we get requests him." He looked up to find Amy's eyes clinging to his. "You trained him well."

Amy rolled her lips, a smile fighting at the corners of her mouth. "I wasn't alone in that. Besides, you were the one that trained me, remember?"

"I remember," he whispered.

He reached out and tucked a loose strand of her hair behind her ear. The silky feel of it lingered on his fingertips, heating his blood.

Amy stepped back, eyes sifting through the rest of the horses. "Where's Thunder?"

Logan stiffened. Of course she'd ask about Thunder. That black stallion had always been one of her favorites, along with Lightning. He curled his fists around the fence rail.

"Logan?" Amy's hands covered his, her face creased with worry. "Where is he?"

Logan glanced at Dominic. He winced, his dark eyes moving to hover over the stables in the distance.

Logan sighed. He should've prepared for this. Should've had something ready to say. The last thing Amy needed right now was bad news and he didn't want to be the one to deliver it. Unfortunately, there was no way around this.

Logan shoved off the fence and took Amy's hand in his, rubbing his thumb over the fragile skin of her wrist. "Come on. I'll take you to him."

AMY SHIVERED. THE warmth of the sun faded and the approaching darkness sent a chill through the air. It sliced beneath her flesh and traveled to her bones, forcing her to huddle closer to Logan's side. His big hand tugged, leading her away from the paddock and down the winding trail to the stables.

The tight set of Logan's jaw and his continued silence froze the blood in her veins. She scanned the path before them, following the familiar curves to the stable where she'd spent the majority of her childhood days.

Every morning, she'd raced to the stalls to plop at Logan's feet and watch him groom the horses. And every afternoon, she'd returned to lean in the doorway and wait for his return. The image of him mounted on his horse, slowly crossing the field, seemed emblazoned on her memory. She was certain the image of her idolizing expression remained imprinted on his.

Her face flamed despite the cool bite of winter air. Amy lifted her chin and straightened the collar of her blouse with her free hand. None of it mattered. There wasn't any point in seeking out old comforts. Or reliving past humiliations. She wasn't staying long enough to enjoy one or endure the other.

She craned her neck, peering past the open doors of the stable for a glimpse of Thunder's dark hair. She knew the exact shade. Years ago, when she'd delivered the foal, she'd stayed to watch Thunder rise on trembling legs then spent the next week smoothing her hands over his black mane.

Logan's hand tightened around hers and he slowed his step. "There was an accident a couple of months ago." He stopped inside the stable entrance, drawing her to a halt. "One of the guests took Thunder out without permission. Some arrogant young suit on vacation, playing at being a rancher for the week."

His mouth firmed into a tight line, throat moving on a hard swallow.

"He knew Thunder was a jumper. Drove him over a few fences and off the lot." He released her, hands shoving deep into his pockets. "Raintree probably looked endless to him, being a city boy and all. He left the ranch and ran Thunder right into the highway." He looked back across the empty fields, shoulders sagging. "Those transfer trucks don't stop for anything out here. Don't know if he was trying to race or didn't see the truck coming, but their paths crossed."

Amy froze. Thunder was a strong stallion, ripped

with muscled bulk and impressive speed. But he'd be no match for a transfer truck. Not the kind that sped along the isolated highways surrounding Raintree.

"Was he…?" Her throat constricted, the question catching.

"No." Logan's black eyes shot to her face and his deep voice softened. "You know Thunder. He's not going down without a fight." A grim smile curved his lips. "He reared, bucked that boy off him and jumped. Almost made it out of the way." His expression darkened. "But almosts don't cut it. He got clipped and was banged up pretty bad. We thought for sure he wouldn't last the night but he did. He's not the same, though. Whole thing scarred him bad. Turned him wild. None of us have been able to make any headway with him."

Amy scanned the empty stalls lining the stable, eyes scrambling from one to the next.

"Only thing that saved the guest was Thunder's instincts," Logan said. "That kid came out of it with a few cuts and bruises. A lot less than he deserved." He cleared his throat. "I wish I'd kept a closer eye on him. He was a reckless rider. And a selfish one to boot."

Amy took in the hard set of Logan's jaw. He'd always been controlled and practical but he had a soft spot for his horses. Often went to extremes to protect and care for them. It was one of the many things she still admired about him.

She touched his arm, fingers resting lightly against the hard curve of his bicep. "You're not meant to control people any more than horses. You can only lead them. How many times did you tell me that over the years?"

Amy's gut clenched, a surge of shameful heat flooding her. Logan had repeated the mantra a thousand times when she'd struggled with training a horse. She could still see his somber expression as he'd delivered the sentiment, but she'd never really listened. Instead, she'd pushed the boundaries of their friendship and tempted him into a different relationship. Had tried to control him all the same.

Logan withdrew his hand from his pocket, capturing hers and smoothing his thumb over her wrist. "He's not the same, Amy. You still want to see him?"

She nodded.

Logan took her elbow, guiding her down the aisle past the empty stalls to a large one tucked in the back. An eerie stillness settled around them. The front of the stall remained empty, a dark bulk huddling in the back corner.

Heart pounding, Amy leaned closer and secured her purse strap on her shoulder with shaky fingers.

"Hey, boy," she whispered.

There was no response. Only the stallion's heavy breathing disturbed the silence.

"Thunder?" She took a small step forward, palm pressing to the stall guard and fingers wrapping around the bars. "Hey, b—"

A hoof slammed into the bars, the edge of it ramming against her knuckles and rattling the stall door on its frame. Amy jumped back, heels clacking over the bricked floor and catching on the slight crevices in between. One cracked loose in the process.

Logan's strong arms wrapped around her right before she slammed into the floor. Her purse dropped from her shoulder and tangled around her ankles, contents spilling out. The relentless pounding continued, Thunder's kicks increasing in intensity and echoing around them.

"Are you okay?" Logan reached for her injured hand.

"I'm fine," she choked.

She drew her throbbing fingers to her chest, cradling them and gritting her teeth.

"Let me see." Logan's brow creased and he tugged at her wrist.

"It's fine," she bit out, stifling a grimace. "He skimmed me."

The kicking stopped. Amy glanced up as the strong pull and push of Thunder's heaving breaths grew close. His broad head appeared against the bars. A savage scar stretched across his chiseled face and down his muscular neck. Amy winced at his glare, the whites of his eyes stark against the wide and wild depths of his pupils.

"He's been through a lot," Logan said. "It's changed him. In the beginning, I thought there was still a chance I could bring him around. But I lost his trust along the way. I'm out of options. I have to put him down."

"No," she whispered.

Thunder's lips drew back and he cried, the sharp sound screeching through the air and splitting her ears. He slammed his front hooves against the door then jerked away to pace the stall, his pained cries turning fierce.

Amy's legs shook. She bent carefully to gather up the contents of her purse. Shoving the scattered items back inside, she caught sight of the bundle of crumpled divorce papers. She snatched them up and drove them deep into her purse.

Metal clanked as Thunder dove forward and butted the stall door with his head. Eyes flaring, he fixed his gaze to hers and stared deep, tearing past the layers of her polished appearance and creeping beneath her skin. He jerked his head, screaming louder and kicking harder.

Amy choked back a sob and shoved to her feet. Logan was right. Thunder wasn't the same. But to consider ending his life…

"You can't put him down, Logan," she said, turning away and stumbling on the loose heel of her shoe. "Not without giving him a fair shot."

Logan held her arms and steadied her. "I have. Nothing has worked. He's a danger to himself and the other horses and he's especially aggressive around the boys. There's not one single rehabilitation outfit willing to relocate him after laying eyes on him." He sighed. "I can't, in good conscience, allow him to exist in fear and isolation with no quality of life. I'm sorry. There's nothing else that can be done."

Amy ducked her burning face. "That's not true," she said, pushing past him. "There's always a way."

The urge to return to Thunder was strong. To stay at his side, try to coax his spirit back and give him a fighting chance. But that would mean staying. And it was time to move on.

She dragged her purse strap back onto her shoulder and brushed at her clothes. But even though the creases in the material released, the guilt remained. It clung to her skin and clogged her throat, suffocating her. Just as it had every day for the past four years.

Her steps slowed, legs stilling of their own accord. She cast one last look at Thunder's violent attack on the stall. "Surely, there's something you can d—"

Thunder's screech overtook her voice, the words dying on her lips.

"He fought hard to survive, Amy." Logan's expression turned grim, his thumb spinning the ring on his finger. "But, sometimes, that's just not enough."

She spun, taking swift strides out of the stable and away from the stallion's broken state. She'd worked hard to survive, too. And she couldn't gamble the new life she'd fought for to recapture a past full of failures and sins.

Logan's eyes bored into her back. Amy hurried up the hill, thighs burning. Thunder's painful cries lingered on the air, hovering around her and haunting the path to the main house.

Chapter Three

"Hold on to your heart, girl."

Amy whispered the words and pressed her fingertips to the cold metal of Logan's truck. By the time she'd made her way back from the stables, the sun had disappeared and night had settled in. The full moon and stars cast a hazy glow over the surrounding fields, lengthening the shadows stretching from the fences and barn.

She grazed her throbbing knuckles over the ring hidden beneath her collar and grimaced, recalling the band on Logan's hand. Her chest tightened. She shook her head, reached into the bed of Logan's truck and hefted out one of her black bags.

"Here." Logan's chest brushed her back. He reached around her for the bag, his fingers brushing hers. "Let me."

"I've got it."

Amy hoisted the bag and leaned over to retrieve the second one. Logan scooped it up first. He flicked the cuff of his flannel shirt back and examined the glowing hands of his wristwatch.

"It's almost six," he said. "We better get a move on."

He led the way up the drive toward the main house, the strong line of his back and lean jean-clad hips moving with confidence. Amy's belly fluttered. She tore her eyes away and surveyed the entrance to the main house which was bathed in the soft glow of the porch lights.

Massive mahogany doors were adorned with lush green wreaths and red ribbons. The colorful cheer extended beyond the wreaths to the crimson ribbon wrapped around the large columns. Poinsettia blooms nestled in the nooks and crannies of the railing lining the porch and the warm glow emanating from inside the house enhanced the twinkling of the white lights draping the posts and eaves.

Christmas. Amy's steps faltered on the slippery ground. It'd been so long since she'd spent the holidays at home with family. Since she'd left Raintree, the color and comfort of Christmas had faded and the holiday had contorted into a pale passing of a day. A low and lifeless one she'd grown accustomed to spending alone.

Amy swallowed the lump in her throat and strived for a light tone. "Why are all the decorations out already? Mama used to say it was a sin to put up Christmas lights before Thanksgiving was over."

Logan glanced over his shoulder, his words reaching her in puffy, white drifts. "I imagine Betty was beside herself last night when we didn't make it back like we'd planned. She probably got overanxious and decided to keep herself busy."

Amy smiled. Next to cooking, her mother's second favorite pastime was decorating. Not a single holiday passed without Betty celebrating it in style.

"Betty knows how much you used to love Christmas at Raintree." Logan waited for her to reach his side, his big palm wrapping around her upper arm to assist her up the steps. "She wants to make this visit perfect for you. We all do."

Amy's blood rushed at the husky note in his voice and she curled her fingers around the handle of her bag, tamping down the urge to lean in to him.

Hold on to your heart. This time, she wouldn't mistake friendship for love. What she felt for Logan was old-fashioned lust and misguided hero worship. She'd do well to remember that.

A loud jingle sounded, both wreaths swinging on their doors as a small figure burst out of the house.

"Amy."

Betty's red bangs ruffled in the night breeze, her green eyes glistening with moisture.

Amy's vision blurred. "Hi, Mama."

She drew her bag in against her thigh and dipped toward the floor of the porch, the length of her limbs becoming awkward. Betty's short stature had always made Amy wither, trying not to loom over her.

Betty's warm palms cradled her cool cheeks then traveled down her arms to caress her wrists. She gently lifted Amy's arms out to the side, trailing her gaze from the top of her head to the tips of her shoes.

"You look beautiful. I think you grew another inch since I saw you last. You're just as tall as your father was." Betty dabbed at the corners of her eyes and smiled. "I'm so glad you came home." She stretched up on her tiptoes, her kiss grazing the curve of Amy's jaw. "I've missed my sweet girl."

"I've missed you, too."

Much more than she'd realized. Amy wrapped her arms around her mother in a tight embrace. The rich scent of cinnamon and butter lingered on Betty's white chef's apron, releasing in sweet puffs with each of Amy's squeezes.

Amy giggled and nuzzled her cheek against Betty's silken hair. "You smell like cookies."

"That's because I've been baking your favorite ones all afternoon."

"Cinnamon and sugar?"

"Stacked a mile high," Betty said, laughing. She released Amy and tugged at Logan's shoulders, kissing his cheek when he bent his head. "Thank you for bringing her home safely, Logan. I was worried the storm would keep you from making it."

"You think we'd let a bit of ice keep us from your cooking?" A crooked grin broke out across Logan's face and his dark eyes sparkled. "Not a chance."

Betty patted his broad chest, her smile widening. "I made your favorites, too. The green bean casserole and sweet potato soufflé are ready and waiting." She shivered and rubbed her arms. "Let's get inside. It's too chilly out here for comfort."

Logan nudged the small of Amy's back, spurring her step on. She followed Betty's jubilant advance into the cheery interior of the house and found the spacious foyer as warm and welcoming as it'd been in the past. The rich grain of the hardwood floors gleamed, several coats hung from a hall tree bench by the entrance and festive garlands draped elegantly from each banister of the winding staircase.

The low rumble of voices, children laughing and silverware clinking sounded from a large room on the right. Two teenage girls dressed in green-and-black chef uniforms strolled by carting pitchers of iced tea and water.

"You've hired some help, I see," Amy said, noting the girls' bright smiles and energetic expressions.

Betty nodded. "Raintree has done well the last two years. We've had to renovate the family floor and expand to accommodate more guests." Her eyes brightened. "Logan and Cissy started an apprenticeship program for high school students last year. We have positions for students interested in culinary arts and equine management and the school gives them class credit on a work-based learning program. The kids learn and make money at the same time. And, believe me, those teenagers are a Godsend in the kitchen around the holidays." She smirked. "Wish I could get your sister to peel potatoes as willingly as they do."

Amy laughed. "I'd pay good money to see that."

She glanced at Logan, warming at his lopsided grin. It was reminiscent of him as a teenager. Even then, he'd taken an eager interest in the business side of Raintree and had been determined to build it into a successful guest ranch. From the looks of things, he'd succeeded.

"Seems you're doing a great job managing Raintree," she said. "You must be proud."

Logan shrugged. "It was mostly Cissy's doing. She and the twins didn't have much when Dom brought them to Raintree, and she knows how some families struggle. She wanted local kids to have as many opportunities as possible to succeed." His smile widened. "Dom's even getting in on the action. He's trying to talk a friend into partnering so he can offer bull riding clinics."

Amy smiled. "That's wonderful."

The warmth in Logan's smile traveled upward to pool in his black eyes. The pleased gleam in them calmed her pulse and parted her lips. Lord, how she'd missed him. Missed talking to him, sharing dreams and celebrating successes. She missed her best friend.

"There's our girl," a deep voice rumbled.

Amy spun, a giggle escaping her as a tall, gray-haired man approached. Tate Slade, Logan's father, had always held a special place in her heart. Having lost her dad to a heart attack at age seven, Amy had found a second father in Tate—or Pop, as everyone called him—as soon as they arrived at Raintree. His familiar gait and handsome smile provoked a fresh surge of tears. Pop pulled her close for a gentle hug and she pressed her cheek to his broad chest.

"It's so good to have you home for a while," Pop murmured.

"I'm glad to be back."

He kissed her forehead, stepped back and nodded at Logan. "You made it back right on time. The guests have already settled in for Thanksgiving dinner and Betty has almost finished setting up the family table."

Logan slipped the bag from Amy's shoulder. "I'll get Amy set up in a room and we'll be there in a minute."

"Don't think that's possible." Pop hesitated, splaying his hands. "A lot of guests missed their flights yesterday because of the storm. We've had to extend their stays and ended up with double bookings. Everything's packed tight. Except for y'all's—" he winced, nodding at Logan "—I mean, your room."

Logan flushed. His knuckles tightened around the handles of the bags and he shifted from foot to foot. Betty fidgeted with the hem of her apron and Pop studied the toes of his boots. The silence lengthened and Amy's heart ached at the awkward discomfort.

Logan cleared his throat. "I'll stay in one of the bunkhouses. You can have my room."

"Thank you, Logan." Amy rubbed her clammy palms over her pants legs and forced a smile. "Mama, how about I help you finish setting the table while Logan puts my bags up?"

Betty's face creased with relief. "Perfect. I'll go get Cissy. It's high time the two of you met."

"And I'll round up the boys." Pop winked as he left. "Lord knows where they are."

Amy started toward the kitchen, faltering when Logan gripped her arm.

"You've got to tell her about the move..."

"I will." Amy sighed, a sharp pain settling behind her eyes. "But I'm not going to spring it on her this second." She rubbed her brow with her fingertips. "I'll tell her later. At a better time. Let's just have a pleasant dinner for now, okay?"

She pulled away and headed down the hall. Her gut churned at the thought of telling her mother and sister about moving so far away. The last thing she wanted to do was upset anyone during her first visit home in ages. But, eventually, there'd be no way around it.

The light aroma of cinnamon enveloped Amy as she entered Raintree's large kitchen. She inhaled, pulling in a lungful of the familiar scent. A red platter piled high with cookies sat on the edge of the kitchen island and her mouth watered.

Out of habit, Amy snuck a look over her shoulder at the empty doorway, half expecting Betty to spring into the room and shoo her away. As kids, she and Traci had never been successful at snagging a cookie before dinner without Betty pointing a finger and ushering them out. She smiled and made her way over to the cookies.

She reached out and stopped, hand hovering in mid-air. Small, grubby fingers fumbled over the pile of sugar cookies. Mud-streaked fingertips curled around the edge of one and tugged it toward the edge of the plate.

Amy leaned over and found the top of a blond head pressed below the edge of the counter. The head swiveled and deep blue eyes widened up at her in shock. She bit back her grin and narrowed her eyes, taking in his features. Could be Kayden. But the twins were so similar in appearance it was hard to be sure.

"Shhh," the boy whispered. "Don't tell."

"Boys." A short woman with blond hair peeked around the door and leveled a stern expression across the room. "Stop that and get over here."

The boy jumped, his head banging into the edge of the counter. He jerked his hand from the cookies and several scattered to the floor. Another blond head shot up from the other side of the island. This one was definitely Kayden. He sported the same cavalier expression he'd displayed earlier when Logan had chastised him. The boys stood together, Jayden with a bowed head and Kayden with raised brows.

"What'd we do, Aunt Cissy?" Kayden asked, a dab of red cinnamon icing smudged across his cheek.

"You know very well what you did," she said. "Now, get those cookies up and go wash your hands. You're about to eat supper."

The boys groaned but complied, gathering up the broken cookies and tossing them in the trash.

The woman winced and shot Amy a rueful smile. "Sorry about that. Those two are always looking for trouble. You must be Amy. I'm so glad to finally meet you. I'm Cissy, Dom's wife."

Cissy entered the kitchen, stepping carefully and pressing a palm to the blue sweater stretched across her heavily pregnant belly. Amy froze. Her eyes clung to the roundness of Cissy's midsection and her arms drew in against the flat emptiness of her own. Weight dragged at her legs, rooting her to the floor.

Amy swallowed hard and held out a shaky hand. Cissy covered it with both of hers. She was a tiny thing, her shoulders barely reaching Amy's chest. But her blue eyes were rich with welcome and happiness.

"I've heard so many wonderful things about you," Cissy said.

Amy masked her expression with a polite smile. That couldn't be the case. There weren't that many good things for anyone to tell.

"Dominic talks so much about how you two got up to no good back in the day," Cissy added with a laugh.

That sounded more like it.

"So this is where you boys snuck off to." Betty swept in, smiling as the twins rushed over and wrapped their arms around her waist.

"We're hungry," Jayden said, tipping his head back and pouting.

"Yeah." Kayden frowned. "And Aunt Cissy won't let us have a cookie."

"I'll let you have one," Cissy said. "*After* supper. I'm sorry, Betty." She flashed an apologetic smile. "The boys were supposed to be washing up with Traci. Not sneaking away and stealing cookies."

"Aw, come on, Aunt Cissy," Kayden said. "You can

smell 'em all the way down the hall. And we only wanted one."

"You can have one after you eat dinner. Not before."

Kayden poked a grubby finger at Amy. "But she's gonna eat one."

Betty ruffled their shiny hair and laughed. "Well, she should know better. I never let her or Traci get away with grabbing a cookie before dinner either."

Jayden elbowed his brother. "Hush, Kayden. Aunt Amy didn't rat *us* out, you know." He nodded up at Betty. "Aunt Amy can have one. We'll wait 'til later." He jerked his chin at his brother. "Come on."

The two boys scampered out, pausing to press a quick kiss to Cissy's belly.

"Can't blame them for trying." Cissy giggled and rubbed her palm in smooth circles over her protruding midsection. "Even the girls kick harder when I get close enough to smell your mother's cookies."

Girls. Amy stared at Cissy's middle. She'd almost had a girl of her own. *Sara.*

The ache behind Amy's eyes spread, streaking in painful bolts to her temples. Heaven help her, she thought she'd gotten past this. Thought she'd set this pain down long ago.

"Congratulations," Amy managed to choke out on a strangled whisper.

"Thanks." Cissy laughed. "We're having twins. Once you add the boys, Dom and I are in for quadruple the trouble. But I wouldn't have it any other way."

Betty's arm curled around Amy's waist and squeezed. Lines of worry creased her brow.

Amy lifted her chin, hugged Betty closer to her side

and summoned up a sincere smile. "I'm so happy for you both. Dom's a good man."

Cissy nodded. "One of the best."

Betty lifted to her toes and kissed Amy's cheek. "Well, I think it's about time we got a home-cooked meal in you. Whatcha say we get this table set?"

Ten minutes later and only five minutes beyond Betty's designated six-o'clock dinner hour, the family Thanksgiving table was packed. Utensils clanged, napkins flapped in the air and settled in laps. Dishes stuffed with sweet and savory samplings were passed from one end of the table to the other.

The twins, tucked snugly between Cissy and Dominic, barely paused to breathe between bites. Traci ate with the same enthusiasm, shooting smiles Amy's way between each extra helping. Logan went for seconds, his muscular arm brushing against her as he stretched across the table.

Amy shifted in her seat, still whirling from the rush of reunions and welcomes. The only moment she'd had to herself was when the men had left to check on the guests while Betty and Cissy rounded up the boys and Traci. Amy had seized the opportunity to sneak off and stow her purse in her bedroom.

She winced. *Their* bedroom. Hers and Logan's. The same room they'd first shared on the night of their wedding, dodging each other's eyes with tight smiles and stiff limbs as they'd prepared for bed. Her guilt and his anger at her betrayal had made it difficult to enjoy the occasion.

Amy's leg quivered at the brush of Logan's thigh under the table. She slid to the side, lifting her cold glass of sweet tea and taking a deep swallow. The liquid coated her throat and forced its way past the lump lodged there. A chill swept through her, raising goose bumps on her arms.

There was no way she'd be able to sleep in that bed. Not with all the memories filling that room. And not with Logan's familiar scent of soap and pine lingering on the sheets.

She put the glass down with trembling fingers and picked a loose strand of hair off her neck, tucking it back into the topknot that had almost fallen loose.

"Here, baby girl."

Pop stretched across the table and tipped the large pitcher of tea toward her glass.

"No, thanks, Pop. I've got plenty."

"Saving room for the sweet stuff at the end, huh?" he asked, setting the pitcher down.

Amy nodded, trying for a small smile.

"She gwanna eat le cookies wif us." Kayden's mouth gaped around a lump of potatoes.

"Ew." Traci wrinkled her nose. "Swallow your food first, squirt."

Dominic chuckled, wiping Kayden's mouth with a napkin. "Use your manners, buddy."

Jayden snickered at his brother.

"You, too, Jayden," Cissy said, plucking a bit of turkey from his lap and putting it on the edge of his plate.

They all laughed and some of Amy's tension eased. She took a bite of green bean casserole.

"Nothing quite like a full house." Pop sat back in his chair and sighed with satisfaction. "Sure is nice having all of you kids back home at the same time."

Betty murmured an assent, casting a wistful look at Amy. "It's wonderful. I'm so grateful to have you back for a few weeks. I just wish it was longer. Will you be able to visit again this summer?"

The painful throb returned behind Amy's eyes. She'd have a new job by then. There was no chance of her being able to take time off work again that soon after moving to Michigan and hope to make a good impression. She shrugged with stiff shoulders.

"I don't think so, Mama. I'd hate to take up a room during the busy season. You told me yourself Raintree is always full now. Especially around the holidays." Amy gestured toward the closed door leading to the public dining room. "There's a crowd out there."

"Yeah, but those are guests." Pop smiled, eyes warming. "You're family. We always have room for family."

Betty squeezed Amy's arm. "And your seat's been empty for far too long." She smiled at Logan. "We're all so happy you've come home."

"That we are," Logan added in a low voice, his warm palm smoothing over her back.

Amy's face heated. She straightened, the cup tilting in her hand and ice clinking in the empty glass.

"Switch gears," Dominic said, propping the mouth of a wine bottle on the edge of her glass and sloshing red liquid into it.

"No, thanks. I'm good." Amy nudged the bottle away.

The red stream splashed against the ivory tablecloth. The formal one with the fancy cutwork and scalloped lace edges. Betty's favorite.

Amy gasped and dabbed at the rapidly spreading stain with her napkin. "Oh, I'm so sorry, Mama."

Betty tsked, shaking her head and stilling Amy's hand. "Don't trouble yourself. We've got more where that came from."

"You sure you don't want a glass of wine?" Dominic asked, concern clouding his features. "You had a long trip down here. It'll help you relax a bit."

Amy pressed harder at the soaked tablecloth with her napkin. "No, I'm fine. A bit tired is all."

Dominic exchanged a glance with Logan before averting his face and returning to his meal.

"She needs a good night's rest," Logan murmured. "We had a long day and a run-in with Thunder earlier." He took the napkin from her hand, leaning close and gently examining her swollen knuckles. "How're they feeling?"

Amy's skin tingled under his tender touch. She shrugged, peeled her eyes from his dark five-o'clock shadow and chiseled jaw and ignored his enticing male scent.

"We're sorry about Thunder," Pop said. "Real sorry, Amy. We all know how much you love that horse. Wish we didn't have to put him down."

Amy's throat closed and she couldn't bring herself to meet Pop's eyes.

"Whatcha mean, put him down?" Jayden's brow creased.

"Yeah," Kayden said. "What's gonna happen to him, Aunt Cissy?"

Cissy moved to speak but stopped, shaking her head and looking down at the table.

"He doesn't have to be put down," Traci said, blinking back tears. "You could help him, Amy."

Logan leveled a look across the table. "Traci, Thunder is beyond anyone's help. And now's not the time to discu—"

"When *would* be the time?" Traci asked, shooting

a pleading look at Betty. "Tell her, Mama. You know she's the only one that could do it."

Betty sighed but asked gently, "Have you given any thought to working with him, Amy?"

"That would take a lot of time," Amy said. "More time than I have."

"But they're gonna put him down." Traci's voice rose. "Please, Amy. I'll help you. I've been training the other horses and Logan said I have a way with them. Just like you. Isn't that right, Logan?"

Logan nodded slowly, his steady gaze causing Amy's cheeks to tingle. "She's not where you were at her age but she's good." His smile was tender. "It must be in your blood."

"See?" Traci scooted forward in her chair and rested her fists on the edge of the table. "Come on, Amy. It won't take us that long. And if it does, surely you can stay for a few extra days."

Amy fixed her eyes on the red stain bleeding toward the edge of the table. "I can't."

Traci glowered. "Why not?"

"Traci," Betty admonished.

"Not 'til she tells me why."

"That's enough, Traci." Logan's arm tensed against Amy. "It's too dangerous. And she just said—"

"I know what she said but she can't mean it." Traci's voice shook. "They're gonna *put him down*, Amy. Don't you care about Thunder at all?"

"I care. But I can't stay."

Amy closed her eyes briefly, her good intentions fading. Now was as good a time as any to tell them. This might be the best opportunity she'd get to break the news.

"I can't stay any longer than I'd planned because I've been offered a management position. It's one I've worked really hard for and I start in January."

Betty smiled. "That's wonderful news. Is it with the same insurance company?"

"Yes, but it's at a new branch." She licked her lips. "In Michigan."

Her quiet comment pierced the comfortable companionship at the table and thickened the air around them. The clatter of utensils silenced.

"Michigan?" Betty's chin quivered and her eyes glistened. "But that's so far away."

"It's not that bad a trip by plane, Mama," she said gently. "You and Traci can visit as much as you want. I'll buy the tickets."

Amy glanced at Traci. Her eyes flooded and tears streamed from her lashes down her cheeks.

"You told me you were moving to a new apartment. Not to a different state." Traci's ragged whisper broke the silence at the table.

She rose, pushing back her chair and leaving the room.

"Come on, boys," Cissy said, pulling the twins' napkins from their laps and nudging them to their feet. "Time for your bath."

Kayden scowled. "But we ain't had no cookies yet. You said we could—"

"I'll get you some on the way," Dominic said. He stood, helped Cissy up with a hand on her elbow then took each of the boys' hands, leading them out of the room.

"Have you thought this through?" Betty asked, fingers clutching the collar of her shirt. "Maybe you need to take some time and decide if it's really what you want to do."

"I'm sure, Mama."

"But…" Betty's gaze hovered on a red-faced Logan. "What about…?"

"Things have been over for a long time between me and Logan," Amy whispered. "You know that. It was my fault. I was too young and too much happe—" Her voice broke and she cleared her throat. "It's time we both moved on."

The implication fell hard, slamming into the silence and echoing around the room. Betty winced and looked at Pop. A burst of laughter traveled from the guests' dining room, the sound muffled by the closed door.

"Logan?" Pop frowned, his gaze sharp on his son's face.

Logan's jaw clenched. He looked down and slumped back in his chair.

"Excuse me," Betty whispered, shaking her head and leaving the table.

The sound of her sobs faded with each of her slow steps.

"I'll just…give you two a minute." Pop squeezed Logan's shoulder briefly before he left, too.

Amy stayed silent, flinching at the harsh rasp of Logan's heavy breaths and staring at the empty chairs. She bit her lip, her teeth digging hard into the soft flesh, and a sharp metallic flavor trickled onto her tongue. Red drops of wine dripped from the tablecloth and plopped onto her leg, the crisp material of her pinstriped pants soggy beneath the stain.

The moment was so familiar. Almost a perfect replica of another meal she'd shared at this table. When she'd announced her pregnancy with gleeful, nineteen-year-old abandon, shocking and saddening those around her. Betty's tears and Pop's disapproval had been just as strong. And Logan's shame just as apparent.

Amy jerked to her feet and headed for the door with unsteady steps. She shouldn't have told them tonight. It hadn't been the right time. But she'd done so anyway because it was easiest for her.

Here, she was still the same disruptive girl she'd always been. If she stayed at Raintree, she'd only bring more of the same. Discord and trouble. She should never have come back.

Chapter Four

It'd be so easy to let her go. To turn around, trudge to their room—which had been empty of her for so long—and continue with the status quo.

Logan frowned, examining the stiff line of Amy's back through the window. He clutched the bottle of beer in his hand, the cold wetness seeping into his warm skin. It was Amy's favorite brand. The only kind she drank. And he'd kept it on hand for four years, fool that he was, having picked it up out of habit during every trip to town.

He'd grabbed the bottle quickly from the fridge minutes earlier, ducking out of the kitchen to the low murmurs of Pop consoling a tearful Betty, then made his way toward the front porch. To do the right thing. To talk to Amy and pick up the pieces. Again.

He rolled his shoulders, trying to ease the knot in his upper back. His mind urged him to walk away. It practically screamed at him to go in the opposite direction. Just as it had yesterday morning when he'd sat in his truck debating whether or not to make the trip to bring her home.

But, just like then, something inside propelled him toward her. It burned hot in his chest, searing his hands and making him desperate to hold on. Even though he knew it was a high risk. Amy's passionate nature had never been predictable and it was even less trustworthy.

He gritted his teeth. Hell if he'd be like Pop and stand in Raintree's dirt drive watching his wife drive away. Crumple into a weak heap as she left her family behind. He was stronger than that.

Logan looked away, peering past the Christmas lights strung along the porch rail to the dark night beyond. Pop had been little good to himself back when his wife left. Much less to his sons. Ten at the time, Logan hadn't sat idly by. Instead, he'd picked up the reins of the ranch, hustled through the daily chores and watched out for his wild younger brother, refusing to allow himself to dwell on his mother's absence or his father's grief.

His mother had made the decision to leave and Logan had accepted it. It was her loss, not theirs. He just wished his father had seen things the same way. The way Logan should accept Amy's decision to leave now.

He dropped his gaze, tracing the trails of condensation on the glass bottle. Amy's movements brought his eyes back to her. She shifted from one ridiculous high heel to the other, leaning down to prop her elbows on the porch rail and wrap her arms around herself with a shiver.

Logan sighed. It was barely above thirty degrees outside and there his stubborn wife stood. Freezing her tail off.

His heart tripped in his chest. *His wife. His Amy.*

He should leave things alone. Let her go her way and him his, as Traci had urged in the office lobby of limbo. But despite it all, he needed her back. Needed *them* back. The way they were before she'd shot their relationship to all hell and beyond.

Amy owed it to him. And they both owed it to their daughter's memory. Otherwise, their baby girl would be nothing more than a mistake. An almost that never drew breath. A wrong that was never righted.

He closed his eyes and hung his head, muscles flinching on a jagged streak of anger. At himself. At Amy. God forgive him for feeling it but it was there all the same.

Logan made his way outside, boots scraping across the floor and drawing to a halt behind Amy. He set the unopened beer on the porch rail and drew in a lungful of icy air.

"Here." He shrugged off his denim jacket, draping it over her bent form.

Amy wanted to refuse it. The urge to decline was written in her drawn brows and scrunched nose. But she accepted it.

"Thanks." She hunched into the coat and turned back to the dark emptiness before them.

Despite his ill mood, a smile tugged at his lips. Amy had always been stubborn. Head thick as a brick but sharp as a tack, she'd fought him at every turn. It'd started the day they'd met. At eight years old, she'd given him a run for his money. She'd sized up his twelve-year-old frame, curled her lip and dared him to race her. And damned if she hadn't won.

Logan eased his hip against the rail and crossed his arms, a low laugh escaping him.

"You still know how to make an entrance." He nudged her and eyed the tight line of her mouth. "Family dinners always were a lot more interesting with you around."

Her shoulders stiffened and she leaned down, propping her elbows on the porch rail and twisting her hands together.

"You plan on spending the night out here?" he asked.

"Maybe."

"Doubt you'd last long, cold as it is."

She glanced up then, emerald eyes fixing firmly on his face. "I'd last long enough."

Logan grunted. He scooped up the beer bottle, snagged the cap on the porch rail and snapped it off. He tipped the bottle up and tugged deeply, swallowing several mouthfuls of the smooth brew and sighing with pleasure.

Amy's gaze clung to him, following the movements of his throat and darting to his hand. He took another swig. Her eyebrows lowered into a glower.

Logan's belly warmed, sending a sweet thrill up his spine. She'd had the exact same expression the night of her nineteenth birthday. He'd given in to her badgering and had taken her up to the local pool hall to celebrate.

She hadn't been satisfied with flashing her ID at the door. Nope. She'd done her best to sweet talk him into going to the bar and getting her a beer. He'd brought her fried cheese sticks and a milk instead. She'd been beyond ticked.

The warmth spread to his face and pulled at the corners of his mouth. He tipped the bottle up again, grinning as her frown darkened. It was good to see a little life in her.

She jerked her chin. "Your daddy ever tell you it's impolite not to share?"

A chuckle rumbled deep in his chest. The kind he hadn't had in years. He let it loose, relishing the feel and sound of it.

Her gaze wandered over his face to linger on his smile. Her lush mouth parted, the edges tipping up and her face lighting with pleasure. That was all it took.

Before he knew it, he was leaning over, savoring the curves of her lips under his. The sweet flavor of her mingled with the crisp coolness of the beer on his tongue.

She tasted the same. Warm and comforting. Like his own personal sun in the middle of winter. She tasted like home.

It didn't last. She pulled away, squaring her shoulders and stepping back.

"This can't happen, Logan," she whispered.

"Why not?" He straightened, setting the beer back on the porch rail. "You're still my wife."

"I haven't been that for a long time. And I wouldn't have been in the first place if you'd had a choice."

"That's not true—"

"It's not?" She leaned forward. "You mean if I hadn't lied to you and gotten pregnant, you would've chosen to marry me?"

He hesitated, scrambling for the right words. The ones he'd chosen so carefully on the drive to bring her home.

"You've never lied to me, Logan. Please don't start now," she stated softly. "Would you have married me back then if you'd had a choice?"

Not then. Not at such a young age. And not before they'd had a chance to experience life beyond the ranch.

His jaw clamped shut. He couldn't say that out loud. Not now. Not when she looked so vulnerable. So hopeful.

"Would you have given in to me to begin with if I hadn't trailed you so hard? If I hadn't pushed so much?" she pressed, her voice catching.

No. He wouldn't have.

She sighed and looked away. "We grew up together. We were friends. I should've left it at that."

That cool mask returned. It settled over her features like a glaze of ice, freezing out all emotion in her expression.

"You were right," she said, knuckles turning white from her grip on the porch rail. "I was naïve and foolish. It was nothing but misguided hero worship."

Logan flinched, an unexpected pain spearing his chest. He'd spent so much time in the past trying to reason the idea with her. Trying to get her to understand what she felt for him was nothing more than a crush. That, at four years her senior, he was easy to look up to and become infatuated with.

But, as she'd grown, he'd had to work harder at talking himself into believing it, too. And on that ride home from the pool hall the night of her nineteenth birthday, she'd turned to him, put her hands on him and touched that beautiful mouth of hers to his.

And, heaven help him, he'd given in. Over and over again during the next two months. Helpless to put a stop to it. Not even wanting to.

She'd sent his self-control up in flames more times than he cared to remember. Had continued to push for more until he was so desperate not to lose her altogether that he gave in whenever she wanted.

Logan squeezed his eyes shut. He should've been more responsible back then. Wiser. Shouldn't have blindly accepted her word that she'd been protected. That she'd taken care of things.

He learned later she deliberately hadn't. And, as a result, they'd made a daughter then lost her. He'd almost lost Amy, too. All because of her selfish obsession.

"But you didn't leave it at that," he gritted, facing her. "You had to have your way."

"I never meant to hurt you." Her face flushed. "Not then and not now. As hard as it is to believe, that's God's honest truth."

"We both have regrets, Amy." He sighed and shook his head. "You were so young. You think that sits well with me? That I didn't step up? Put a stop to things?"

She smiled. It was small. A joyless tilt. "I knew what I was doing, Logan. Even at nineteen. And even if you were my first."

"I was never interested in being your first."

"I know. You wanted to stay friends. Wanted me to grow up. Live and learn." She released the rail, wrapping her arms around her middle. "Well, I have. I'm not that girl anymore. I've learned and I won't ever be like her again."

He clenched his eyes shut. She was right. He'd wanted to wait. Had spent so much time waiting. Waiting for her to mature. Waiting to see if her adoration grew into something real. Something he could trust. Her friendship had been too important for him to risk it.

"I really and truly thought back then that all you needed was a little push," she said. "That if I could show you how I felt, you'd understand and feel the same. That

you'd want the same things and I could make you happy."
A humorless laugh burst from her. "It was such a stupid
teenage thing to do. So ridiculous. And you called me on
it. Do you remember what you said to me?" she asked.
"When I told you I was glad I'd gotten pregnant? That
it'd been my intention?"

His stomach roiled, a roaring sounding in his ears.

"You told me I was selfish. That I had a selfish obsession."

"I was angry." Dragging his tongue from the dry roof
of his mouth, he said, "I should've been less blunt. You
were so young—"

"But it was the truth, wasn't it?" She kneaded her
nape with both hands. "I was selfish and obsessed. I
never had a clue how to be a real friend." She shook her
head. "But that was the best lesson I ever learned. I've
learned how to be a good friend, Logan. I have. And I
finally did the right thing and filed. You don't have to
pay for my mistake anymore."

A mistake. Their daughter a mistake. Their marriage
a mista—

"Marrying you was not a mistake," he rasped. "I
chose to make you promises and I intend to keep them."

"That's my Logan," she whispered. Her fingertips
rose, bumping gently across the creases on his forehead
and following the hard line of his jaw. "Always doing
the right thing. The honest, honorable thing. That's how
you got into this mess to begin with." She leaned in, her
breasts brushing his chest. "We both have a chance to
get out of this. To get our lives back. All you have to
do is sign."

He caught her wrists and pressed a kiss to her palms.

"I vowed to take care of you and love you every day of my life. I don't break my promises."

She stilled, her expression lifting. "And do you? Love me?"

He eased his hold on her when the dig of fragile bone hit his flesh. "You were the best friend I'd ever had. I've always cared for you."

"That's not what I'm asking." She stepped closer, the heat in her eyes burning into him. "You said you swore to love me. What does that mean to you?"

He clamped his jaw so tight he thought his teeth would shatter. *Damn words.* Every time he was near her, they jumbled up. They tied together in knots, clogging his throat and never escaping the way he intended. But not this time.

This one time, the bastards were sharp, clean and at the ready. And, he had no clue if they were the ones she wanted to hear.

"Tell me, Logan." Her voice firmed. "What does loving me mean to you?"

"It means you have my loyalty. My fidelity and protection. And my support."

Her face fell. The spark in her eyes faded, her long lashes swooping down and masking them. She placed her hand on his chest. Her favorite spot. The place she'd always clung to the hardest whenever he'd moved into her. Over her. The spot she'd nuzzled her cheek against every time he'd held her.

"Those are all very important things," she said. "Very practical things. But what about your heart?"

His heart. Something so much weaker than his head. Erratic. Just like his mother's when she'd abandoned her family for some other man. Like his father's when he'd failed to function for months after she'd left. And like Amy's all those years ago when she'd tempted him down a path he'd never meant to travel.

There were no sure things or guaranteed happy endings in life. Just chance and disappointment. Loyalty was much more tangible and steadfast.

Logan shook his head. "Hearts are unpredictable. Untrustworthy. The kind of love you're asking for doesn't exist, Amy. It's just some notion thrown into kids' fairy tales."

Releasing her wrists, he smoothed his hands around her back, pulling her closer and trying not to plead. "I don't break my promises. I'm offering you something real. Something you can depend on. Something we've both already sworn to each other."

She straightened. That beautiful back of hers drew up into a proud tilt against his palms, breasts thrusting and stubborn chin jutting.

"That all sounds so nice," she said. "But I'm not tying either of us to a vow we made as a result of my stupid teenage lie."

"Amy—"

"You loved me as a friend. A young friend that just happened to grow up on the same ranch as you. I should have recognized that a long time ago." She stepped back and trailed her hands from him. "I won't take anything more from you. And I won't let you sacrifice anything more for me. If I did, I'd be no more of a woman now than I was at nineteen."

Logan's gut roiled. So, she'd leave instead. He wouldn't have her at all and it would amount to nothing more than a mistake. Another regret.

"I'm sorry, Logan," she whispered. "More sorry than you'll ever know."

He clenched his teeth, half-afraid they'd crumble, and studied the tense curve of her jaw. They'd both always been hardheaded and Amy could hold out longer than anyone. But he'd never known her to be able to walk away from a challenge.

"It's one thing to say it," he said. "Why don't you show me, instead?"

She glanced at him, features clouding.

"Stay," he said. "Do right by your family. Do right by me."

She shook her head. "It's too late for that."

"No. That's just your excuse." He shoved away from the porch rail and moved to the door, turning to say, "You haven't changed. Don't know a thing about loyalty. You're no different now than you were back then. The girl that stood right in front of me and lied to get her way is the same woman that's turning her back on her family now. And I'm your family, too, Amy. You worked hard to snag me. You oughta have the guts to stick it out."

She flinched, body stiffening and face paling.

He watched. Waited. Then forced himself to turn on his heel and jerk open the door.

"Wait."

He froze, the sweet sound of her voice sweeping over him. Turning, he watched her pick at her pants leg and shift from foot to foot. She came to a decision, stilling and drawing to her full height.

"I'll stay," she whispered. "Long enough to work with Thunder."

"Absolutely not." Logan held up a hand. "That horse is dangerous."

"I can help him. You know I can."

"Neither one of us knows that for sure, Amy." He blew out a breath in frustration. "You could get hurt. Badly."

"Then help me."

He hesitated. If he refused, there was a good chance she'd leave or, worse yet, put herself in even more danger by trying to work with the horse on the sly. But his throat tightened at the thought of her approaching the maddened stallion.

She interpreted his silence as agreement.

"So it's settled. I'll stay. Just until it's time for me to take up the post in Michigan. I'll work with Thunder and help ease Mama into the idea of the move. But as for us," she said, shaking her head, "I can't stay in this marriage, Logan. It's not good for either of us. We'd both be miserable."

"What makes you so sure?" His muscles tightened, a wave of nausea flooding through him. "Is there someone else?"

"No," she stated firmly.

He forced the next question past his constricted throat. "You're not still hoping for another baby, are you?"

She recoiled, fear flooding her features, and shook her head.

He stepped forward and cradled her arms. "I'm sorry, Amy. I know how hard it was for you to accept that you can't have any more children. But after Sara—" he swallowed hard, eyeing her pale cheeks "—I have no desire to have another child, either. So what's to stop us? It'll keep the family together." He rubbed his thumbs gently over her skin. "Plenty of marriages have been based on a lot less than the friendship we have."

"Had," she stressed, moving away. "We lost our friendship along with everything else. And I won't stay in a marriage out of duty."

"That's a damn sight better than throwing it away." He spun the ring on his finger with jerky movements of his thumb.

Amy kicked off her shoes, slamming the loose heel against the porch rail to break it off, then did the same with the other and rolled up her pants legs.

"What are you doing?"

"Getting started," she said, slipping her shoes back on and scooping up the beer bottle. "The sooner I begin helping Thunder, the better."

She made her way down the porch steps, plucking the pins from her hair with one hand as she went and combing through the long, dark waves with her fingers.

"It's too cold out, Amy." He fell in line behind her, body tightening with a surge of heat at the supple sway of her hips. "Come back inside and get a good night's sleep. It'll wait 'til morning."

"No time like the present."

And that was it. That was all he got before she tipped up the beer and quickened her step, raven hair swinging as she disappeared into the dark night.

Logan stopped, rammed his hands into the pockets of his jeans and headed back to the house. *Stubborn, hardheaded woman.* Only Amy would camp out in a stable in the dead of night, freezing her tail off. Hell if he'd encourage her.

He took long strides across the lawn only to halt at

the foot of the stairs. He should let her go. Walk away. It was the sane, sensible thing to do.

And he almost did. Almost kept right on going. Into the house and an empty bed. Away from Amy. Away from the mess of their marriage. Only, his legs wouldn't budge.

"Damn."

Logan spun back around and followed the same path Amy had taken, moving swiftly across the field toward the stable.

Chapter Five

"She's dead."

Amy inhaled, her peaceful hold on sleep slipping with the intrusive whisper.

"Nah," a second voice declared. "She just breathed, see?"

"No, she didn't. She freezed to death."

That was Jayden. The uncertain tremor and concern in his voice gave it away.

A small hand poked Amy's chest and the warm presence of two small bodies closed in at her sides. Her mouth twitched. She kept her eyes shut and shifted on the stable floor, pressing deeper into the heat at her back, reluctant to release her relaxed state.

A strong hand flexed on her hip. Amy stilled, her stomach flipping as she recognized the familiar strength at her back.

Last night, Logan had tried his best to talk her into going back inside but she'd been determined to stay by Thunder's stall. The stallion had been left alone too long, cooped up away from everyone. She couldn't stand the thought of him spending another night in isolation. Instead, she'd settled on the cold stable floor, keeping a vigilant eye on Thunder.

She'd hoped Thunder would relax after getting used to her scent again. Had thought it might even help him settle down and find comfort in having someone close. It'd worked to a certain extent. Even though Thunder had started his usual intimidation tactics when they'd arrived at his stall, he'd eventually quieted down after a couple of hours. After which, she must have fallen asleep.

Logan, true to his word, had stayed at her side, gathering her against him and throwing a blanket over them. And, as usual, she'd settled right back into his arms. Even in her sleep.

"If she's dead, then that means Uncle Logan's dead, too." Kayden's whisper tickled her ear. "He was with her. And he ain't moving neither."

"Uh-uh," Jayden argued. "If Aunt Amy's dead, it's 'cuz she freezed to death. But Uncle Logan wouldn't die 'cuz men don't get cold."

Logan's chest shook. His gentle breaths of silent laughter ruffled her hair. Apparently, he was playing along, too.

"I know how to check," Kayden said.

Amy cringed as the tip of Kayden's tiny finger jerked her eyelid up, making her eye roll with discomfort. He released it and sat back with a sigh.

"Yep," Kayden said sadly. "She's dead."

"Do something." Jayden's voice turned anxious.

"What do you want me to do?" Kayden's tone was long-suffering.

"Give her CRP."

"What?"

"CRP," Jayden said. "You know? Blow air in her mouth."

Okay. That was enough playing along. Amy opened her eyes.

Kayden sucked in a mouthful of air, held it with puffed cheeks and leaned forward.

Amy held him off with a hand. "That's not necessary, Kay—"

The sharp slam of Thunder's hoof against the stall door sounded, an earsplitting crack of wood cutting through the air and causing them all to jump. Logan's arms shot out, snagging the boys close. He bundled them all together and rolled over, pressing against the wall and covering them.

"What's happening?" Jayden cried, his arms tight around Amy's neck.

"That mean horse is trying to stomp on us." Kayden burrowed his blond head into her middle.

"No." Logan's voice, calm and soothing, rumbled at her back. "He's just letting us know he wants his space."

Thunder's assault on the stall door ceased. Logan tensed, holding them all tight in the wake of the silence, then eased back. He stood and tugged them, each in turn, to their feet.

"Land sakes, what have the boys done now?"

Betty stood in the stable entrance, Traci at her side, and eyed the twins.

"Nothing," Amy said hastily. "Thunder's being rowdy is all."

"Rowdy's an understatement," Logan said, frowning. "He's about to take that door down. We need to turn him out so I can work on it. Don't want to chance him breaking it down tonight."

"He wants out," Jayden murmured.

His sad eyes lingered on Thunder. He took a hesitant step toward the stall. Thunder resumed kicking, his hooves slamming against the stall walls and echoing around the stable.

Logan jumped in front of Jayden and examined the door for damage. "We're about to turn him out, buddy."

"Why can't we let him out *now*?" Jayden slipped between Logan's parted legs, stretching up on his toes and reaching for the latch on the stall.

"No, Jayden." Logan spun him gently toward Betty. "You leave this to me and keep your distance from him. He's dangerous."

"But—"

"No buts. Thunder's wild when he's loose. He needs to be fenced in." He ruffled Jayden's blond hair and nudged him toward the door. "You and Kayden can watch Thunder all you want once we turn him out. For now, you keep out of the way."

Jayden glanced up at Amy, his chin trembling and blue eyes glistening. "He doesn't like it in there. He wants out."

Amy's chest tightened. She patted his cheek and smiled. "I know he does. And we're going to let him out for some fresh air soon."

"Well, in that case, you boys go on in and get some breakfast," Betty said. "Give Logan and Amy time to get a handle on Thunder, then you can come back out to watch later on."

Kayden grumbled on his way past Betty and Jayden trudged behind but both boys picked up their pace at hearing pancakes and bacon were waiting on them.

"Pop told me he found the two of you out here with Thunder last night," Betty said. "We got worried when you didn't show back up." She tilted her head at Amy, expression cautious. "I guess this means you changed your mind about working with Thunder?"

Amy nodded. "I don't know how much progress I'll make with the little time I have but I promised Logan I'd give it a shot while I'm here."

Betty glanced at Logan. "I'm glad to hear that."

Logan ducked his head and resumed examining Thunder's stall.

"I brought a pancake and bacon sandwich out for each of you." Betty smiled, placing two foiled bundles in Amy's hands. "Figured if y'all were gung ho to stay out here all night, you wouldn't take a break long enough to eat this morning. The hands were wolfing them down so fast, I didn't think there'd be any left by the time you did get around to coming in."

The thick weight of the packages warmed Amy's palms and the sweet aroma caused her stomach to growl. The rumble was loud and long, triggering Logan's deep chuckle at her back and a giggle from Traci.

Amy joined them, the laughter lifting her spirits. For a moment, it felt like home again. The way it used to before things went so bad. When the ranch was full of comforts, family and laughter. A time when she'd never wanted to leave.

"Take a few minutes to eat before you start working," Betty said. "You can't make it through a long day on no sleep and an empty stomach."

Betty smiled but her eyes were puffy. Dark circles hovered beneath them and a red tinge lined her lashes.

Amy winced, a lump rising in her throat. Betty had probably stayed up half the night, too. Worrying and weeping. And she'd been the cause of it.

"Thank you, Mama." Amy hugged her close, murmuring near her ear, "I'm not going anywhere yet, you know?"

Betty sighed, squeezing her tight. "I know. I'm glad to have you home for however long you're able to stay." She pulled back and smiled. "I'm happy about your new job and I'll help in whatever way I can. For now, let's just have a great Christmas together, okay?"

Amy grinned, the pressure easing in her chest. "Yes, ma'am."

Betty looked at Logan. "Dominic and Pop said they'd handle the trail rides for you today. So make sure you eat, too, before getting started."

Logan dipped his head and winked. "Yes ma'am."

Betty left, calling over her shoulder, "I gotta get back to the kitchen. Sun's coming up and there's a hungry crowd of guests that needs to be fed."

Amy tugged at Traci's arm as she turned to leave. "You're still gonna help me out with Thunder, right?"

Traci's brows rose. "Do you want me to?"

"Of course. I wouldn't have it any other way." Amy placed the foiled sandwiches in Traci's hand. "Can you do me a favor and hold on to these? I need to change out of these clothes before we get started, then you can watch me work on getting Thunder out of the stall." She laughed. "Or, at least, try getting him out. Do you think you can round up a couple sticks and strings? We'll need a rope, too."

Traci beamed. "No problem."

Amy changed into a gray hoodie, jeans and boots then joined Logan and Traci outside. The strong morning sun had broken out above the horizon and burned off the frost from last night. The air turned warmer and the wind less fierce. Amy tilted her head back and pushed up her sleeves, absorbing the heat.

Figured. Georgia weather was unpredictable at best. It could be thirty degrees at night then spring back to seventy by noon. She'd learned a long time ago to just take it as it came.

She, Logan and Traci took up residence on the white fence lining the paddock. They lingered over the sweet and salty breakfast Betty had provided, watching the horses stroll across the dormant brown grass of the fields. The pleasant chatter of guests sounded and, soon, Raintree's grounds were speckled with visitors, all soaking up the pleasant late–November day.

After eating, Logan brought the hose around and they scrubbed their hands under the spray, cleaning the traces of grease and sweet aroma of the sandwiches away. The fewer strange smells introduced to Thunder, the better.

Amy brought the hose to her mouth, swallowing a few gulps of the water, the metallic taste of the nozzle clinging to her tongue. Logan followed suit, splashing the spray over his face and rasping his palms over the stubble lining his jaw. The thick muscles of his shoulders and back rippled beneath the tight pull of his shirt with each movement.

Amy's palms itched at the display, a deep longing to smooth her hands over his broad shoulders and weave her fingers through the dark waves of his hair overwhelming her. She turned away and faced Traci.

"Did you round up everything?"

"Yep." Traci handed the items to her. "Rope, sticks and strings, just like you asked for."

Amy thanked her and attached strings to two of the training sticks.

"You ready?" Logan asked, turning off the faucet and shaking his hands dry.

Amy nodded, handed Logan the rope and one of the sticks then led the way into the stable. Her heart tripped in her chest.

A finger threaded through her back belt loop and tugged. She stopped and looked over her shoulder. Logan's eyes peered into hers, the sensual curve of his lips pressing into a firm line.

"Go easy, Amy," he said.

She swallowed hard, ignoring the warm flutter in her belly, and walked to the back of the stable to stand in front of Thunder's stall. The stallion pinned his ears and tossed his head back, nostrils flaring on sharp pulls of air.

Amy's thighs trembled. The shaking traveled down her knees to her shins, leaving her lower half weak and unstable.

"Easy," Logan repeated.

He stood a few feet away, a tic appearing in his jaw. Traci hovered behind him.

Amy waited as Logan prepared his rope, studying the movements of his strong hands. The thick, twisted fibers seemed like such a weak support against a frightened, thousand-pound animal. She closed her eyes and placed her hand on the latch of Thunder's stall.

LOGAN MOVED CLOSE to the stall, keeping an eye on Thunder as he whipped the rope overhead and lassoed him. The stallion cried and kicked the wall with his back hooves, thrashing against the pull of the rope.

"It's okay, boy," Amy murmured.

Thunder stopped at the sound of her voice, pinned his ears back and pawed the ground. Logan's throat closed.

"Go wait for us outside, Traci." Logan firmed his hold on the rope, then nodded after Traci left. "Let him out."

Amy unlatched the stall and pulled it open, raising her arms and directing Thunder's feet toward the exit. The stallion backed away, jerking wildly, but eventually exited with her encouragement.

It took several minutes to maneuver Thunder out of the stable and into the round pen. Logan removed the rope and let him buck around the pen until he settled down and drew to a halt on one side.

Amy moved toward the entrance of the pen, her tender expression causing Logan's mouth to run dry.

"He's not like you remember, Amy. He's aggressive now. Likes to dive and bite. You have to start hard and end hard." Logan lifted his training stick, jiggling the string and motioning toward hers. "Use that thing on him if you need to."

She frowned. "I've never whipped a horse and I won't start now."

Logan shook his head. "I've never done it, either. But the last time I tried to work with him, he almost forced me into a position where I had no choice."

"This time will be different," she said, walking to the gate.

He bit back a curse. "How you figure?"

She stopped and faced him. "Because you have help. We're doing this together."

Together. Logan glanced away, focusing on Thunder

and ignoring the pleasurable tingle sweeping through him. There was no room for distractions in that pen.

He cleared his throat. "We start hard and we end hard."

Amy opened the gate and they entered, walking to the center of the round pen. Thunder pinned his ears and pawed the ground, dipping his head and snaking it from side to side as if to attack. Logan immediately threw his left hand up and whipped his training stick behind Thunder's heels, lashing the ground with the string.

"Move," he shouted.

Thunder started then ran left, making it halfway around the pen before he stopped. Amy stepped in, striking her stick against the ground behind him and forcing him forward. Thunder balked, rearing and spinning his back to her.

Amy slapped the ground with the stick again, regaining Thunder's attention. She pointed in the air and shouted, "Right."

Thunder complied, running around the curve of the pen, but stopped again. He laid back his ears again and made to charge.

Logan ran him back, thrashing the ground with his stick and yelling, "Move!"

They continued the tactics, shouting commands and running Thunder around the pen until he began to respond.

"Good boy," Amy praised, easing off when Thunder obeyed a request the first time it was issued.

Logan returned to her side. They stood still, breathing hard and watching Thunder trot around the pen.

"He's doing good, huh?" Traci called from the other side of the fence.

Amy's eyes followed Thunder's progress. "Looks that way." She turned, glancing up at him with excitement. "It's an improvement, right?"

Logan smiled. "Yeah. But he still has a long way to go." He took a step back but stayed close to her side. "When he comes around, ask him to face you. See if he'll give you both eyes."

Amy did as instructed, dropping her arms and maintaining her stance. Thunder drew to a halt, faced her and pricked his ears forward.

"Remember me, beautiful?" she asked.

Thunder huffed and ducked his head.

Amy took a step forward. "It's okay, boy." Then another.

Thunder licked his lips and Amy moved close. She murmured phrases of affection and rubbed his forehead.

"Can we try to saddle him now?" Traci asked.

"Not yet," Logan said. "This is just the first step. It'll take a lot of attention and time."

Traci eased closer to the fence, eyes glued to Amy's actions. Thunder relaxed even more with each of Amy's touches and eventually, he allowed Amy to smooth her palm over his neck. He leaned into her hand, tilting his head slightly when she scratched a favorable spot.

Amy giggled and smiled. "He might put up a hard front but he's still a softie underneath." She crossed carefully to Thunder's other side and continued the tender touches. "You like getting attention. Huh, handsome?"

A low rumble of pleasure sounded in Thunder's throat and he leaned closer to Amy.

Logan chuckled. She was good with a horse. Always had been.

"Ready to give him his space?" Logan opened the gate.

Amy nodded and they exited the round pen.

"You're stopping?" Traci's brows furrowed as she moved to Amy's side.

"Yeah," Logan said. "Horses learn as much from the release of pressure as they do when you exert it."

"Thunder's worked hard and he's been cooped up in that stall for a long time." Amy squinted against the afternoon sun, shielding her eyes with her hand. "He deserves a chance to burn off some energy."

As if on cue, Thunder cried and tore around the pen. His black mane rippled and clods of dirt sprayed from his hooves on every pass.

"How's the training going?"

Logan turned to find Cissy strolling toward them. The boys skipped ahead of her, their blue eyes bright and excited.

"You might want the boys to stay back, Cissy," Logan said. "He's making progress, but he's still dangerous."

Cissy hurried forward and pinched the boys' shirts, tugging them away a few feet. The boys grumbled and strained against her hold, gazes flicking expectantly from Thunder to Amy.

"He seems angry today," Cissy said.

"No more than usual. They've done wonders with him already," Traci said, grabbing the railing as if preparing to duck down. She glanced at Amy. "Want me to help you run him the next round?"

"Not yet." Amy threw out a hand. "Stay there. And help Cissy keep the boys still."

Thunder noticed the onlookers, his eyes growing wild and his cries increasing.

"He just wants out," Jayden said, pulling agains Cissy's hold.

"Shhh." Cissy tapped a finger against her mouth. "Amy and Logan are helping him. You have to be quiet if you want to stay."

Logan tensed, shifting from one boot to the other, and kept an eye on Thunder. The stallion remained at the opposite end of the enclosure, bucking and rearing. Each kick of his hooves against the fence clanged louder than the one before it.

The muscles of his neck and chest stood out in sharp relief. His midnight hide gleamed almost blue in the sun. The long black strands of his mane and tail flew in strong arcs with each of his head tosses and kicks.

"It's okay, boy," Amy soothed, slipping back through the fence.

"Amy," Logan said. "Wait." He caught her wrist and tugged. "He's too worked up."

"I'll be fine," she whispered, pulling away.

She straightened and lifted a hand. The shiny length of her raven hair rippled across her back as she approached the center of the pen with graceful ease. The stallion backed up, calming slightly at the sight of her.

Logan's eyes clung to them, admiration surging through him. A crack of laughter rang out from a neighboring field. Two guests cackled from their saddles as their friend struggled to mount his horse with a ranch hand's assistance. Thunder bucked. His hooves struck with violent smacks against the fencing again.

"Go ahead, boy," Amy said. "Kick all that steam out."

The click and creak of the paddock gate rang out.

"No, Jayden!" Cissy shouted.

Logan spun, eyes shooting to the gate. Jayden clung to the top of it, releasing the latch and swaying as it swung open. Cissy ran toward Jayden as fast as the girth of her belly allowed, stumbling over the ground and falling hard to her hands and knees.

Hooves pounded at Logan's back, increasing in intensity and heading straight for Jayden and Cissy. Logan shoved away from the fence and sprinted toward them.

"Move, Amy," he yelled, racing past.

Logan shoved the gate as he ran, thrusting Jayden out of Thunder's path and barely rolling Cissy out of the way as Thunder charged. The stallion barreled past, eyes wild and lips drawn, kicking up a spray of dirt. It stung Logan's eyes, caking his lashes and obscuring his vision. He rubbed the back of his arm across his face and blinked hard.

Shrieks and yelps from the guests shattered the cheerful atmosphere as the startled stallion darted wildly in different directions, alarming the other horses and causing them to bolt. One of the horses saddled up for the next trail ride reared. The man on his back toppled off and slammed to the ground.

Logan knelt at Cissy's side and cradled her against him. She sat up with his assistance, chest rising and falling on ragged breaths.

"Are you okay?" Amy asked, rushing over and placing a hand to the curve of Cissy's belly.

Cissy nodded and pushed to her feet. "I'm fine."

"Don't force it," Logan said, supporting her arms. "Sit for a minute."

"I'm okay, really," Cissy said. She tried for a smile. "Just clumsy nowadays." Her blue eyes darted beyond Logan's shoulder, voice trembling. "Jayden?"

Logan glanced toward the gate. Traci stood beside it, hugging both crying boys against her legs.

"Are they okay?" Logan called out.

Traci nodded. "They're fine."

The yells from guests continued. Confused by the crowds, Thunder gathered speed and leapt over a fence into an adjoining pasture, galloping through groups of horses. They scattered and took off in all directions.

"Get him," Cissy gasped, waving a hand in Thunder's direction. "Before he hurts someone else."

Amy spun and took off. Logan tore his eyes from Amy and tightened his hold on Cissy's arms. He skimmed his gaze down her length once more for injuries. There were none visible aside from the scrapes on her hands.

"Go," Cissy insisted, patting his chest. "I'm fine. Go help Amy."

"Aunt Cissy?" Kayden ran to her side and reached a hand up to her belly.

Logan grabbed it and tugged the boy around to face him. "You and your brother go straight to the house and tell Mrs. Betty she's needed down here right away."

Kayden blinked, blue eyes darting over the chaotic fields surrounding them.

"Kayden." Logan shook him. "Do you hear me?"

"Yes, sir." He motioned to his brother and they ran toward the safety of the main house.

"Traci, stay with Cissy," he said. "You're not to leave her side until your mom gets here. Understand?"

Traci nodded and wrapped an arm around Cissy. Logan hesitated, stomach dropping as Amy gained more distance.

Cissy shoved at his chest. "I'm fine. Go."

Logan scrambled around in the dirt for the rope. Fisting it, he tore off after Amy.

She was ahead of him, climbing over the fence. Logan ran faster, slowing as he approached the pasture Amy had entered. Thunder paced at one end, tossing his head and eyeing the chaotic movements of guests. Amy stood several feet away, motionless, with her right side facing Thunder.

Logan froze. Thunder was scared and confused. And Amy would be no match for a thousand-pound animal that fought to protect itself. If Thunder felt threatened enough to attack…

She's dead.

Logan flinched. Jayden's innocent whisper from earlier returned, spearing his gut and reverberating in his skull.

His hands shook. Exactly as they had years ago. The night he'd sat beside Amy's hospital bed, watching her work her way silently through the dark delivery of their stillborn daughter. Unable to help her. And unable to save their baby girl.

She's dead.

Logan's heart slammed against his ribs, his eyes blurring. "Get out of there, Amy. Let me handle it."

She glanced at Thunder and walked a few steps away from him. "Just give him a minute."

Logan frowned and studied her determined expression. She wasn't leaving that pasture and there was no way he could drag her out without spooking Thunder even more.

Thunder eyed Amy, jerking his head and shuffling from side to side. Amy moved further away, stopped then murmured words of affection.

They watched and waited. After several restless movements, Thunder stilled and took a hesitant step toward her.

She walked a few more steps, slowing as Thunder approached and halted calmly at her side. Amy reached out, stroked Thunder's forehead with the back of her hand and eased away. She applied and removed her touch on both sides of the stallion, speaking to him in soothing tones.

A few minutes later, she walked away again. Thunder followed, stepping behind her and waiting for direction. Logan sighed as Amy stroked Thunder's forehead with one hand and held her left side with the other. A small amount of blood seeped through her shirt.

"You're hurt," he rasped, stomach dropping to his knees.

"It's only a scratch." She glanced at the cut then him. "A nail caught me when I was going over the fence."

Logan held her stare, shoulders sagging with relief. The wind rifled through the trees lining the pasture, scattering rust-colored leaves around the fence and sweeping over them in a quiet whisper. Thunder leaned further into Amy's soothing touch and dropped his head.

"Good boy." Amy gently scratched Thunder's neck, her gaze lingering on Logan's mouth. "I think we can work with this."

Logan's chest tightened, heat buzzing in his blood at her coy grin. She looked so much like she used to. Vibrant and strong. Eager to gain his approval. Scaring him with her impulsive actions and impressing him in equal measure.

He smiled. "We're still a helluva team, yeah?"

"The best one around," she said.

It all rushed in at once. The flirtatious gleam in her eye and confident tilt of her chin. The excitement lighting her expression. Every bit of her as wild and unpredictable as that horse she gentled.

Logan's fist tightened around the rope in his hand. He'd never wanted her so much. Had never been more drawn to her. Or, so terrified.

Chapter Six

"I told him, I'm fine," Cissy grumbled.

She shifted beneath the stark, white sheet covering the exam table and huffed. A strand of blond hair slipped down over her eyes. Cissy batted it back only for it to fall again.

Amy smiled. She reached out from her seat beside the exam table and tucked it behind Cissy's ear.

"I compromise on a lot, Cissy," Dominic said, pausing his restless movements and leveling a stern look on her. "But I'm not taking any chances with this."

Amy winced. It was a wonder Dominic hadn't worn a hole in the floor with the amount of pacing he'd undertaken over the past hour. At this rate, he'd be in a hospital bed alongside Cissy for high blood pressure.

Cissy sighed. "There's no winning with Dominic when he's in this mood."

Amy smiled and squeezed Cissy's hand. She glanced at Logan hovering in the corner on the other side of the room. He crossed his arms over his broad chest and planted his feet wider apart. There was never any winning with him, either. Both Slade men could bow their back up better than a bull. Dominic had proved as much a few hours earlier.

After successfully moving Thunder back to his stall, Amy and Logan had returned to the main house to find Dominic bundling Cissy into his truck to make the drive to the nearest hospital. Amy and Logan followed close behind in Logan's truck, leaving the boys in Betty's care.

They'd ended up spending the afternoon and early evening waiting in the emergency room near the revolving entry doors. Dominic's agitation had grown with each passing hour and remained after they were ushered into an exam room then to an ultrasound lab. He stopped pacing momentarily and crossed the small room to touch a kiss to Cissy's forehead. "There's no way we're leaving here until I know my girls are safe." His voice lowered and he placed a hand on her belly. "All of them."

Logan shifted, dragging a hand over his face and closing his eyes. The dark stubble across his chiseled jaw matched the black night that had fallen outside. His broad shoulders tensed and he maintained his silence.

Amy's chest ached. She'd only ever seen him this anxious once before. When she'd been the one in the hospital bed and they'd shared the same worry as Dominic and Cissy. And the outcome had been exactly as they'd feared.

Logan caught her eyes on him. He drew his head back, composed his features and turned to stare at the open doorway. She couldn't blame him. This was the last place she wanted to be, too.

Amy slipped a hand under her sweater to rub the throbbing cut on her side, careful not to dislodge the bandage covering it. A warm dampness met her fingertips and she stifled a wince. It'd been a close call earlier but they'd all been lucky. She just hoped their luck for the day continued a little longer.

A nurse swept into the room and closed the door behind her. "Sorry for the long wait." She smiled with apology and sat on a stool by the exam table, tugging a latex glove on each hand with a snap. "It's been a busy night."

Amy's gut churned and sweat broke out across her brow.

"Let's have a look at these beautiful babies and make sure they're comfortable," the nurse said.

Logan squeezed Dominic's shoulder and strolled to the door. He hovered on the threshold, looking expectantly in Amy's direction.

"We'll wait outside," Amy said, releasing Cissy's hand.

"No," Cissy grabbed the sleeve of her sweater. "Please stay."

Her chin trembled but she grinned and held up her other hand which held Dominic's. She wiggled it and laughed nervously.

"What with the boys, I've gotten used to having both hands full," Cissy said. "It's more comforting."

Amy hesitated at the fear shadowing Cissy's eyes. She knew how it felt to lie on a bed waiting for the world to crumble. To hear your worst nightmare as a mother spoken out loud by a stranger.

Amy sighed, forcing a small smile and taking Cissy's hand again.

Logan shifted restlessly at the exit. "Amy—"

"I'm staying, Logan."

He frowned but didn't argue, leaving and shutting the door behind him.

"Thank you for staying," Cissy whispered.

The nurse tugged the hem of Cissy's hospital gown from underneath the cover and Dominic tucked the sheet around the underside of her bare belly.

"I told my husband this wasn't necessary." Cissy laughed nervously. "It really wasn't that hard of a fall, and I feel perfectly fine."

The nurse smiled and rolled closer on the stool, squeezing a glob of jelly onto Cissy's protruding middle.

"It never hurts to double-check," she said. "Besides—" she winked at Dominic "—I think this proud papa will rest easier knowing all of you are okay."

Dominic nodded, jaw clenching and dark eyes worried. Amy tightened her hand around Cissy's and did her best to put on a calm front.

The next few minutes stretched on for an eternity as the nurse moved the probe over Cissy's belly. She searched around then hovered in one spot. A strong throb pulsated around the room, evoking a heavy sigh of relief from Dominic. Locating the second heartbeat, the nurse eased back on the stool to give them all an unobstructed view of the monitor.

"There," she said. "You can relax. Mom and babies are safe and comfortable."

Dominic's smile stretched wide.

The nurse packed up the equipment and wiped Cissy's skin clean, pausing on her way out to say, "You two better get plenty of rest. The opportunity will be gone in a couple months."

Dominic chuckled. He bent, showering kisses all over Cissy's belly, then cradled her face in his big palms and touched a tender kiss to her lips.

The bittersweetness of the sight warmed Amy's chest

and tears welled in her eyes. She dropped her gaze, the cut on her side throbbing stronger than ever.

Cissy laughed. "Can we go home now?"

"Yep." Dominic straightened. "I'll help you get dressed and we'll check out."

Amy's skin heated beneath the weight of Dominic's scrutiny.

"Amy?" Dominic's warm palm touched her arm. "Why don't you and Logan head back home? It's been a long day for y'all, too."

Amy nodded.

"Do you mind checking on the boys for us when you get back?" Cissy asked.

"I'd be glad to."

Amy moved to the door, pressing a fingertip to the corner of each eye as she turned away. Dominic's heavy tread sounded behind her.

"Thanks, Ames," he said, pecking a kiss to her cheek. "Thank Logan for me, too, okay?"

Amy left and joined Logan in the hall.

"The babies are fine," she said. "And so is Cissy."

Logan released a heavy breath. He shoved away from the wall and stepped close. His dark eyes hovered on her face. He swept the pad of his thumb over the wetness lining her lower lashes.

Drawing his hand away, he rubbed his thumb and forefinger together and his mouth drew into a tight line. "Let's get outta here."

His big hand engulfed hers and squeezed, pulling her to the exit.

The drive home was silent. Only the sporadic clicking of the truck's blinker and jingle of keys hanging from the ignition filled the cab. Logan squeezed Amy's hand for the length of the ride, releasing it to change gears or navigate a turn then clasping it tight again.

They pulled to a stop in front of the main house. The truck's headlights flooded the front porch, highlighting the boys and Betty huddled on the steps under a blanket.

"Their little butts should be in bed." Logan cut the engine and thrust the door open.

"Don't be so hard on them. They had good intentions."

Amy sighed at his glower. She trailed Logan to the porch, wincing as the boys' eyes widened up at him. They scrunched together, tugging the blanket up over their heads.

"What are you two still doing up?" Logan pulled the cover down.

"They wanted to wait for Cissy to get home." Betty stood and ran the back of her hand across her forehead. "We've all been worried. But, at least, we've been able to rest a little easier since Dominic called from the hospital to say they'd be on the way back soon."

"Well, that'll take some time, yet," Logan said. "Everything's fine. There's no need to wait." He steered Betty toward the door. "Take a break and put your feet up. We'll look after the boys."

Betty nodded gratefully, saying over her shoulder, "Pop and Traci are still out in the stables. They had a lot of horses to calm down but they should be in soon."

Logan waited as the door closed behind Betty, then glared down at the boys.

"Do you have any idea how much chaos you created this afternoon?"

Kayden sat up, face twisting. "Uh-uh. Don't look at me, Uncle Logan. I ain't do it this time. It was all Jay—"

"You." Logan snapped his fingers at Kayden, then pointed to the door. "Bed. Now."

Kayden clamped his mouth shut, jumped to his feet and scurried inside.

"Hate to say it," Logan murmured, "but Kayden's right this time." He narrowed his eyes on Jayden. "What were you thinking, Jayden? This is the kinda thing I'd expect from your brother. Not from you."

Jayden's lips quivered. "I wanted to—"

"Didn't I tell you to keep your distance from Thunder and let us handle it?" Logan shook his head. "I told you he gets wild when he's let loose. And, yet, you did the exact opposite of what I told you to do."

Jayden's eyes flooded, big tears spilling over his lashes and streaming down his cheeks.

"But he was sad," Jayden whispered. "He wanted out—"

"He's not sad," Logan clipped. "He's wild. So wild he almost ran you and your aunt Cissy over." He bent, pinching Jayden's chin between his fingers and tilting his face up. "Not to mention the babies."

Jayden's face crumpled, his sobs overtaking Logan's words.

"Okay, Logan." Amy removed his hand and stepped between the two. "You've made your point."

She helped Jayden to his feet. Jayden wrapped his arms around her waist and pressed his flushed face against her belly. His tight hold dug into the wound on her side. A fresh rivulet of blood trickled over her skin and dampened her sweater. Amy grimaced, shifting him to a more comfortable position.

"I j-just wa-wanted—"

Jayden's muffled words stopped, his shoulders shaking.

"Shhh," she soothed, smoothing a hand over his blond head and rubbing his back. "It's all right now. Everything turned out okay."

Logan's face darkened. "Amy—"

"He knows he did wrong." She touched her lips to Jayden's shiny hair. "Don't you, Jayden?"

"Y-yes, ma'am," he choked out. He squeezed her waist and buried his face in her sweater again. "I'm s-sorry. I just wanted to…"

His voice turned small and trailed away.

"To help." Amy smiled gently and peered into Logan's angry eyes. "You just wanted to help Thunder be happy. Right?"

"Yes, ma'am," Jayden whispered. He glanced up at Logan and scrubbed the heel of his hand over his cheek. "I just wanted to help, Uncle Logan."

"He's learned his lesson," Amy stressed.

Logan's mouth flattened into a hard line. His dark eyes moved from Jayden's face to Amy's and back again. She held his stare, determined to win this one. Logan shifted restlessly and shoved his hands in his pockets.

"When I give you a rule, Jayden," he said, "I expect you to obey it from now on. Otherwise, I can't trust you."

"Yes, sir," Jayden whispered.

Logan bent, cupped Jayden's head with a broad hand and kissed his forehead. He opened the door and held it, gesturing toward the warmth emanating from inside the house.

"Put him to bed, Amy." Logan glanced at her side and frowned. "Then come to the bathroom and let me change that bandage."

She raised a brow and nudged Jayden. "Your uncle Logan's kind of bossy. I don't think he knows the magic word."

Jayden smiled. He whispered, "It's *please*, Uncle Logan."

Logan's mouth twitched. Those beautiful eyes of his lifted and locked on hers. "Please," he said, voice husky.

Amy's belly warmed. She ducked her head and slipped past him into the house. She was as much a sucker as he was.

Amy led Jayden to his bedroom, helped him and Kayden wash their faces and brush their teeth, then tucked them into bed. Kayden returned her good-night kiss, snuggled into his pillow and watched with interest as Amy sat on the edge of Jayden's mattress, smoothing her fingers through his blond hair.

"What you did today was wrong, Jayden," she said. "No matter how much you think you were doing right."

"Yes, ma'am." Jayden hiccupped. "I won't never do it again."

"Promise?" Amy narrowed her eyes.

"Promise."

"He deserves a butt whoopin'," Kayden proclaimed. "Can I give it to him?"

Amy forced back a smile and cast Kayden a stern look. He shrugged and turned over to face the wall, dragging the covers up over his shoulder.

"Are you gonna give me a spanking, Aunt Amy?" Jayden asked. His blue eyes widened, engulfing his face.

She smiled and ran a finger over his forehead, tucking back a blond curl. "No. I think you've learned your lesson, don't you?"

He nodded, expression earnest.

"Okay." Amy stood. "I want you both to close your eyes and go to sleep. That way you'll be well rested and ready to deliver a good apology to Uncle Dominic and Aunt Cissy in the morning."

She crossed the room and flicked off the light, tugging on the doorknob as she stepped into the hallway.

"Aunt Amy?" Kayden poked his chin above the covers. "Can you leave the door cracked so we can hear when Aunt Cissy gets home?"

"Of course," she whispered. "Now, close your eyes and go to sleep."

"Yes, ma'am," they said in unison.

Amy released the doorknob, allowing a slant of light to pierce the dark quiet of the room. She took a few steps down the hall but paused when the rustling of bedsheets sounded.

"I'm glad we got two aunts now." Jayden's hushed voice carried into the hallway. "They're better than a mama any day."

A bed creaked.

"Yep. Aunt Amy's cool," Kayden said. "But you're lucky she didn't give you a butt whoopin'. A mama woulda burned your tail up."

Jayden sighed. "Yeah, pro'ly. We'd both have us a thousand butt whoopins by now."

It was silent for a moment.

"Maybe," Kayden whispered. "But we ain't got one yet."

A burst of muffled giggles rang out. Amy grinned, covering her mouth to silence her laughter and cradling her side at the sharp sting running through the cut. She leaned against the wall and closed her eyes.

The moment was so familiar. Full of laughter coming from little ones tucked in their beds. She'd imagined it a million times when she'd been pregnant with Sara. And, had her luck been as good back then as it had been for Cissy earlier, the laughter would be coming from her children. Hers and Logan's. Safe in their beds. Loved and protected.

She'd been so sure back then that she could've made Logan happy. Could've won him over, earning a loving husband and strong family. But she'd gone about it the wrong way and ended up losing everything.

Amy sighed. All that was in the past. It was just a teenage crush she'd worked hard to overcome. She'd gotten over her unrealistic hero worship of Logan. She wasn't that desperate girl begging for his attention any more. She was moving on.

She made her way to their old bedroom, shutting the door quietly behind her. It was exactly as she remembered. The small fireplace on the far wall was still charming and the deep polish of the cherry furniture shone as bright as ever. Her purse sat on the dresser and her overnight bags were lined up against the wall by the wide, king-sized bed.

Amy rubbed her hands over her arms and crossed to the dresser. She rifled through the contents of her purse, pulling out the crumpled divorce agreement and smoothing the creases.

The bathroom door opened and Logan exited, his bare feet whispering over the carpet as he crossed the room. He reached out, plucked the papers from her and flicked them down on the dresser.

"Come on." His strong hand wrapped gently around her elbow, tugging her to the bathroom.

He'd discarded his shirt and the thick muscles of his bare back tightened with each of his movements. Amy swallowed hard. It was a physical reaction. Nothing more. She tried to convince herself she'd have the same response to any other well-built man she came across.

Logan stopped in front of the sink. He sifted through the medicine cabinet, retrieving alcohol wipes, fresh gauze and tape.

Amy flicked her eyes around the bathroom, trying to focus on anything other than the broad expanse of his chest. A sprinkling of dark hair arrowed down his abs toward unsnapped jeans hanging low on his lean hips.

Logan's tanned hands gathered the hem of her sweater.

"I can do this myself," she said, stilling his thick wrists.

"You can't reach it properly."

"Yes, I can. Clear out and I'll take care of it."

"Amy, it's been a hell of a day. Just let me do this and let's get some decent sleep. In a bed, this time." He raised a brow and flashed a crooked grin. "Please."

Her body sagged, his gentle expression melting her defenses. She raised her arms, squeezing her eyes shut as he lifted the sweater over her head and dropped it to the tiled floor.

"I swear, Amy, you're about as hardheaded as those boys…"

She glanced up. His eyes clung to the ring dangling from her necklace and the strong column of his throat moved on a hard swallow.

Her face flamed. She should've taken it off long ago. Her hand shot to her chest, pressing over the metal. The stone cut into her palm.

"Logan—"

"Lean to the side," he said, voice hoarse and strained.

She sighed and twisted to the side.

His broad hands moved slowly against her skin, peeling off the old bandage and sweeping an alcohol wipe across the wound. Amy winced at the sting. Logan lowered his dark head, blowing gently across the cut until she relaxed.

"There," he whispered, pressing the last bit of tape over the gauze and a kiss to her rib cage.

Amy tucked her chin to her chest, cheeks burning under his scrutiny. "Thanks."

Logan rose, running his hands along her sides. The heat from his sculpted abs and wide chest pulsed against her front. His fingers caressed her hips and tugged her closer.

She tensed her stomach, trying to ignore the warm flutters spreading beneath her skin, waiting for the moment to pass. It was a physical reaction, nothing more.

Logan's calloused fingers slipped underneath the ring and lifted it.

"You still wear it," he murmured.

Amy blinked, eyes tracing the gray grout outlining each of the square tiles on the floor.

"For how long?" he asked, tugging the ring. "Since you left?"

She looked up and nodded.

Logan's brow creased. His dark eyes clung to hers. He hesitated, his mouth opening and closing, voice finally emerging in a choked rasp.

"There've been no other men?"

Amy cringed. She wished she could lie to him one more time. Tell him he no longer mattered to her. That what she'd felt for him had never been real. That she'd forgotten him long ago and fallen for another man along the way.

That would be enough for him to give in, give up on their marriage and let this go. Then she could move further into her new life. Away from her past sins and embarrassments.

Only, that's how they'd ended up here to begin with. Her past lie still stood between them, casting a shadow and undermining his faith in her. She'd forced his hand back then and didn't deserve his trust now.

Still, she wanted it. Even if she wasn't worthy of it. Amy recoiled, feeling as small as Jayden. Wanting to do so much good and failing in every respect.

Logan's face flushed, the redness flooding his lean cheeks and racing down his broad chest. The muscles in his abs rippled on an indrawn breath.

"Amy?"

A soft tremor shook his voice, highlighting the dark uncertainty in his eyes and deepening the lines of pain on his face.

Amy sighed, shoulders sagging. It was just as Cissy had said. There was never any winning with a Slade man. Especially Logan. He wouldn't let this go. And she couldn't lie to him again. Or to herself. No matter how much she wished she could. Like Jayden, she'd learned her lesson.

She closed her eyes, curled her fingers into his tousled hair and tugged him close. His forehead was warm against hers and she smoothed her palms down to cup his jaw, the only fair words there were leaving her. Honest ones.

"There *are* no other men, Logan. Not like you. They don't exist."

A strangled groan rumbled in his throat, vibrating against her lips as his mouth plundered hers. She wrapped her arms around his broad shoulders, bending beneath his tender advance.

She should stop him. Should finish this before it started. But the hard heat of his chest and the rough rasp of his stubble-lined cheek against her skin renewed old longings.

The longing to be seen by him. To be desired by him. To be loved by him.

His tongue parted her lips and his fingers pressed through the fall of her hair to knead the back of her neck. His hands slid down her back to cradle her bottom, lifting her and wrapping her legs around his waist.

Her chest swelled and a lick of heat curled low in her belly. His masculine scent and gentle touch enveloped her, permeating her senses and settling back into their rightful place in her heart. And, God help her, she'd had no idea how empty she'd been.

She hugged him closer as he carried her into the bedroom and tossed them both onto the bed, the plush bedding cushioning her back and his hard length spanning her front. The moist warmth of his mouth left hers to travel across her skin, lingering on her breasts, thighs and everywhere in between, dispensing with their clothes along the way.

Gasping, she nuzzled the hard curve of his bicep as he settled between her thighs. He pressed deep and a soft cry escaped her, body adjusting, remembering.

He murmured warm words of apology against her lips, then continued with extreme care, body rigid and quaking. She tucked her heels around his thick thighs and pressed her nails into his muscular buttocks, urging him on.

"I won't break," she whispered, kissing his temple. "Let go. Make love to me."

He sucked in a strong breath and moved with greater strength and purpose, limbs steadying. Her hand moved of its own accord, pressing tight to his chest, absorbing the comforting pound of his heart and taking everything he would give.

"Make love to me," she repeated. "Make love to me."

The phrase fell from her lips with each of their movements, hovering on the air between them. She didn't know when the mantra changed. Didn't notice when the words rearranged or when some dropped away.

She only realized it after they both found release. When he rolled to his back, arms wrapped tight around her and she followed. When she replaced her hand at his chest with her wet cheek. Just as she had the first time they'd been together.

The plea lingered on her tongue, breaking the silence, just as it had all those years ago. It echoed around them and within her, mingling with the thundering beat of his heart and the searing heat sweeping over her skin.

"Love me. Love me."

And she wanted him more than she ever had before.

"I'M SORRY."

Logan grimaced. He knew it was the wrong time to tell her. Could feel it in the stiffening of Amy's spine beneath his fingertips and the slow lift of her face from his chest. But he needed to say it. Needed to pry it from his gut and put it down. So they'd at least have a fighting chance.

"For everything," he said. "All the way back to the very start."

Amy rose to her elbows and faced him. Her brow creased, her lush mouth parting on shallow breaths. The light sheen of sweat on her flushed cheeks glistened in the lamplight.

His body tightened. He dropped his gaze, studying the raven tangles of her hair pooling against the white blanket beneath them.

"I remember the exact day things changed between us." He dug deep for the right words. The ones he'd arranged so carefully. "I was twenty. Had finished a good day's work and took off on my own. Rode hard. Decided to stop off by the creek to let the horse take a breather. I was half asleep propped up against that old oak tree when I heard you coming." His mouth curved, a small smile fighting its way out despite his unease. "Your feet snapped a twig or two and I figured you were sneaking up on me. Pulling a prank like you always did. So I kept my eyes shut and played along."

Amy's flush deepened. "Logan—"

"But that's not what you wanted." His mouth tightened. "You kissed me, instead." He tapped a fingertip to his lips, warmth spreading from the spot and heating his face. "Right here."

She squirmed against him and he curled his hand over the curve of her hip, stilling her.

"I was just to practice on, you said. That some guy had caught your eye and you wanted to be prepared." He laughed, the sound grating over his ears. "You turned beet-red. Just like now."

Amy winced and looked down. The long sweep of her hair cascaded over her shoulders, hiding her face.

"I was still a kid," she whispered.

"You were sixteen. Had that beautiful hair and flirty grin. And I knew you were lying." He reached out, brushing her hair back and rubbing the strands between his fingers. "It caught me by surprise. I'd only ever thought of you as a friend and was under the impression you felt the same way about me." His gut churned. "I remember wishing you'd shift that attention to Dom or some other boy closer to your age. Because all I could think was…if I don't put a stop to this, I'm not just gonna lose my best friend, I'm gonna break this girl's heart."

She glanced up, gorgeous green eyes welling.

"And, damn me to hell, Amy," he choked, "that's exactly what I did."

She shook her head and placed her palm to his jaw. "You tried to let me down easy. I know it had to be awkward for you, and you did your best to set me straight over the years."

"My best wasn't good enough."

"You tried. That's the important thing," she said, looking away. "What happened later was my fault. And none of it matters now."

His throat tightened, heart bleeding for her. For the innocent girl she'd been. And the guarded woman she'd become. He lifted his hands, cradling her cheeks and dropping gentle kisses across her face.

He may have made mistakes by eventually giving in to Amy. By not keeping his distance. But when he'd learned of the pregnancy, he'd chosen to marry her despite the fact that she'd deceived him. As her husband, it'd been his job to protect her and he'd failed her. His throat closed. It'd been his job as Sara's father to protect her, too.

Sara.

Logan froze. A wave of nausea swept through him, flooding his mouth. Just their daughter's name was enough to bring the pain back. Enough to remind him of how much they'd lost.

"It doesn't have to all be for nothing, Amy." His voice sounded strange, even to his own ears. "However we got here, this is where we ended up. We still have a chance to build something solid. Something real." He looked up, hating himself as much as he hated the hard glint in her eyes. "You're not still looking for a fairy tale, are you?"

Her mouth tightened. She turned away again, gazing blankly beyond his left shoulder.

"No."

Logan sighed. "We can make this work."

"No. We can't."

Amy pulled against his hold. His hands shot out, tugging her back against him.

"Why not?" He pressed his forehead to hers. "We were best friends once and can be again. That alone will make our marriage strong. We're good together. We proved that earlier with Thunder and just now."

"What just happened was a mistake. One we're not going to repeat."

A mistake. Logan's chest burned. "We're still married."

"Not for much longer." She tossed her hair over her shoulders. "I've been truthful with you this time around,

Logan. You knew exactly what my intentions were coming here."

"I heard you say it. But I can't believe it's what you really want. Raintree is your home. Your family's here." He curved his hand around her jaw, her skin warm under his palm. "I'm here. I want you with me and I want this marriage to work."

She shook her head. "Only because you feel obligated. You didn't want to be married to me. Didn't love me that way—"

"I cared for you." He gathered her against his chest. "I still do. I know that doesn't sound impressive. But love is just a word, Amy. One that people throw around as an excuse for reckless behavior."

Logan's mouth twisted. His mother had used it often enough. She'd said it every time she'd placed her needs before his or Dominic's. Had whispered it when she'd wanted to manipulate Pop into giving in to another one of her selfish demands. And, eventually, had used it as an excuse to abandon her family for a richer man, shrugging off all responsibility for her actions.

Amy had used it, too. She'd said it to him over and over again after getting pregnant. As though that justified her deceiving him and trapping him into marriage.

He shook his head. "It's just a word. A fantasy. The friendship we had was strong. It was real and my loyalty is, too. We're a good team. Always have been."

Her brow creased, eyes roving over his face, dull and heavy. "As good as Dom and Cissy?"

He clutched her hard and nudged a thigh between hers. "Better. We have history."

A scornful laugh burst from her lips. "Bad history."

"I remember the good. The rest can be forgiven."

"And have you? Forgiven?" Her lips trembled. "And forgotten?"

He stiffened. He wished he could tell her what she wanted to hear. Ease her mind and put the light back in her eyes. But he couldn't.

"I'm trying, Amy. We'll try together. Take things slow. Work at forgiving and trusting each other again."

The forgetting he wasn't so sure about.

Her breasts lifted against him on an inhale. "Let's just be for now. I'm tired."

She sounded it. The husky note in her tone and heaviness in her limbs proved it.

Logan moved to his back, holding her close and trailing his fingers in wide circles over the smooth skin of her back.

"Then go to sleep," he said. "I'll be here when you wake up."

And he would be. Every day. He could get things right this time. Remind her how good they could be together and prove their marriage wasn't a mistake. That their daughter hadn't been a mistake. He owed it to Amy and they both owed it to Sara.

He shifted, bundling Amy against him and sliding beneath the covers. She drifted off before he tucked the sheet around her, hand resting over his heart and quiet breath whispering across his chest.

Logan tried to follow. Closed his eyes and tried to dream. But he couldn't silence his thoughts. Could only continue wondering silently how Amy could be right in his arms but still feel a million miles away.

Chapter Seven

"Over this way, Amy."

Logan tapped the brim of his Stetson lower on his brow and leaned over the fence rail. Amy stood in the center of the round pen edging around Thunder's frantic bucks. Just as she'd been doing every day for the past three weeks with no progress to show for it.

Amy passed one palm after the other farther up the lead rope, stepping slowly across the ground toward Thunder. Logan tensed.

"Something's off." Dominic shifted at his side and propped a boot on a low fence rung.

"I know," Traci said. She grabbed Dominic's shoulder and pulled, leveraging herself up to straddle the fence. "Thunder gets more aggressive every day."

Logan sighed. He hated to admit it but it was the truth.

Every morning for the past few days, he'd woken before dawn to find Amy gone. By the time he yanked on clothes and made it outside, she'd had Thunder in the round pen, attempting to run ground work.

Attempting was the only word for it. She'd been at it for hours today, just like all the others, with no change in the stallion. Thunder ducked his head and attacked on several occasions, causing Amy to scale the fence more than usual. And every time Logan or Dominic tried to help, Thunder became more violent and left Amy even more discouraged. It seemed as though whatever ground she'd gained with Thunder, she'd lost it just as fast.

Logan grimaced and scraped his boot over the ground. Amy hadn't been herself since he'd brought her home but she'd definitely been more out of sorts lately. The only explanation for it was their sexual encounter three weeks earlier.

He didn't blame Amy for backing away. He blamed himself. With everything that had happened between them, he should've been more controlled. Shouldn't have let the chaos of that day and one shared moment of success coax his guard down.

It seemed his body was as intent on betraying him as much now as it had before. But despite that, he couldn't bring himself to regret making love to her. He'd missed her over the years and it'd felt good to comfort her. To be comforted. To hold her again.

But he felt as removed from Amy now as he would if she were already in Michigan. And only a couple of weeks remained before she left.

Logan balled his fists. *Time.* He'd never been on good terms with it. The earth could crack under his feet and the fool sun would still rise. But as soon as a moment of peace arrived, night would swallow it whole. Time kept ticking no matter what occurred.

"There he goes again." Dominic smacked his palm on the fence, rattling it under Logan's elbows as Thunder lunged and missed Amy by inches. "I'm worried she's gonna get hurt. He's starting to wear her down."

"She's being careful," Logan murmured.

Hell if he knew who he was trying to reassure. Dominic? Or himself?

"Angle over this way, Amy." Logan waved a hand, keeping his tone calm. "I can boost you over if he charges again."

Dominic sighed. "I know she doesn't want to hear it but have you talked to her? Asked her to ease off a bit? Take a break?"

"I've tried," Logan said. "But she's adamant she can bring Thunder around. Keeps fantasizing that he can be saved."

"It's not a fantasy, Logan. There's always a chance. But she needs to take a step back. Rest and regroup. Let us take over for a while."

"That won't help," Logan said. "Thunder trusts us less than he does her. And no amount of time is going to change the final outcome."

"So, that's your solution?" Dominic cocked an eyebrow. "Just give up? She can handle him, Logan. More than handle him if she gets her bearings again." He jerked his chin at the enclosure. "She's gentled more horses in that pen than I can count."

"This is different."

"How? There's a horse and a round pen. Same as before."

"It's not the same—"

"Shhhh."

Logan jerked his head back around to find Amy scowling in their direction. Thunder, rattled by her hiss, snaked his head and charged. Logan shot over the top rail, catching Amy as she jumped out of Thunder's path and assisting her over the fence.

She pushed his hands away, tossed her hair back

and frowned. "I can handle myself. Could've handled Thunder, too, if the two of you hadn't been running your loud mouths."

Dominic cast a halfhearted smile at Amy. "We know you can, Ames." His face softened. "We're just worried about you. You've had a lot of close calls with Thunder lately and we don't want you getting hurt. If anyone can help Thunder, you can. But you can't be effective in that pen if you run yourself into the ground. You haven't been yourself for a while and Thunder's picking up on it."

Amy rubbed her forehead. "I know that. I'm just frustrated."

She glanced behind her, shoulders sagging. Logan followed her gaze to the far side of the enclosure where Thunder kicked and stomped.

"I'm doing the same things I've always done," she whispered. "I don't know why he won't respond."

Logan studied her weary expression and cringed. Dominic was right. She needed some space. Some time to relax.

Logan plucked a piece of dead grass from her sleeve then rubbed his hands up and down her arms. "Well, forcing it isn't going to help you or Thunder. You need to take a break and clear your head."

Squeals broke out behind them. Jayden sprinted across the field at high speed, his brother chasing close on his heels. They kicked up clouds of dust that hovered in sunlit particles behind them and drew to an abrupt halt at the fence.

"I won." Jayden doubled over, air rasping between his lips.

"Only 'cuz you cheated." Kayden shoved his brother

then swaggered over to Amy. He propped his hands on his hips and squinted at Thunder thrashing in the pen. "You ain't whipped that horse, yet, Aunt Amy?"

"She's not gonna whip anything," Jayden huffed. "She don't give spankings." He skipped over and tipped his head back to look up at Amy. "Ain't that right?"

Amy laughed and hugged the boys to her legs. Her entire demeanor changed. The rigid tension in her body released and the tight lines on her brow eased.

Logan's chest swelled. This was Amy. As she had been. Bright and energetic. Warm and inviting. The way she was before they'd lost so much.

"Oh, you know what I mean," Kayden drawled, squinting up at Amy. "You could whoop any horse into shape. Uncle Dominic said so."

Amy glanced at Dominic. "That's nice of him to say. But I don't think Thunder likes me messing with him. I think he'd prefer to run me over."

"You want me to help you?" Kayden puffed his chest out. "I won't let no horse come after you."

Amy smiled. "Thanks for the offer, Kayden." She bent and kissed his cheek. "But I wouldn't want to risk you getting hurt."

Kayden shrugged, his features firming. "Okay. But if Thunder shows his butt, you tell me and I'll whoop him for ya so you won't have to."

"Me, too," Jayden said, sharing a conspiratorial look with Kayden. "We'll both give him a butt whoopin'."

The boys dissolved into a fit of giggles, wrapping around Amy's legs and snorting.

"Lord have mercy," Traci muttered, grinning. "Any horse would take off as soon as they saw the two of you coming."

"Uh-uh," Kayden jeered. "Besides, I know what Aunt Amy's doing wrong."

Kayden darted between Dominic's legs and climbed onto the fence rail next to Traci.

He rubbed a grubby hand over his face, leaving a streak of dirt on his cheek. "She ain't spitting."

Traci issued a sound of disgust. "What does that have to do with anything, squirt?"

"Everything." Kayden lifted his chin. "Mr. Jed said if something's broke on a ranch, it just needs some spit-shine and elbow grease." He smiled, teeth gleaming. "She needs to spit on him."

Dominic laughed and ruffled Kayden's hair. "I think you're spending entirely too much time with Mr. Jed. Why don't you give the hands a break and let 'em work without you underfoot today."

Kayden's nose wrinkled. "Mr. Jed ain't no hand. He said he's a bone-a-fine cowboy. Like you and Uncle Logan."

"That's *bona fide*." Traci said, lips twitching.

"Yeah, that's what I said." Kayden pursed his lips in affront then grinned. "Anyways, Mr. Jed likes us helping him. He gives us good jobs, and he pays us."

Logan smiled. Grumpy Jed probably came up with something all right. The boys had started trailing Jed the second they were released from school for Christmas break yesterday and hadn't stopped since.

"What kind of job did he give you today?" Amy asked, smoothing a palm over Jayden's back.

"He gave us a dollar to sit by the fence he painted and make sure it dried." Kayden shrugged. "But that got boring so we left. Then we couldn't find him."

Amy laughed. "Well, that's his loss."

Jayden tugged at Amy's wrist. "Are you a bone-a-fine cowgirl, Aunt Amy?"

She smiled down at him. "I don't know. Depends on who you ask. Everyone has their idea of one. Do you think I'm one?"

"Yep." Jayden grinned. "That's how come you can whoop any horse into shape."

"Yeah and Uncle Dominic said you can beat anyone on a horse," Kayden said, flashing a sly look at Logan. "Said you used to beat Uncle Logan every time y'all raced."

Logan narrowed his eyes at Kayden. "Not every time. I won on occasion."

"Sometimes, but not often," Amy said, laughing.

Jayden's eyes widened with excitement. "Are you gonna race Uncle Logan today?"

Amy's laugh tapered off and she glanced back at the round pen. "I don't have time for a race. I need to work with Thunder some more."

The shadows returned to her eyes and her expression fell.

Logan shook his head. "Not a good idea. You've been at it long enough."

"But—"

"No buts. Jayden has a good point. You need a break and so does Thunder. I think a ride is a great idea." Logan pulled at Jayden's belt loop, pausing to unwind the boy's arms from around Amy's legs with a chuckle. "Let your aunt Amy go, buddy. She's already taken."

Jayden frowned. "Who's takin' her somewhere?"

Logan returned Amy's grin. "Me."

Kayden sprang down from the fence, ran over and

stood beside his brother. Both boys put their hands on their hips and narrowed their eyes up at Logan.

"Where you takin' her?" Kayden asked.

"For a ride on a horse," Logan said.

"How far?"

"Far."

The boys pondered that, their wide blue eyes moving from him to rest on Amy.

"You wanna go with him?" Kayden asked.

Amy smiled and nodded.

Jayden huffed, jutting his chin out at Logan. "You better bring her back."

"I will," Logan murmured, body tightening at the warmth in Amy's green eyes. Her throat moved on a hard swallow and she looked away. "I promise."

"Hey." Kayden darted off and yanked at Dominic's jeans. "Is it time for the bonfire yet?"

Logan grinned at the excitement gleaming in Amy's eyes. Every year, Raintree kicked off the week of Christmas with a special celebration for family and guests. The night consisted of tasty treats, games for the kids, lighting the large cypress tree behind the main house, and a big bonfire.

Every child on the ranch received an ornament, painted their name on it and hung it on the tree. Then, the bonfire would be lit to make sure Santa had a clear view of all the names. Pop used to say the bonfire was Raintree's way of getting the Nice list to Santa.

Logan shook his head. He'd never been conned into believing it. But as children, Dominic and Amy had. The flames had burned so bright and high they had believed the message reached all the way to heaven.

Logan remembered how excited Amy had always

gotten over the annual Christmas bonfire as a kid and her joy for it had never diminished. It'd been years since she'd been home for one.

"Not yet," Dominic said. "Needs to be good and dark first, then Uncle Logan will get it lit."

"Can we light the bonfire, Uncle Logan?" Kayden asked.

Logan suppressed the shudder sweeping through him. It wouldn't take the twins more than ten seconds with a match to send Raintree up in flames.

"No," he said. "I think it's best to leave that to the grown-ups."

Dominic winked and nudged Kayden's chin with a knuckle. "Uncle Logan lights it every year. We don't want to break tradition, do we?"

Kayden frowned but shook his head.

"How 'bout we go in for some hot chocolate?" Dominic suggested. "Traci and I will get you fixed up with some marshmallows. After that, we can help Mr. Jed and the rest of the hands get the wood stacked for the bonfire."

The boys squealed at that. Jayden ran over and tugged at Traci's arm.

"Can I get the big marshmallows this time? I don't like the small ones."

Traci hopped down off the fence and took Jayden's hand in hers. "They both taste the same, Jayden."

"No, they don't."

"If Jayden gets the big ones then so do I," Kayden grumped.

"Rein it in, Kayden, or you won't get any marshmallows." Dominic scooped Kayden up and settled him atop his shoulders, holding his hands as he started walking across the field.

Jayden scampered after his brother and Dominic, pulling Traci behind him and hollering over his shoulder, "You better bring Aunt Amy back, Uncle Logan. You promised."

"Keep it quiet when we get inside, boys," Dominic said. "Your aunt Cissy's probably still napping."

Their *Yes, sirs* faded into the distance.

"You don't want to ride, Dom?" Amy called.

Dominic twisted, tossing a dimpled grin over his shoulder. "Nah, I've had my share of riding. I want to check on Cissy."

The group ambled off toward the main house.

"He's changed." Amy stared after Dominic as he made his way across the field.

"Yeah," Logan said. "Took a while, but he finally decided to settle down. Cissy and the boys had a lot to do with that."

She glanced at him. "Does he still compete at rodeos?"

"No." Logan shook his head. "The last time he rode a bull was over a year ago. He talks about starting up that bull-riding clinic but he's been preoccupied with preparing for the babies lately. When it comes to Cissy, those bulls don't stand a chance with Dom."

Amy looked back at Dominic making his way up the wide, front porch steps, Kayden on his shoulders and Jayden at his side. "He left the circuit for her?"

Her lips barely moved over the quiet words. Logan's chest tightened at the air of yearning that surrounded her. That familiar wistfulness was in the stillness of her body and the features of her face. It was an air that had clung to her over the years. One he'd first seen shining in her eyes when she'd kissed him by that oak tree all those years ago.

"She's his wife." Logan moved close, touching her jaw and bringing her face back to his. "A man stays with his family. That's the way it should be."

Her eyes dropped and her resigned half smile hit him hard in the gut.

Heaven help him, he missed her. Missed *them*. He wanted to rebuild their friendship and remind her of who she used to be before her spirit was broken. Return that sweet look of wistfulness to her face and feel it warm his skin when she looked at him.

You better bring her back.

Logan smiled. Jayden was on to something, all right. And that was exactly what he was gonna do. "Now, let's go for that ride."

AMY TILTED HER head back and strained to catch the faint touch of warmth from the setting sun. The late afternoon air had grown colder over the course of her ride with Logan across Raintree's grounds.

A wave of dizziness swept over her, causing her weight to shift off-center in the saddle. She grabbed the saddle horn and straightened. Lightning huffed beneath her and shook his head. His white mane tossed about, settling in disarray over her fingers.

Amy made herself heavy, re-centered her balance and weighed her seat down. She blinked rapidly, clearing the dancing spots from her vision and refocused on the horizon.

It was nothing new. For the past week, she'd had the same type of spell almost every day and had felt...*off*.

It had to be stress. She'd had her fair share of it since she returned home, and working with Thunder only exacerbated her emotional state.

Amy relaxed as the world centered again. She delivered gentle pats to Lightning's neck. He nickered and slowed his steps, the day's dying light caressing his pale mane in a glow of pink.

It'd be dark soon and would only get colder. There was so much work that still needed to be done with Thunder. It was past time to turn back.

"It's still Saturday, yeah?"

Logan's deep tenor disrupted her thoughts. He cut her a sidelong glance, dark eyes narrowing beneath the brim of his tan Stetson. His broad hands pulled back on his reins to fall into step beside her.

She frowned and nodded. "Why?"

He shrugged, broad shoulders stretching his blue shirt, and grinned. "Just wondering why you're taking a Sunday stroll."

Amy warmed at his sly look. She dropped her gaze, only to find it hovering over the tight denim covering his muscular thigh.

"I'm enjoying a relaxing ride," she said. "Taking a break like you suggested."

"At this rate, it'll take two weeks to cross the grounds. Feels like we've been trudging along at this pace for days already." He jerked his chin toward Lightning. "He's restless."

As if on cue, Lightning tossed his head and stomped.

Amy's mouth tightened. "No, he's not."

"Yeah. He is."

She raised a brow at his deliberate tone. "So what are you suggesting?"

His grin widened. "A harmless competition between friends."

"I take it you want to race."

"Isn't that how our rides always used to turn out?"

Amy smirked. "Pretty much. And, if memory serves, Kayden was correct in saying I always won."

"Not always."

"Yeah. I did."

Logan laughed, the deep, sexy rumble surrounding her and tingling on her skin. "Then you shouldn't have a problem defending your title."

Amy hesitated, gaze lingering over the warm depths of his eyes and teasing grin. It was a bad idea. She should be back at the round pen, at least trying to run Thunder through the paces.

She'd promised to bring the stallion back to his old self and hadn't made a lick of progress. Thunder was the last hurdle she had to overcome before leaving. One that would enable her to pack her bags and walk away to a fresh start, leaving the empty ache in her chest behind.

Only, it was becoming harder to believe she could ever banish it altogether. The four-year absence from Raintree had left her longing for home. These last few weeks had reminded her how much she missed it. And most—*or worst*—of all, making love with Logan had reminded her of exactly how much she missed *him*.

They'd continued to sleep beside each other in the same bed. Most nights, she'd fallen asleep on her side, carefully keeping her distance. But each morning, she'd woken up in Logan's arms, then slipped away quickly while he slept. She'd never been able to give Logan her body without handing over her heart. Still couldn't. And

Logan's heart was something he'd never been willing to share with her.

Amy sighed. Could what Logan offered be enough? Maybe he was right. Maybe she was too hung up on a fantasy. The kind that didn't exist. Maybe what he offered was as real as love could get.

"You're thinking too much." Logan moved his mount closer and placed his big palm on her thigh.

Amy's leg tensed. His tender caress penetrated her jeans, slipped beneath her skin and danced in her blood. It rushed higher and filled her chest with a sweet heaviness. The same sweet welling of heat that bloomed when Logan held her, his heart beating beneath her cheek.

Amy closed her eyes and squeezed the saddle horn tighter. She wished that feeling could last. Wished she could carry it with her, possess it forever and never feel alone.

"Just once," she whispered, clarifying at his confused look. "We'll race one time."

That would be enough. Then she could set this longing down and move on. Let Raintree go. And leave Logan, along with the girl she used to be, behind.

She straightened, tossing her hair over her shoulder and re-centering her seat. "How about we up the stakes, though? You win, I muck the stalls. I win, the hat's mine?"

Logan's mouth twisted, his tone hesitant. "Don't know about that. A man should never be parted from his hat." He tapped the brim with his finger. "And this is a damned good one."

She laughed. "So, you know you're gonna lose."

He knuckled the Stetson up an inch, narrowing his eyes and smiling. "Didn't say that, babe."

Amy's heart tripped in her chest. Logan's flirtatious gaze seared over her, heating her skin. How many times had she wished for that look from him over the years? And to get it now…

A man stays with his family.

How she still wanted that. Wanted Logan at her side every day. His child in her arms.

His child. Amy froze. Dizzy spells for a week. Feeling *off.* Her hand touched the flat plane of her belly. *How long had it been since…?*

She'd arrived home on Thanksgiving Day and she and Logan had made love the night after. Her mind scrambled to count the days, which quickly added up to weeks. *Three weeks.* Almost three weeks to the day since they'd—

No. Her shoulders slumped, a heavy weight settling over her. There was no need to worry on that account. There was next to no chance of it. What had the doctors said after she'd lost Sara? Her chances of conceiving were—*greatly diminished. Highly improbable.* And, in the event of a successful conception, pregnancy was… *inadvisable.*

Amy swiped the back of her hand over her forehead, whisking away cold beads of sweat. *Placental abruption. Stillborn. Hemorrhaging. Scarring.* Cold clinical terms for something so horrifying.

No. It was highly unlikely. It had taken several times for her to get pregnant before. They'd only been together the one time and she'd been late more than once over the years. But never this late.

Amy's stomach churned, her palms growing sweaty. She didn't know which emotion railed at her more. The paralyzing fear of possibly being pregnant. Or the over-whelming pain of never being able to conceive.

A frigid wind swept through, masking the sun's fading warmth. A streak of adrenaline shot through her veins and shook her limbs, the urge to bolt hitting her hard.

The endless acres before her beckoned, the dormant ground unobstructed and ripe for the taking. Amy tightened her legs around Lightning. He jerked his head, drawing to a reluctant halt.

Lightning wanted to run. So did she. More than anything.

"Whatcha say, handsome?" Amy asked, combing her trembling fingers through Lightning's coarse mane and striving for a calm tone. "Want to show him up?"

Amy lowered her torso, lightened her seat and clutched the reins. The command from years ago bloomed in her chest, rose to tickle her tongue and escaped on a panicked whisper.

"Fly, boy."

Lightning heaved forward, hooves pounding over the ground, spraying up dead grass and clumps of mud. Amy moved with him, staying steady and centered. The stallion's powerful lunges stirred excitement in her veins. It buzzed in her blood, strengthening her posture and dancing on the surface of her skin.

Each foot of distance brought back her balance and soothed her senses, reminding her of how she used to feel. Brave. Carefree. *Alive.*

She hooked the reins around the saddle horn and rose up, firming her grip with her thighs and stretching her arms out to catch the rush of wind with her palms. Cold air licked through her hair, teasing her neck and slipping beneath the billowed back of her shirt.

The throbbing gallop of Logan's stallion sounded at her side. Amy glanced to her left. Logan leaned forward, his muscular thighs hugging his horse's middle, his powerful build steady, keeping pace with her.

He smiled. "That all you got, babe?"

Amy laughed, a rebellious energy she hadn't felt in years firing through her body. The wind roared by her ears, her heart pounded and a sweet sense of freedom overcame her. She renewed her hold on the reins and gave Lightning permission to charge faster. They regained the lead, sprinting a foot ahead and swallowing up the spacious fields before them. Logan remained hot on their heels.

Lightning stretched his legs in long, galloping leaps following a familiar path until they crossed the edge of the open field. He slowed to a walk as they came to a cluster of trees lining a rushing creek and carefully maneuvered between them until they reached the bank.

"Good boy," she crooned.

Amy kissed Lightning's sweaty neck, drew him to a halt and glanced over her shoulder. Logan stroked his horse's neck and eased up beside her. She examined his devilish expression, narrowing her eyes on the sexy curve of his smile.

"You held back and let me win."

Logan chuckled. "Are you implying you couldn't have outrun me otherwise?"

"No. Just making an observation."

"So, considering that, I get to keep my hat."

"I don't know," she said. "I'll have to think about it."

She swung her leg over Lightning's back and hopped

down, watching as the stallion walked to the creek and began to drink. Logan followed suit and led his horse over to join Lightning.

Amy turned, eyeing the scattering of trees and noting one in particular. She sighed as she surveyed the solid strength of the oak tree. Its impressive shape and towering height was familiar and stirred an ache in her chest.

She winced, absorbing the rush of embarrassment. It was the same tree Logan had leaned against when she'd first kissed him. It had taken every drop of bravery she'd had to touch her lips to his all those years ago. To risk so much for what she knew would be so small a reward.

She'd loved Logan just as strongly then as she loved him now. There was no need to fight it or run from it. It just was. She had to accept it as something she could never change or leave behind.

Amy walked over and leaned against the oak's trunk. She closed her eyes and absorbed the whispering rush of water from the creek and the rough bark at her back, allowing herself to imagine, just for a moment, how different things might have been if she hadn't lost Sara. If she hadn't pushed Logan so hard. If she'd given him a chance to love her back.

She felt fabric sweep past her shoulders and a strong heat drew near to her chest. She opened her eyes to find Logan leaning close, his dark eyes on her mouth and his muscular arms braced against the trunk on both sides of her.

Her belly fluttered as his lips parted, his head dipping.

"Wanna give it another try?" He tapped his mouth with the blunt tip of his finger.

Amy shook her head, heat racing up her neck. She pressed her palms tight to the tree behind her, digging her fingers into the uneven crannies of the bark.

Logan's gaze left her mouth and traveled over her face. His lips tipped up at the corners.

"Come on, babe," he whispered, taking one of her hands in his and holding it to his chest. "Try me."

She pressed her lips together, stilling as his eyes darkened and returned to her mouth. The heavy throb of his heart beat against her palm and coursed down to her wrist, coaxing her pulse to join its rhythm.

"Let's make a better memory," he urged. "One we can enjoy remembering."

God help her, she wanted that. Amy sighed, closing her eyes and touching her mouth to the rough stubble on his cheek. She nuzzled her nose against his skin and breathed him in, savoring his masculine scent. He pressed close and slipped his fingers underneath the ring hanging from her neck.

"Friend, lover, husband…" His husky voice tickled her ear, sending thrills over her skin. "Call it whatever you want." He nudged a leg between hers and lifted his head. "I'm yours, Amy."

Her palms tingled. She wanted nothing more than to hold on to him. To find comfort in his strength.

She slipped her fingertips under the brim of his hat, weaving them through the thick waves of his hair, and parted his lips with hers. A low growl throbbed in his throat and he explored her mouth with gentle sweeps of his tongue. His knuckles brushed her cheek, skimming her shoulders and uncurling to secure a grip on her hip.

Heat speared through her and traveled low, making her ache with need. Seeking a distraction, she burrowed her fingers further into his hair and dislodged his hat, swooping up his Stetson and settling it firmly on her own head. It sat a little loose and knocked against his forehead as he kissed her.

His deep chuckle rumbled. He smiled wide against her mouth, his teeth bumping her lips. Amy grinned, savoring the delight in his eyes and cherishing the abandon in his unrestrained laughter.

"That's my favorite one." He drew back, pinching the hat and centering it on her head. "I should've known better than to risk it with you."

Amy's grin slipped. It was a teasing statement. Benign and meaningless. But it managed to cut.

Logan winced. He framed her face with his warm palms and kissed her forehead.

"Hey," he whispered. "This is a better memory, yeah? A good one."

She nodded, closing her eyes as he claimed her mouth with the softest of kisses. He rubbed his hands up and down her arms in brisk movements and smiled.

"It's getting cold. Let's head back for the bonfire so you can show off your trophy." He tapped the Stetson and grinned. "I know you gotta be chomping at the bit to gloat to Dom."

Amy thumped the brim of the hat and beamed, slowing her speech to her best hick drawl. "A girl's gotta lay claim to her bragging rights, sir. Ain't my fault you held back."

"This time." He laughed, turning to amble away toward the horses. "I might not on the next run. So you better hope you remember everything I taught you."

She dragged her palms over her jeans and ducked her head. That was the biggest problem. She couldn't forget. Any of it. The good or the bad. They were impossible to separate.

Logan whistled. Lightning left the creek and trotted toward him.

Logan turned, stretching out his upturned palm. "Come on. Let's head home."

She placed her hand in his, skin heating at his touch, and mounted Lightning. Logan smiled and left to remount his horse.

Amy eyed the wide expanse of land barely visible between the tangle of trees. A strong wind swept across her overheated skin. It rushed through the long strands of her hair, jerking them over her shoulders and in front of her face in wild arcs.

Lightning stomped, his muscled bulk shifting beneath her as he shook his head, ready to take off again. Amy rubbed his neck and murmured soothing words. The wind whipped with greater strength, causing the trees to sway, limbs to dip and the swift current of the creek to intensify. Even the ground trembled with excitement beneath her as Lightning took a few impatient steps.

Amy inhaled, chest rising and shoulders lifting. The moment was so familiar. Raintree as it had been. Alive and exciting.

Logan laughed. "You look all of nineteen again in that hat."

Amy opened her eyes to find him at her side.

He swept a strand of hair over her shoulder and his tone deepened. "Ready?"

She nodded, nudging Lightning and undertaking a relaxed pace across the grounds. The wind continued to push at their backs and the festive Christmas lights draping the fences of Raintree's front yard peeked out from the dark stretch of land before them, guiding their way.

Amy squared her shoulders and pushed Logan's Stetson down firmer on her head. Raintree's call grew louder. It beckoned with each sweep of cold air, twinkle of white lights and creak of their saddles. She glanced at Logan, returning his smile with a more cautious one.

Even now, she could feel the girl she'd been unfurling inside, stretching and waking up. Wanting nothing more than to keep riding straight into the warm embrace of the main house and stay in this beautiful place. Needing so much from it and from Logan. Wanting everything despite the cost.

Amy pressed a trembling palm to her midsection, smoothing it hard over the flat plane of her belly. This dance with Logan was dangerous. He and Raintree belonged to the rebellious girl she used to be. Not the honorable woman she'd grown into. She had to remember that. Because she wasn't sure if there was room inside her for both.

Chapter Eight

Logan pushed away the cup of "eggnog" Jayden held out and smiled politely. He had lived long enough to learn the value of self-preservation, and any concoction the twins offered was suspect.

"No, thanks, buddy."

Logan glanced at the massive cypress tree, glowing with white lights. The annual Christmas tree lighting had become a crowd favorite at Raintree. Guests and locals alike turned out every year to help decorate the tree and huddle around the warmth of the festive bonfire.

The group of guests had dwindled down on account of the late hour and most of them had retired to their rooms for the night. Only family remained, along with a few hands who were finishing off the last of their sweet desserts or beer on hay bales used as makeshift seating. Logan spotted Amy silhouetted in the bonfire's blaze, recognizing the familiar shape of his Stetson atop her head.

He grinned. The only time she'd removed it since their ride several hours ago had been when she'd let Kayden climb onto her shoulders to hang a cloth angel on a high branch of the Cypress tree. And, even then, after lowering Kayden to the ground, she'd scooped the hat up and put it right back on.

"But you ain't had no eggnog yet." Jayden stepped on top of Logan's boots and thrust the cup closer to his face.

Logan frowned and examined the liquid. The flickering light from the bonfire blazing several feet away enabled him to make out the white liquid filling the lower half of the clear mug. It looked safe enough. But the thick, red film floating on top turned his stomach and called for hesitation.

He twisted his lips and glanced at Amy. She had her back to him, sharing a laugh with Cissy, Betty and Traci. At least, she wouldn't witness him being a heel.

"Nah, I think I'll pass." Logan lifted Jayden off the tops of his boots and set him back on the ground.

Dominic and Pop shifted at Logan's side, cocking their heads and leveling disapproving frowns on him. *Well, hell.* He'd get no support from them.

"Come on." Dominic nudged Logan. "Don't want to disappoint the little fellas, do you?"

Logan sighed and surveyed the boys. Jayden and Kayden stood side by side, blinking up at him with wounded blue eyes.

His stomach dropped and he shifted uneasily. Nothing stripped your defenses better than kids.

He rubbed a hand over his brow then reached for the cup. "I'm not that big on eggnog, fellas."

"But it's good." Kayden smiled. "We made it special, Uncle Logan."

That, he believed. The strong scent of spices wrinkled his nose as he lifted it to his mouth. He hesitated, holding the cup to his lips.

"Please try it," Jayden said. "Just one taste?"

Logan's mouth twitched. Whether it was from laughter or distaste of what he was about to put in it, he wasn't sure. But he proceeded, tossing back a healthy swallow of the goop.

A flash of heat engulfed his gums and scorched a path down his throat, choking him. He spewed the last globs of it out of his mouth and doubled over. His eyes watered and tears coursed down his cheeks as he gasped.

"Lord, have mercy, Logan."

Betty approached, her shocked voice barely rising over the gales of laughter from Pop and Dominic. A hand slapped his back, pounding hard, then shook his shoulder.

"Get it all out, son," Pop chuckled.

"What in heaven's name have you done to him?" Betty pressed against his side, clutching a glass of sweet tea and peering into his face. "You okay, Logan?"

He snatched the glass from her hand and tossed it back in one gulp. The cold beverage masked the fire coating his throat, allowing him to catch his breath.

Dominic winked. "He just had a taste of the boys' special brew."

"Oh, Dom." Betty clucked her tongue. "I told you to throw that stuff out."

Logan sucked in a lungful of cold air and glared at Dominic. "You mean to tell me you knew what was in that?"

"Of course he did," Betty said, taking both glasses from Logan's hands. "The boys used up every bit of my cayenne powder making this gunk. They thought it was cinnamon. Heaven knows what else they put in it."

Dominic held up his hands and adopted an innocent expression. "Easy now, big bro. I only knew because I got talked into trying it, too."

Logan choked back a laugh, stretched around Pop and grabbed a handful of Dominic's shirt. "You little shi—"

"Language, boys," Cissy admonished.

The rest of the ladies had arrived. Traci covered her mouth as a fit of giggles overtook her and Amy smiled a mile wide. Cissy, however, shoved between the men and rose to her toes, prying Logan's fist from Dominic's shirt.

"Not in front of the little ones." Cissy smoothed her hands over Dominic's collar and the corner of her mouth kicked up. "Besides, my husband looks especially nice tonight and I'd like to keep him that way."

Dominic tugged her close and whispered in her ear. Cissy's cheeks reddened. She batted at Dominic's chest, disentangling herself from his hold and started for the main house.

"Time to go in and get a bath, boys. It's getting late and you both need your rest."

The twins groaned.

"Aw, come on, Aunt Cissy." Kayden scowled. "Just a little longer. We ain't got no school all week."

"That's, *we don't have any school this week*. And from the sound of those double negatives, I think they should've canceled vacation and kept you in class."

"But—"

"I said, no." Cissy stabbed a finger at the ground and smiled. "Now, do your good-night rounds and get your tails over here."

"Best do what she says, Kayden," Dominic whispered, expression grave. "Santa's watching."

Kayden pouted but delivered his good-night kisses to everyone. Jayden followed suit but after kissing Amy's cheek, he wrapped his arms around her hand and pulled.

"Will you come in, too, Aunt Amy? I want you to tuck me in."

"Yeah," Kayden chimed, grabbing Amy's other free hand. "And will you read that same story you read to us last night? No one else does the voices good as you."

She smiled. "I'd love to."

"You gotta do your good-night kisses before you go in," Kayden said solemnly. "It's Aunt Cissy's rule."

Amy laughed. "Well, we don't want to break any rules, do we?"

She pressed a swift kiss to Dominic and Pop's cheeks then peppered a few more all over the boys. They gurgled with giggles and she laughed harder in response. Logan's chest warmed at the sight. The heat from the fire had painted her cheeks a cherry red, making those gorgeous green eyes shine like emeralds.

He'd heard her laugh on several occasions throughout the evening and each delightful bout of it melted away another lost year between them. It was easy to recall the teenage years she'd spent at his side by the Christmas bonfire, plucking marshmallows from his roasting stick and sneaking sips of his mulled wine.

She caught him staring and blushed even more. "Are you coming in?"

"Soon," he said. "I'm gonna help clean up."

"Come on, Aunt Amy." Kayden shoved at her hip. "Give Uncle Logan his good-night kiss so we can go in."

Logan grinned and arched a brow. Amy hesitated,

glancing down at the boys. Their wide blue eyes moved from her to him and back again.

Amy sighed and stepped closer. She brushed her lips against his cheek, lodging a sweet ache in his belly. Logan curled his hand around her hip, tugging her close and nuzzling her neck.

A small hand shoved between them. Jayden scowled up at him and wrapped his arms tight around Amy's leg.

"You already got your good-night kiss, Uncle Logan."

He laughed. "Guess you're right, buddy."

Amy stepped back and tapped the brim of the Stetson with a fingertip. "Good night, gentlemen."

Amy left with the boys, following the other ladies and laughing on the walk back to the main house. Cissy looked over her shoulder and blew a kiss to Dominic.

"I hate to call it quits early, but…" Dominic rubbed his chest and grinned, dimples denting.

Pop held up a hand and smiled. "Say no more, son. We'll wrap things up out here."

Dominic jogged off, catching up with Cissy and hugging her close as they made their way up the path. Amy trailed behind the couple with the boys, pausing every few steps to point at the sky and answer the boys' questions.

"Amy sure has a way with those boys," Pop murmured. "She looks good with 'em."

Logan stiffened. He turned away to watch the hands laugh and pass around another round of beers. Amy did look great with those boys at her sides. But he couldn't shake the last image he'd had of her holding a child.

Their child. Sara. And the sight had been gut-wrenching.

Pop shifted, his elbow brushing against Logan's. He remained silent for a moment, then cleared his throat.

"It's nice having Raintree full again," Pop said. "It'll be even nicer when Cissy and Dom's girls get here. I hate that Amy might not be here when the babies arrive." He hesitated, rocking back on his heels. "How much longer is she staying?"

"A couple weeks." Logan rasped a palm over the stubble lining his jaw and turned away.

"Don't mean to pry but have you talked with her any more about things?" Pop's gaze heated his skin. "I thought Amy might've changed her mind about leaving after she settled in."

"No." Logan shoved his hands in his pockets. "I'm still working on getting her to stay put."

"You two seem a lot closer now than when she first came home." Pop nodded as if in reassurance. "That girl still loves you. Always has. No amount of time or distance will change that."

"You sure about that?" Logan faced him. "You thought the same thing about Mom and we all know how that turned out."

Pop held up a hand. "That was different."

"How so?"

Hues of red and orange from the bonfire flickered over Pop's face. He kneaded the back of his neck as his eyes roved over the acres stretching out around them.

"Gloria never wanted to come here. Raintree was always my dream, not hers. She tolerated it because she loved me but she wanted something different." His mouth twisted. "And she found someone else that would give it to her."

Logan sighed. "We were better off without her, anyway."

"You think so?" Pop glanced at him. "I wanted your mother from the first moment I saw her, but we both knew we weren't a good match. She was happy in the city and I was a rancher just passing through." A short bark of laughter escaped him. "That short skirt and high heels of hers did me in, though. I fought it but it didn't take long for the rest of her to win me over, too. We knew the odds were stacked against us but we loved each other enough to give it a shot." His smile dissolved. "She ended up being miserable here and wanted to go back to her old life. I tried my best to talk her into staying. It didn't work out because neither of us was willing to give up one path for the other."

Logan scoffed. "Except her path had another man on it."

"Not at first. But she did meet him and she ended up choosing a life with him instead of here with us. Wasn't much I could do about it and still keep my dignity. There are things in life you can't control, Logan. At least, your mother was honest. Told me how she felt before she acted on it."

"And that excuses it?"

"No." Pop's tone turned sharp. "It was one thing to walk out on me. But my boys—" He swallowed hard and looked away. "I wasn't proud of myself back then. No matter how much I hated your mother for leaving y'all, I still loved that woman in equal measure. Probably always will. And that's how it is. You don't get to pick who you fall in love with. It just happens. If it works out, you end up living with 'em. If it doesn't," he said, and shrugged slowly, "you find a way to live without 'em. It took me a long time to learn that."

Logan dropped his head, focusing on the shadows cast by the bonfire.

"Guess that's why I've never blamed Amy for going after you like she did," Pop said. "I knew what it felt like to want someone that much. That girl's always had a strong spirit and loved you the second she laid eyes on you. As hard as it may be to understand, she was just fighting to keep you."

Pop's hand curled around his forearm. Logan tensed, lifting his eyes to face him.

"I wish you'd open up for once. Tell me what you're thinking. Feeling. You're closed so tight—" He kicked the ground with a boot. "But that's my fault. I put too much on you when your mama took off. Left you to tend to your brother. I had so much trouble holding myself together I didn't realize how much you boys needed me."

"We turned out fine, Pop."

"Fine's not good enough. Not for me or my boys. You've always been careful and independent. Even as a kid. But sometimes living safe keeps you from the best things in life." Pop watched Amy disappear into the darkness, then peered back at him. "Amy used to enjoy life. Showed you how to at one time. She could be the best thing that ever happened to you." His grip tightened on Logan's arm. "But if you want a real shot at saving your marriage, you've got to open up."

"I'm trying."

"No, you're not." He shook his head. "You're pushing Amy away like you do the rest of us because you're afraid of things going bad." He hesitated. "You've gotten worse since y'all lost the baby."

The baby. Logan's muscles tensed. *A mistake.* "Her name was Sara."

"I'm sorry," Pop murmured, touching his arm. "You haven't been the same since you lost Sara. And it's time for you to…"

"What?"

Pop sighed. "Move on. You've spent so much time worrying about Amy, it's time you worked on yourself. Time for you to let go of what happened. Time to forget—"

"Forget Sara?" Logan's throat closed, tightening to the point of pain.

Pop winced. "No. I didn't mean that."

"That's exactly what you meant." Logan's gut roiled. "And that should be easy, right? Because I'm a man? Because I didn't know her? That's the same thing everyone else said after we lost her."

"Logan—"

"I knew my daughter." His voice turned hoarse, tearing from his throat in rough rasps. "Sara knew me, too. I put my hand on Amy's belly every day and Sara kicked every time I spoke to her." His breath shuddered from him. "That's how I knew something wasn't right. I put my hand over her that morning and talked to her and she didn't move." He shook his head. "Amy didn't think anything was wrong. Not until later. But I knew that morning."

Logan stared ahead, the flames of the bonfire licking higher and the smoke growing thicker.

"We'd lost her that night while we were sleeping." His lungs seized, choking him. "Sara died right there in that bed beside me and I couldn't do a damned thing about it."

"No one expected you to, son. Nature has a way—"

"Of taking care of things. I know." Logan grimaced, eyes blurring. "That's why I can't understand it. When we saw her, she was beautiful. So perfect. She just didn't cry." He shoved his trembling hands in his pockets. "I kept holding her, thinking they'd got it wrong. That she'd wake up. She would've been due in two more weeks. I can't understand how she could be that perfect and not cry. How she could *almost* make it…"

Pop kneaded the back of Logan's neck, his words low against his ear. "It's okay to mourn for Sara. To miss her. But it wasn't your fault or Amy's. You have to accept this was something you couldn't control and choose to move on. For your sake and hers."

"Every choice I've ever made has been for Amy's sake." Logan pulled away. "It's called loyalty. Something a lot stronger than this illusion of love everyone keeps holding on to. It's something Mom knew nothing about. Even Amy didn't have a clue what it was, lying to me the way she did. And I have no intention of trading it off for this reckless fantasy all of you keep trying to sell. The only thing that's ever been certain in my life has been my word. Everything else—*everyone* else—has been a damned disappointment." He motioned to the hands across the field and called out, "Let's get this fire out. It's time to call it a night."

They nodded, tossing their beers in the trash and rounding up buckets of water.

"Logan, you can't build a future when your hands are holding on to the past."

"The only thing I'm holding on to is my wife. I made a vow and I'm standing by it because it's the right thing to do." His lip curled. "The only *dignified* thing to do.

Surely you can understand that." He shook his head. "Amy and I may have been dumb kids back then but we're not now. I'm not going into this blind, and Amy knows exactly where I stand." His mouth ran dry and he forced his words past the lump in his throat. "I knew my daughter. Sara was not *a mistake*. And neither was my marriage."

Logan spun on his heel and joined the hands, grabbing a bucket of water and heaving it over the pit. The hiss and sizzle of dying fire sounded and smoke billowed out with fury. He grabbed another and repeated the motion, muscles screaming with every throw.

Things would be different this time. He wouldn't fail Amy. And thank God they'd never have the chance to fail a child again.

"Mmmm." Amy closed her eyes in bliss and wrapped her hands tighter around the warm mug. "Mama, you make the best hot chocolate in existence."

Betty smiled. "It's all about balance, baby girl. You have to make sure the bitter matches the sweet. Besides, you can't break in Christmas properly without a decent hot cocoa."

Amy took another sip and rolled it over her tongue, savoring the peaceful stillness of the empty kitchen. She and Traci had helped Cissy get the boys bathed and tucked in bed. Traci and Cissy had called it a night but Amy had lingered, reading three bedtime stories before the boys' eyelids finally fluttered shut.

Amy smiled. She could've stayed in the boys' room for hours, reading in gentle tones and listening to their soft breaths. It hadn't taken long for their rambunctious sweetness to slip into her heart. She'd grown so close to them it'd be painful to leave.

Betty set her cup down and reached across the table to squeeze Amy's forearm. "It's good to see you smile again."

Amy drummed her fingers against her cup. "I smile enough. Matter of fact, we have plenty of laughs when you and Traci visit me in Augusta."

Betty shook her head. "They're not like the ones you had out by the bonfire tonight. You looked like your old self again wearing Logan's hat and grinning. I don't know what he did to coax it out of you but he did it right."

Amy's face flamed. She sat back, dodging Betty's narrowed gaze. "We went for a ride, is all. I just haven't ridden in so long it was nice to race again. I forgot how much I enjoyed it."

Betty released her arm and retrieved her cup. Amy dug into the plastic bag of marshmallows on the table, plucked one out and plopped it into her cocoa. It bobbed around in the dark liquid, melting in white streaks around the edges.

She pressed the cup to her lips and the sickly-sweet foam of the melted marshmallow clung to her gums, rolling her stomach. She dropped the mug to the table with a clang and pressed the back of her hand to her mouth.

"Are you okay?" Betty leaned forward, brow creasing.

Amy nodded and swallowed. "Yeah. I haven't been feeling well, lately."

Her hand shook. Betty's gaze clung to it. Amy shoved it between her knees below the table.

"Baby, you know you can come to me for anything, right? No matter how old you are?"

"I know."

"Well, I'm here if you ever want to talk." Betty shifted forward, mouth opening and closing a time or two. "About your new job or the move." She shrugged, fiddling with the handle on her cup. "Or Logan."

Amy's lips twitched. "Smooth delivery, Mama. Real smooth."

Betty flushed and waved a hand in front of her face. "I forget you have so much of your father in you." She smiled. "He never had much use for tact, either."

Amy laughed, the churning in her gut easing. Betty was right. Her dad had always been blunt. They reminisced about his many missteps and before long, Betty joined her, doubling over and holding her belly as she chuckled. At the same time, Betty's eyes darkened with sadness over the loss of her husband.

The nausea returned and Amy's laughter broke away, fading with each jerk of her shoulders. Amy fought for air, her lungs burning. She pressed a weak fist to her chest, fighting to regain composure at Betty's shocked expression.

"I'm scared, Mama."

Betty moved quickly to the seat beside Amy and hugged her close. "Of what?"

Possibly being pregnant. Losing another child. Losing Logan. Her throat closed and violent chills racked her body.

"Try to relax, Amy."

Betty's voice trembled. Her hand moved in warm circles over Amy's back, slowing as the spasms subsided and resting between her shoulder blades.

"Now, what is it you're afraid of?"

"Everything," Amy whispered. "Leaving. Staying." She clamped her trembling lips together. "*Myself.* I don't know who I am anymore."

Betty smoothed her fingers through Amy's hair, tucking a long wave behind her shoulder. Amy leaned into her, craving the soothing touch as much as she had when she was a child.

"Maybe that's because you're trying to be someone you're not," Betty murmured, gesturing toward Amy's necklace. "When did you take that ring off your finger and string it around your neck?"

Amy bit her lip. "What does that have to do with anything?"

"Everything." Betty squeezed her hand. "I know losing Sara was difficult. I knew you needed to heal and I thought leaving here for a change of pace was the best thing for you at the time." She shook her head. "But you carried it with you."

Amy licked her lips, the taste of salt lingering on her tongue.

Betty grabbed a cloth napkin from the table and dabbed at Amy's cheeks. "I think you've been so determined to get some distance from the bad that you forgot about the good."

"What good?" A scornful laugh burst past Amy's lips. "Not one single thing I did was good. I lied. I hurt Logan. Not to mention Sara—" Her voice broke. She stilled Betty's hand, taking the napkin and wiping her eyes. "But I've been trying to be someone good. Someone better. What's wrong with that?"

"Nothing," Betty whispered. "So long as you remember that no one can be perfect no matter how hard they try. We're, none of us, saints or angels. We all make mistakes." She tugged Amy's hands to her lap and eyed her. "If you don't mind my asking, who is it you're really doing all this changing for?"

Amy ducked her head and picked at the hem of her shirt. "Logan, I suppose."

Betty sighed. "I know I should be objective right now. Tell you how proud I am of you for being so repentant and selfless." She slid closer, smile tight. "But I won't. You're my girl, Amy, and I'm proud of you. Always have been. I'd hate to see you change the things I love most about you to impress a man. Even if he is a good one."

"There's more to it than that."

"Is there?" Betty asked. "You used to like who you were and were proud of it. You were so brave and headstrong." She smiled. "I remember watching you fall off a horse more times than I could count. Was scared to death you'd hurt yourself. But you'd get right back up, brush yourself off and try again. Every time. And you kept on trying until you got it right."

"Or got it wrong," Amy choked out. "I kept right after Logan, too, and look how that ended up."

Betty took Amy's hands in hers and squeezed. "You've always lived hard and you love just as hard. Your heart was in the right place no matter how wrong you went about it. Your daddy was the same way and you remind me so much of him. That's why it's so hard for me to let you go." Her eyes watered. "I'm not going to lie to you. I don't want you to move so far away. But I do want you to be happy. If that means moving to Michigan then I'll support you. Traci and I will visit you just as we've been doing." Her features firmed.

"But no matter what you decide, I won't help you hide yourself away. I love you too much to support you in that." She tapped a finger against the ring at Amy's neck. "That one mistake has been weighing you down long enough. It's past time to set it down, forgive yourself and live again."

The tension in Amy's muscles eased, the tightness seeping away and leaving a soothing stillness in its place. She hugged Betty, absorbing her strength.

"Now." Betty squeezed Amy close. "How 'bout I sneak us a few sugar cookies and we pile on the couch and watch a late movie together like we used to?"

Amy sniffed and smiled. "I'd like that."

They stayed up and watched the last hour of one of their favorite holiday comedies, nibbling on cookies and sharing laughs. Betty's eyes grew heavy and Amy kissed her cheek, suggesting it was time to turn in.

Betty paused at the door and smiled. "You're loved, Amy. No matter where you are or what you do. I wasn't the only one that loved the girl you used to be. Logan did, too. And would again if you'd give him half a chance."

Standing motionless in the living room, Amy watched her mother leave. The house was quiet. All the guests had turned in for the night and Logan would be coming in soon. A steady ticking from the clock on the wall marked the time, bringing the future closer in small moments that weighed on her shoulders.

Amy glanced down at her boots. They were as banged up and muddied as they'd been when she'd run reckless as a teen. They felt as comforting now as they did back then. As if she could bound effortlessly across the ground with every step.

She wondered if the girl she'd been then was still inside her, the good and the bad in equal measure. She continued to ponder this long after she'd crawled into bed.

Logan joined her soon after, wrapping his arms around her and falling asleep. The gentle rhythm of his breathing offered comfort but sleep escaped her. She eventually gave up and slipped out of his arms, dressing and leaving the room quietly.

It was dark save for the light of the stars as she made her way to the stables. The path seemed to stretch farther than ever in the chill of the night air. She stopped more than once, almost turning back, but continued to put one boot in front of the other until she reached Thunder's stall and placed her palm to the bars.

"Hey," she whispered.

Thunder's dark bulk shifted. He stomped a time or two and tossed his head.

"Not getting any sleep, either, huh?" Amy smiled. "Want to come with me? Take a night stroll like we used to and stretch your legs?"

He kicked, hooves striking the stall door. The sharp crack of wood split her ears. Amy held her ground, keeping her hand flat against the bars.

Thunder kicked again then paced, growing calmer and slowly approaching her hand. His nose drew closer, nostrils moving rapidly with strong pulls of air.

"Remember me?" Her throat closed and her vision blurred. "Because I think I need you to."

He nudged closer, his wet nose and swift breaths tickling her skin. She reached with slow movements for the lead rope hanging on the wall.

"We'll take it one step at a time," she whispered. "Until we trust each other again. That okay with you?"

Thunder tossed his head and pawed the ground but she managed to get the lead on him and move him to the round pen. She slipped the rope off him once they made it inside the enclosure. He took off, bucking and kicking at the fence.

Her heart pounded against her ribs but she pushed on and walked him back several times, moving through the familiar routine and feeling the strength return to her trembling legs.

"Easy," she murmured, lifting her arms.

The glow from the starlit sky pooled over him. His dark mane ruffled with each push of the wind. He tossed his head up, crying and stomping the ground, eyes flaring with fear.

Amy's arms grew heavy but she kept them up, palms out. "I'm here," she whispered. "Right here. Whenever you're ready."

Thunder pinned his ears and ducked his head.

"I'm right here," she repeated.

Her body quaked. She closed her eyes, the lump in her throat tightening. Thunder's hoof hit the ground, the solid thud disturbing the stillness of the night, and his heavy pulls of air rasped across the distance between them.

It was silent for a moment. Then the familiar pounding of hooves sounded.

Amy tensed as the rapid slams increased in speed, growing closer. She opened her eyes, pushed her arms higher and advanced, pushing him back.

Thunder cut right, sweeping back with heavy stomps. His cry slashed through the air, piercing her ears. He tossed his head then nestled against the fence and stilled.

Amy waited for several minutes then advanced slowly toward his hip. Thunder jerked as she touched his back but stilled when she moved her palm over him with soothing whispers. His breathing slowed and Amy's followed the same, calm rhythm, her breath passing past her lips in white puffs on the frigid air.

"I'm sorry," she rasped.

Her throat tightened, cutting off the sound, and tears scalded her cheeks. The cry echoed inside her. It burned her chest, leaving her gasping and mouthing the soundless words.

I'm sorry.

And God help her, she was. Sorry for Thunder's pain. For betraying Logan. For every day that passed without her beautiful daughter in it.

Her arms dropped, her hands clutching her middle, and she cried. For Sara. For Logan. For the girl she used to be. And what could have been.

She didn't notice how much time passed. Didn't realize when the tears finally stopped. But the knot in her chest untied and her shoulders sagged with sweet release. The kind she hadn't known in years. A sense of peace. A welling of hope and forgiveness. Silent comforts that had escaped her for so long.

Thunder remained still, head lowered and body relaxed.

"I'm right here," Amy whispered. "Whenever you're ready."

She began walking, moving slowly along the curve of the fence and rounding the pen. The wind slowed to a gentle breeze and she inhaled, the clean air filling her lungs and refreshing her spirit.

It was on the ninth pass that Thunder followed. He took hesitant steps at her back but kept time with her, matching her step for step.

They completed one lap. Then another and another until Amy lost count. The only reminder of their efforts was the sheen of sweat collecting beneath her shirt and coating Thunder's hide.

The air warmed and a hint of red peeked above the horizon. Dawn approached and the tendrils of sunlight had never looked so bright or felt so warm. Amy stopped, soaking in the glow of the sun.

Something warm and wet nuzzled her palm. Thunder's broad head nudged her arm up. Smiling, she turned and looped her arms around his neck, pressing her forehead to his warm neck and praising him.

Thunder's heat spread to her belly. A gentle throb pulsed in her veins, flowing through her blood and pooling in her middle. She knew the feeling. Recognized it immediately, even though she hadn't experienced it in years.

It lit her up on the inside, fighting off the frigid air and blazing bright in her chest. She was hopeful. And that feeling was strong. More all-consuming than ever.

Amy smiled, wrapping her arms tighter around Thunder's neck, holding on to it all and savoring every delicious thrill. The hope of a miracle. Another chance at being a mother.

The sweet promise of the future had never felt this good before. And she knew the only reason it did now was because she'd felt the bad.

"Are you tired, boy?"

Thunder snorted, nudging her with his nose.

She laughed. "Neither am I. Wanna run? Like we used to?"

She left the rope behind, exited the pen and left the gate open for Thunder to join her. Amy gripped his withers and made to jump but a strong pair of hands wrapped around her waist.

"That's my girl." Logan's deep tenor rumbled at her back as he lifted her.

Amy settled astride Thunder and glanced down. "How long have you been out here?"

"Long enough." He looked up at her, his dark eyes warm and tender.

"Well, I'll be damned."

Dominic stood several feet behind Logan. The boys stood on either side of him, bulky coats zipped up and wide smiles across their faces.

"Yeah," Kayden drawled, crossing his arms like Dominic, "I'll be damned."

Dominic cringed and clamped a hand over Kayden's mouth, sneaking a peek over his shoulder. "All right, now. Don't say that around your aunt Cissy."

Amy laughed, the sound bursting from her chest and mingling with Logan's. Jayden ran over to beam up at Thunder.

"Is he happy now, Aunt Amy?"

She nodded. "He will be."

Logan lifted Jayden. "Give him a good pet. Your aunt Amy's gonna take him out for a while."

Jayden patted Thunder's neck, smiled and whispered, "Thanks for making him happy, Aunt Amy."

She returned Jayden's smile with her own. In that

moment, the bitter in her life was balanced with the perfect amount of sweet. The kind of sweet promise she deserved to hold on to. Even if it meant letting Logan go.

Chapter Nine

"Blue wrapping paper, silver ribbons, name tags, cowboy hats and—"

"A partridge in a pear tree?" Amy winked as Traci dumped a pile of shopping bags on the wide leather couch in the family room.

"No, but if the store sold 'em, I'm sure Dominic would've bought those, too." Traci puffed a strand of dark hair out of her eyes. "He settled for a trampoline instead."

"A trampoline?" Cissy's blond head shot up. Her hands froze over the present she wrapped, a bit of tape clinging to her fingertips.

Amy grinned. The past few days had flown by in a flurry of shopping, wrapping and hiding. She'd helped Cissy hide more Santa presents for the boys in two days than she could remember receiving over all her childhood years put together. Since it was Christmas Eve and stores closed early, Cissy had felt it safe enough to send Dominic out for more wrapping supplies without him returning with another armful of toys.

"Now, don't get upset, baby." Dominic edged sideways through the living room door, his dimpled smile as wide as the load of firewood weighing down his arms.

Cissy frowned. "I asked you to get more wrapping paper, not more gifts. At this rate, there won't be enough gift wrap in the world to cover the boys' presents."

Undeterred, Dominic dumped the wood in a basket by the blazing fireplace and crossed the room to kiss Cissy's forehead.

"It's Christmas," he murmured, smoothing a hand through her hair. "Only comes once a year."

"But you're spoiling them, Dominic." Cissy flushed, eyes fluttering shut as he feathered more kisses to her cheeks and the tip of her nose.

"Mmm-hmm. Gonna spoil my girls, too." He placed a gentle hand over her belly. "Anyway, I didn't buy the hats. That was all Logan's doing."

Logan walked in, holding a couple of thick oak logs. "I didn't see anything wrong with buying my nephews one more present. The boys have been good this year." His brow furrowed and a crooked grin broke out across his face. "For most of it, anyway."

Cissy sighed, blue eyes dancing. "You'd think two big, muscle-bound men could stand up to a couple of little boys. Turns out, you and Dom are the biggest push-overs in existence."

Amy laughed. Logan's dark eyes locked with hers.

"That," Logan murmured, "we might be."

Amy looked away and shifted closer to the lamp-light at her side. She concentrated on slipping flannel shirts into boxes for the boys and savored the gentle flutters in her belly.

Since her breakthrough with Thunder, she and Logan had taken the stallion out for a ride every day over the past week. During which, Logan had sweet-talked her into several more races and a dozen years' worth of kisses.

She glanced up as Logan crossed to the fireplace and stowed the logs in the basket. A few strategic turns of wood with the poker and he had the fire flaming high again. The red flames and glow of yellow light accentuated his muscular profile.

Amy pulled the gift boxes closer to her belly and tried to calm the tremors running over her skin. *Four weeks.* It'd been four weeks now since they'd made love and her hopes of a possible pregnancy had grown stronger than ever.

Despite her excitement, she hadn't been able to follow through with confirming it. The past week with Logan had been especially sweet and she wanted to hold on to it. They smiled and laughed together often. They'd become more than best friends again. Only, she wasn't quite sure what they'd become.

She knew Logan was aware she loved him. But she'd never heard it from him and it was time to face the possibility that she never would. Friendship was the strongest bond he offered.

Logan turned, his expression cast in darkness by the flames at his back, his face as difficult to read as his carefully controlled emotions.

How would he handle the news of another pregnancy? He'd made it clear that he didn't believe it was possible for them to have another child. And four years ago, he'd reminded her of how dangerous a pregnancy would be every time he'd given in to her persuasions.

Amy curled her fingers around the corners of the gift boxes in her lap. Back then, things had played out exactly as Logan had predicted. They'd had no luck conceiving. But now...

Now, there was a real chance. She stilled her bouncing knee. As excited as she was, she was equally dismayed. She wanted Logan, but having him out of obligation was no longer something she could accept. She needed more than loyalty and so would their child.

"Sustenance for Santa's elves," Betty chimed.

Betty and Pop entered with trays of hot chocolate and set two red mugs in front of Amy and Cissy.

"Bless you," Cissy murmured, picking up her cup and sipping.

Traci and Dominic each grabbed a mug and plopped down on the floor in front of the fireplace. It was quiet for a few minutes, save for the snap and crackle of the wood burning. They sipped their sweet beverages and watched the flames burn brighter.

An additional crackle sounded at Amy's back. She frowned, glancing over her shoulder to find four small hands reaching over the arm of the couch and digging around in the shopping bags.

"Boys," Amy whispered, "there's no peeking at Christmas."

Their blond heads popped over the arm of the couch and two pairs of wide blue eyes blinked at her.

"Oh, for goodness' sakes," Cissy grumbled. "Haven't I told you two to stay out of this room until tomorrow morning? Santa's going to fly right over the ranch if he finds out you've been sneaking into presents early."

Both boys jumped out from behind the couch and held up their hands.

"We ain't took nothing, Aunt Cissy," Kayden said. "Promise."

Cissy sighed. "You mean you *haven't taken any-thing.*"

"That's right." Kayden nodded, his face scrunching up with confusion. "I ain't took nothing." He turned to his brother. "Did you?"

"Uh-uh," Jayden protested, waving around his empty hands. "We ain't took nothing, Aunt Cissy."

Cissy smiled and shook her head. "I give up."

They all laughed. Logan walked to the couch and rummaged around in the bags, a slow smile lifting his cheeks.

"Well, you're in luck, boys," he said, pulling out two small cowboy hats. "These, you can have now."

The boys whooped and jumped around, barely holding still long enough for Logan to settle a tan hat on each of their heads.

"What do you say?" Cissy asked.

"Thank you, Uncle Logan," they both chimed, hugging his legs.

Kayden strutted away to stand beside Dominic, poked his chest out and propped his hands on his hips. "We're bone-a-fine cowboys now, Uncle Dominic. Like you, Uncle Logan and Mr. Jed."

Traci snorted. "Like I keep telling you squirts, it's *bona fide.*"

"That's what I said," Kayden argued.

The bag rattled again. Jayden burrowed around in it. "There's another one, Uncle Logan. Who gets it?"

Logan reached over Jayden and tugged out a black straw hat. A row of silver-toned rhinestones circled the band, giving it a classic, stylish look.

"This one's for your aunt Amy," Logan said, placing it on her head. His broad hands moved over the brim, bending and shaping the edges. His narrowed eyes roved over her face as he adjusted the hat then stilled with satisfaction. "Beautiful."

"Thank you," she whispered.

Logan nudged the brim up and kissed her. "You're welcome. Thought it was time you had one of your own."

"You're a real cowgirl now, Aunt Amy." Jayden beamed with pride. "You got a hat and everything."

Amy smiled. "I suppose so."

"It's stunning," Cissy said. "Don't you think so, Betty?"

Betty beamed. "It's gorgeous." She blinked rapidly, gathering up the dirty mugs and pausing on her way out. "You boys better get ready for bed if you want Santa to drop by."

The twins darted to the window, shoved aside the curtains and peered out.

"Is he on the way now?" Jayden asked.

"Will be soon," Cissy said.

"What'd you ask Santa for, Aunt Cissy?" Kayden scampered over, placing his hands on Cissy's knees and leaning in.

Cissy winked and rubbed her belly. "Your baby cousins, Grace and Gwen."

Kayden scowled. "Is that all?"

Dominic laughed. "You'll think differently once they get here. You'll be like their big brother." He nodded at Logan. "Someone they can look up to."

Amy's chest swelled as the Slade men shared a smile. It was wonderful seeing them so close again. It seemed Dominic's return to Raintree had worked all sorts of magic on the family. A magic she was beginning to feel herself.

Jayden looked thoughtful then whispered something in Kayden's ear. He seemed to agree and the two took off, clutching their new hats to their heads.

"Best get them to bed, pronto." Dominic moved toward the door. "Looks like they're up to something."

"I'll give you a hand." Pop laughed, following him out of the room.

"All right," Cissy said, "I think we deserve a break. Thanks for the help with the shopping, Logan. We never would've gotten it done without your help."

"No problem." Logan grinned. "Why don't you get a bite to eat? I'll get the other presents out of the truck. The wrapping can wait. I have a feeling it'll be a while before Dom gets the boys settled."

Right on cue, the twins barreled back into the room, shoving past Amy and Traci toward the fireplace. They carried a large bucket between them and sloshed water onto the hardwood floor with every step.

"What in the world?" Cissy murmured.

"Hold up there, boys," Dominic shouted, rushing in behind them.

It was too late. Kayden and Jayden dumped the entire contents of the bucket onto the fire, killing it with a sizzle and sending billows of black smoke into the room.

Amy shut her eyes and waved a hand in front of her face, the mass of smoke choking the air from the room. Violent bouts of coughing sounded as she grappled her way over to the window. She struggled to unlatch the lock, the dark clouds of smoke making it difficult to see.

Logan's big hand covered hers, unlocking the window and heaving it open with a shove. Amy took off her hat and waved it wildly, ushering the smoke outside and blinking as it cleared.

Dominic stood by the fireplace. Each of his hands clutched a twin by the waistband, holding them in the air.

"Why did you do that?" Dominic sputtered as he shook them gently. "I know I won't understand but go ahead and tell me. Why?"

Jayden scrunched his nose and twisted his head up to answer, "So Grace and Gwen won't get hurt."

Dominic blinked. "What?"

"That's what Aunt Cissy asked Santa for." Kayden squirmed against Dominic's hold. "The fire's hot and the babies will get hurt when he comes down the chimney with 'em. So, we had to put it out."

Dominic's face went slack and he burst into laughter. Amy joined him, dropping her hat to the windowsill and glancing over at a chuckling Logan.

Cissy shook her head. "We talked about this, boys. The babies won't come for a few more weeks. I thought you understood the babies were in here," she said, patting her belly.

Amy's heart tripped as she studied Logan's profile. A muscle in his jaw ticked and his posture grew rigid.

The boys cocked their heads and studied Cissy's belly with a frown.

"So you asked Santa for 'em, he made 'em and then put 'em in there?" Jayden asked.

"No," Kayden declared, smacking a hand on his brother's arm. "Santa don't do all that. That's what the elves are for." He glanced up at Dominic. "Ain't that how babies are made?"

Dominic cleared his throat "Not exactly."

"Then how?" Kayden asked. "How are babies made?"

"Go ahead, Dominic," Cissy said, laughing. "Explain it to us."

Amy slipped her hand in Logan's. He glanced at her, smile tight and eyes bitter.

Her chest ached. There was no way Logan would react well to the news of a possible pregnancy. The pain of losing Sara was plain in his expression.

"Amy?" Logan squeezed her hand, his deep voice low against her ear. He studied her, his face creased with concern. "You okay? You went pale there for a second."

She leaned her head out of the window and sucked in a lungful of icy air. "I'm fine. Just took in a little too much smoke, I guess."

"See there, boys," Dominic boomed, "you owe Aunt Amy an apology."

"Are you avoiding the question, Dominic?" Cissy asked.

Dominic chuckled. "No. I'll be more than happy to explain it to you tonight, baby. In the meantime, you boys go apologize to your aunt Amy, then help me clean up this mess."

The boys ran across the room and tugged at Amy's jeans.

"Sorry, Aunt Amy," Kayden said.

"Me, too," Jayden added.

Grateful for the distraction, Amy knelt and drew the boys close. They wrapped their arms around her and pecked a kiss to her cheeks.

"Y'all better be on your best behavior for the rest of the night," Logan said. "So Santa doesn't hold it against you."

"We will," the boys chimed, nuzzling their warm faces into Amy's neck.

Logan scooped up Amy's hat from the window-sill and placed it back on her head. His warm palm smoothed through her hair and curled around her shoulder, causing her heart to beat faster.

"Santa won't be mad with us," Jayden whispered against her ear. "It's all right 'cuz everything turned out okay. Right, Aunt Amy?"

Amy hugged the boys close against her middle, spirits lifting at the thought of comforting her own child in her arms. A possibility that became more real with each passing day.

"Yeah," she whispered. "Everything's okay."

It would be. Either way. Life was moving on and there was a chance things might change. That she might become a mother, after all.

She hugged the boys tighter, straightened her hat with her other hand and smiled. It was the time of year for gifts. And the smallest ones, it seemed, held the biggest promise of all.

"HE CAME!"

Logan jumped, eyes flying open and arms clutching Amy tighter to his chest. The mattress beneath him dipped to one side then bounced. The springs squeaked and the bed frame rattled.

"Santa came!" Kayden jumped up and down at the end of the bed. "He ate all the cookies we left and he drank all the milk and—"

"He left presents," Jayden shouted, scrambling onto the bed and bouncing with his brother. "Lots and lots of presents! They're under the tree and in the hallway and in our room—"

"And he left a trampoline outside," Kayden gasped. He stopped jumping and dropped to Logan's chest, his small knees jabbing into Logan's ribs. "A trampoline, Uncle Logan!" His face contorted. He raised his fists and shook them on a primal yell. "A *tram-po-line!*"

Logan winced, his voice leaving him on a painful groan. "Then why aren't you using it instead of me?"

Gentle breaths of laughter brushed his ear, causing the skin on his neck to tighten. He rolled his head to the side. Amy smiled up at him, green eyes warm and excited. Her cheeks flushed a sweet shade of pink and her raven hair clung to her face in mussed waves.

Logan's chest warmed. Christmas morning was definitely much more beautiful with Amy at his side. Friends, like they used to be. The relationship familiar, safe and inviting.

He cleared his throat, leaning in and whispering, "Merry Chr—"

"Come on, Uncle Logan," Kayden said, smooshing his hands against Logan's cheeks. He leaned in, the tip of his nose brushing Logan's. "Get up. Aunt Cissy said we can't open presents until everyone's up."

"Yeah, get up, Aunt Amy," Jayden hollered, tugging at Amy's nightshirt.

"Boys, I told you to keep your tails out of here." Dom stuck his head inside the room, his hand covering his eyes. "You two decent, I hope?"

Amy laughed and Logan joined her.

"Yep," he said.

Dominic dropped his hand and smiled, dimples

flashing. "Then get your butts out here and let's get this party started."

Five minutes later, Logan and Amy were dressed and in the family room. The boys pounced on the presents while the adults sipped warm drinks and watched with smiles. The next several hours passed in a blur of squeals, torn wrapping paper and excited hugs.

It didn't take long for Logan to get swept up in the twin tornado. He, Pop and Dominic assembled new gadgets for the boys and helped them test out their new toys. It had taken the boys over an hour to tear into them all. Then, they spent hour upon hour afterward testing out each one. At one point, the boys couldn't decide whether to eat or play. They ended up grabbing a handful of sugar cookies, eating them with one hand and shooting their toy guns with the other.

Eventually, Logan crashed into a heap on the floor. His eyes grew heavy as they lingered on Amy but even her delighted smile couldn't keep the exhaustion at bay.

"Logan."

A hushed whisper swept by his ear, the sweetest voice he'd ever heard calling his name.

"Logan."

The familiar scent of strawberries lingered on the air. A long sweep of hair poured over his shoulder and gentle lips touched his cheek. Logan opened his eyes to find Amy leaning over him. Those emerald eyes of hers more gorgeous than ever under the wide brim of her black hat. They trailed over his face, heating his skin and causing his heart to trip in his chest.

"I hate to wake you," she whispered with a smile. "But it's getting late."

Logan blinked, focusing on her expression. The same

sweet one she'd first given him so long ago. Full of hope and admiration.

He shifted, lifting his arms to pull her close and claim her mouth but his elbows were glued to the floor.

Amy laughed and glanced at either side of him. "They're knocked out, too. You've all had a long day."

Logan turned his head to find Kayden draped face-down over his left arm and Jayden sprawled on his back over his right one. They clutched half-eaten peppermint sticks in their hands, each rhythmic snore puffing between their sticky red lips and brushing over his chest.

Logan smiled. He'd fallen asleep and, apparently, the boys had joined him. Amy was right. It had been a long Christmas day. Full of fun, food and family. And, of course, gifts. He lifted his head off the floor and scanned the mountains of torn wrapping paper, piles of toys and scattered ribbons littering the family room.

Presents. Logan chuckled. There'd been acres of them.

"Where is everyone?" he asked, clearing his throat to erase the husky note from his voice.

"Cissy was worn out so Dom and I sent her to bed. Dom and Pop are checking the stables, Mama and Traci are watching a Christmas movie marathon in the living room." Amy winked. "And the partridge is still in the pear tree."

Logan's smile stretched his cheeks. Lord, she was beautiful. He wanted to tell her. Wanted to tug her close. Hold on to her and the moment.

"Come on," she whispered, sliding her hands under Jayden's arms, "it's time to put our nephews to bed."

Our. Dear God, he wanted…

He caught her elbow as she lifted Jayden off his arm. "Hey."

She paused and glanced at him, expression expectant. He swallowed hard.

"Merry Christmas," he whispered.

She grinned, the pink flush of her cheeks causing his body to tighten. "Merry Christmas."

Jayden grumbled as she lifted him upright and held his hat to his head. Logan rolled to a seated position, then tugged Kayden to his chest and stood. He made swift work of settling a twin on each hip and they made their way quietly down the hall and into the boys' bedroom.

Amy took the boys' hats off and hung them on the bedposts, then motioned Logan into the bathroom. She wet a washcloth with warm water and he held the boys while she gently wiped away the sticky peppermint and scrubbed a toothbrush over their teeth to the tune of their sleepy grumbles.

Soon, they'd put each of them into their beds and tucked the covers snug around them. Logan bent and placed a kiss on Jayden's forehead. Amy did the same for Kayden.

"Aunt Amy?"

Logan stopped, watching as Amy tiptoed back to Kayden's bed.

"What is it, baby?" she asked, smoothing a hand over his blond curls.

"Can I sleep with my hat on?"

"Of course, you can." She plucked it off the bedpost and placed it gently on his head. "There. You're a bone-a-fine cowboy even when you sleep."

"And you're a real cowgirl," Jayden murmured sleepily, pointing to her hat.

"Dang sure am," she said.

The boys giggled.

Kayden curled his arms around Amy's neck, tugging her close. "I love you, Aunt Amy."

"Me, too," Jayden murmured.

Logan's chest clenched, a warm ache spreading over him and making him catch his breath. She hugged Kayden, a gentle smile appearing.

"I love both of you, too," she whispered, kissing Kayden's nose then Jayden's. "Very much."

The boys hunkered down under the covers, eyed each other, then sang out with sleepy smiles, "Merry Christmas."

Amy laughed. "Merry Christmas. Now you two go to sleep."

"Yes, ma'am," they whispered, snuggling into their pillows.

She tucked the blankets a little tighter around them and left the room. Logan followed her into the hallway, pulling the door closed behind him. Her long legs carried her farther away, that beautiful raven hair of hers swinging across her back.

Logan fisted his hands at his sides, his body shaking. "Amy?"

She stopped walking and turned, the wide brim of her hat skimming the curves of her dark eyebrows and casting a shadow over her mouth.

"I want…" His throat closed.

He wanted her. Wanted her so much it scared the hell out of him. Made him lose his logic and good sense.

"I want to…"

Hold her every night. See her first thing every morning. Have her in his life every day.

"To wish me Merry Christmas again?" she teased, crossing her arms under her full breasts. "I seem to be getting a lot of those lately."

Logan shook his head. He took long strides across the floor, wrapped his hands around her hips and nudged her against the wall.

Those gorgeous green eyes of hers softened. "What is it you want, Logan?"

He swallowed hard, shoved down the lump in his throat and pressed close. "I want you to stay," he whispered. "For good."

His heart raced and his hands trembled. The ache in his chest grew, becoming intense and all-consuming. He steadied his hands around her hips and slipped his leg between hers, striving for control. Hating this weakness. This dependency on her.

Her brows lifted and moisture sheened her eyes. She asked hesitantly, "You do?"

Logan nodded, touching a kiss to her mouth.

"Why?" she whispered.

He ducked his head, pressing his hot cheek to her cool one, then trailed his mouth down her neck, nipping and kissing. She softened beneath him, her arms sliding over his back and sweet moans escaping her.

"Logan." She tugged his head up and drifted a fingertip over the seam of his mouth. "Tell me. Why do you want me to stay?"

He firmed his jaw. "Because you're my wife."

The slow movement of her finger stopped. Her eyes dimmed. He kissed her, coaxing a response from her. Her sigh of pleasure heated his blood, his body hardening at the cushion of her breasts and rapid pound of her heart. He lifted her in his arms, carried her down the hall and covered her on their bed.

Logan took his time, touching and tasting her as if he never had before. He kept his eyes open, committing to memory every blush that heated her silky skin, every gasp that parted her lush mouth and every movement that lifted her supple hips. He pressed between her thighs, stilling when her lips parted several times soundlessly.

"What is it?" he urged, brushing her hair from her cheeks and trailing a hand over her breasts.

She hesitated, then shook her head, put a hand around his neck and tugged him close. Her lips parted his, the sweet taste of her filling his mouth and her body wrapping tight around him. He lost himself in her, losing track of where he ended and she began.

Afterward, he held her close until she fell asleep, smoothing a hand over her back and tucking her head beneath his chin as he had every time before. But something was missing. Something that had always been there. The absence of it sent a wave of dread through him.

Logan tightened his arms around Amy, wishing he would hear it. That she would look up at him and say it. But the words never came.

The desperate need weakened him, prompting his heart to pound and his hands to shake against her. He didn't know what scared him the most. The fact that Amy no longer asked him to love her or what he would say if she did.

Chapter Ten

"No, Kayden."

Logan sprang behind the line of large racks housing the New Year's Eve fireworks, scooped Kayden up and tossed him over his shoulder. Kayden squirmed as Logan carried him back across the safe line.

It was almost midnight and so dark Logan couldn't see his hand in front of his nose. Chaotic bursts of laughter, movement and music clamored on the air across the fields beyond them, but the dark night cloaked everything and very little was visible.

"I distinctly remember telling you and your brother to keep your distance." Logan flicked his flashlight upward three times and called out, "Found him, Dom."

The rustle of boots moving over the ground sounded and Dominic stalked out of the darkness surrounding them and into the low lights surrounding the work area. A tall, muscular man ambled up behind him with a pretty redhead at his side.

"I ought to tear your tail up, boy." Dominic blew out a frustrated breath. It hovered on the air in a white puff. "Your aunt Cissy's fit to be tied. You ever run off like that again—"

"Uh-oh," the man at Dominic's side rumbled. "Better take off now, Kayden. Dom's on the warpath."

"Hey, Mr. Colt," Kayden shouted, writhing in an attempt to get down.

Logan laughed and released him, watching as he skipped over and high-fived the man. Colt Mead. One of Dominic's fellow bull riders and playboy extraordinaire.

"Glad you could make it, Colt." Logan shook his hand. "Dom said you might take a break from the circuit and stop in."

"Yeah." Colt ran a broad hand through his blond hair. "Gotta get off the road once in a while or you forget where you are."

"Just as long as you don't stay in one place too long." The redhead nudged Colt with her elbow. "There's a lot of competition out there. You fall behind quick if you don't stay on top of it."

Colt cocked an eyebrow and smiled. "Never met a woman who likes to race as much as Jen does. She might get good at it one day."

"Keep telling yourself that," she said.

Logan chuckled. *Good* was an understatement. From what Colt told him, Jen Taylor was steadily climbing the ranks of barrel racers. She was fast, focused and dedicated. Poised to be at the top of her game if she kept at it.

She traveled with Colt and his cousin, Tammy. The trio was a band of close friends and Logan always enjoyed their visits to Raintree.

Jen smiled. "When there's a break between events, there's no better place to be than Raintree."

"Yep," Colt said. "Even though Dom does his level best to talk me into partnering with him every time I visit. Keeps saying it's time I retire from the circuit and settle down." He chuckled. "I still have plenty of rodeo years left in me, though."

Logan nodded. Next to Dominic, Colt was the most die-hard rider he'd ever met. The man was pure nomad and daredevil. Dom was wasting his time asking him to abandon the rodeo life. Colt wasn't the type of man to stay put anywhere for very long. Or settle down. He enjoyed the circuit—and women—too much.

Kayden tugged on Jen's arms for a kiss and chattered a mile a minute about Santa's recent visit and the approaching fireworks show.

Kayden paused then flashed a hesitant smile. "You can help light the fireworks with me, Ms. Jen."

"Oh, no," Dominic stressed. "You're coming back with me so I can show Aunt Cissy you're still in one piece."

Kayden frowned. "But I want to stay back here and help Uncle Logan with the fireworks."

Logan shook his head. "It's way too dangerous, Kayden. You can see 'em fine from across the field and it's much safer for you over there."

"But Aunt Amy said she's staying," Kayden argued, scrunching his nose.

"Well, there's not much I can do about it." Logan grinned. "She's a hardheaded woman."

"I heard that."

A jaunty bounce of light grew closer and Logan smiled. He flicked his flashlight up and the glow cascaded over Amy's curvy form as she approached. Jayden clasped her hand and skipped along at her side.

"You're in trouble, Uncle Logan." Jayden giggled. "Better say you're sorry."

Logan met them halfway, tapping Jayden's hat and

touching his lips to Amy's ear. "Sorry, babe. But it's true."

Amy harrumphed, her expression playful but strained. Logan knuckled her hat straighter on her head and smoothed a finger over the curve of her cheek, tamping down his frustration.

He'd spent the majority of the week following Christmas coaxing her into bed with him. Her rosy skin glowed, her kisses tasted sweeter than ever and her curves seemed to grow fuller every day. He damn well couldn't get enough of her and every day that passed heightened his anxiety. She still hadn't agreed to stay.

"You must be Amy." Jen reached over the boys and held out a hand. "It's nice to finally meet you."

Pleasantries were exchanged and it wasn't long before Jen was regaling Amy with tales of the barrel racing circuit. Her enthusiasm for the sport was obvious. Colt tensed, shoving his hands in his pockets when Jen described her most recent close call in the arena.

"One of these days, she's not gonna come out of it so lucky," Colt grumbled.

Jen shook her head. "Don't start, Colt. That warning's ironic coming from a bull rider." She smiled at Amy. "*Men.* They're under the mistaken impression that we're the weaker sex."

Amy laughed.

"Fact is," Jen continued, "we all have our dreams. And if they're worth imagining, they're worth chasing." She winked down at the twins. "I'm determined to reach mine."

The boys beamed.

"It's about time to get the show started," Logan said, clapping his hands together.

The boys practically vibrated with excitement and Kayden begged again to stay behind and light the fireworks.

Amy shook her head. "I hate to say it but Logan does have a point." She nudged the twins in Dominic's direction. "It's much safer for you two to watch from the field with everyone else."

The boys groaned in disagreement but darted over to Dominic and pushed at his legs.

"Then let's go so we can get the best seats," Kayden said.

Dominic shook his head. "We had the best seats until you ran off from them."

He smiled and led the boys away. Colt and Jen said their goodbyes and followed, all of them disappearing into the darkness.

Logan waved an arm, signaling to a crew of men to start the proceedings. Scattered shouts from the hands rang out as a couple of the crew moved around, testing and reaffirming everything was in order. Logan took Amy's hand, leading her away from racks of fireworks and farther behind the safety line.

They reached his truck and he released her long enough to rummage inside the cab for another hard hat and set of earplugs.

"Are those really necessary?" Amy asked as he draped the earplugs around her neck.

"Yes." He hooked a finger under her straw hat, swapping it for the hard one. "These aren't backyard firecrackers, Amy. They're extremely dangerous."

She glanced up at the brim of the hard hat. "I guess it'll be worth it." She smiled. "They might be dangerous but you've always put together the most beautiful displays I've ever seen."

"Still do." He smiled. "Wait 'til July rolls around. I'll really impress you then."

His smile slipped. If she was still here.

Amy hesitated, shadows creeping into her eyes. "We need to talk, Logan. About tomorrow."

Logan tensed. The tight note in her voice unsettled him. *Tomorrows*. He'd never been on good terms with them.

She tucked her hair behind her shoulders, fingers trembling slightly. "This was the last day I had on leave from work. I planned on heading back to Augusta first thing tomorrow to start the move."

"But that plan's changed." His chest tightened. "It has changed, hasn't it?"

She stilled, her mouth drawing into a hard line.

"Hey, Logan." Jed waved a flashlight from his stance by the racks of fireworks. "Countdown's about to start. You wanna lead?"

Logan frowned and waved him off. "Nah, you go ahead. You know the drill, yeah?"

Jed nodded and signaled with his flashlight to the rest of the group. They began running final checks for the fireworks show.

"Please tell me you're staying, Amy." Logan's gut churned at her stoic expression. "Things have gone well between us the past few weeks and they can continue that way."

Amy held up a hand. "I want to stay. I really do. But…"

"But, what?" Logan shook his head.

"There's another consideration," she whispered. "A small one."

"What kind of consi—"

"I'm pregnant."

Logan froze. He watched her mouth and waited. Waited for her to take it back. To say she'd misspoken. That it was all a mistake.

A mistake. God help him. *Sara.*

"That's not possible." He bit his lip, a sharp metallic taste seeping onto his tongue. "The doctors said—"

"The doctors said it was highly unlikely." She shook her head, features softening. "Not impossible. We're lucky—"

"*Lucky?*"

"Yes." Her mouth tightened. "We're lucky to have another chance whether we were looking for it or not. Good things can happen just as much as the bad. Life's given us another gift."

Her hand dropped to cover her belly. His gut churned and he swallowed hard, looking away.

Sporadic yellow lights flickered over the ground as the hands moved about with flashlights on the other side of the lot, checking the racks and getting into final positions.

"How long have you known?" His voice sounded strange, even to his own ears.

"It was confirmed a couple of days ago. I didn't want to mention it until I knew for sure." Her tone gentled. "I'm sure now."

Sure. Logan's mouth twisted. She'd been sure when she'd gotten pregnant with Sara. Had been sure their daughter was okay even when he'd insisted something was wrong. Sure they'd deliver a healthy baby girl.

Logan shoved his hands in his pockets and moved away. There was no such thing as being sure. Nothing was ever certain. Not for this pregnancy and not for Amy.

What if...

"We can't go through this again," he choked. "What happens when we lose this baby? You think it'll hurt any less than before?"

"I want this child." Amy squared her shoulders. "I was told that as long as I'm careful, things may work out. There's a chance nothing will go wrong this time."

"As much chance as there was the first time? With Sara?" His voice cracked, his throat tightening to the point of pain. "What about her? She was once part of our family, too. Have you forgotten her?"

She winced, whispering, "I've never forgotten Sara. Not for one day. And I never will." Her chin lifted. "But nothing you or I did caused us to lose her. It just happened. I won't let the pain of losing Sara stop me from living." She touched his arm. "Life goes on, Logan."

He flinched, pulling away. *"It shouldn't."*

A searing heat washed through his chest, flooding it as though his heart was bleeding out.

The shaking in his hands was becoming a violent tremor. "What if something happens to you? I just got you back."

"You've never had me," she said. "Not really."

"You're my *wife*."

Amy's smile was sad. "That's just a word, Logan. One you throw out to excuse the lie I told. What you use to console yourself every time you give in to me. Something you say to feel honorable for keeping your promise and sticking it out." She shook her head. "I'm not your wife. I'm just an obligation. Another one of your regrets."

Pain swept over Logan, leaving him hollow and weak.

"That's not true," he said.

A voice boomed over the loudspeaker, signaling the start of the New Year's Eve countdown. Portfires burst into bright red flames across the lot as the men approached the fuses. The crowd, hidden in the darkness, cheered and the chant began.

Ten. Nine…

"That's not true," he repeated.

Seven. Six…

She blinked, her wide green eyes lifting and meeting his.

Four. Three…

"I can make this work, Amy."

One. Happy New Year!

A massive round of explosions cracked through the air. The black sky burst into color with scattered streaks of light. The boom from the firecrackers echoed through the ground beneath their feet, smoke and ash scattering all around them.

Amy cringed, the green light from above casting an eerie glow over her. Logan pressed his hands over her ears and held her close as the pyrotechnics continued, the explosions sounding closer together and growing louder.

The fireworks stopped. The cheers of the crowd took over and smoke billowed in big, dark clouds around them.

"I can make this right," he rasped.

Amy yanked at his wrists, pulling his hands from her

ears. "There's no wrong to be made right. This pregnancy will not be another obligation. This baby and I deserve to be loved."

"*Loved?*" Logan shook his head. "You don't know what that means—"

"Yes, I do. You're the one who doesn't know what real love is. Everything you offer comes with conditions and expectations. You only accept people when they live up to your standards and can't forgive them when they don't." Her fingers wove into his hair and rubbed over his nape. "You have to believe love exists to be able to feel it. My love isn't enough for you and your loyalty isn't enough for me. Neither of us can win. It's time for us to go our separate ways."

His legs grew weak. "You can't go through this pregnancy alone."

"Yes, I can," she said. "I'd rather be alone than with someone who could never truly love me for who I am."

Amy took the hard hat off her head, slid the earplugs from her neck and held them out. Logan took them.

"This pregnancy might not work out," she said. "I might lose this baby like we lost Sara. It may even hurt worse than it did before." She hesitated, looking away. "Or, things could turn out differently. I might end up with a healthy child and be happier than I ever thought possible." She faced him again, her small smile determined. "Maybe I'm a dreamer. Maybe I am still chasing a fairy tale. But I'm not giving up on it. No matter what happens, I don't want to just exist. I want to live."

She grabbed her hat from the truck and left, her long strides taking her farther and farther away. Logan balled his fists and tried to take a step. Tried to follow. But he couldn't. His heart, heavy with pain and regret, rooted him to the ground.

Cheerful shouts from the crowd echoed over the field and the rhythmic pound of music drifted on the night air. The smoke cleared and the stars shone brighter than ever.

Logan stood alone again, stuck between the present and the past, waiting for Amy to return. And watching life move on without him.

FIVE O'CLOCK. AMY TUCKED her watch beneath the sleeve of her sweater and raised her head, looking out at the dark fields before her. The glowing hands on her wristwatch haunted her vision and floated in bright smudges across the landscape on the other side of the porch rail.

She rocked back in her chair and sighed. New Year's Eve had officially ended and she'd spent the first five hours of New Year's Day rocking on a porch, staring into the darkness and waiting. Something she'd never been any good at, even under the best of circumstances. And Logan had still not returned to the main house.

She'd known the news of the pregnancy would be hard for him. Had expected it to unsettle him. But she'd also hoped he'd seek her out after recovering from the shock. That she'd have an opportunity to say goodbye on better terms and reassure him that he'd always be welcome in their child's life.

Only, Logan hadn't sought her out. The one glimpse she'd had of him since the fireworks show had been his moonlit figure as he'd entered the stable then left with Lightning.

The screen door creaked open. A tall figure emerged

onto the porch, taking long strides toward the line of rocking chairs and halting abruptly in front of hers.

"Damn, kid," Dominic boomed. "You crackin' dawn in for everyone or what?"

Amy smiled despite her ill mood. "Is that how you say good morning these days?"

Dominic chuckled, plopping down in the chair beside her and cradling a cup in his hands. "Good morning." He tipped his cup at her, the pleasant aroma of coffee rising with each curl of steam. "You want? Your mama just brewed a fresh pot. It'll help wake you up."

She shook her head. "I've been up."

"Couldn't sleep?"

"Didn't want to." She forced a half smile. "I've slept more than my fair share over the last four years."

Dominic's grin slipped. "I won't argue with you there. It's good to have you back." He sipped from his mug, glancing out at the horizon and rocking. The wood chair creaked with each of his movements. "Sun's comin' up soon. That what you've been out here waiting on?"

"No. I've been waiting for you." Which had become true at some point in the wee hours, when she'd given up on Logan returning…

He smiled, his expression tinged with amusement. "'Course you have." He propped his boots on the porch rail. "I'm always in high demand."

Amy laughed and smacked his arm. Dominic's wisecracks alone were enough to clear the grit from her eyes and lift her spirits.

"I was hoping you'd drive me to Augusta today," she said. "It seems I've lost my ride."

He frowned. "You're still leaving?"

She nodded.

"Why?" At her silence, Dominic added, "I thought you and Logan were getting along better lately."

"I'm pregnant."

His boots dropped from the rail with a thud. "Well. I guess y'all are getting along *a lot* better lately."

Amy swallowed hard, vision blurring. "Not anymore."

Dominic stilled. "He didn't take it well?"

Hot tears scalded her cheeks, rolling slowly down her face and dripping off her chin. "No."

"Ah, hell, Ames." Dominic set his cup on the porch rail with a thunk and crouched at her side, wrapping her hands in his. "I hate that that happened. But he's had a hard time coming to terms with losing Sara. Give him some room. A little time to adjust—"

"That's something I can't give him." She tugged her hands free and scrubbed them across her face. "We've lost too much time already. Both of us."

"So you're gonna leave? Just like that?" Dominic shook his head. "That'll kill him, Amy."

She sighed and rocked back in the chair. "No. Losing Sara already did that. When Logan looks at me, all he sees is the past. We've both spent enough time there. I have to move on for this baby, and maybe if the reminder's gone, he'll finally move on, too."

"I can't help you do this." He stood and took a step back. "I can't do this to Logan."

"It's the only thing I *can* do. I already love this baby as much as I loved Sara. This child deserves a fair shot at life and all my support to thrive. I can't provide that buried underneath Logan's guilt and regret." She raised a hand in appeal. "Logan doesn't love me. I've faced that. Come to terms with it. And I won't stay here just to be tolerated."

Dominic turned away, but didn't immediately leave.

She straightened. "It's time for me to move on, Dom. I'm leaving. With or without your help. But I'd be lying if I said I didn't need it. I could really use a friend right now."

He slowly turned back to face her. His frown dissolved and a tight smile took its place. "How soon do you want to head out?"

Amy finished packing within an hour, throwing in everything she'd brought with her except for two items she decided to leave behind. She slipped the necklace over her head and dropped the ring onto the papers on the dresser, swapping them out for her black straw hat.

She took her bags to the kitchen, hugged Pop and Cissy and said the rest of her goodbyes in the driveway while Dominic loaded her luggage in the truck.

"Remember you're loved," Betty whispered, hugging her tighter. "No matter where you are."

Traci wiped away tears and tried to smile. "I want first-class tickets, sis. Not crappy economy."

It was hard saying goodbye to Betty and Traci but it was sheer torture walking away from the boys.

"But who's gonna take care of Thunder and keep him happy?" Jayden looked down and twisted the toe of his shoe in the dirt, his cowboy hat hiding his face.

"I was hoping you and Kayden could do that for me. And maybe look out for your uncle Logan, too?" Amy glanced at Kayden and he nodded with a brave smile.

"We can do it, Aunt Amy." Kayden elbowed his brother, mouth quivering. "Can't we, Jayden?"

"Yeah," Jayden whispered. His wide blue eyes peeked

up at her from beneath the brim of his hat, glistening with tears. "But who'll keep you happy? You won't have Thunder no more. And you won't have us."

Amy's heart squeezed. She knelt down and hugged the boys close. "Oh, I'll always have the two of you, baby. I'm carrying you both with me." She leaned back and placed a hand over her heart. "Right here."

With Sara. And with Logan... She smiled, blinking back her own tears and forcing down the lump in her throat.

"Just like you both will have me." She touched her hands to their chests. "Right here."

Kayden rubbed his eyes with his fists. "Will you come back and visit?"

"Of course," she said. "And your aunt Cissy and I already talked about you coming to see me in Michigan. Maybe next Christmas?"

She felt excitement stirring at the hope of holding her own child on Christmas morning. She straightened Kayden's hat and squeezed his arms.

"There's real snow up there," she said. "You and Jayden can make huge snowballs and throw as many as you want. It won't hurt like the ice."

Jayden perked up. "Real snow? Lots of it?"

"Mountains of it. As far as the eye can see."

Grins broke out across their faces.

Amy kissed the twins once more, hugged Cissy and waited in the truck while Dominic assured Cissy one last time that he'd return safely, soon. He hopped in and they strapped on their seat belts.

Amy glanced up at the sunlight beaming through the windshield. She noticed Logan then. He was several yards away, sitting astride Lightning in the center of the adjoining field. His Stetson was pulled down low and he remained motionless, watching them.

"He's hurtin', Amy," Dominic murmured. "As much as you were."

"I know." She twisted her hands together in her lap, resisting the urge to fling the door open and run straight to him.

"You sure you wanna leave?"

"No." Amy tore her eyes away from Logan, straightened and faced the road ahead. "But I'm done standing still."

Dominic nodded, cranked the truck and drove away.

Chapter Eleven

Divorce Settlement Agreement.

Logan smoothed his fingertips over the words. The papers crinkled under his touch, the edges worn. He bent them in half then folded them over. Once, twice then a third time, and returned the bundle to the dresser.

The action had become a habit over the past week. One he'd undertaken every night before crawling into an empty bed and every morning when he finally gave up chasing sleep to face the day.

The day. God help him. The things kept coming. Rolling in with the sun, spanning what seemed like thousands of hours and hanging on through the darkness. A darkness he failed to find relief in.

He ached for Amy. His chest burned for her and his hands turned numb from clenching empty air every time he reached for her in the night. Every part of him wanted to follow her but the heavy weight in his chest held him hostage where he stood.

Logan sighed and dragged a hand over his face. Every day, he tried to make himself go and bring Amy back. And, every day, he failed.

"Uncle Logan?"

He spun from the dresser to find the boys hovering in

the bedroom doorway. Jayden picked at the legs of his jeans and Kayden peeked up at him with a concerned expression. The same one he'd worn every afternoon for the past week as he'd followed him close, at Logan's heels around the ranch after school.

"Hey." Logan cleared the husky note from his voice and strived for a cheerful tone. "You two are up early for a Sunday."

Jayden nodded, hands clutching his hat in front of his waist. "We asked Uncle Dominic to get us up. We wanna help you with the horses today."

"You sure you want to spend your day off school working? It'll be a long one."

"Yes, sir," Kayden said.

Jayden put his hat on his head, straightening the brim with both hands, and stuck out his chest. "We promised Aunt Amy we'd take care of Thunder for her." He tried for a smile but it drooped at the corners. "So, can we help?"

Logan nodded. "There's nothing I'd like more."

He crossed the room and held out his hands. They latched on to them and they took their time making their way to the stables, just as they had every afternoon over the past week.

Winter was in full swing and this morning was no exception. The January air whipped through their clothes with cold gusts of wind as they strolled down the winding path, flushing Kayden's cheeks and making Jayden shiver. Logan stopped, bending to fasten the top button on their jean jackets and tug their hats down firmer around their ears.

"We're all right." Jayden batted his hands away and strutted on with his brother.

"Yeah," Kayden said. "We don't get cold no more."

"Oh, yeah?" Logan's mouth twitched. "Why's that?"

Kayden jerked his chin. "'Cuz we're bone-a-fine cowboys now. Mr. Jed said they don't never get cold."

Logan clamped his lips shut, choking back his laughter. It was probably best to let that one go. Wouldn't do for him to question Mr. Jed's knowledge. The boys didn't take too kindly to others criticizing the ranch hand's words of wisdom.

They spent the first couple hours of the morning turning horses out and mucking stalls alongside the hands. When the twins' shoulders began to sag, Logan took the shovels from them and suggested a break. He led them outside and lifted them to the top rail of the white fence lining the paddock, keeping an arm snug around each of the boys' backs.

"We got a treat for Thunder." Jayden dug around in his pocket then drew out a small, colorful lump. "It's oats and carrots and the sugar stuff mixed together."

"Yeah," Kayden said. "Ms. Betty helped us make it last night."

Logan held Jayden's palm and tilted it from one side to the other. No sign of cayenne powder this time.

He smiled. "I think he'll enjoy that. Hold it out and let him have a taste."

Logan clucked his tongue and steadied Jayden's outstretched arm as Thunder walked over. The stallion moved gracefully, his muscles rippling. Thunder nudged Jayden's hand with his nose then wrapped his lips around the treat and nibbled.

Kayden giggled. "He likes it."

Thunder's soft breaths and chomping teeth filled the silence that followed until the treat disappeared. The stallion licked Jayden's palm, setting off another round of laughter from the boys, then turned and strolled away.

Kayden tilted his head back, glancing up at him. "Uncle Dominic said you're the best trainer there is. 'Cept for Aunt Amy." He blinked and lifted his chin. "I ain't scared of Thunder no more, and I can learn to ride him like Aunt Amy does. You think you could teach me one day?"

"One day. But not quite yet. Thunder might be having more good days than bad, but he's still adjusting."

Jayden pursed his lips. "Bet he misses Aunt Amy."

Logan's gut churned. He looked away, focusing on the other horses milling about in the field. "I expect so."

Kayden sighed and picked at Logan's sleeve. "We miss her, too."

Logan tightened his arms around the boys, tugging them closer and whispering, "So do I."

The twins huddled into Logan's chest and wrapped their arms around his back. They stayed silent for a while, gazing across the fields and listening to the gentle sounds of the horses.

A breathless cry and pounding feet shattered the silence.

"It's time!"

Logan glanced over his shoulder. Traci loped down the path from the main house. She stopped, bending with her hands on her knees and struggling to drag in air.

"Time for what?" Jayden asked, squirming against Logan's chest.

"Time..." Traci gulped and grinned "...for the babies." She straightened and pointed to the main house. "Mama and Pop just left for the hospital with Dom and

Cissy. Mama said to come get you so you could drive the rest of us."

Traci darted back up the path, flapping her hands and sputtering over her shoulder, "Well, come on."

Logan made short order of loading Traci and the boys into the truck and took off for the hospital as fast as safety allowed. The drive seemed to take longer than usual and Logan's hands shook harder against the steering wheel with every giddy exclamation from Traci.

"I can't wait to see Grace and Gwen," she gushed, biting her lip and bouncing in the passenger seat. "Bet they'll be beautiful."

"Yeah," Kayden drawled, kicking the back of her seat, "'til they start cryin' and poopin'. Mr. Jed said that's all babies do."

"Hush up, squirt." Traci glanced in the rearview mirror and narrowed her eyes. "Mr. Jed's full of hot air. You oughta be glad you're getting cousins."

Kayden wasn't impressed. He curled his lip and turned to stare out of the window, remaining quiet for the rest of the journey.

The waiting room was crowded, and they filled up the last row of empty chairs by the window. Pop and Betty walked around the corner, a smile wreathing both their faces.

"Everything's well underway," Pop said. "The doc told us things are moving fast. So it shouldn't be long now."

"Dominic's a nervous wreck." Betty laughed. "Good thing it'll be over with soon."

Logan shifted in his seat and hoped that was the case. He ran his eyes over the others in the waiting room. Fathers, siblings and grandparents all moved with excited energy around the chairs. They tapped their toes, flashed nervous grins and sprang up for hugs at the delivery of good news.

This continued throughout the course of the morning, carrying over into late afternoon. For the other families. There was, however, no happy word on Dominic and Cissy, and the silence stretched into late evening.

Logan shoved to his feet and paced the waiting room. His legs tingled, blood rushing back in and tight muscles stretching.

Traci's knees bounced with jerky movements and Betty wrung her hands in her lap. The twins hunched in their chairs, hats shielding their expressions. Pop left for the third time in the past hour to check for more news.

"You boys want to run down to the cafeteria and grab something to eat?" Betty smiled and crouched in front of the boys.

They shook their heads.

"Are you sure?" Betty asked. "It's been a long time since y'all had breakfast and you didn't have any lunch or supper."

"I'm not hungry," Jayden mumbled.

"I wanna wait for Aunt Cissy." Kayden's hat tipped up as he looked around the room. "Lots of other people got their babies already." His voice shook. "Why ain't ours here yet?"

"I don't know," Betty said gently. "But they'll get here eventually. Sometimes, it takes a while." She glanced up and stood. "Here comes your uncle Dominic now. Maybe he'll have some good news for us."

Or maybe not. Logan's stomach dropped as he watched his brother stride swiftly across the room. His hair stood up at odd angles and his face was shadowed. Pop followed a step behind with the same grim expression.

The boys ran to Dominic and he squatted, drawing them both between his knees, squeezing their arms and kissing the tops of their heads.

"Are the babies here yet?" Kayden asked.

Dominic's throat moved on a hard swallow. "Gwen is." A smile flitted across his lips. "She's got dark hair—" he tapped their noses "—but her eyes are as blue as yours."

"What about the other one?" Jayden asked.

Dominic stood and nudged the boys toward Betty. "Grace will be here soon, too. Now, go sit with Traci and I'll come get you when it's time."

"Come on, boys," Pop said. He took their hands and led them over to join Traci.

Logan stepped close, eyeing the worried glint in Dominic's eyes. "What's going on?"

"Grace—" Dominic's voice cracked. He bit his lip and looked away. "Grace is showing signs of distress. They said the cord prolapsed and she's not getting enough oxygen so they took Cissy for an emergency C-section. If they don't make it to Grace in time…"

"Oh, Dom." Betty patted Dominic's arm. "You hang in there. There are good doctors taking care of your girls."

Dominic nodded, his gaze moving over her shoulder. Kayden scrambled into Traci's lap. She hugged him close and surveyed Dominic with a worried expression.

"Cissy asked me to check on the boys," Dominic said. "She wanted me to let them know everything was gonna be okay."

"We'll take care of them," Betty said, moving away

to drop a kiss to the twins' foreheads. "You tell her not to worry."

Dominic stood, watching the boys, shoulders sagging and mouth twisting. Logan's throat closed.

"I've got to get back." Dominic pressed his thumb and forefinger to his closed eyelids and dropped his head. "Cissy's exhausted and worried sick about Grace. I've never seen her this terrified." He looked up, eyes hovering on Logan's, and whispered, "And there's not a thing I can do to help either one of them."

Logan froze. Sara was on Dominic's mind. It was right there in every defeated line of his brother's body. And seeing that kind of pain hanging on Dominic burned in his chest.

He gripped Dominic's shoulder and squeezed, forcing sound out of his constricted throat. "Cissy's strong. She's gonna pull through this. And if Grace inherited even half of the grit you and Cissy have, she'll come out either smiling or swinging a fist."

There was no way to tell how much truth was in the words. The outcome would remain uncertain to the last second, no matter what anyone said. But it comforted Dominic and that was all that mattered.

Dominic nodded. "Cissy *is* strong. The strongest woman I've ever met." He managed a small smile. "Aside from Amy."

Dominic strode across the room toward the hall but stopped, turned back and said, "I'm glad I came home. Glad Cissy and I settled at Raintree. Don't think we could make it through this without all of you." He smiled, the fear in his eyes still present but determination overcoming it. "Having people you love around makes you stronger. No matter how tough it gets."

Logan watched him leave. He'd never seen Dominic stand so tall or move with such strength. In that one moment, Logan was the proudest he'd ever been of his little brother.

Logan returned to his chair. Jayden leaned onto the arm of it, staring down at his boots and frowning.

"Hey," Logan said, "wanna sit with me for a while?"

Jayden nodded, his blond curls slipping onto his forehead. Logan sat down and settled him in his lap. He caught sight of Jayden's hat lying upside down on the floor.

"Did you lose your hat?" Logan reached for it.

"No." Jayden stilled him with a hand on his forearm. "I just ain't no bone-a-fine cowboy no more."

"Why not?"

Jayden glanced up, blue eyes blurred with tears. "'Cuz I'm scared."

"For your aunt Cissy and Grace?"

Jayden nodded. "Mr. Jed said bone-a-fine cowboys are always brave. That they don't never get scared."

Logan winced. He knew the weight of that worry. The need to be strong. The need to always be perfect and never make a mistake. Otherwise, what would there be for anyone to respect? To admire? To love?

Love. He tensed, Amy's words returning.

Everything you offer comes with conditions and expectations.

Logan tipped Jayden's chin up with a knuckle and peered into his eyes. "It's okay to be afraid. Most everyone is at some point or another. It's pushing through the fear that makes you brave."

Jayden blinked and asked, "So I can still be a bone-a-fine cowboy?"

Logan nodded. "Yep. And a bone-a-fine cowboy always looks better wearing a hat." He scooped it off the floor and placed it on Jayden's head. "A man needs his hat."

Jayden brightened, a smile stretching from ear to ear. He snuggled against the left side of Logan's chest— Amy's favorite spot—settling in for the long wait.

You only accept people when they live up to your standards and can't forgive them when they don't.

Logan cringed. He'd never lived up to his own standards. Had never pleased himself with his own actions, much less been impressed by anyone else's. He'd been so fixated on flawlessness that he'd failed to see the good qualities in others.

Dominic had left the circuit for Cissy. Not because he had to but because he wanted to. For her and the boys.

Even though it'd almost broken him, Pop had stayed behind at Raintree instead of following Gloria. Not because he hadn't still loved her but because he loved his sons more.

Amy had held the memory of their marriage in her heart for four years. Had remained loyal to it and to him. Not because she had to. But because she loved him.

You have to believe love exists to be able to feel it.

He *had* felt it. Every time he held Amy, hands shaking against her. Every time his body rebelled against his mind, reaching for her and getting lost in her over and over again. And he'd felt it burning in his chest when he'd held Sara.

He'd fought feeling it to avoid pain and regret. To avoid the risk of losing Amy and being hurt. Turned out, his heart was stronger than his head. It had remained steadfast to Amy through the worst.

I'm just an obligation. Another one of your regrets.

He didn't want Amy because of a piece of paper. Or to make up for any mistakes they made. He wanted her because he needed her. He needed her spirit and smile in his life. Needed her hardheaded stubbornness and tender touch. Needed her because she challenged him and made him feel more alive than anything else. The love he had for her was stronger and more comforting than any pain life's disappointments could bring.

Logan's throat thickened. He'd never told her he loved her. Not once. Hell, he hadn't even been able to acknowledge it to himself.

The next few minutes ticked by in slow motion. One hour passed and then another. The boys' eyes drooped but they stayed awake, Kayden in Traci's lap and Jayden in Logan's. Pop paced and Betty wiped tears away a time or two.

Dominic burst into the waiting room, his smile as wide as his step. "Cissy's doing well. They moved her into a room. Get over here, boys. You have an aunt asking for you and two cousins to visit."

"So Grace is okay?" Pop's smile shook.

Dominic hugged him. "Yeah. She's perfect. All my girls are."

Relief flooded Logan's chest. The boys squealed and hopped to the floor, clamoring across the room to barrel into Dominic's legs. They each looped an arm around his thighs and stood on his boots, laughing as his strides carried them down the hall.

"Well—" Dominic's brow quirked "—y'all waiting for an engraved invitation, or what?"

They all laughed and followed Dominic. Logan stayed back, waiting in the hall as Betty and Traci cooed over the girls. Pop's deep voice sounded as he spoke in soothing tones to Cissy and the babies and the boys' proud chatter filled every corner of the room. Everyone was there.

Everyone except Amy. Logan closed his eyes. He wanted a new life with her and their baby. Wanted to hope again for the dream he'd lost so long ago with Sara.

Maybe I am still chasing a fairy tale. But I'm not giving up on it.

Amy's words warmed his blood and lifted his head. He opened his eyes, excitement buzzing in his veins at the possibility. The hope of happiness. Of something bright and beautiful growing out of something that was once so bleak.

"We're heading back now," Pop said, stepping into the hall. "Dom's spending the night here. You coming?"

Logan shook his head. "I'm gonna stay with Dom for a while. Can the boys and Traci ride back with you and Betty? It's late and I don't know how long I'll be."

Pop smiled. "Of course. Take your time."

Betty and Traci passed, discussing plans for the new twins' wardrobe. Kayden and Jayden smacked noisy kisses to Cissy's cheeks, then skipped into the hall.

"What'd you think?" Logan asked.

Kayden tilted his head and shrugged. "They ain't bad. Kinda small but they're okay, I guess."

"We like 'em," Jayden said. "We're gonna take good care of 'em."

"I know you will." Logan swept them against his legs for a squeeze before they scampered off to join the rest of the crew walking down the hall.

Logan inhaled, holding his breath and edging his head into the room. Dominic sat at Cissy's bedside. He smoothed one hand over her blond hair and the other over the babies nestled in her arms.

Logan cleared his throat and asked, "Got time for one more visitor?"

They glanced up and smiled.

"Of course," Cissy said. "Come meet your nieces."

Logan walked slowly to the bed. "You feeling okay?"

Cissy laughed. "I'm feeling great right now. It's tomorrow when the meds wear off that things will change."

Logan nodded and looked at the bundles in her arms. The boys had been right. The babies were small. The pink blankets cocooning them parted slightly to reveal dark hair, flushed cheeks and rosebud mouths. Every bit of which reminded him of Sara.

Logan flinched, pain shooting through his chest. Not as sharp as before but enough to cut.

"They're beautiful, aren't they?" Dominic bent and kissed their foreheads.

Logan nodded and searched their peaceful faces, waiting for their eyelids to flicker or their mouths to part.

"Would you like to hold one of them?" Cissy asked.

Her eyes were patient and gentle. Understanding.

Logan swallowed around the lump in his throat. "Please."

Dominic stood and Logan took his seat, watching with coiled muscles as Dominic gently lifted one of the babies and carried her over.

"Here you go, Grace," Dominic whispered, lowering her into Logan's arms. "Meet your uncle Logan."

Grace's light weight hardly rivaled a feather and if he didn't have his eyes on her, Logan could've sworn

Dominic had never put her in his arms. He held still and studied her face. She didn't move. Didn't make a sound.

Sara.

Logan froze. A knot formed in his chest. He pulled Grace closer.

"There's something wrong."

Heaven help him, he knew the thought was irrational. Knew it to be untrue. But he couldn't stop himself from voicing it.

"No," Cissy whispered. "She's just sleeping."

Logan shook his head. His eyes burned. The dark, downy head blurred in front of him, the delicate features distorting.

"She's not breathing—" Tremors stole his voice and racked his body as he studied her chest.

"Yes, she is." Cissy's hand touched his forearm.

He tore his eyes away from Grace and focused on Cissy's face.

Cissy smiled. "She's perfectly fi—"

A cry pierced the air, cracking the stillness and echoing around the room. They all started. Logan curled his hands around the bundle, the warmth of her seeping into his palms.

"Here." Dominic reached out, his face shadowed with concern. "I think Grace is gonna turn out to be the fussy one. You can hold Gwen."

"Wait, Dominic."

Logan barely registered Cissy's words. Grace demanded his attention. Her face scrunched up and an angry flush engulfed her cheeks. That small mouth parted and the biggest, shrillest cry he'd ever heard broke free, causing Dominic to cringe and provoking wails from Gwen.

Something cracked wide open in Logan's chest and every heavy pain he harbored came rushing out. Tears poured from his eyes in scalding streaks and rattled free of his body with each shudder ripping through his limbs.

His chest shook then. It jerked with strong bursts of laughter and he blinked away the tears to smile down at the howling bundle in his arms.

"Cry, baby girl. You cry all you want. Let the whole damn world know you're in it."

Grace opened her eyes. Those beautiful blues widened up at him, her cries fading away. She blinked and took up squirming, the pink blanket shifting with each thrust of her legs and arms. One tiny fist broke free and made its way to her mouth. Her lips moved with sucking sounds and she frowned. The fist flailed and Grace released a more demanding cry.

Logan looked up, returning Cissy and Dominic's smiles with one of his own. "You were right, Dom. She's perfect."

For once, Logan's arms were heavier than his heart.

Logan made it back to the ranch in record time. He refused to wait for the sun to rise. Instead, he threw essentials into his overnight bag, grabbed the packet of papers and ring then stuffed them into his pocket.

He hopped into his truck, twisted the key in the ignition and slammed his foot on the pedal. He could just make out Raintree's main house in the rearview mirror as he drove away, the taillights casting a red glow through the haze of dust billowing up behind him.

Logan smiled. It still hurt to look back but it felt good to move forward.

"Do you need another box? There's more in the break room."

Amy puffed a strand of hair out of her face and stretched a strip of packing tape across the top of the box in her office chair. She glanced up, smiling at the receptionist hovering in the doorway.

"No, thanks, Kimberly. I think this will do it."

Amy smoothed a hand over the tape, then sighed with satisfaction. It had taken several days to finish packing up everything at her apartment and her office but the task had been a welcome distraction since she'd left Raintree. Everything was taped up and ready to go. Except for her heart.

"You'll be missed around here." Kimberly sighed, studying the two boxes stacked on top of the mahogany desk. "I sure hope the newbie coming in knows their stuff."

Amy laughed. "I imagine that's what someone is saying about me right now in Michigan."

"Maybe so. But I've really enjoyed working with you. I know this is a good opportunity but I wish you didn't have to go."

Amy's smile slipped. She'd wished the same thing over the past week. Wished she didn't have to leave Raintree's sprawling fields or her family. She missed Betty's cooking, Pop's bear hugs, Traci's good-natured banter with the boys, Dom, Cissy and... *Logan*. She missed Logan so much more than she ever had. She wished she could go back to Raintree for good. Wished—

"I wish I didn't have to go, either," Amy said, straightening her shoulders. "But sometimes, you have to move on whether you want to or not. Take the bad right along with the good."

Kimberly nodded, calling over her shoulder as she left, "I'll be right out front if you need anything."

Amy closed her eyes, unable to stop herself from wishing one last time that things were different. That this move would be to Raintree instead of in the other direction. That Logan would be at her side, hoping for the best for this baby and making their family complete.

She placed a hand over her belly and focused on the good. *Six weeks.* New life had thrived within her for six weeks. A life she and Logan had created.

Today was difficult. Driving to the airport in the morning would be even worse. But the next day would be better. So would the next. Eventually, more good days would come. And she'd appreciate them more than ever before because she had known the bad. Of that, she was certain.

Amy smiled and lifted the last box from the chair, setting it on top of the desk with the others. A heavy tread sounded down the hallway followed by the rapid click of Kimberly's heels.

"Sir, please." Kimberly's breathless voice echoed in from the hall. "Wait one minute so I—"

"I'm through waiting."

Amy's head shot up at the low words. Logan strode into the room, closed the door and rounded the desk. She caught a glimpse of the determined set of his jaw and warm, dark eyes before he claimed her mouth.

His lips parted hers, the familiar taste and masculine scent of him overwhelming her. The heat of his touch spread from her shoulders down her back and over her bottom, his broad palms kneading and caressing along the way. The tender advance continued, Logan's touch faltering when a soft cry escaped her.

His hands stilled on her waist. He lifted his head, nuzzled his cheek against hers and whispered in her ear, "Just so we're clear, babe, that wasn't for practice."

Her heart flipped over at his gentle grin. "I don't think you need any."

"Ask me."

She blinked. "Ask you what?"

"Ask me why I wanted you to stay."

Amy hesitated, belly fluttering. "Wh-why did you want me to stay?"

His big palms cradled her face, thumbs sweeping over her cheeks. "Because I love you, Amy. Always have in one way or another. I was so afraid of things not working out that I didn't trust it. Didn't want to risk losing you or make a mistake. And, after losing Sara, I didn't want to take a chance on anything. But I want to now. I want to move forward. With you."

He kissed her again, each sweep of his tongue and glide of his hands making her knees weaker. A low moan escaped his lips and entered her mouth.

She trembled, leaning back and trying to catch her breath. "Say it again."

He smiled. "I love you," he repeated. "Always have. Always will."

"I love you, too, Logan."

He brushed his hand through her hair, dark eyes locking with hers. "Thank God for that." His palm slid around her waist to cover her belly. "I'm ready. For everything. Anything. No matter what happens."

"Does that mean you're here to bring me home?"

"No. You're my home. Wherever you go, I follow."

He stepped back and pulled the pack of divorce papers from his pocket. His tanned hands held them up and ripped them several times over. The torn pieces fluttered to the floor in a soft, white shower of chaotic disarray.

"I want to start over." He took her hand, slipped her ring on her finger and ran his fingertip over the band. "Live every day of my life to the fullest, with you in it."

She fought to ignore the heated rush of her blood and studied his face. "Things may not work out any better with this pregnancy than they did before."

"Or they might." He slid his hands over her hips and pressed a kiss to her forehead. "Whatever happens, we'll pull through it. The good and the bad because we're stronger together." His expression softened. "We'll make our own fairy tale."

He kissed her again, his mouth tasting and teasing. Amy wrapped her arms around his neck and returned his kiss, holding him tighter.

Her rapid breaths mingled with his. "Let's start home."

"To Raintree?" He brightened at her nod, a wide smile stretching across his lean cheeks. "Are you sure?"

Amy kissed him again, whispering against his lips, "Everything I love is there. There's no place in the world I'd rather be."

Epilogue

Hope. One syllable with so much promise and the richest reward. The most comforting word in existence.

Logan smiled and spun the crib mobile with his fingertips. The silver stars dangling from the center glinted in the low light of the bedroom lamp with each twist. His son's eyes followed the movement, wide with wonder.

"Give it a try, Ethan," he whispered.

Ethan curled his knees to his chest and kicked his feet against the mattress. His gaze refocused on the star above and he stretched his arms up. At four months old, he had difficulty controlling the direction of his movements but he gave it his best shot anyway. His small hands opened and closed, his fingers dancing in the air as he tried to capture the shiny object.

"You can do it." Logan held out his finger, raising it just beyond his son's reach.

Ethan shifted his attention to Logan's hand and his grasping fingers followed. He caught hold of Logan's finger, wrapping it tight in his palm. His eyebrows lifted and a smile broke out across his face as he gurgled with delight.

Logan chuckled. "That's my boy."

"Are you two still playing?"

Slim arms encircled Logan from behind, hands splaying over his chest and soft curves pressing against his back. His body tightened, flooding with warmth. He turned, wrapping his hands around Amy's hips and tugging her close.

"Feeling left out?" he teased, touching a kiss to her nose. "Because I'd be more than happy to schedule extra playtime for us if that'd raise your spirits."

"Hmm. That might be a good idea…"

Her head tilted back as he kissed her neck. He moved his mouth over her skin, breathing in her sweet scent and touching the tip of his tongue to the pulse at the base of her throat.

He closed his eyes, savoring the taste and feel of her, and knew he'd never get enough. His love for Amy grew every day and this one was no exception. They'd had an extra busy Christmas morning with family, followed by a boisterous afternoon playing with the kids, and they should all be exhausted. But it seemed none of them were ready to call it a night.

A disgruntled cry emerged from the crib. Logan groaned, stealing one more kiss as Amy edged around him.

"What's the matter, handsome?" Amy slipped her hands under Ethan and lifted him to her chest, murmuring soothing words.

Logan grinned and stroked his palm over Ethan's downy black hair. "We've gotta work on your timing, son."

"Oh, he'll settle down soon." Amy kissed the top of Ethan's head and rubbed a hand over his back. "He just likes a stroll before bedtime."

She crossed the bedroom and stood by the window, humming a Christmas tune and swaying from side to side. Ethan's eyes grew heavy and eventually fluttered shut, his rosy cheek pressed tight to Amy's chest.

A wave of sweet heat rushed through Logan. Dear God, they were beautiful. The most precious parts of his life.

"Logan." Amy glanced over her shoulder, mouth parting with excitement. "Come look."

He moved close, wrapping his arms around them both and looking out the window. The glow of the white Christmas lights lining the porch rails of the house spilled over, illuminating the space below their window. A silent shower of puffy white flakes fluttered to the ground. They piled up to form a festive blanket that tucked up against the edge of the house.

"A white Christmas." She laughed softly. "In Georgia. Can you believe it?"

"Yeah." Logan squeezed Amy closer and smoothed a palm over his son's back. "Anything is possible."

They stayed awake, watching the snow fall, and Logan's heart filled up. Like his arms, it overflowed. With love, happiness and hope.

* * * * *

LET'S TALK
Romance

For exclusive extracts, competitions
and special offers, find us online:

...might just be true love...

MILLS & BOON
MEDICAL
Pulse-Racing Passion

Set your pulse racing with dedicated, delectable doctors in the high-pressure world of medicine, where emotions run high and passion, comfort and love are the best medicine.

Medical stories published every month, find them all at:

millsandboon.co.uk

MILLS & BOON
True Love
Romance from the Heart

Celebrate true love with tender stories of
heartfelt romance, from the rush of falling
in love to the joy a new baby can bring,
and a focus on the emotional
heart of a relationship.